Hallows Hill

In addition to writing novels, Olivia Isaac-Henry is a crime drama lover, and occasional keyboard player and backing vocalist in the band The Protagonist. She grew up in Worcestershire but now lives in London, where she loves the theatres, food markets and festivals.

Also by Olivia Isaac-Henry
Someone You Know
The Verdict

Sorrow Spring

Hallows Hill

OLIVIA ISAAC-HENRY

HarperCollins*Publishers*

HarperCollins*Publishers* Ltd
1 London Bridge Street
London SE1 9GF
www.harpercollins.co.uk

HarperCollins*Publishers*
Macken House, 39/40 Mayor Street Upper
Dublin 1, D01 C9W8, Ireland

First published by HarperCollins*Publishers* Ltd 2025
1

Copyright © Olivia Isaac-Henry 2025

Olivia Isaac-Henry asserts the moral right to
be identified as the author of this work

A catalogue record for this book is available from the British Library

ISBN: 978-0-00-865641-6 (HB)
ISBN: 978-0-00-865642-3 (TPB)

This novel is entirely a work of fiction. The names, characters and incidents portrayed in it are the work of the author's imagination. Any resemblance to actual persons, living or dead, events or localities is entirely coincidental.

Typeset in Sabon LT Std by HarperCollins*Publishers* India

Printed and bound in the UK using 100%
Renewable Electricity at CPI Group (UK) Ltd

All rights reserved. No part of this publication may be reproduced, stored in a retrieval system, or transmitted, in any form or by any means, electronic, mechanical, photocopying, recording or otherwise, without the prior written permission of the publishers.

Without limiting the exclusive rights of any author, contributor or the publisher of this publication, any unauthorised use of this publication to train generative artificial intelligence (AI) technologies is expressly prohibited. HarperCollins also exercise their rights under Article 4(3) of the Digital Single Market Directive 2019/790 and expressly reserve this publication from the text and data mining exception.

This book contains FSC™ certified paper and other controlled
sources to ensure responsible forest management.

For more information visit: www.harpercollins.co.uk/green

To Mum.
Thanks for your endless encouragement and support.

TWENTY YEARS AGO

FOLLY

Chapter 1

The five stone pillars crowning the summit of Hallows Hill were known as the Hags Ring, or more irreverently as the Toff's Garden Gnomes, because the stone circle was not the remnant of a sacred Neolithic site, but the caprice of an eccentric eighteenth-century nobleman. A folly.

From the foot of the hill, Mia looked up and counted the stones.

Then she blinked and re-counted.

Long ago, Mia and her friends had each chosen a pillar and carved their name at the base of it – assigned in height order. Darcy, the dancer, charismatic and mercurial, light and elfin, had taken the smallest, slenderest stone. Next came Chrissy, plain, clever and super organised. Mia herself, the group's calming influence, etched her name into the middle stone. The two tallest belonged to the boys: Ed's a little shorter than Noah's; always in his shadow, always looking up.

Five stones. One for each of them.

Today, however, in late October, nearing dusk with the low sun drenching the hilltop in hazy red, Mia could see a sixth stone. It had to be the peculiar autumn light casting odd shadows. She peered up more intently at the Hags Ring.

Now she saw that the sixth stone was moving – not a stone at all.

Her throat tightened. Had the others seen it too? Darcy and Chrissy were too busy fiddling with the torch settings to notice. Noah and Ed had been drinking cider since noon and were probably seeing ten stones.

Mia turned to them.

'Shouldn't we wait for Leanne?' she asked.

'She's not going to come now, is she?' Darcy said. 'I knew she'd chicken out.'

'I bet she's gone straight to Alicia's party,' Ed said.

'Maybe five more minutes?' Mia pleaded.

'We have to be up there by sundown or it won't work.' Darcy flicked her torch beam towards the wooded path that led to the hilltop.

Mia looked to the stones again.

Only five now. Yes, it had been a trick of the light or, perhaps, the prod of a guilty conscience. Either way, the hilltop was now bare save for the five pillars of rock. Mia's breathing slowed. With no phone reception on this side of the hill, her deceit wouldn't be discovered.

By now the sun had dropped lower and the hill was perceptibly darker, the air cooler. A tendril of cold slid beneath Mia's wool scarf, making her shiver.

'We've got something to warm you up,' Noah said. 'Hot toddy.'

'My recipe. Dad's whisky,' Ed said proudly.

From a backpack, Noah produced a Thermos and poured a darkish liquid into its plastic screw-lid cup. Mia didn't know what a hot toddy was, but she took the cup from him. It steamed in the cold air and carried with it the musty scent of forest floor: fungi devouring fallen leaves. She would have poured it away if Noah hadn't been watching. These days he only had eyes for Darcy and it made Mia feel good that he remembered her. She knocked back the whole cup to get it over with. The moment it hit her tongue she wanted to gag. It tasted worse than it smelt – mouldy, rotten and rancid. Who drank this stuff? She swivelled from them to hide the disgust on her face, before turning back and handing Noah the cup.

'Thanks,' she said.

Noah gaped in disbelief.

'All of it. Wow.' Ed started laughing.

'What's so funny?' Mia asked. 'Wasn't I supposed to drink the lot?'

'Oh, no, you drink as much as you like,' Ed said. 'More?'

Mia looked at Noah.

'That's enough for now, right, Mia?'

'Right,' she said.

Ed was smirking towards Noah, who was busying himself shoving the flask back into his pack. What was so funny? Had she done something wrong?

'We need to get going,' Darcy called.

Mia stood staring at the boys, neither of whom would return her gaze. Instead they walked towards Darcy and the torchlight.

Overhanging conifers formed a tunnel above the path that led through the woods to the summit of Hallows Hill. The ground was uneven and crisscrossed by tree roots. Darcy's ballerina poise allowed her to skip along, her feet barely touching the ground. The boys, Noah and Ed, were too drunk to think their repeated stumbles anything but hilarious.

Chrissy, prepared as ever, in her walking boots, strode sure-footed next to them. Mia brought up the rear.

Without her own torch and wearing flimsy canvas shoes, she struggled, more than once slipping on the loose earth and tripping over roots. Soon she fell behind, leaving herself further from the light. Beneath the branches the darkness was so dense, it was difficult to believe night had yet to fall.

It was after Mia tripped for a third time and she twisted her wrist, that she heard the footsteps. A low thud somewhere behind her. When she stopped, so did the steps. She thought of how a sixth stone had appeared at the Hags Ring and reminded herself that just as that had been a trick of the light, this was a trick of the atmosphere, the damp air amplifying and distorting her own footsteps. If it was Leanne, she would have shouted out.

Still Mia hesitated.

'Can you hear something, Chrissy?'

Chrissy stopped and turned. 'Hear what?'

'Someone behind us,' Mia said.

Chrissy shone the torch back down the path. Its beam threw Mia's shadow against the trees, her head and fingers elongated, her body small and hunched.

'There's no one there,' Chrissy said. 'It was probably a deer.'

A deer. One of the little muntjacs. Mia had seen them often enough. They were the size of sheep and nothing to be frightened of. And yet . . .

'Look, Chrissy, I don't like this. We should go back.'

'They're waiting for us,' Chrissy said. 'Walk with me. It'll be fine.'

Mia looked at the dark trail below her. If Chrissy

wouldn't come, she'd have to go back alone and in the dark. Reluctantly, she turned up the hill and followed Chrissy and the torch beam.

She was concentrating so hard on staying upright that the disc of light at the end of the path came as a shock.

Darcy was the first to run out of the trees onto the hilltop. The five stones of the Hags Ring loomed as a dark halo above her before she sped to their centre, stood on her tiptoes, tipped her head to the sky and brought her arms down in a 'V' to her sides. Noah rushed after her and, lifting her by the armpits, twirled her around. Ed whooped and jumped into the ring before dropping to his knees and bringing two more cans of cider from out of his backpack.

Chrissy jogged after them.

Mia held back, halting just beyond the wood's boundary, hovering between the dark and the light. She'd been here hundreds of times, but today the circle seemed different, the stones distorted and malevolent, emitting a faint hum as if electrified. Again she looked back at the dark tunnel of trees, before finally stepping out onto the hill.

In the stone circle Noah had let go of Darcy and was drinking more cider with Ed.

'Can't you two lay off it for a bit?' Darcy said. 'Why are the girls the only ones taking this seriously?'

''Cos this is bollocks and we should be at Alicia's party, not carrying out some dumb dare,' Ed replied, chugging on his can.

'It's not a dare,' Darcy said. 'This is a serious ceremony.'

She looked to Noah. He nudged Ed's elbow.

'Come on, mate. It'll only take a few minutes.'

Ed rolled his eyes, but put the can down. Mia felt a surge

of jealousy. Noah had no more interest in the ceremony than Ed. He just wanted to impress Darcy. Until the last couple of months he'd only seen Darcy as Mia's mate. Then something changed, and Mia felt left behind and excluded by her two oldest friends. She'd only come today because she didn't want it to be just those two together.

'We need to start,' Darcy said. 'The sun's about to set.'

As Mia walked across the thin grass to join them in the circle, the humming intensified. Could the others not hear it?

'I guess Leanne's not coming then,' she said.

'She'll be at the party already,' Ed said. 'Not freezing her arse off like us.'

'I told you, Ed, we're going to the party later. This first. We agreed,' Darcy said. She looked to the west. Only the tiniest sliver of red was visible on the horizon. 'We have to start now.'

The chill evening air wormed its way beneath Mia's scarf once more and was creeping down her spine just as Ed's foul-tasting brew started bubbling in her stomach.

'Do you really think we should be doing this?' she said.

'Scared?' Noah asked.

'Of course not.'

'Then let's get on with it.' He looked to Darcy for approval. She flashed him a brief smile.

But it wasn't fear that made Mia hold back, rather something she sensed – a presence; neither malignant nor benign, but best left alone. She shook her head to dispel the thought.

'We need to sit on the floor, inside the circle,' Darcy said. 'Have your back to the stone with your name on it.'

They slumped to the ground, in rough alignment to their named stones.

The last ray of sun ran across Mia's stone as a streak of blood. Her insides turned cold.

The Hags Ring dare was a rite of passage for the youth of All Hallows. Most of the school's fifth form had tried at some point. You called the name 'Bella' three times and she rose from her grave and spoke your fortune. Jodie Lawson and Everett Collins had gone there last year on midsummer's eve. Jodie swore she'd had a weird creepy feeling, which was explained when, only a week later, her dog died. Dom Chandler and Adam Robbins called for her at New Year, both so drunk on vodka they fell asleep and were later hospitalised with hypothermia.

Mia remembered it was Leanne who had suggested they came tonight, Halloween. She had explained that if calling to Bella was to work, wouldn't it be on the night of the year when the veil between the worlds of the living and dead was lifted?

Chrissy's mind must have been drifting in the same direction because she said, 'It's weird Leanne bailed. I mean, this was her idea.'

No one replied.

Mia was using her finger to draw a circle in the loose earth next to her. Ed was still mumbling to Noah about Alicia's party, and Darcy was preoccupied with balancing her torch on the ground at the centre of the circle so its beam pointed upwards. Lighting them from below, it gave each youthful face an ancient and cadaverous form.

'Close your eyes and join hands,' Darcy said.

They reached for each other. Mia took Chrissy's hand.

It was cool and trembled slightly. On her other side, Noah's was warm, and a glow spread up Mia's arm to her neck and face.

Darcy was seated opposite, taking a long deep breath. 'Close your eyes,' she said again.

Like Mia, Ed kept his eyes open. He grinned at her, his teeth wolf white in the torchlight.

'We come to you, Bella, on Halloween, as the curtain between the living and the dead lifts and our world blurs into yours,' Darcy said. 'We respectfully call upon you to speak our fortune.'

Ed's brew was fermenting in Mia's guts and she was starting to feel nauseous.

'We call upon you, Bella, once.' Darcy emphasised the final word.

The torch flickered like a candle and, though the evening was still, the trees started to sway, their movement becoming a wild dance, their shapes nearly human.

Mia sat, mute with fear, the bile rising in her throat.

'We call you, Bella, twice.'

A long shape detached itself from the woods below the summit and slid towards the circle. Mia blinked hard. *It's not real. They're just shadows.* Something crackled. A rustle of footsteps approached the circle. The stones' humming was becoming so intense, she could feel the vibrations through the earth.

Mia jumped to her feet.

'Sit down,' Chrissy said.

'Something's coming.'

'There's nothing there, Mia.' Chrissy pulled her back to the ground.

The long shadow, which had reached halfway to the Hags Ring, was no longer moving. It was now motionless, ready to pounce.

'You need to stop this, Darcy,' Mia said.

'There's nothing there,' Chrissy repeated. 'What's wrong with you?'

The torch flickered again. Darcy's breath was coming fast and shallow; she was barely audible when she said, 'We call you, Bella, a third time.'

Mia's eyes remained fixed on the creeping shadow. Chrissy's hand was still gripping her wrist, fixing her to the ground.

They sat in silence. The last glow of the sun had disappeared. Then the torch flickered again and went out.

'Damn,' Chrissy said.

She let go of Mia's arm and Mia could hear her banging the torch on the ground. It came back on, lighting the circle.

Something rustled close by. Mia was up on her feet again. Whatever had risen from the woods had used that moment of darkness to bridge the gap to the Hags Ring. It was outside of the stones, circling them.

'Mia, you need to sit down,' Chrissy said.

The torch threw long shadows of the stones fanning out across the hilltop. Five stones, six shadows. One moving anticlockwise around them.

'She's here,' Mia said.

'Oh my God,' Darcy said. 'You can see her.'

Mia was spinning around, transfixed by the shape circling them.

'What was in that drink you gave her?' Chrissy asked.

Ed snickered. 'Just some shrooms. She'll be fine.'

Chrissy came and stood close to Mia.

'Whatever you're seeing, it's not real,' she said.

Darcy was also on her feet. 'Bella, Bella, is that you?'

'That's enough,' Chrissy said. 'There's nothing there, Mia. Ed gave you magic mushrooms. They have the same effect as LSD.'

Mia wasn't listening. She stepped to the edge of the circle and caught the scent of rotting vegetation and damp bark.

'Miaaaaa . . .' The sound of the wind through dry leaves.

'What do you want?' Mia asked.

The shadow started to run, twisting and turning until it took solid form. A woman, her skin made of bark, her hair of ferns, twigs and birds' nests, sloe berries for eyes. She had no mouth and her voice was the rustle of leaves.

'You came to find me, Miaaaa,' she said.

'No, it wasn't me. It was Leanne.'

'Shit. That stuff must be good,' Ed said.

Suddenly the figure stopped running. It halted between two stones, beckoning to Mia with a twig finger. She felt as if she were being drawn forwards on a string.

'Don't step outside the circle, Mia,' Darcy said.

The tree woman raised a twig finger and pointed at Mia. She was right at the edge of the circle now, so close Mia could see a spider weave a thin thread through her hair.

'Who are you?'

'You know who I am,' the figure said.

'Is it her? Is it Bella? Ask her for our fortune,' Darcy said.

Mia wanted to move away, to turn her head from the sloe eyes and scuttling spiders. She remained frozen to the spot. 'Leave me alone. I don't want to know.'

'We do. We want to know,' Darcy said.

The sloe eyes glistened. Bella unfurled a single twig finger, on which stood six ripe green buds, bold and proud.

Six buds swelled and burst into leaf. Then, one shrivelled and died.

'What do you mean?' Mia asked.

Bella's laugh was a hiss on the wind.

'What do you mean?' Mia repeated.

But Bella was on the move again, whizzing around the circle in a flurry of branches. Mia lurched after her, tripped on the torch, fell and cracked her head on one of the stones.

For a second time the torch went out.

A scream ripped through the darkness. So loud and so anguished it froze Mia's blood.

The hilltop lay silent, black and bare. Then she saw it. A sheet of purest white floating above them, bright and shapeless against the night sky. Mia had seen it before and knew what it meant. The shroud was a portent of death. It evaporated into the night air just before a large object thudded to the ground close by.

Chrissy banged the torch again and it flickered back to life. She came over with Noah and Ed. Mia pressed her fingers to her temple and felt the warm sticky flow of blood.

'See what you've done,' Chrissy said.

'We didn't think the shrooms would be that strong and work that fast,' Ed said.

'Well, now you do. And forget Alicia's party. We need to get Mia to the hospital.'

Mia rolled to a kneeling position, which increased the throbbing at her temple and her rising nausea.

'I just want to go home.'

Ed was still grinning, but Noah seemed to have sobered up.

He reached out for her hand. 'Let's get you back,' he said.

As she raised her arms to him, he suddenly jerked away. 'Was that you who screamed earlier?' he asked.

Slowly Mia shook her head.

'Then who?'

The shroud. Death. One of them was missing.

'Darcy,' Mia shouted. 'Darcy.'

She used the stone to haul herself to standing.

'Darcy,' she screamed into the dark.

A wail came from the opposite side of the circle.

Chrissy swung the torch round.

Darcy was kneeling before the west-facing stone. Propped up against it sat Leanne, her eyes open and unblinking. The blood seeping into her scarf had started pooling on the ground beneath her.

Chapter 2

Wyrd and Wonderful Ezine

The Hags Ring Curse Strikes Again

The disaster at the Caverwell factory may have been dominating the headlines but here at *Wyrd and Wonderful* we've been focusing on another incident – the murder of Leanne Tattersall at the Hags Rings stone circle in Worcestershire. Several of you have contacted us, asking for some background to this story. Don't worry, we're on the case. As far as we're concerned, the police have been too quick in declaring 'nothing to see here' when dismissing any link to the occult. Our discerning readers will have noticed the striking similarities between Leanne's death and another murder (reported in our second ever Ezine) that occurred in the exact same spot over sixty years ago. In 1942 a woman's body was found in the Hags Ring. Like Leanne, she had been propped up against the west-facing stone and her heart pierced by a thin blade. The woman's identity has never been established, but the locals call her Bella after Isabella Verne-Fontaine, wife of the eighteenth-century lord of the manor.

Official records state she died in childbirth, but according to local legend, the fifth Viscount Verne-Fontaine murdered his wife inside the Hags Ring as part of a satanic ritual.

As always, *Wyrd and Wonderful* has set out to find the truth;

All Hallows or Wraithshollow?

Originally a hamlet and called Wraithshollow, All Hallows is first mentioned in the tenth century texts written by the monks of Worcester Cathedral. However, it was not listed in the Domesday Book, meaning it was either forgotten or deliberately avoided by the King's commissioners. If the latter, the monks' reports of the place would provide an explanation. In the year 926 Brother Wilfred notes that the village

> ... has weather quite apart from the surrounding county, where orchards hang heavy with fruit and, in the fields, wheat reaches to the sky. In Wraithshollow strange vapours fill the air, and both the crops and the people raised there grow crooked and spare.
> It is an unholy place, whose inhabitants are impervious to the word of God. With no patch of consecrated ground, the deceased join their ancestors, whose restless souls roam Wraiths Hill, itself strewn with the graves of the ancients.

Wilfred goes on to report that in olden times the heathens enacted 'monstrous rites', though there is no elaboration on what these might be.

Then, abruptly, Wraithshollow vanishes from written

records, only to reappear several centuries later when Charles II granted the land, along with a newly created viscountcy, to the Verne-Fontaine family. By this time the village had been renamed All Hallows and had acquired a church and a priest. The Verne-Fontaines, whose ancestors arrived with the Norman conquest, already held a much smaller estate thirty miles to the south. They quickly erected a large brick manor house, only for it to be pulled down a couple of generations later in order for the fourth Viscount to erect a Neo-Palladian mansion: All Hallows Court.

And here's where it gets interesting, because whilst the first few generations adhered to strict Christian principles, Arthur Verne-Fontaine, the fifth Viscount, had other ideas. An enthusiastic member of the Hellfire Club, he founded his own group, the Crimson Circle, after its demise. One of its members, named Redford, a close friend of the Viscount's, was also a keen historian and archaeologist. He told Verne-Fontaine that under instruction from the local bishop the village's original name of Wraithshollow, meaning valley of the undead, had been changed to All Hallows, meaning all saints, in order to erase its pagan past. Moreover, Redford maintained that Wraiths Hill, now Hallows Hill, contained many Iron Age barrows – that is, prehistoric burial mounds – which tallied with Brother Wilfred's account of 'the graves of the ancients'. It was this information that led Verne-Fontaine to place a stone circle atop the hill, much to the fear and indignation of the villagers. Stories of blood sacrifices had filtered down through the generations, and whispers of the Viscount's 'goings-on' with the Hellfire Club in London troubled them. Were the ancient rites to be revived?

When Verne-Fontaine's wife, Isabella, died, their worst fears were realised. Although her husband claimed she died of puerperal fever a few days after the birth of her daughter, rumours circulated that she had been murdered or, more accurately, sacrificed in the Hags Ring. A shepherd stumbled across her body inside the stone circle, her heart pierced, the stiletto blade still in her breast. Verne-Fontaine dismissed the man as a drunk and a mischief maker. How could he repeat such foul slanders at this time of grief? With no other witnesses – all the servants having been dismissed from the manor house by the time of Isabella's death – and as Verne-Fontaine was the local magistrate, the official record stood.

It was after this that the legend around the Hags Ring grew. Locals believed that as Isabella was buried on unconsecrated ground in the nearby woods, if you entered the stone circle and called for her three times, her restless spirit would rise, return to the spot of her murder and reveal your fortune.

As the years passed, belief in the story waned, and with the scientific advances that defined the twentieth century, there seemed little to fear from either the Hags Ring or the Verne-Fontaines. That was until 1942, when the body of a second woman was found in the Hags Ring, propped against the west-facing stone, in the same spot as Isabella was said to have been killed. Those with long memories recalled the old tales and labelled this murder a second sacrifice. The villagers nicknamed the unknown victim Bella in a nod to the similarity between her fate to that of Isabella Verne-Fontaine.

And now a third young woman has been found in the same spot, murdered in the same manner as the woman in

1942. Can this be a coincidence? The police quickly arrested a man named William Nicholson, but was he acting alone or is he part of a wider occult movement? *Sub judice* laws severely curtail *Wyrd and Wonderful*'s ability to speculate in this article, but surely given the site's history, police need to provide a convincing reason for dismissing the connection between Leanne Tattersall's murder, the two previous deaths and the occult.

Tell us what you think. Are you from All Hallows? What are people saying? Drop us a line here at *Wyrd and Wonderful*.

Chapter 3

Haverton Herald

Sick Occultists Disrupt Leanne Tattersall Trial

Scuffles broke out today outside Haverton Magistrates' Court as William Nicholson, the man accused of murdering Leanne Tattersall, appeared for the first time. Since his arrest, Nicholson has become a hero figure for sick occultists, who claim Leanne's death was a necessary sacrifice. On the steps of the courthouse the Crimson Circle wore T-shirts bearing Nicholson's face as they chanted his name. Their leader, Rex Pender, taunted Leanne's family, claiming they should be honoured their daughter was chosen. Leanne's father, Tony, tried to rip Pender's T-shirt from him, and was then surrounded by other members of the Crimson Circle before police stepped in.

Pender and four other members of the organisation were arrested for affray and breach of the peace.

Oleana Jenkins, head of the local Wiccan order, slammed the Crimson Circle.

'There's no evidence druids practised blood sacrifice.

Wiccans, such as our coven, celebrate nature and the changes of the seasons. We hold all life as sacred. People like the Crimson Circle have hijacked and distorted ancient beliefs to justify their own sick fantasies.'

Leanne had moved to the area from London only a few months before her body was found in the Hags Ring stone circle, the site of another murder in the 1940s. The previous victim was also a young woman who had been stabbed through the heart in an identical manner. At the time, similar rumours circulated, alleging that the killing was linked to the occult and mirrored the murder of Viscountess Isabella Verne-Fontaine in the eighteenth century.

Police have repeatedly stated that there were no indications of a ritual killing in relation to Leanne's death and the location of her body was a matter of coincidence.

Pender will appear before magistrates tomorrow.

Chapter 4

Haverton Herald

No Justice for Leanne

Leanne Tattersall's family were left angry and confused today, as Judge Jane Harding instructed the jury in William Nicholson's trial to dismiss the charge of murder and instead convict on the lesser one of manslaughter on the grounds of diminished responsibility.

Leanne was killed on Hallows Hill when trying to join her friends for a Halloween dare. It's believed there was a mix-up about where they were to meet and she took a different route up to the stones and ran into William Nicholson before she could reach them.

Nicholson admitted to killing Leanne but claimed voices told him she was a witch who had laid a curse on him, one that could only be lifted by her death. He was deemed unfit to appear in court.

Flanked by his wife, Susan, Leanne's father, Tony Tattersall, tore up his prepared statement and blasted the justice system.

'The only thing that could bring us any closure would be to see the monster who murdered our daughter punished. By rights Nicholson should be at the end of a rope. Instead he's been allowed to hide behind mental health jargon and is going to spend a few years in some hospital or other. And what's that going to be like? Just Butlin's for crazies. This isn't justice. It's a joke.'

'The judge has blood on her hands,' Mrs Tattersall added. 'Not just Leanne's but that of the kids who are going to die because every sicko knows all they have to say is that they heard voices and the law can't touch them. We can't move on from this. As a family, we have nowhere to go. That lot in there – the judge, the lawyers – they can all go home and hug their children tonight. But my Leanne's gone and she's never coming back. Tell me how I'm going to explain to Leanne's little sister what happened today. How do you tell a four-year-old that the man who took Leanne from us, who admitted killing an innocent girl, isn't even going to jail?'

Mrs Tattersall then broke down in tears. Her husband stepped in.

'No one believes Nicholson acted alone. Her friends know more than they're saying, and instead of being questioned as suspects they're being treated with kid gloves.'

'That lot were never her friends,' Mrs Tattersall added. 'There's more to come out about this.'

DCI Archibald, who led the investigation, stated that he understood the family's frustration.

'The police can only gather evidence, put it before the court and hope for the right decision. And although Nicholson won't be going to prison, given this crime's serious nature and his ongoing delusions he's unlikely ever to be released.

As for conjecture that Nicholson acted with one or more accomplices, all I can do is reiterate that the evidence, including the witness statements, points to him acting alone. Darcy Alderwell, Noah Campbell, Christine Parker, Edward Fields and Maria Collier are five young people who've been through an extremely traumatic experience. The inaccurate and malicious speculation being circulated is causing them acute distress and we would strongly discourage it.'

There was a heavy police presence at the court to prevent further disorder from the Crimson Circle, who had threatened to come and celebrate the verdict.

In a statement their leader, Rex Pender, said, 'Freedom of expression is dead in this country. We will be marking the occasion in private.'

Chapter 5

Midlands Today TV news at 6.30

Fury at Hags Ring 'Ritual'

PRESENTER: **Following the funeral earlier today of William Nicholson, the killer of schoolgirl Leanne Tattersall, we've received disturbing reports of so-called pagans, the Crimson Circle, enacting a ritual to celebrate his life. We're going live to the top of Hallows Hill now.**

> Cut from studio to a reporter standing in front of the Hags Ring, the smouldering remains of a bonfire at its centre.

REPORTER: **Yes, that's right, Shakti. Last year, Nicholson was sent to a high-security psychiatric hospital. Shortly after his arrival, he was diagnosed with terminal cancer and he died last week. His funeral was held this morning with only a priest in attendance. Earlier this afternoon, however, a member of the public secretly recorded Rex Pender and his Crimson Circle celebrating Nicholson's** life and praising the killing of Leanne Tattersall. You can see the remains of their fire inside the Hags Ring stone circle behind me, where Leanne's body was found.

Cut to grainy images of Rex Pender in flowing green robes addressing his followers.

PENDER: In sacrificing Leanne, Nicholson also sacrificed himself. He was murdered by the authorities and a web of lies created around his illness.

Whilst reviled by the general populus, we, the enlightened, know he was not a monster but one of the most selfless individuals of our time. Leanne's friends too should be praised for bringing her here, to the Hags Ring on Halloween.

These guardians of morality are quite happy to sacrifice innocent people every day in pursuit of profit or power. They talk of just wars and collateral damage. Strange how these arbiters of justice always manage to line their pockets and extend their influence in the process.

The Crimson Circle suffers from no such hypocrisy. The sacrifice of innocents is an end in itself. A sign that we are willing to prostrate ourselves before greatness and grind our miserable human desires into the dust in order to touch a higher plane of existence.

The same friends and family who quail at your beliefs are the ones who read every inch of the papers when a murder such as Leanne's occurs. How else can they quench their blood lust and still believe themselves to be pure and pious? They revelled in Leanne's death far more than William Nicholson's. He was compelled to take her life. They were not compelled to read about it.

Pender lights the bonfire.

FOLLOWERS: **Nicholson. Nicholson. Nicholson.**

Cut back to live.

REPORTER: **We contacted Oleana Jenkins, the head of another local pagan group, for comment.**

Cut to earlier footage.

OLEANA: **The level of ignorance shown by these people is unbelievable. The Hags Ring is not Stonehenge. It's a folly. Five lumps of rock put in by the local aristocrat a couple of centuries back as a tourist attraction. It makes me livid that people like Pender grab all the headlines, when our religion celebrates love, tolerance and respect for nature.**

Cut back to live.

REPORTER: **Police said they were unaware the ceremony was going to take place and are looking into possible charges that could be brought against Pender's group.**
The Tattersall family have declined to comment.

Chapter 6

The Hags Ring Five Forum

Ingmar
they totally killed her right. that pender guy's onto them. no one believes nicholson acted alone.

> **Dodo**
> defo. they offered leanne as a sacrifice.

Ingmar
there was an orgy first. all of them at it before they stabbed her through the heart.

> **Dodo**
> wish i'd been there. the darcy girl is hot, hot, hot.
> i heard they got paid thousands.

Ingmar
it wasn't the money christine got a place at oxford and the girl don't look that smart to me. someone in high places is pulling strings. i wouldn't do her though. but that darcy – hell yeah – every day of the week and twice on sunday!!!

Dodo
man yeah!!!And if the maria bird wants to join in, let her.

Amanda
You're totally sick. A girl died at the hands of a madman and you turn it into some sordid sex fantasy.

Dodo
you're in the wrong forum little bo peep.

NOW

OCTOBER

Chapter 7

Halloween this year is one of those days where dawn is simply the sky's transition from black to grey and, with the thick mist, little is distinguishable from the train window as I rattle along the branch line taking me to All Hallows. Every instinct tells me to stay away and yet here I am, meeting up with the old gang: Darcy, Noah, Chrissy and Ed.

I convinced myself that returning to the village two decades after Leanne's death is an act of bravery: facing my demons, drawing a line under the past.

Darcy's invitation arrived in my inbox while I was sitting at my kitchen table. Arrogance and fear made me reply with an immediate refusal, when all the reasons for my later acceptance were staring me in the face: the empty wine glass, the empty takeaway carton, the empty room.

All Hallows is the only place I've ever belonged. Since leaving, I've been unable to forge a connection with anywhere or anyone. Not even with Jake, my husband. Possibly the reason for our impending divorce, and why he currently lives in Harpenden with Lisette, who's expecting their first child. More than ever, I need company because *Bella* feeds on loneliness. Like the dark, it makes her stronger.

Work acts as a shield. I paint and repaint canvases in the sugared-almond shades that have become my trademark. Pinks, lilacs, blues and yellows swirl into fairy castles, sprites and unicorns. Critics consider my pictures kitsch and ironic. They're neither. The folds of light and pastel hues hold the dark at bay. Hold *her* at bay. And I've been lucky. In the first newspaper report of the Hags Ring murder, a typo had me down as Maria and they used my stepfather's surname, Collier. Subsequent articles repeated the mistake, so no one associates the artist Mia Raine with the girl in the Hags Ring case.

To me, Leanne's death is not a painful memory, like the loss of a grandparent or a broken limb. It's not even like it happened yesterday. It feels like it's still happening, as if I'm living through that period of my life. With my username TC123456, so anonymous no one can trace it back to me, and never commenting, I spend hours trawling true crime sites, combing Reddit posts and listening to podcasts for any mention of the Hags Ring murder. Like playing with a loose tooth, it's both painful and addictive. And though I worry about my part in events becoming the subject of online conjecture, exposure is not my greatest fear.

Bella. I hardly dare say her name. Her shadow lingers in the corners of rooms a split second after I switch on the light. At night I wake to find her standing over me, sprig fingers brushing my skin, the scent of rotting vegetation thick in the air.

October and its shortening days embolden her. In the autumn gales her figure rises, spins and reforms in the eddies of fallen leaves. Bare branches stretch out, twig hands beckoning to me. She whispers my name on the wind that whistles around the eaves and rattles the window frames.

By the time I received Darcy's email, I feared for my sanity. Even then, I held back.

Darcy wrote again. It was coming up to the twentieth anniversary. No one else will ever understand. We only have each other.

Darcy is the sister I never had. We used to do everything together. We shared clothes, flats and lovers, including Jake and Noah – sort of.

I began to weaken.

Finally, I received a text from Noah.

> Darcy's not doing great. We need to do this for her. And, Mia, you're my oldest friend. I miss you. Please come.

After that, I booked my train ticket and Darcy emailed me a file with the details of our accommodation.

I know it's a mistake. But when my husband left, loneliness crept back into my life and all my painting, gallery openings and invitations to lunch couldn't hide the fact that my only meaningful conversations were the weekly calls to my mother. Until our separation, I was able to suppress the guilt and confusion I felt about Leanne's death. With Jake, my life was filled with dinners, parties and holidays with our friends. After we broke up, I realised our friends were actually his friends. None of them ever contacts me, and when I've phoned them they sound embarrassed and make excuses to end the call. I want to be back with my real friends, to be young again, drink cider on the swings in the park with Ed, listen to the latest bands at Noah's house, curl up on Darcy's bed while she applies make-up and tells me about the older boys she's dating, and have Chrissy make a colour-coded revision timetable for me. *That's the bare minimum, Mia.*

I know we cannot return to the past, and yet I feel its tug as a physical sensation.

Bella mocks me on my journey north, singing my name in the screech of metal on the tracks, winking at me from the bushes that appear and disappear in the mists along the line. As we near the village, the sun breaks momentarily through the clouds, the fog clears and Hallows Hill rises before me. The dense atmospheric conditions distort the standing stones to many times their size, twisting them into human form. Then the clouds close in around them. The stones disappear and we pull into All Hallows Station.

Stepping out of the train, I scan the platform, half expecting news of my arrival to have spread and a group of angry locals to be waiting for me. But the only other people are fellow passengers, their shoulders hunched, their heads bent against the chill wind as they stream for the exit, as oblivious to me as they are to each other. Still, I wait until everyone has left before heading towards the narrow gate leading out of the station.

If Leanne's death occurred today, we would not survive. The murder of a beautiful girl, hints of the occult and whispers of a wider conspiracy would have YouTubers, podcasters and web sleuths banging on our doors, demanding the truth and constructing ever wilder theories as to why five ordinary teenagers would kill their friend. Photos from social media posts at a party six months ago or on a holiday two years before, would be dissected and the most innocent comment or symbol interpreted as a sure sign of satanic influence. Even back then we couldn't entirely escape – the guilt heaped upon us by others adding to that we heaped upon ourselves. It left me unable to leave the house for many months, and when I did find the courage to venture out alone, I regretted it.

There are no taxis at the station and the route to the house Noah has rented takes me along All Hallows High Street. In the shop windows pumpkins grin, witches fly and skeletons dance. Later, children will wander the streets in costumes and masks, collecting coins and sweets in brightly coloured buckets. Halloween has become a rollercoaster ride, a contained fear to make the pulse race whilst disposing of genuine peril. If people truly believed dark forces stalk the land on 31 October, they'd stay indoors.

I stop outside the newsagents, half expecting to see the old signs advertising the *Sun* and Silk Cut. Instead it's a Spar, bright red lettering with the green fir tree symbol. If I am going to lay demons to rest today, I should start here, where I made my first foray into the outside world after Leanne's death. Mum and Bernard, my stepfather, tried to shield me from the furore surrounding the case, although some of what was being said leaked through to us. We had left Leanne alone and were responsible for her death. While more truth lay in these rumours than I cared to admit, I was young and restless. Staying cooped up was driving me insane. So at eleven o'clock, on a school day, when I was certain not to run into one of my classmates, I braved the outside world and went into the village to collect my art magazines.

The newsagents was ten minutes from home. I walked fast and kept my head down. I remember the cold morning, pavements thick with frost and the wind nipping the tip of my nose, giving me an excuse to wrap a scarf tight around my face. Disguise, however, proved pointless.

I was about to exit the shop when Leanne's mother, Mrs Tattersall, entered, holding her daughter by the hand. Cara was about five years old and looked cute in a padded red coat with a fur-trimmed hood. The same one she'd been wearing on Halloween of the previous year, when it was her sister's hand she'd been holding. That had been the last time I'd seen Leanne alive.

Mrs Tattersall didn't see me at first. When she did she stopped. Her face transformed from a mask of grief to one of hatred.

'Don't you dare even look at my Cara,' she said. 'You stay away from her. From all of us.'

I longed to tell her I was sorry. If I could have gone back and said or done something to stop Leanne coming to the Hags Ring alone that night, I would have. But I was unable to say any of this. All I could do was stare back into the eyes of a mother who held me responsible for her daughter's death.

My lack of reaction only provoked her. She stormed towards me and ripped the magazines from my hands.

'You're no better than Nicholson,' she screamed.

I looked to the other customers to intervene. They stood and watched in silence.

'Why should you get to swan around the village, happy and carefree, while my Leanne's lying cold in her grave? Nicholson didn't act alone. You know something. Tell me.'

I backed away. Cara's wide frightened eyes peered up at me through the fur trim.

'There's blood on your hands. You as good as killed her,' her mother raged. 'You should be the one six feet under, not my beautiful daughter.'

She raised a fist. I thought she was about to strike me. Instead her face cracked and crumpled into tears. Two customers rushed over and led her away to a chair at the back of the shop, where sobs shook her whole body. One of her rescuers, whom I recognised as Alicia's mother, threw me a filthy look. If only we'd gone straight to her daughter's party that night instead of carrying out that stupid dare.

The newsagent looked on, impassive. Cara stood staring at me, screwing up her face as if trying to remember something.

I left the magazines on the shop floor, their pages soaking up the melting frost and ran out of the door.

What I didn't realise at the time was that Mrs Tattersall's accusations were some of the kinder ones circulating.

Chapter 8

Darcy's file listed our accommodation as the Dower House, the only surviving structure of the Verne-Fontaine estate. From a module we did on local history at school I know that in the eighteenth century, the same capricious nobleman who erected the Hags Ring folly, built All Hallows Court, a Neo-Palladian mansion on the site of an older manor house. Our teacher, Mr Thomas, was unusually animated as he told us how the Court was destroyed in the war: a Luftwaffe pilot dumping his bombs on it after failing to find his target in the towns and cities to the north of the village. A just punishment, some said, for the twelfth Viscount Verne-Fontaine, whom many believed to be a Nazi sympathiser. His flight to South America as soon as an Allied victory was assured, added weight to these accusations. Last spotted in Buenos Aires circa 1947, his only son had died and his more distant relatives had neither the money nor the inclination to rebuild. The Court's remaining walls were pulled down and the land sold off to build a housing estate that more than doubled the size of the village.

I remember the details not because of any interest in local history but because of our teacher, Mr Thomas. His face was ashen, his cheeks hollow and his clothes fell loose around him. It was as he described the misdeeds of the Verne-Fontaines that a white sheet floated down from the roof of the prefab hut that served as our classroom. No one else saw it. But in the suffocating heat of a summer's day, I shivered because I had seen it before and I knew its portent. It was not a sheet but a shroud.

We returned to school in September to learn that Mr Thomas had died over the holidays. It was that same term that we went up to the Hags Ring and I saw another shroud before Leanne's death. I told no one of these visions. I would have been thought strange, even before Leanne's death.

Mr Thomas forgot to mention that a small piece of All Hallows Court had remained unscathed and unsold – the Dower House. Until her death in the 1980s, a Verne-Fontaine cousin lived there, after which it fell into disrepair. Although I was never invited, kids from my school used to go to the abandoned building for parties. The bass lines pumping out could be heard in the heart of the village.

Then a few years ago, an entrepreneur bought it for pennies, restored it and now rents it out as an Airbnb and occasionally as a film set.

My route there skirts the housing estate and I have to drag my suitcase along a narrow pavement before turning left onto a small country road lined with holly hedges. The Dower House is the only building. As I approach, I feel like someone crawling through the desert as they near an oasis. Soon I will be among friends. Not colleagues or acquaintances, but friends who know and love me. For tonight, at least, I will not be alone. For one evening Bella might let me be.

The near-derelict house I remember, with missing slates and graffiti-sprayed walls, is gone. Now the ornate iron gates bearing the Verne-Fontaine crest – an oak and a falcon – combined with the ivy-clad walls give the house a fairy-tale quality; *Sleeping Beauty*, perhaps. I sprint forwards, the wheels on my suitcase crunching along the gravel drive.

Darcy opens the front door before I get there. She bounds over and gives me a hug. The rose and vanilla scent of her signature Coco Mademoiselle fills my nostrils and her oversized mohair jumper, which tickles my chin, is not thick enough to cushion the xylophone ribs sticking into me. She grabs my hand and runs with me into the hall, placing a finger over her lips to demand my silence.

'The others are in the lounge, but I wanted to talk to you first.'

'Why?' I mouth.

She motions for me to follow her upstairs.

The walls of the Dower House are decorated with portraits of the Verne-Fontaine family, all long noses and narrow eyes. They must be reproductions because the originals perished in the bombing. Still, it's strange to imagine what that ancient family would have made of our rag-tag group invading their house for the evening.

Darcy takes me to the room furthest from the stairs.

'We're sharing – that's OK, isn't it?' she asks.

'I thought this place had six bedrooms,' I say.

'Only five and one's out of use. The boys won't share and Chrissy wants her own room because the twins wake her up at six o'clock most days and she deserves a lie-in.'

Our room has damask wallpaper of China blue with silver foliage; the twin beds have matching coverlets. Darcy has already placed her nightdress on the one nearest the door. I put my case down next to the one by the window and try to figure out which way we're facing. South. The direction of Hallows Hill and the stones. They're not visible from the house, but I sense their looming presence and close the curtains. I'm pleased I'll be sharing and won't have to sleep alone.

Darcy pats the bed and I sit down next to her. 'I'm worried about Sandy.'

'Mum? She's fine,' I say.

'Are you sure? She popped over before I left to give me a blouse you forgot last time you went to see her.' She hands me a plastic bag. 'Do you think she's lonely? She's always making excuses to come and see us.'

Mum has plenty of friends and can't abide Darcy's mother, Marielle Alderwell. It's more likely she's been checking up on Darcy because she knows I worry about her. The beautiful, brilliant Darcy, who was going to be a prima ballerina, then an aristocrat's wife, is now unemployed and living at her parents' home in All Hallows. Since moving back her weight has plummeted, her hair thinned and on the few occasions I do see her she has unexplained cuts and bruises. Once or twice I've broached the subject. Is it an eating disorder or self-harm? Each time Darcy has bitten my head off and filtered my calls for over a month.

'Mum's fine,' I say. 'She probably just wants to escape Bernard for a while. You know how boring he can be, droning on about golf and the Conservation Club.' My stepfather is a kind, but dull man. I'm still not sure why Mum married him, but she seems contented enough. I put the blouse on top of my suitcase. 'Shall we join the others?'

Darcy remains seated. 'There's something I have to tell you.'

She's not making eye contact. My mind spins away from eating disorders and self-harm to degenerative diseases and cancer.

I sit back down and reach for her hand. 'Tell me.'

'It's Noah,' she says.

This is the last thing I'm expecting.

'I wanted you to be prepared, before we all go in there and get drunk and he blurts it out.' She bites her lip. 'The thing is, he's just got engaged.'

It's a good thing I'm not standing. My knees feel watery and the damask foliage on the walls begins to wobble.

'I didn't know he was seeing anyone,' I say.

'Penny.' Darcy says the name as if it should mean something. 'His PA.'

A vague image comes to me of an earnest young woman in glasses, scuttling around Noah's apartment, a tablet in one hand, a coffee in the other. The sort of plain and efficient personal assistant, whose boss describes her as his Girl Friday before dumping his dry-cleaning on her desk and demanding she drop her weekend plans to prep for a meeting in Frankfurt first thing Monday.

Was this really the woman Noah intended to marry? Even before his finance app made him a millionaire, Noah had endless girlfriends. It was rarely worth learning their names. None of them made the slightest imprint on his life. Even the ones who moved in with him carried an air of impermanence. None of them lasted long enough to change the curtains.

If he ever did marry, I always imagined it would be one of

the society girls he occasionally hooks up with, an up-and-coming actress, the daughter of Lord Such-and-Such. Instead, he's asked Penny. I've no idea of her background but the plain, quiet young woman I met didn't fit any of these descriptions. If he was going to choose someone ordinary . . . no, my mind mustn't stray there. And yet . . .

My mum and Noah's used to laugh about how well we two got on and how we'd probably end up marrying one day. I didn't realise it was a joke. I thought we'd always be together. That illusion evaporated when he fell for Darcy.

We were only fifteen. But I can recall the sharp stab of seeing them together for the first time. I was walking home from school when I turned a corner, saw them holding hands and experienced the sharp spike of betrayal. They let go of each other the moment they saw me, which made it worse. Both of them knew it counted as cheating, though Noah and I had never been more than friends. I had no right to say anything so kept my hurt and confusion to myself. The truth is, I would have chosen Darcy over me. Everyone always did. Even Jake, my husband. He and Darcy dated briefly during my final year at art college. It's only because she went off to Italy that Jake and I got together.

Noah and Darcy's relationship was equally short-lived. It was nothing more than a fling on Darcy's side, and after Leanne's death she went to France to further her dance career, and Noah's father sent him to boarding school to do his A levels. I've never been sure of his feelings towards her. That he insisted on this weekend, because Darcy needs it, suggests some residual affection. Which I resent as much as I did twenty years ago.

Darcy sits quietly next to me.

To break the silence, which is becoming awkward, I say, 'I always thought Noah would end up with an Anoushka or a Tamara.'

'He says he's sick of socialites and women just after his money.'

'How does he know Penny's not after his money? They can't have been going out for long.'

'She's worked for him for a couple of years,' Darcy says. 'I don't know how long they've been an item. Ask him.'

'You know I can't,' I say. 'Is that why he suggested this gathering, to share the good news, because I don't know why we're here? We could have met anywhere. I know you don't like to travel, Darce, but you could have gone to Haverton at least.'

'You've spent too long pretending it never happened,' she says. 'I did the same but, you know, coming back is healing in a way.'

I want to say she doesn't look like she's healing. She looks like she's falling apart. The radiators are cranking out near tropical levels of heat and she still has that thick jumper on. What's she hiding?

'If people found out we were here, there'd be trouble,' I say.

'People do know,' she says. 'I've been back two years now and no one's said anything. The people who do remember, sympathise with me. They know it wasn't our fault. It was just a few idiots online.'

'If a few idiots decide to write their own narrative about what happened to Leanne it could ruin our lives. The truth doesn't matter to those people. Clicks do. Imagine if they found out we'd all met here, not two miles from where it happened, on the twentieth anniversary of her death. You're not planning on going up there, to the Hags Ring, are you?'

'Of course not,' Darcy says. 'That's not what this is about.'

'Then what is it about?'

'I told you, healing, forgiveness.'

She's eager and hopeful. A sickness grips my stomach. 'You've not invited Mrs Tattersall, have you?'

'God, no. I'm not sure she's still alive. And I know she'd never forgive us. We all have survivor's guilt. The forgiveness is for ourselves.'

But I don't feel guilty because I survived. I feel guilty because if it weren't for my jealousy and spite, Leanne would still be alive.

After a quick change of clothes, swapping my sweatshirt for a blouse, Darcy and I go downstairs. The stained glass at the front of the house carries the family crest I saw on the gates, as do two carvings at the top of the stairs: the oak and the falcon.

As we descend, Darcy says, 'I'd forgotten this place exists until Noah booked it. Ed said the same. Odd, it's only just outside the village.' She darts a furtive glance at me. 'By the way, Mum thinks we're meeting up in Oxford. If she finds out I'm just down the road, she'll find an excuse to come by. Ed's told Molly the same, so she doesn't expect him to go home tonight.'

'I'm hardly in a position to lecture on marital bliss, but can't he just tell her he wants a night away.'

'Nah. She won't like him and Chrissy sleeping in the same house. She thinks he's staying at Noah's and that Chrissy's at yours.'

'Ed could have asked me before including me in his lie,' I say.

'Noah's not pleased either, but Molly needs to get over it. Ed and Chrissy were kids. It was finished long before he even met Molly.'

I run my hand along the smooth mahogany of the balustrade, not knowing what to say.

Was Darcy really warning me about Noah? We were kids. I should get over it.

At the bottom of the stairs, I ask, 'This isn't going to be some sort of group therapy session, is it?'

Darcy laughs. 'Can you imagine Ed in therapy?' She mimics his gruff tones. 'We need to move on from the past, do we? What's your PhD in, the bleeding obvious?'

I can't help smiling. It's exactly what Ed would say.

'That stuff I said about reconnecting and facing our demons. It makes it sound loads heavier than it is. We're having dinner and a few drinks, that's all.' She sounds breezy. But it was Darcy who brought Leanne into our group and she was far fonder of her than the rest of us were. The light tone doesn't match what I know of Darcy and how sensitive she is. She seems far more concerned about me and sounds nervous as she asks, 'Look, you're cool about Noah getting married, aren't you?'

'Sure,' I say.

She smiles. 'I knew you would be. Noah was a bit worried.'

'Oh, come on. That was before I met Jake.' I've only just stopped wearing my wedding band and my ring finger feels suddenly light.

'Let's get in there and grab a drink before Ed necks the lot. He stopped off at the Fontaine Arms for a pint on his way over.'

'If I know Ed, it was more than one. We'd better go and rescue the Chardonnay.'

Darcy glides towards a door from where the strains of Outkast's 'Hey Ya!' can be heard. She still moves like a dancer, however unwell she appears.

I hover before the large mirror on the wall next to the front door. My hair's a mess. I pat down flyaways and wipe smudged mascara from under my eyes before opening them as wide as I can.

'Congratulations, Noah!'

The mirror reflects a maniac with an insincere grin.

I try again.

'Congratulations!'

Feigned rapture only emphasises the fine lines around my eyes that will soon become crow's-feet.

As I start to move away, the light coming in from the porch is suddenly obscured and there's a rustle against the front door.

'What are you doing?' Darcy asks.

'I thought I heard someone outside,' I say.

'The wind's getting up. It'll just be dried leaves,' she says.

That's what I'm afraid of. Bella taking shape in the dying vegetation. I take a step towards the front door.

'Come on, Mia,' Darcy calls.

It's silent now.

I turn and follow her into the lounge.

Chapter 9

My mother and Noah's, Natalie, were childhood friends. Both grew up in All Hallows and both moved to London for work, where they met and married their respective husbands. Noah and I were born a few months apart. In a strange city, with their husbands working long hours, most of their days were spent together and, in consequence, so were Noah's and mine. Not that I remember those early years. When I was two, my father died of cancer. Mum could no longer afford to live in London and so moved back to All Hallows. Noah's mother persuaded her husband to move back too. He spent so much time abroad doing something lucrative in IT no one understood, it seemed only fair that his wife should get to choose where they lived in England.

After Mum married Bernard, we ended up living on the same road as Noah and Natalie. Given the size of All Hallows, this is not as much of a coincidence as it might sound. Some of my earliest memories are of Noah and me being pushed along by our mothers in the park or tumbling around in our back gardens. Having known him all my life – long before either of us knew the others – I feel I have some sort of ownership.

Ed's father worked with my stepfather. They came to the parties and barbecues that Bernard loves to throw. Ed joined Noah and me in our rumbustious games, whilst the adults chatted and sipped cold beer. And although Noah's a little younger than Ed, Ed always looked up to him and still does.

Chrissy and I sat next to each other at primary school. We had both been marked out as gifted and were given extra classes. My gift appeared to be that I was slightly ahead of the other children. When they caught up, I fell back into being 'quite bright'. Chrissy, on the other hand, continued to be a stellar student, at school and university, becoming an academic specialising in psychology.

Darcy and I met at ballet. Naming her after the principle dancer at the Royal Ballet, Mrs Alderwell held grand ambitions for her daughter, and Darcy was marked out as a future star. I only attended the local dance school because it was offering three free taster classes. I lasted two before it became very obvious that I had little co-ordination and zero interest. During my second lesson I asked to be excused and sneaked off to read my book. At the end of class, I was found outside in the corridor, my head buried in *Alice in Wonderland*. Mum agreed with the ballet teacher that my time would be better spent elsewhere. The other girls lined up in their leotards, their hair in perfect globular buns, regarding me with a mixture of amazement and horror. All the girls except Darcy. She came over, looked at the cover of my book and asked if she could borrow it. I said, yes, and of course after that she had to come and borrow another and then another. Our friendship sprung from there.

All our childhoods were so intertwined, our adolescence so full of shared fun and mischief, that Darcy, Noah,

Chrissy and Ed forgot who forged our group. And that while Darcy was the beauty and Chrissy the brains, Noah the entrepreneur and Ed the joker, I was the glue. We were different but the same. We balanced each other out. We occasionally squabbled but never argued.

Until Leanne Tattersall came to our school.

Chapter 10

In the living room more fine-featured Verne-Fontaines stare down from wood-panelled walls, as if the Viscount might arrive at the Dower House at any moment to visit his widowed mother, ensconced in a Bath chair. Noah and Ed care nothing for the grand surroundings. They're lounging on a fat leather sofa, scrolling through Spotify and arguing good-naturedly about whose noughties playlist is better. The table in front of them is strewn with beer cans and a few packets of crisps. Chrissy is seated opposite on a matching sofa. Plain Christine Parker has transformed herself into the rather glamorous Chrissy Banks. Her frizzy hair sculpted into shiny waves. The pear shape Darcy's mother, Mrs Alderwell, once taunted her about is now swathed in loose but expensive fabric, lending her a svelte, chic nonchalance. She is the first to spot me and jumps to her feet, runs over, hugs me and gives me a kiss. Ed follows, then Noah. He looks a little nervous, and of course I go for the wrong cheek and our lips nearly brush and we both pull back and laugh as if it's nothing. And, to him, it is. Eventually I plant my lips on the correct cheek and splutter something about his engagement, congratulations being in order and Noah being a dark horse. I hope my face is doing a better job of expressing joy than it was in the hall mirror.

My acting must be passable because Noah relaxes a little. 'Thanks, Mia. It's a bit of a surprise to me, to be honest. How are things with you?'

Unconsciously, I start to finger the indentation where my wedding band should sit.

'Not too bad. Busy with work. I've got an exhibition at a Berlin gallery in March.'

'Fantastic,' he says. 'I'd love to come. So would Penny. She's a big fan of yours.'

Noah comes to all my exhibitions and invariably buys something. He's a big art collector, but my work is so different from his other paintings that I can't help thinking loyalty rather than personal taste prompts his purchases.

'Great. I'd love to see you there. We'll have to have a night out in Friedrichshain,' I say. 'But we should all meet up with Penny before then and before the wedding. Y'know, bring her into the gang. Have you set a date?'

'No date, but she'd love that,' Noah says.

It's one of those lies we all choose to perpetuate, that our partners will be accepted and welcomed into our group. They won't. Not Ed's wife, Molly. Nor Chrissy's husband, Mark. Jake was so resentful of my closeness to my friends, I'm wondering if he'll cite it in our divorce papers. His antipathy was made worse because he never believed my feelings for Noah were purely platonic any more than Chrissy does now. Not fooled by my performance, she gives my arm a squeeze.

'Drink?' she says and points me to the sofa while she goes over and pulls back one of the wooden panels to reveal a fridge. 'Cool, huh?'

Noah, who used to be happy guzzling cans of White Lightning cider and bottles of WKD Blue, has stocked the fridge with the sort of wine and champagne that could pay off our mortgages. A bit wasted on someone like me, who's happy with three-for-the-price-of-two minis from my local Tesco Express. I suspect Chrissy's the same.

'How about some fizz?' she says.

'Why not?'

Noah clears his throat. 'Go easy. We've got dinner first. Then we can go for it.'

I jump as something thuds against the window.

'It's just the wind,' Chrissy says.

Outside the eaves whistle and branches groan. *Miaaa*. I thought I'd be safe in a brightly lit room surrounded by friends. Yet even here *she* reaches for me. *Miaaa*.

I shut my eyes.

'Are you OK?' Chrissy asks. 'Go and sit down. I'll bring your drink over.'

I slump onto the sofa opposite the boys.

The others are looking at me. I don't want to make a fuss. My friends don't know about Bella. No one does. At first when I used to wake in the night, screaming, my neck damp with sweat and Bella leaning over me, Jake would hold me and tell me it was just a dream. Later he moved into the spare room to get some rest. Now he resides in the Home Counties and lies in the arms of a woman who sleeps soundly. He made a point of telling me this in our last conversation and went on to say that my night terrors were probably a result of my artistic temperament combined with trauma – 'the thing with that girl when you were a teenager'. I should probably see a therapist, just in case.

Just in case of what? Just in case I really am seeing a dead woman set on vengeance?

'Dom Perignon?' Chrissy says brightly, and hands me a coupe.

Anything fizzy tastes the same to me, so whether it's my lack of sophistication or the continuing whispering of the trees outside, the bubbles bursting on my tongue taste sour.

'Turn the music up, will you, Ed?' I say.

He does so and Bella recedes.

Darcy joins us on the sofa. She takes a coupe from Chrissy but doesn't drink.

'When was the last time we were together?' Chrissy asks. 'All of us, I mean, not just in twos.'

'Dad's funeral,' Ed says. 'Three years ago.'

'Really? That long?' Chrissy says. 'What happened to us?'

'Nothing happened to us. Our circumstances changed. We're not living within five minutes of each other; we have careers, families, lives.'

I only have one of those things and Darcy has none.

'Ed, only you and Chrissy have families,' Noah says.

'Yeah, but you'll be joining us soon,' Chrissy says.

I look away because I don't want to see the smile I sense spreading across Noah's face.

Chrissy's never had any romantic interest in Noah, so she can ask him anything without raising suspicions of an ulterior motive. 'So why Penny, after all the others?'

I hear Noah exhale. 'I guess 'cos she's so normal. She'd rather stay in and watch Netflix than go to some celeb gala. She shops at Zara and eats at Nando's. My other girlfriends were all designer this and Michelin-starred that. It's a buzz at the start, then it gets boring. I just want someone I can hang out with. Plus, I do want a family of my own, preferably before I go grey.'

Ed ruffles Noah's hair. 'You may be a little late for that.'

He's right. A lamp shines directly on Noah's head and highlights the smattering of silver in his dark mass of curls.

'But seriously, be careful what you wish for,' Ed says. 'If I were you, I'd wait until you're at least fifty.'

'Stop it, Ed,' Chrissy says. 'You'd be lost without Molly and the boys.'

Ed pulls a comedy-clown sad face, one of his stock expressions, which makes it impossible to tell how serious he's being. 'They're great. But we were too young. I wish I'd gone out and had more fun first. Why do you think I told Molly I'm in London this weekend?'

'I'm missing my two,' Chrissy says. 'But at the same time, I'm looking forward to a lie-in.'

The talk of children makes me uncomfortable. Jake wanted some, but I never did, and I don't know how Ed and Chrissy went through with it, knowing what's out there and what could happen to an ordinary girl like Leanne. I want to tell Noah he's being irresponsible. It's obvious to me he doesn't love Penny. He could 'hang out' with anyone. He just wants to be a father, and she's the right girl at the right time.

'Chrissy, you and Mark waited. And look at your career, look at Noah's and Mia's.'

'You can't compare me to Noah,' I say. 'I've done all right, but I'm not going to be able to buy Jake out of the flat after the divorce, and it's a two-bed in Tufnell Park, nothing like Noah's.'

'Move in with Noah then,' Ed says. 'His place is big enough.'

It's a joke, but I wince. Ed doesn't notice. Noah does and interrupts.

'The flat's not that big,' he says.

'Flat? You make it sound like two rooms squashed between a laundrette and a caff. Have you been there, Mia? It's massive, like something a Bond villain would live in.'

No, I have not been to the place Noah moved to earlier this year. He's never invited me. But I know the building because I made a point of walking past it on the opposite side of the river. It's as impressive as it is ugly, a huge modern development with balconies overhanging the water.

'A Bond villain would have his own island. And I'm working on it. But seriously,' Noah spreads his hands, 'Penny's the big change in my life, not the flat.'

Penny. The reason I've not seen Noah in the last twelve months, let alone his new place. And whilst my marriage was disintegrating, the confirmed bachelor decided to get hitched.

'Mia?' Chrissy says sharply.

I look up. 'What?'

'I was asking what you've been up to?'

'Work,' I say. 'Oh, and divorce.'

I try to make it sound like a joke.

'You're well out of that,' Ed says.

'Ed!' Chrissy says.

'It's OK, Chrissy. Ed's right. We weren't suited,' I say. 'We can't all be like you and Mark.'

Chrissy met her husband when they were both students and they moved in together immediately after graduation.

They waited until her career took off before having their two kids, Layla and Macey. If Chrissy still harbours any romantic feeling towards Ed, she hides it well. His reaction is less clear as he resumes editing the Spotify playlist.

'Actually, things aren't great with us,' Chrissy says. 'Mark's lost his job. I mean, we'll get through it – it's just this wasn't the best time to come away.'

'It's only one night,' Darcy says.

'I know. But I've had to take on extra work to plug up the finances. I'm not home so much and Mark's feeling neglected.'

'Then he should get a job,' Ed says, showing the playlist hasn't absorbed his entire attention.

'He's trying,' Chrissy says.

Ed sniffs and looks unconvinced. Mark never lasts long anywhere. Like me, he went to art college; unlike me, he's never made money from his work and has ended up doing a string of dead-end jobs. Whenever we meet, he implies that his *oeuvres* are too intellectual for commercial success and making a living from my paintings is a sure sign of their inferior quality.

'Maybe he should try a bit harder. Or train to do something,' Ed says.

'Don't be so judgey,' Darcy says, speaking for the first time.

'I didn't mean you,' Ed says. 'You're not asking Chrissy to support you.'

I expect Darcy to go on to explain she's unemployed and living with her parents. Instead she waits for the next song to come on before saying, 'Is that Franz Ferdinand? I've not heard this song in ages.'

She jumps up and starts to move her hips to the spiky guitars of 'Take Me Out', then seems to think it's too much effort and slumps back on the sofa. I notice she's still not touched her champagne.

'And you, Ed,' Darcy says. 'What have you been doing?'

'Working, being a dad. Same old, same old.'

'So what Noah aspires to, you take for granted,' Darcy says.

'Yeah, well, like I told him, be careful what you wish for.'

'At least we made it. What do you think Leanne would be doing now?'

Darcy just comes out with it, like talking about Leanne is no big deal. We fall silent. It's stupid, we're meeting on the anniversary of her death, yet we've avoided mentioning her. Eventually Chrissy says, 'I think she'd be working as a buyer for an exclusive fashion boutique. She always had a great eye for clothes.'

'Yes, she bought that beautiful McQueen scarf. Do you remember?' Darcy says.

'Of course, Darcy,' Ed says. 'It was the one she was wearing when she died.'

We fall silent again. Noah tries to revive the conversation. 'All the boys thought being from London meant she was too cool to ask out.'

I long to tell them Beckenham, where Leanne came from, isn't really London. I want to show how I can empathise with a girl desperately trying to make an impression but fear I'll sound snide. It was no secret I disliked her. So instead I say, 'Alicia was so keen for her to go to her party because she knew the bass player from that band.'

'So the elephant's stopped stamping around the room and has taken a seat,' Ed says. 'Make that a herd of elephants.'

Noah puts down his drink. 'It's been twenty years since Leanne's death. Don't you think we should ditch the guilt and celebrate? We survived. Not just that night at the Hags Ring, but all the speculation and hate.'

'Can you imagine if it happened now?' Chrissy says. 'I read about some students in the States who had to go into hiding after their roommates were murdered. They had nothing to do with it, but all these online sleuths pinned it on them.'

'We shouldn't have come here,' I say. 'Not so close to the stones. We could have met up in London, or Oxford, or abroad. What if a tabloid or some true crime blogger came and took photos of us here this weekend? They'd twist it and make it into something sinister. I think we've been lucky no one's made a podcast. The case has all the elements: young, attractive victim, occult overtones – that's their meat and drink.'

'Nicholson was caught, and now he's dead,' Noah says. 'The podcasters like to blow the case wide open with shocking new evidence, even if it's entirely invented. I've had a few sniffing around. We always get legal involved early on. If the podcasters know any wild speculation's going to land them in court, they move on.'

'I still think we need to be careful,' Chrissy says. 'You've become well known, Noah. I saw an article about you in the *Financial Times* a couple of months back. And I'm surprised no one's outed Mia yet.'

It does seem more than luck that no one's corrected that first newspaper error, identifying me as Maria Collier. Also, despite lively online discussion on various niche forums, the case didn't ignite in the public imagination. It occurred on the same day as an industrial disaster in which scores of people were killed and injured. And the trial and sentencing happened in the middle of a political sex scandal. All of which meant Leanne's death did not make the headlines you might have expected for such a case.

'You live in the village, Darce,' Ed says. 'Has anyone ever contacted you?'

'I don't think so. Dad would get rid of them if they did. And you know I don't do any social media. The thing is, we did nothing wrong. We were victims too.'

'That didn't stop people blaming us and making stuff up back then,' Chrissy says. 'And it wouldn't stop them now.'

'I was so nervous catching the train here, Noah,' I say. 'Normally I drive to All Hallows, but Jake's got the car now. Walking up the High Street made sick me with nerves.'

'Look, no one knows we're here,' Noah says. 'Penny booked it. I just thought we should get together and mark the occasion somehow, because however much we wish it away, it did happen and it changed us in ways we probably don't even realise.'

'Jeez, if I'd known this was going to be a therapy session, I'd have stayed in the pub,' Ed says. 'Darcy and I both live in the village. No one's ever come knocking on our doors. So we're safe. And as for facing our demons, fuck it. We were kids messing about, the way kids do. It was sad, but I don't feel guilty. If you do, see a shrink, don't spoil a good evening.'

Noah looks hurt. In the past Ed has always deferred to him. Perhaps it's more than our proximity that's changed.

'We just need to acknowledge that it happened,' Noah says.

'Fine. I acknowledge it,' Ed says. 'Now pass me another beer.'

Despite disliking the champagne, I look down to see I've drained my glass. Noah sees it too.

'We should eat,' he says. 'The caterers left everything under foil in the kitchen. Most of it just needs heating up.'

'I'll do it,' I say, pleased to get out of this overheated room and the talk about Leanne.

'I'll help,' Noah says.

'Sit down,' Chrissy says. 'You've paid for everything. I'll go with Mia. You can lay the table.'

'It's already laid.'

'Then have a drink and catch up,' Chrissy says.

'You don't need to ask me twice.' Ed leans back and puts his feet up on the coffee table.

'I need to talk to you,' Chrissy whispers as we leave the room.

Chapter 11

I'm unsure where the kitchen is and at first I go to the door directly opposite the lounge, which is locked.

'I thought we had use of all the rooms,' I say to Chrissy.

'Do we? I only scanned that document Darcy sent. These old houses always have a north facing kitchen. Here.' She opens a door to the side of the staircase.

The kitchen's more Ikea than Downton Abbey, all clean lines and stainless steel. Metal trays are laid out covered in tin foil.

'It reminds me of school dinners,' I say.

'I don't think our school dinners contained truffle oil,' Chrissy says as she removes the cover from puréed potatoes, releasing the fungi's sickly aroma.

I had expected Noah's menu to be something 'cheffy', but it's more the sort of nineties dinner-party fare I remember Mum preparing for Bernard's friends. *Coquilles St Jacques* for starters and *boeuf bourguignon* with the aforementioned puréed potatoes for the main. The instructions for heating and serving are taped to the table.

Our limoncello semifreddo dessert has to be removed from the freezer an hour before serving.

I try to figure out the oven controls. I rarely use my cooker and, anyway, this one's a different make. Chrissy steps in and sets the dials to the correct mode and temperature. There's something calming in her unfussy domestic efficiency. But I can't help remembering where we are and what night it is.

The small high windows reflect the kitchen's interior so I'm unable to see out and can't tell how close the trees are on this side of the house.

'What did you want to talk to me about?' I ask.

'Darcy – do you think she's all right? She looks ill but I didn't want to ask her if something's wrong.'

'She doesn't tell me anything any more,' I say. 'The few times I've asked her, she's got defensive. But no, she's not well. I only hope that having two doctors in the family will mean she's getting what she needs.'

'If people don't want to see something, they won't. I don't trust the Alderwells to look after her.'

'It's impossible to know. If she won't talk to us I don't know what we can do.'

'And what about you, Mia?' Chrissy says.

I can't help thinking this is the real reason Chrissy wanted to get me on my own.

'I'm fine.'

'You keep staring and listening, like you're expecting someone. Are you?'

'No.'

'Then what is it? You totally ignored me when I was talking to you in the lounge, like you were in a different world. You're not yourself.'

'How can I be? Here, tonight of all nights.'

'Anniversaries are meaningless. They're just a pattern we

fix upon passing time,' she says. 'Years, months, days, they're determined by how the planet moves through space. We've gone twenty times around the sun since Leanne died, so what? It's no different to one and a half times or seventeen and three-quarters.'

'So why does it feel different?'

'It's deeply ingrained. Nearly everyone's earliest memories involve celebrating a birthday.'

If anyone can help me it's Chrissy. She has a PhD in psychology. I'm too scared to see a doctor, afraid of what they'll say or where they might send me.

'It's more than that, Chrissy. I see stuff. I hear stuff.'

She stops unwrapping the ready-prepped vegetables, but doesn't appear surprised.

'What sort of things?'

'Don't tell anyone else.'

'Course not.'

'That night at the Hags Ring twenty years ago wasn't the last time I saw Bella. Sometimes I wake up in the night and she's standing at the end of my bed.'

'Anything else?'

'In the day, I can hear her saying my name in anything that rustles or screeches. And her figure appears in the shadows and swirling leaves. She's coming more often. It's getting worse. I've never told anyone before. Not even Jake. Am I going mad?'

'No,' she says calmly. 'It's classic sleep paralysis, seeing a figure at the foot of your bed. It's described in all cultures, sometimes called a sleep demon or old hag. People used to think they were real. But it's just the brain waking before the body; it creates a hallucination to make sense of a situation where you're awake but you can't move. It's not happened to me, but I've seen studies . . .'

'You study this stuff?'

'Yeah. I've written papers on it.'

'Wow. I should have come to you sooner.'

I feel guilty because I've never taken the slightest interest in what Chrissy actually does. All I've ever known is that she's a high-flying academic. I make a note to try to read one of her papers.

'There's no cure for sleep paralysis,' she says. 'But it's linked to trauma. I could recommend a good counsellor.'

'No. Not that,' I say.

'OK, but now you know what it is it should be less frightening. And you need to reduce your stress levels. I know you're going through a divorce. What about yoga?'

'I'd sooner see a therapist.'

'Just don't go down Ed's root, with the self-medication.'

I think of all the empty wine bottles I've saved to recycle at the supermarket because I'm too embarrassed to leave them in the communal bin. OK, I'm not Ed and I don't drink every day, but it's creeping up from the odd glass with dinner.

'What about the stuff that happens during the day?' I ask.

'Hypnagogic hallucinations are the flip side of sleep paralysis. They happen when you're falling asleep but you can experience them during the day, especially if you're not sleeping well at night.'

'But it happens when I'm not tired, like earlier, when I came downstairs with Darcy, I heard Bella outside the door. The leaves were brushing against it.'

'What we went through as teenagers, seeing our friend bleeding out in front of us – you don't just walk away from that stuff. You've got PTSD, Mia. Your brain's firing off danger signals in response to harmless stimuli. If Pavlov's dogs had been beaten when he rang the bell rather than given food, they would have whimpered not salivated when they heard it.'

Just then, a bell does ring. We both jump.

'It's the front door. We're not expecting anyone else, are we?' Chrissy asks.

'Oh my God, it's her. Leanne's mother. Darcy said she wouldn't come.'

'It can't be.'

We stand still and strain to listen. Footsteps cross the hall. The door opens. Low greetings are exchanged.

I pace the kitchen for a couple of seconds, then run and poke my head out into the hall.

Although the front door is now closed, a cold draught circulates and small twigs have blown in onto the floor. Noah is ushering two people, a man and a woman, into the room that was previously locked. I don't get a good look at the woman but she's far too tall to be Mrs Tattersall.

The door clicks shut behind them.

The scent of rotting vegetation fills my nostrils. A sudden draught moves the twigs, which settle into the shape of a beckoning hand.

Who have you let into this house, Noah?

Chapter 12

In the kitchen Chrissy is waiting by the door.

'Was it Mrs Tattersall?' she asks.

I shake my head. 'A woman and a man I don't recognise. Noah let them in.'

A shadow of concern crosses Chrissy's face.

'We shouldn't be inviting other people here,' she says. 'Not tonight. I'm going to speak to him.'

I go towards the door but Chrissy is out into the hall first. She brushes the pile of twigs away with her shoe.

'That room.' I point.

We're halfway to the door when it opens and Noah comes out. He stops abruptly, startled at our presence.

'Who are they?' Chrissy asks.

Noah looks sheepish. 'I invited them,' he says.

'That doesn't answer my question. What are they doing here? It's meant to be just the five of us.'

'They're the after-dinner entertainment.'

'You never said anything about entertainment,' Chrissy says.

'I wanted it to be a surprise.'

'Are you insane, Noah?' she says. 'We've just been

discussing how important it is no one knows we're here on the twentieth anniversary of Leanne's death, so close to the stones. And you invite strangers into the house.'

'Privacy is as important to me as it is to you. These people,' he lowers his voice, 'they're very discreet.'

'Are they linked to Leanne?' I ask.

'Of course not,' he says. 'Come back to the sitting room. And don't say anything to the others. I told them the caterers had forgotten something.'

I look at Chrissy. She gives a slight shrug and appears unconcerned, then watches for my reaction. I think of what she's just told me, take a couple of deep breaths and look down at the twigs. They're now in a small heap against the wall. Of course there's no beckoning hand. There never was. My mind imposed a pattern onto them, just as Chrissy said. But the twist in my guts tells me our visitors aren't jugglers or mime artists. In fact, I can't imagine what sort of entertainment Noah would want and why he thinks we need it. If he's tricking us into some sort of group therapy, I'm sure Ed will walk out and I'll go with him.

After placing all the trays in the oven and setting the timer, we return to the lounge. One of our favourites from back in the day, Daft Punk's 'One More Time', is pumping out of the speakers, but neither Darcy nor Ed are dancing. Darcy's where I left her, on the sofa with her legs curled under her chin, and Ed's leaning over the coffee table, tipping white powder out of a small plastic bag. He proceeds to chop it up with a credit card before scraping it into two lines.

'You're kidding me,' Noah says.

'Who's gonna know?' Ed says and snorts a line.

Noah looks furious. So does Chrissy.

'What sort of example are you setting Tyler and Ellis?' she asks.

'Like I do it in front of the kids. It's once in a blue moon, which, by the way, is about as often as I get out. Want some, Mia?'

'No.'

Ed's the last person who should be dabbling with drugs. He's always taken things too far. Only our experience on Hallows Hill the night Leanne died stopped him doing shrooms every week they were in season. Fortunately, Ed doesn't notice my judgemental tone because he's too busy neatening up his second line.

'Excellent. More for me,' he says before snorting it.

'Put it away,' Noah says. 'You're making everyone uncomfortable.'

Ed looks like he's about to argue but on seeing Chrissy's furious expression he pockets the packet of powder.

Darcy says nothing. She did a fair amount of coke in her wild London days. Now she sits quietly and her glass of champagne remains untouched.

Chrissy pours another one for me and I sit down.

I overhear Noah telling Ed that he needs to sort himself out. 'You drink like a fish and now you're into coke.'

Ed replies by calling him a boring old fart and picking up another can.

The dining room is at the back of the house, the other side of the staircase from the kitchen. It's in the faux medieval style of the lounge. We eat at a mahogany table laid with silver cutlery and ornate candlesticks. None of us enjoys the meal.

My anxiety about Bella and our unannounced guests leave me with no appetite. Ed pushes his food around the plate in between slurping on his beer. Darcy barely eats at the best of times. Only Noah and Chrissy pile their plates and, as we forgot to take the semifreddo out of the freezer, we decide to have pudding later.

I wish I'd never come but it's too late to get home by public transport. Mum's only down the road; I could go there, but that would mean explaining why I'm back in the village with Darcy, Noah, Chrissy and Ed on the anniversary of Leanne's death.

Chrissy's thinking the same.

'This is a mistake,' she whispers to me. 'If I hadn't drunk so much already I'd drive home.'

Ed overhears her.

'Look, I'm sorry about the drugs,' he says. 'I've put them away, OK? We're all back to our boring lives next week. Let's just have some fun. I've made a wicked playlist. It'll be like the old days.'

'You talk like we were normal teenagers,' I say.

'You make everything about Leanne,' Ed says. 'We *were* normal teenagers up until then – drinking, partying, no work, no bills, no parenting.'

Although I can remember those lost times of carefree fun and it's why I came back here tonight, Leanne's death is like a drop of blood in a glass of water. It taints the whole.

'I can't forget what happened,' I say. 'We shouldn't forget.'

'We were kids,' Ed says. 'Are we going to punish ourselves for ever?'

'That's not what I'm saying.'

'Ed's right,' Noah says. 'Earlier you asked me why I'm marrying Penny. I wasn't entirely honest. In the past I always ended relationships before I felt the need to discuss what happened with Leanne. I couldn't get serious before that conversation – it would have been lying by omission. With Penny it was different. It was so easy to tell her. She's suffered trauma and loss of her own. She's the one who's shown me how to move forward with my life – emotionally, I mean.'

'More therapy talk,' Ed says.

Noah ignores him.

'Penny made me see, it's something I have to deal with. If we're not guilty why do we feel guilty?'

'I don't,' Ed says.

'Your alcohol intake says otherwise,' Noah says.

'Thanks, Sigmund Freud, but I drink because I like it. And Penny doesn't even know us. Is that the only reason you're willing to hang out with your old friends now? Because she tells you to?'

Noah sighs. 'I don't need someone to tell me to hang out with you guys. And I saw you a few months ago, Ed. But Penny did suggest we all came here tonight.'

It's a punch in the guts. Their engagement is not just right time right place. Penny has a hold on Noah. Noah, who's always been a leader, is now in thrall to a woman we barely know. I thought it was him who wanted me here, when in fact it was his fiancée.

I can't keep the bitterness out of my voice as I ask, 'Did Penny arrange for those people in the other room?'

Ed puts down his can of beer. 'What other people?'

'They're in the morning room. I wanted it to be a surprise,' Noah says.

'Strippers?' Ed says and grins.

'Shut up,' Chrissy tells him. 'Who are they, Noah?'

'Don't get freaked out. It's going to sound weird but I know what I'm doing. The woman is Madame Castanese. She's a medium.'

We all stare at him.

'You're not serious,' I say.

'Sure. Why not?'

'After what happened to Leanne, we don't want to mess with that stuff – the occult.'

I look at the others for support. No one says anything. It's Darcy, who I realise has been unnaturally quiet all evening, who finally speaks.

'Madame Castanese isn't some charlatan. She has the gift.'

'You knew about this?' I ask.

Darcy gives a slight shrug and, in a flat tone, says, 'I'm thirty-six and still living in my childhood bedroom. I can't escape All Hallows. I can't escape Leanne. Everyone blamed us – Mum, Mrs Tattersall, the entire school. I blame myself. I need to know if Leanne does. Or has she forgiven us?'

'Leanne's dead. She can't blame or forgive anyone,' Chrissy says. 'And if this Castanese woman claims she can speak to her, then sorry, Darcy, but she is a charlatan.'

'You're so good at analysing everyone else, Chrissy,' Darcy says. 'But you never analyse yourself. You use fancy words and science so you don't have to face the truth. You were there. You saw what happened that night. We called Bella and she came. Leanne was murdered.'

'William Nicholson killed Leanne,' Chrissy says. 'He was a sick, dangerous man. All that occult stuff was invented by Rex Pender and the Crimson Circle. Even other pagans agree the Hags Ring has no significance. It's a folly. And if these two idiots,' Chrissy indicates Noah and Ed, 'hadn't spiked Mia's drink, we wouldn't be having this conversation.'

'Bella showed Mia that Leanne was going to die,' Darcy says.

'Mia ingested psilocybin. A hallucinogen that messes with your neurotransmitters. She had sensory misalignment. It's frightening, it's not supernatural. So can we stop with all this garbage? I expected better from you, Noah.'

'We reached out to evil and it came,' Noah says. 'I used to be like you. I drowned myself in code and algorithms. Everything had a logical explanation. But that's not working any more. Penny made me see that. I want to know if Leanne blames us.'

'And you think some sideshow freaks are going to tell you that?'

'I don't know, Chrissy,' Noah says. 'But we need to start talking about Leanne, her death and the effect it had on us.'

'Then let's talk about her. We can go on a retreat or book a therapy session. Not this.' Chrissy throws her arms in the air.

'I've been in therapy for years,' Noah says. 'It didn't help, and no matter how many hours I worked, how much money I made, how many models I screwed, it was always there like a second shadow. It wasn't until I met Penny—'

'Cunt struck,' Ed says.

'Fuck you, Ed. Penny's suffered so many bereavements, she nearly lost her mind. Castanese helped. We can't doubt our own senses. We have unfinished business.'

'These people prey on negative emotions, guilt, loss, despair,' Chrissy says. 'Anyone can look up the Leanne Tattersall case.'

'Penny booked us under a false name and if you don't believe, then what are you scared of?'

'I'm not scared. I'm worried about you.'

'That's kind, Chrissy, but I'm fine.'

'Mediums tell you what you want to hear.'

'She can't possibly know what I want to hear. You don't have to come but I'm going in. So's Darcy. Ed? Mia?'

I should refuse. It rankles that Penny has manoeuvred us here. Was she making notes on that iPad, her brain ticking over as she slid inconspicuously around us in Noah's old flat? Has she anticipated that I wouldn't want the others going in without me? I'm ninety per cent certain Castanese will turn out to be a fraud. But what if she's not and she's able to tell them the truth about what I did?

'I'll come,' I say. 'And I'll feel better if you're there, Chrissy.'

'No way. We can't reward these people. They're parasites feeding on guilt and grief. They make it dark and spooky so you're halfway to believing before they've even opened their mouths.'

'That's why we need you, Chrissy,' I say. 'To spot what she's up to.'

'Yes, we need you,' Darcy says. 'If she's scamming us, you can tell us how.'

Chrissy looks at Noah and Ed. 'All right,' she says. 'I'll come. I don't want us to fall out over this.'

Noah exhibits no sign of triumph.

'If Chrissy's going, so will I,' Ed says 'Let's face it, if these people could actually predict the future they'd be working in Downing Street or the White House, or they'd be sunning themselves on a yacht in St Tropez, frittering away their lottery winnings, not holding sweaty palms for a few quid.'

'It's a seance, not palmistry,' Darcy says.

'Whatever.'

Ed's derision eases my anxiety. He may play the fool, but like many fools he's laid bare the truth: it's impossible that the claims of people like Castanese hold water.

We follow Noah across the hall to the morning room, where I saw the two people enter earlier. He knocks on the door. A young man opens it.

'Hi. This is Leon, everyone,' Noah says.

Leon's wearing thick glasses, his head is shaved and the sleeves of his smart black suit strain to contain his biceps. He looks us up and down with a sharp eye, as if we're underage kids trying to get into a nightclub. When his eyes fall upon Darcy, his expression softens. He spends some time examining her before she returns his gaze and he looks away. Even to a man a couple of decades younger, she's still incredibly beautiful.

'Why does she need a bouncer?' Chrissy whispers to me.

I shrug.

'Is everyone sober?' Leon asks Noah.

'More or less.'

Leon looks less than pleased. 'Intoxication of any kind can lead to unpredictable outcomes,' he says.

'We've only had a couple of glasses of wine,' Noah says.

'If you say so,' Leon says. 'And I'll need your phones.'

'No way,' Ed says. 'My wife freaks if I'm out of contact for more than ten minutes.'

Leon crosses his arms. 'If you want Madame to do the reading, you need to give me your phones,' he says. 'We've had people try to discredit Madame. Journalists, podcasters making recordings and trying to catch her out. When you influence important people, you make enemies.'

Ed scoffs. 'What important people?'

'If I told you the names of those who've consulted Madame – royalty, politicians, captains of industry – you wouldn't believe me.'

'Well, that's one prediction you've got right,' Ed says.

Leon starts squaring up to Ed.

Noah steps in. 'Look, don't mind us. It's Madame's international reputation that drew us to her. We have nothing but respect.'

Glaring at Ed, Leon says, 'In that case, you'll understand about the phones.'

No one is going to call me and I hand mine over first. The others follow.

Leon places them in a bag and goes back into the room, closing the door behind him.

'Do you think politicians really use astrologers?' I ask.

'Elizabeth I had her own astrologer, as did Ronald Reagan,' Noah says.

'You didn't believe all that about the famous names, did you?' Ed says. 'They make it up so they can fleece you for more. How much did you pay for this, Noah?'

'It doesn't matter,' he says.

'Yeah, well, rather you than me. As a test, I'll ask her if she can give me the score for the Villa match next week. I suppose the no intoxication rule means I can't take a beer in.'

'You need to take this seriously,' Darcy says. She clings to my arm and I notice she's shaking.

'You don't have to go in there,' I say to her. 'We can go back to the lounge and listen to music.'

'We agreed to do this together. Darcy's fine,' Noah says.

'I would be if Ed stopped messing around,' she says.

'Soz,' Ed says, and tries to look serious.

Leon returns. 'Madame will see you now. But she told me to warn you that if you enter with malice in your hearts, that is what will leave with you.'

Ed rolls his eyes and we file through the door.

Chapter 13

The room is dimly lit, the 'dark and spooky' Chrissy predicted. Candles on the central table send distorted shadows across the wood-panelled walls and cast a shimmering yellow light over the paintings hung there. Unlike the portraiture of the other rooms, these are of local scenery: the Neo-Palladian splendour of All Hallows Court before it burnt down, the Dower House in summer and Hallows Hill crowned by the Hags Ring stones. It's painted at dusk with the setting sun bathing the hilltop red. Chrissy and I stare open mouthed. Did Noah know about this? Was it put here deliberately to remind us of what happened up there?

The painting is sufficiently distracting that at first I don't notice Madame Castanese, which is amazing, given her striking appearance. Standing in the corner with her back to us, the blond ringlets piled on top of her head, make her over six feet tall. Her black taffeta dress skims the floor and its voluminous sleeves quiver as our entrance disturbs the air.

'Sit down,' she says in a deep, melodious voice that carries a non-specific foreign lilt.

We take our seats around the table. I decide to sit between Ed and Chrissy. Their cynicism offers reassurance.

When Madame Castanese turns to us, it's a shock. The girlish curls don't match her face, which is gaunt and deeply lined, the eyes lost behind heavy black mascara. She has to be at least sixty and that hair must be a wig.

She returns our scrutiny, her eyes skimming over each of us.

'I am Madame Castanese,' she declares. 'Leon was not entirely satisfied with your attitude.' Ed smirks like a naughty schoolboy. 'You're not the first to come to me with an inelastic mindset. A limitation too common for me to take offence. But for your own safety, do not show such disrespect towards the spirits. Leon has already warned you that the only malice in this room is brought from outside. *Honi soit qui mal y pense*. Evil to he who thinks evil.'

She glides towards the table and sits down. One chair lies empty. Castanese glances towards it and nods, as if it's occupied. Beneath the table, Chrissy presses my foot, drawing my attention to this piece of theatre: a prop to unnerve us before we've begun. Why then, knowing this, do goosebumps creep up my arm?

'Your names?' Castanese asks.

Noah introduces us by first names only. Castanese merely nods before drawing herself up in her seat. Her thick eyelashes flutter before her gaze lands, not upon us, but an undefined space in the middle distance.

'Fear stalks this room,' she says. 'Some of you are afraid to believe in spirits. Others of what they have to say.'

The candles flicker though the air is still.

Castanese removes a purple silk shawl at the centre of the table to reveal an orb of intense black.

'Obsidian,' she says. 'Brought back from the Americas by

Sir Francis Drake. Cut from the same Aztec mine as the mirror owned by Elizabeth I's alchemist, Dr John Dee. It has been passed down through the women of the Castanese family, gathering power with each generation.'

Chrissy presses my foot again.

'Dee was a great man. But he was limited, catching only glimpses of other realms in his mirror. The women in my family are born simultaneously into both the corporeal and the spirit world. To us that world, the past, present and future are as one.'

Next to me Ed's shoulders jiggle up and down in laughter but mine remain still and my breath becomes shallow.

'Nothing is hidden from the spirits, no secrets, no desires. Knowing this, and given my warning about your intentions, are you certain you wish to continue?'

'We're sure,' Noah says.

Darcy takes a deep breath. I daren't look at her. Her fear will only fuel mine.

A soft draught blows in from nowhere and Madame Castenese's taffeta rustles like dry leaves. She draws a loose ringlet over her ear.

'We will begin.'

Her hands lie on the crystal ball and she lets her head fall forwards, her long, painted nails tapping lightly on the glass. It seems to me that dark waves are lapping within it. I blink to make the image disappear. As Madame Castanese's fingers still, her body becomes taut.

Eventually she raises her head, eyes closed.

'Someone comes. A man.'

The house is so close to the Hags Ring, my mind leaps to William Nicholson.

'He's here for Chrissy – a relative. Your grandfather . . .' Castanese hesitates. 'No, your great-grandfather.'

We're at an age where we could still have grandparents alive but great-grandparents are unlikely.

'He's worried about you,' Castanese says. 'Your life is not going as planned.'

'Whose is?' Chrissy says.

'Your great-grandfather says marriage is for life and your husband loves you. He says you should concentrate on your marriage. Not your ambition. Nor your carnal desires.'

The ambition bit makes sense. Chrissy's career is important to her and Mark resents her success. The carnal part is a reach. But as Chrissy's wearing a wedding ring and no marriage is perfect, any nod to spousal disputes is going to sound familiar. Chrissy's face shows she's unimpressed.

Castenese doesn't notice as she continues to tap her fingernails on the glass.

'He's gone,' she says.

There's a sense of anti-climax, as if bracing for a blow that doesn't fall.

'Is there anyone else who wants to speak to us? Yes?' She looks up. 'A woman – she's here for Noah. She won't say who she is.' Castanese tilts her head to one side. 'Strange, very strange. She has a message for you. Only one.'

Noah sits up.

'Don't marry that woman.'

Ed shoulders judder with laughter once more. Noah's face turns from surprise to annoyance.

'This isn't what we came for,' he says.

'I cannot guarantee who will appear and what they will choose to reveal. Your fear holds them back. But I sense fear was not all you brought with you. Guilt and deceit have also entered this room. You appear as friends but none of you trusts the others.'

'We trust each other one hundred per cent,' Ed says. 'We've known each other since we were kids. There's no one I trust more. Your blob of glass isn't up to much if it can't see that.'

Castanese's eyes narrow. 'I did not need to consult the orb to make my observation. A collection of people on the verge of middle age, clinging to the friendships of their youth. Friendships that are more memory than reality.'

Only Ed can hold her gaze. For the rest of us her words are too close for comfort.

'Why did you really come here?' Castanese asks.

None of us reply.

'Never mind. The spirits will reveal all.' She places her hands back on the glass, lowers her head again. After some minutes she says, 'The atmosphere is not conducive to communication. Voices swirl around us but they are cautious. They are afraid.'

'Afraid of what?' Chrissy says.

Castanese doesn't appear to have heard her.

'Afraid of what?' Chrissy repeats.

Castanese remains silent. Then, without warning, she slumps across the table, knocking over the obsidian orb. We all look at each other. Castanese remains motionless. Chrissy, though furthest away, is the first to move, pushing her chair back and taking a step in Castanese's direction. But she stops and retakes her seat when Castanese jerks back to an upright position.

Her eyes are open and her mouth fixed in a rictus smile.

Then her head tips slowly backwards and her eyes roll up into her skull so that only the whites are visible.

Darcy lets out a screech. I take Chrissy's hand.

Castanese's jaw drops open and she begins to speak.

'You came. I've waited so long.'

It's not Castanese's voice but that of a teenage girl with a London accent.

This is the moment Chrissy warned us about. The theatrics have led us to a heightened emotional state, leaving us vulnerable to her mind tricks. I wait for the reassuring press of Chrissy's foot on mine. It doesn't come. She's gawping at Castanese because, like the rest of us, while the left side of her brain is scrambling to rationalise, the right side tells her that Leanne Tattersall is in the room.

Darcy starts whimpering. 'We need to stop this,' she says.

'No, carry on,' Noah says.

'It's so dark,' Leanne's voice says. 'Cold and dark.'

'This isn't funny,' Darcy says.

'I've been here too long.'

'Stop this.'

'Others come, every Halloween. But I've been waiting for you. Even your scarf couldn't keep out the cold. But it wasn't for the cold, was it?'

'What scarf?' Ed says.

'It was never meant to be me.' Madame Castanese's head rocks forwards. Her irises become visible and she looks directly at me. 'Nicholson came for you.'

I freeze. Darcy jumps to her feet. Noah pulls her back down.

'Lies. Lies upon lies.' Castanese continues to look straight at me, then points her finger. 'It was supposed to be you. You. You.'

Suddenly the candles gutter and die. The room falls black and the scent of rotten vegetation and damp earth fill the room.

Leaves rustle, twigs snap and a thin torch beam alights upon a dark sloe-berry eye and flaking tree-bark skin.

The eye turns upon me.

Miaaaa.

'No,' I shout.

You've been lonely. You wanted me to come.

'No.'

You want to know, don't you?

Bella holds out her arm, formed of a branch, the hand made of twigs. One finger unfurls. Five ripe green buds, bold and proud, one already shrivelled and brown.

One didn't see the summer. Five won't see the winter.

'Please,' I say. 'Please don't.'

To every thing there is a season...
 A time to be born, and a time to die;

The sloe eye holds me, then closes. A shard of unbearable pain shoots through my torso. The sweet, rancid smell of decay fills my nostrils. My throat constricts. I can't breathe. Darkness engulfs me. I'm going to die, here, at the foot of Hallows Hill.

Then a hand on my shoulder yanks me back into the room. It's Chrissy.

The candles are relit and Madame Castanese is back, slumped across the table. Darcy is clinging to Noah; his head is buried in her hair. Chrissy's face is blank with fear.

I wrap my arms over my chest.

Chrissy gets up and shakes Castanese's shoulder. She jolts awake, blinking as if she's not sure where she is. The rictus smile has gone. She's returned to looking like a tired sixty-year-old woman.

'Do you want me to fetch Leon?' Chrissy asks.

'There's nothing wrong with her,' Ed says.

Castanese ignores both of them and looks straight at me.

'Who was she – that girl, the one that was killed?'

'Don't give me that, you knew who we were before you came here,' Ed says.

Castanese doesn't take her eyes off me as she says, 'The reading is over.'

'You're a fraud,' Ed says. 'A sick charlatan.'

Castanese laughs and shakes her head. 'You think what happened to that girl was bad? Wait until you see what's coming.'

The malice Castanese claimed only we could bring to the room is now dancing in her eyes. Darcy is breathing so hard, I think she's having a panic attack.

'This needs to stop,' Chrissy says.

Castanese sets the orb upright and re-covers it with the silk shawl. 'I warned you before you entered: if the truth frightens you, you should not come to this table.'

'What truth?' Ed says. 'You're just trying to fuck with our heads. Noah, you didn't pay in advance, did you?'

Noah swallows. 'Things have got out of hand. We've finished now, Madame.'

Castanese's eyes swivel back to me. 'Mia, isn't it? You know the truth. Are you going to tell them?'

'What does Mia know?' Ed asks.

Castanese's accent loses its foreign lilt and she breaks

into broad Scouse as she says, 'Don't shoot the messenger. But you'll all be dead by Christmas.'

Ed slams his hand on the table and leans in, his face an inch from hers.

'You spiteful old bitch.'

The raised voices bring Leon into the room. Ed steps back as he bursts through the door, rippling with anger.

Castanese, her previous accent restored, says coolly, 'I've just explained to our clients that the reading is over.'

'You need to leave,' Leon says.

No one moves.

'Madame has told you the reading is over. So go.'

'Come on,' Noah says.

Leon turns to Ed, his face bright with anger. 'Listen to your friend.'

He opens the door and indicates for us to get out. Ed pulls himself up to his full height, then realising he's still a head shorter than Leon makes a show of helping Chrissy, though she's perfectly capable of helping herself. Unlike Darcy, who's virtually carried out by Noah.

I push my chair back and move towards the door. Castanese puts a hand on my arm to stop me. She waits for the room to empty before saying, 'Perhaps we should have swapped seats.'

'I don't know what you mean.'

'No?' She raises a pencilled-in eyebrow. 'The veil between the realms of the living and dead is gossamer thin. Still, most can't see through, even fewer are able to raise it. I have that ability, though it comes and goes. But I've never met anyone like you before. You have the gift. You do not lift the veil – another comes from the other side and lifts it for you. She's reaching for you but you shun her. Who is she? Why does she come?'

A memory comes to me. I am very young and my mother is leaning over me, her face eager and frightened. 'You must tell no one of what you saw. No one. Forget you saw it yourself.'

I had forgotten all but her urgent warning, which she had given years before Leanne's death and before I first saw Bella. What then had I seen? Whatever the answer, I stick to Mum's advice – tell no one.

'Ed's right. You're a fraud,' I say.

'By the time you find out I'm not, I fear it will be too late. The buds will die in the winter frosts.'

I see them again as they shrivel on the branch and I'm robbed of speech.

Leon comes back. 'Are you still here?'

Castanese lets go of my arm and I run from the room.

Chrissy is waiting for me in the hall, which seems darker and colder than before. I feel weak and hollowed out, as if the reading drained something from me, or through me.

'I knew this was a bad idea, Darcy's in a right state,' Chrissy says.

I say nothing. Chrissy peers at me. 'You didn't let her get to you, too? She obviously researched us before we came.'

I move further from the door. 'But how did she make the candles go out? Where did that smell come from? And that woman appeared from nowhere.'

Chrissy looks confused. 'The candles didn't go out, Mia. There was no smell and no woman.'

'But they did, and then . . .' rustling, glinting sloe eyes. 'You didn't see anything?'

She shakes her head. 'You haven't taken anything, have you?' she asks.

'Of course not.'

I see her face change, obviously doing some mental adjustments.

'You're a psychologist. Am I going mad, Chrissy?'

'No, you're not,' she says. 'Right now I need a drink. But we *need* to talk.'

She heads for the lounge. I'm just about to follow her when something scrapes against my face. I reach up and remove whatever's twisted into my hair.

It's a small twig.

Chapter 14

In the sitting room, Darcy is back on the sofa, and despite the heat from the fire and radiator, she has a woollen throw wrapped tight around her shoulders.

'How did she know all of that?' Darcy asks. 'About us? About Leanne?'

'You brought her here, Noah,' Ed says. 'What did you tell her?'

'Nothing. Penny made the booking.'

'Then what did Penny tell her?'

'She didn't have to tell her anything,' Chrissy says. 'Castanese will have researched the house and area before she came. Details of the Hags Ring murders are online. It would take her five minutes to learn about Isabella Verne-Fontaine, that woman in the 1940s and Leanne. She would have looked it up the second the booking was made.'

'Oh my God. This is going to get out, us being here,' I say. 'The tabloids . . . podcasters . . . I knew I should never have come.'

'No one's going to hear about this,' Noah says. 'Leon wasn't lying about the politicians and royalty. Any hint that Castanese talks to the media and her business is finished.'

'Even if she did find out who we are, it doesn't explain how she knew stuff that wasn't even in the papers. Stuff no one knew,' Darcy says.

Noah looks up. 'Like what?'

'You must have heard her,' Darcy says.

'There was nothing she couldn't have got from newspaper reports and true crime sites.'

'She said, "It was supposed to be you." I was the one who was meant to die. If she was right about that, what about the predictions?'

'No, Darce. She was looking at me,' I say.

'She meant me, Mia,' Darcy says. 'Leanne was wearing my scarf. My fake Alexander McQueen skull one. Castanese mentioned it.'

'Nicholson attacked Leanne because she was the first person he came across.'

Darcy shakes her head. 'It was me Nicholson wanted dead. Dad managed to keep it quiet.'

I try to keep my voice as calm as possible when I ask, 'Are you telling us it wasn't a random attack?' I glance at the others to indicate they shouldn't say anything. If we press Darcy too hard, she'll clam up.

'I swore to keep it a secret. I'm only telling you now, so you understand what Castanese said is true.'

Noah's about to say something. I raise a finger to stop him.

'You have to understand, Dad's a great guy and a good doctor,' Darcy says. 'Telling the police wouldn't have made any difference.'

'Telling them what?' I ask.

'That Nicholson was one of his patients.'

'How the hell did you keep that from the police?' Noah asks.

'It was easier than you think,' she says.

'But why lie, Darce?' I ask.

'Do you remember when Granddad died?'

I have a vague memory of being told not to go round to Darcy's house because Mr Alderwell's father has passed away and he was taking it hard. I don't see what this has to do with Nicholson.

'Dad went back to work too soon,' Darcy says. 'He wasn't himself. The patients at Heartfield Psychiatric Unit used to go to Haverton Hospital if they had a physical issue. Nicholson came in complaining of stomach pains.'

'So?' Noah says.

'Dad diagnosed an ulcer, gave Nicholson some antibiotics and sent him away.' Darcy looks close to tears. 'If it had been anyone else, they would have come back when the antibiotics didn't work. But the staff at Heartlands thought Nicholson was attention seeking when he kept complaining. The cancer diagnosis came too late for effective treatment.' She fingers the stem of her still-full glass. 'When Nicholson found out, he threatened to kill our whole family. Dad didn't say anything. There was no point in frightening us when Nicholson was locked up. Then he escaped.'

'But how did he know where you lived, or that we'd be at the Hags Ring?' I ask.

'We think he must have gone to Haverton Hospital, followed Dad home and seen me in the McQueen scarf. Then, because Leanne was wearing it, and it was dark, he mistook her for me.'

I shift in my seat but Darcy's not looking in my direction.

'I still don't understand why you didn't tell the police,' Chrissy says.

'Dad had been a doctor for years, helped thousands of people. He was about to be made Head of Department. It wasn't fair for him to miss out because of one mistake. One mistake, in all those years, when he wasn't himself and under too much pressure. Nicholson was caught straight away. They had to pump him full of sedatives to keep him from being violent. Dad got rid of the paperwork and Heartlands was closed down soon afterwards so no one made the connection. What was the point? It didn't affect the trial.'

It never occurred to me I wasn't the only one carrying a secret about that night.

'You did the right thing,' Noah says.

Ed nods.

Only Chrissy presses her lips together. She believes in obeying the rules. But maybe she's forgotten how we were the target of anger from both the village and online forums. Darcy seemed to get the worst of it because she was so pretty with her pixie face and enormous eyes.

That sort of attention was bad enough, but knowing all the time that she was the intended victim, well, I'm not surprised she didn't cope as well as the rest of us. If any of us did manage to cope. Ed's an alcoholic, Chrissy's a workaholic, Noah's a control freak. And what am I? The one who jumps at leaves tumbling down a pavement or the tap of a stray branch on the window at night.

'But that's not the point,' Darcy says. 'How did Castanese know?'

Chrissy tries to calm Darcy with reason. 'There's been hundreds – literally hundreds – of surveys under lab conditions that show there's no such thing as mediumship or clairvoyance or whatever you want to call it. Not one single experiment demonstrates anything more accurate than guesswork and the laws of probability. "It was supposed to be you." She knows we all have survivor's guilt. Mia thought she meant her. She didn't know about your dad. You just leapt to that conclusion.'

I stay silent, my hand in my pocket, turning the tiny twig that was stuck in my hair.

'Explain how she could have known about the scarf?' Darcy says. 'The police never even noted that it used to be mine. None of the internet sleuths have mentioned it.'

'Castanese must have spoken to someone,' Chrissy says.

'No one knew outside our family and we wouldn't tell anyone.'

'Not even your mum?' Chrissy asks.

'Especially not Mum,' Darcy says.

Darcy's Mum, Mrs Alderwell, used to proclaim that Chrissy's brains were only partial compensation for her plain looks. And, in more recent years, expressed her surprise that she ever found a husband.

'If you say so,' Chrissy says. 'But Castanese used a classic clairvoyant's ploy. Throw out something general and the client interprets it as a specific. Anyone who'd been through what we've been through would have that at the back of their mind: "it should have been me". She's cruel and clever. Look what she did to Mia.'

All eyes turn to me.

'Mia?' Darcy says.

'Nothing. I was upset. Just like you, Darce.' I glare at Chrissy. *Shut up.*

'Sorry,' she says. 'I'm only trying to make Darcy feel better.'

'Can't you make me feel better?' I ask.

'What happened?' Noah asks.

'Nothing. You shouldn't have said anything, Chrissy.'

'Yeah, let's pretend it never happened,' Darcy says.

'For God sake, Darce,' Ed says. 'Castanese is a skilled charlatan. She can tell us about the past because it's on the internet. She can't tell us the future. She picked on you because she can tell you're sensitive and probably because you're so pretty and she's an ageing old hag.'

'That's so sexist,' Chrissy says.

'I would have said the same about a man,' he says.

'But she isn't and—'

'Let's not argue,' Ed says. 'I was looking forward to a night away from the kids and having some fun. The whole Castanese thing was a bad idea from start to finish. She's right, we're all going to die. Everyone does. Just not by this Christmas. I'm going to forget about it and enjoy myself. Who's with me?'

He reaches for his top pocket, thinks better of it and goes and pours himself a whisky instead.

'I've had enough,' Darcy says. 'I'm going to bed.'

'It's not even ten o'clock,' Ed says.

'I don't care, I'm exhausted.'

She looks it. The smudges under her eyes have darkened, and she's still wrapped tight in the woollen throw, even though the heat from the radiators is stifling.

'Noah? Chrissy? Mia?' Ed appeals.

Noah shrugs. 'Why not?'

'One more,' Chrissy says. 'But I need to go up and ring Mark first.'

'I'll go with Darcy,' I say.

I'm worried about her and I'm not in the mood for Ed's enforced jollity.

Darcy walks up the stairs so slowly I think of offering her an arm. She makes it to the top, however. Chrissy's room is next to ours, and she hovers at the door.

'Are you sure you two will be OK?'

'Yeah, why shouldn't we be?' Darcy says.

'No reason. Only . . . you know none of it's real, Darcy. I know that woman got under your skin.'

'Mia's with me,' Darcy says. 'I'll be fine.'

Chrissy gives a tight smile and as she goes into her room she catches my eye and mouths the word 'later'.

I nod.

Chapter 15

While Darcy takes a shower, I boil the kettle to make camomile tea. Although I'm the only one who saw Bella, Darcy is far more shaken. It's ages before the bathroom door opens and she comes out through a cloud of steam, dressed in a thick fleece onesie and with a towel twisted into a turban around her wet hair.

'It's freezing in here,' she says.

It's actually sweltering.

'I made you tea,' I say and point to the mug next to the bed. 'That'll warm you up.'

Darcy goes to pick it up, then stops.

'What did Castanese say to you, after we left the room?'

'She repeated what she said to all of us, we'll be dead by Christmas. Ed's right, she's a spiteful bitch. Don't let it upset you.'

Darcy lets the towel fall to the floor. 'I wish you wouldn't talk to me like that. All of you do it, as if I'm a particularly delicate child.'

'Would you prefer it if we didn't care? I know you hate me mentioning it, Darce, but you don't look well and you haven't for ages.' Her face hardens. I raise my hands. 'I'm not going to ask any questions, but it's natural for us to worry. I mean, you've gone back to living with your parents, you don't have a job, and you don't seem to want to change any of that. I could understand it if you were ill—'

'I've told you, I'm fine,' she snaps. 'You're the one who looks ill. All that concealer isn't hiding how puffy your eyes are. I think you worry about me so you don't have to think about your own situation.'

'What situation? Sure, I'm getting divorced but I've got a flat and a job. I'm not living at home with my mum waiting for life to happen.'

Darcy draws back.

'I'm sorry. I didn't mean . . .'

'There's stuff you don't know,' Darcy says. 'It's difficult. I can't leave Mum. She struggles with anxiety. She needs me. If I wasn't there, I don't know how she'd cope.'

If passive aggression were an Olympic event, Mrs Alderwell would be a gold medallist. I have to make a conscious effort not to roll my eyes.

'I know what you think,' Darcy says. 'But she's getting older, she's nervy. Dad and David are out working all day and she hates being there on her own.'

David, Darcy's older brother, also lives at home. He used to be sweet on me, as Mum termed it. It was embarrassing because although there's nothing of his mother's spite about him, he's dull and unattractive and, as my best friend's brother, it was awkward.

'My mum's older than yours,' I say. 'She would love me to move closer to home. The thing is, she knows my life's in London.'

'Your mum's not on anti-anxiety medication and riddled

with osteoporosis and arthritis. Mum needs sticks to walk now. Soon she'll be in a wheelchair.'

'John and David earn enough to pay for a helper. She doesn't need you twenty-four seven. You could leave.'

'Not when I don't have a job and I'd never find one that pays enough for me to rent anywhere decent. I can't bear the thought of some grotty studio.'

'Can you not at least try and get out more? What about dating apps?'

She gives an empty laugh.

'Guys on there are always ten years older and four inches shorter than their profiles. They say they're solvent then try and wriggle out of paying the bill, and "single" means they've a burner phone their wife doesn't know about. I'm done with dating apps.'

'At least come and visit me next weekend,' I say. 'We can go to the theatre or the ballet.'

'A reminder of my failure. No, thanks.'

'You got injured, Darcy. It wasn't your fault.'

Her laugh is mirthless. 'You don't still believe all that injury rubbish Mum put about, do you, Mia? I wasn't good enough. That's it.'

'But you got into that prestigious ballet school.'

She shakes her head. 'Mum told everyone it was prestigious. No one in the dance world has ever heard of it.'

'Why did you never tell me this before?'

'Because I wanted to believe it myself. That if it wasn't for bad luck I'd be a prima ballerina in one of the top companies. But I'm too old for that. At some point in your life you have to realise who you are. And I'm an Alderwell. I will find a job, but it will be in All Hallows.'

'But you need to get away from the Grange.'

'It's not so bad at home,' she says. 'Mum can be difficult but she's kind underneath.'

I lean back so my face is out of the light, where Darcy can't see it. Mrs Alderwell is not kind at any level. Thinness is the only quality she values in women because, as she'll tell you within half a minute of meeting, she doesn't weigh a pound more than she did the day she left the corps de ballet. That living on apple cider vinegar and cigarettes have left her with crumbling bones and the face of a woman thirty years older is of no consequence. I'm pretty sure the starvation diet decreed by her mother has led to Darcy's poor health. And though normally you'd blame a woman's poor choice in men on the relationship with her father, I blame Mrs Alderwell, who ground Darcy's self-worth so far into the dirt she considers any man caring for her a sign of poor judgement. Her longest relationships have all been with married men or ones who treat her as nothing more than arm candy.

Mrs Alderwell is the reason why my beautiful, brilliant friend Darcy, who even now turns the heads of younger men like Leon, has ended up living this half-life. In the aftermath of Leanne's death, when we became pariahs, the rest of us had the support of our families, whereas Darcy faced as much criticism within the home as outside of it. The horror that spurred the rest of us to make something of ourselves broke her. And looking back, I'm sure Mrs Alderwell was secretly pleased Darcy's dance career failed. No one should outshine her, not even her own daughter. She even resents my success. *I can't believe people pay for those awful daubs of yours.* And Chrissy being an eminent academic, causes even more derision. *No job for a woman. And what do you boffins know anyway?*

I start to unpack my small suitcase to avoid responding to Darcy's assertion of her mother's kindness.

'You know what I think?' Darcy says. 'I think we're cursed.'

'Don't talk rubbish.'

'That night, on Hallows Hill, we did raise something. The spirit of Bella, or maybe something else. It's followed us. And I can make excuses about failing to make my mark at ballet school or it not working out with Alessandro. But I was eighteen when I left Paris and twenty-eight when I broke up with Alessandro. I've had plenty of time to rebuild. I tried to be an artist like you, I tried teaching ballet. I've been on endless dates trying to find "the one". Why do I always end up with nothing and nobody? I can't help thinking my life's a failure because I should be dead.'

Wind rattles the windows; I hear Bella's call.

'You need to stop talking like this,' I say.

'It's not just me, though, is it? Outwardly you lot are successful, but none of us are happy. You never smile these days, Mia. And we both know you despise those paintings that make you so much money.'

I swallow. I didn't realise I'm so transparent.

'Soz. That was harsh,' Darcy says. 'Today's been exhausting. I'm going to get some Zs.'

She takes a couple of small blue tablets from a bottle.

'Sleeping pills,' she says. 'Want some?'

'No, thanks,' I say.

Darcy finishes drying her hair, then gets under the covers.

'You don't have to turn the light off. I've got my eye mask.'

She pulls it over her face and lies on her side. Soon her breathing becomes soft and even and I know she's asleep.

I sit on the bed, scrolling through nonsense on my phone. On Instagram, I see Jake has posted a picture of Lisette's baby bump.

The wine has dulled me. I can't feel anything – not anger, not jealousy.

'Congratulations,' I type underneath.

Then, in a fit of paranoia I go to the usual true crime forums and scroll through to make sure no one's found out about our meeting. There's nothing. I lie back against the headboard. Sleep is far away.

The gift.

Who other than Castanese has used those words about me? The image of a woman in a smart suit comes to me. Mum has taken me to see this person before I start at primary school. The nice lady is going to help me with the slight stutter I've developed. I want to talk nicely in front of all my new classmates, don't I? But the woman doesn't ask me about my stutter. She asks me all sorts of unconnected questions about my father, who died before I can remember him, and my grandmother, whom I met only once. Had I minded when my mother left me with a neighbour and gone out to work? At the end of the session Mum came back into the room and spoke to the lady. They thought they had lowered their voices but I overheard. *The gift.* I now realise the woman was a child psychologist. Why would she be using words associated with mystical mumbo jumbo? Maybe I'll ask Mum when I see her, but I'm not sure this memory is even real.

I'm relieved to be pulled out of my own musing by WhatsApp.

Chrissy
Are you still up? Fancy a nightcap?
> Me
> Yes.
Chrissy
I know what happened to you with Castanese. I'll explain everything. I'm back in the morning room.

I check Darcy is asleep. Then I slip out and go downstairs.

Chapter 16

My hand lingers on the door of the morning room. The memories of what I experienced in there are still fresh. Can Bella still be waiting for me? I know Chrissy is already inside. The light will be on, there will be no shadow in the corner. I push it open.

Under electric lights, the room is ordinary to the point of boring. Even the painting of the Hags Ring loses its menace.

Chrissy is sitting at the same table where Castanese did the reading. She smiles as I enter but it doesn't reach her eyes. Sometimes I wonder why she chooses to hang around with us. She's always been too clever and too sensible. It can only be the old associations, the old bonds.

'I got some more champagne,' she says, and pours us a glass each. 'What's Darcy up to?'

'Sleeping. She took a couple of pills.'

'You'd think she'd make the most of being away from Mrs Alderwell,' Chrissy says. 'I don't know how she can live with that woman.'

'She says she doesn't want to move out to some scummy studio flat.'

'I'd sooner sleep in a cardboard box than in her mother's house.' Chrissy's light tone belies her simmering anger.

'You should go back and see her. Slay the dragon,' I say. 'She's just some sad old woman these days, crippled with osteoporosis and arthritis.'

'I bet it doesn't affect her tongue,' Chrissy says. 'I worry Darcy is going to end up like her. She's so thin. Did you notice, she didn't touch any food or drink tonight?'

'Whatever you do, don't mention Darcy's weight. She'll bite your head off. But I'm serious, go and see Mrs Alderwell. We're not kids any more.'

'I know I should get over it,' Chrissy says. 'It was probably for the best she kept Ed and me apart. You know she was in his ear all the time, telling him that going out with someone so much cleverer was bound to end in tears. It really got to him. He's always had a chip on his shoulder about being less academic than the rest of us.'

'Mrs Alderwell can certainly sniff out people's sore spots.'

'I was pretty heartbroken at the time. I mean, Ed and I would never have lasted. He's better off with Molly and I'm better off with Mark. That's not the point. The point is why did she interfere? It was pure spite. Like telling me I'd never find a husband, as if we're in some costume drama and that's a woman's sole aim in life. I mean, her husband worships her and she's still miserable. She should have stayed single instead of inflicting herself on poor John. Not to mention ruining her kids' lives. We need to get Darcy out of there. Stage an intervention.'

'I've tried getting her down to London. She always makes excuses. What about asking her to come to you in Oxford?'

'She can't stand being around the children. They make

too much noise, apparently, and Mark's always playing the guitar. Besides, I prefer meeting up with you lot away from the house, having a break, y'know? Noah's got us croissants for breakfast. I'm going to take mine back to bed so I can sit in my PJs and get jam all over the sheets and someone else has to clear it up. You won't appreciate that, not having kids. I guess every weekend's a lie-in.'

There's no point telling her I wake up at five most mornings and get out of bed to stop myself falling back into nightmares.

'Can't you and Mark take it in turns getting up for the kids?' I ask.

'Yeah, right,' she says sarcastically.

'Are things OK between you two?' I ask.

'It's difficult with him not working. He insisted we sent the kids to private school and get that big house and now we're up to our eyes in debt and he's being picky about which job he takes. I've had to take on extra work. He doesn't have to take a pressured job. Ed's wife works in a garden centre. Even that would help.'

'I can't see Mark helping old ladies choose their azaleas.'

'When I suggested he trains as a teacher, he went right off on one. Is that all he's good for, lying to talentless brats and their parents that their doodles show promise? He's got as much brains as I have, yada yada yada.'

'No one's got as much brains as you, Chrissy. Well, no one I know.'

'Thanks, Mia, but having a PhD doesn't help me with Mark.'

'You're a psychologist. If you can't make it work, who can?'

Chrissy laughs. 'We're all amateurs when it comes to relationships. Anyway, I don't think it's the right time to invite Darcy down. What was Noah thinking, bringing that woman here? He's the last person I thought would buy into all that rubbish. And Darcy – "it was supposed to be you" – so obvious.'

'I was kind of relieved when Darcy said that because I did think Castanese meant me.'

'That's how they work. Something like that is bound to resonate. The stuff about her dad is just a coincidence.'

'You think the Alderwells should have told the truth?' I ask.

'Yes, but there's no point dragging that up now. What good would it do? I'm sure I read that Leanne's parents are dead.'

'You're right. But it must have eaten away at Darcy, knowing she was the intended victim.'

'We don't know that for sure. Nicholson threatened John, but with his mental state I doubt he could have constructed a plan to go to the hospital and follow him and then follow Darcy. It's more likely to have been a coincidence and Leanne was just unlucky.'

Given that Nicholson had to be sedated the moment he was captured, Chrissy could be right. He was incoherent, more the type to run up to John Alderwell screaming and raging, rather than silently and methodically shadowing him.

'Talking about insanity, you said you could explain what I saw in here.'

Chrissy places her hands on the table and leans forward. 'What exactly did you see?'

'It was like that night at the Hags Ring. I saw Bella. There was rustling and the smell of rotting vegetation. Then she came out of the corner of the room, a shadow at first before she took the shape of a woman made of leaves and twigs.'

'Did she say anything?'

'No.' I don't want to tell Chrissy about Castanese's first prediction, 'You'll all be dead by Christmas', already makes it too real. 'Tell me I'm not going mad, Chrissy.'

She takes her time answering.

'There are many external factors that affect how our senses perceive their surroundings.'

'I didn't drink shroom soup this time.'

'You don't have to take psilocybin to have a hallucination. I told you that earlier.'

I see Bella again, six buds on her hand. One was already dead: Leanne. The others then turned brown and died.

'The thing is, Chrissy, it felt so real.'

'In a heightened emotional state, your brain processes your surroundings in a very different manner. Do you know what a psychomanteum is?'

'A psycho-what?'

'It's a modern take on the Greek necromanteion.'

'Still no idea.'

'It's a small, enclosed area with a candle and a mirror where the recently bereaved can see spirits. There was a podcast recently where a psychic investigator used one. He deprived himself of sleep, watched scary movies and started seeing shadowy figures in the mirror.'

'I didn't just see shadowy figures.'

'It was dark, you've already had one traumatic experience when messing with the occult. Your brain was primed for this. It could even have been a flashback. People get those long after they've taken hallucinogenic drugs.'

'Twenty years later?'

We've gone over the events at the Hags Ring before. Noah and Ed tricking me into drinking shroom soup. I had misremembered the order in which things happened. I could not have known Leanne was dead before Darcy saw the body. Chrissy's reasoned scientific arguments are so convincing. And yet, I know what I experienced that night, and on the many days and nights since. The sight of Bella's twig unfurling, her wind-whistle voice. Castanese saw it too. And whatever Darcy thinks, Castenese's 'it was supposed to be you' was aimed at me.

'You've got so much going on. Not just Leanne. Jake too. Did he leave because of Noah?'

'What? No! Jake met someone else. Why would you think Noah's got anything to do with it?'

'You know it's not normal to fancy the same person you did as a teenager. Especially if they've made it clear they've no interest in you.'

'Well, now he's engaged to Miss Moneypenny, who's probably just another, better-disguised gold-digger, so I think I got the message,' I say.

'You didn't know he was engaged until today, and Jake still doesn't know.'

'You're supposed to be on my side, Chrissy.'

'It takes someone on your side to deliver a few home truths.'

'I never take Mark's side against you.'

'Because you don't like him. You don't like any of our

partners. You want us all to be single, so it's just us, like when we were teenagers.'

'That's not true.'

'You said Molly's boring.'

'She is.'

'And you sneer at Noah's fiancée when you've met her once for about five minutes.'

'*Home truths*. Isn't that the excuse Mrs Alderwell always uses for being a total bitch? Maybe you've more in common with her than you care to admit.'

I stand up, sloshing wine on the table. I go to the door and pull it open. Noah is standing outside. He must have heard everything.

Humiliation washes over me.

'Listen, Mia,' he says.

I push past him, race up the stairs to my bedroom and slam the door behind me. The noise doesn't disturb Darcy. She's curled up in exactly the same position as when I left. I wish she were awake, so I could vent about Chrissy. How unsupportive and disloyal she's being. How patronising and superior.

Being a leading scientist doesn't make you a leading relationship expert. As far as I know, Mark's her only boyfriend apart from Ed, and that hardly counts. How can she understand about Jake? Was I supposed to remain single for ever, waiting for Noah? My life moved on, even if my heart didn't. I never cheated on Jake and always supported him in his career. Not every marriage is a Mills & Boon romance. Some are practical and companionable. And even those that start off with flames of passion burn down to embers eventually. If I didn't act on my feelings for Noah, who was harmed?

I sit on my bed in the dark, unable to sleep. Of course, Noah has always known. But now we can't even pretend.

I hear Chrissy go into her room next door. She's speaking quickly into her phone. No doubt telling Mark what a bitch I am.

Who do I have to call?

Mum will be in bed. Jake is with another woman.

I drift into a half-sleep where sounds from the landing – laughter and slamming doors – merge with Madame Castanese's prophecy. The windows rattle. I dream of the Hags Ring stones coming to life and walking to the Dower House to block our escape. Branches tapping at our window become Bella's beckoning hand, seeking to lure me outside. The wind whistles around the eaves and whispers to me.

You raised something that Halloween on Hallows Hill.
You'll all be dead by Christmas.

Chapter 17

I wake to the pitter-patter of rain against the window. A grey light seeps from underneath the curtains. In the next bed, I can see Darcy is still curled up on her right side. She's not moved an inch since last night.

You'll all be dead by Christmas.

I jump out of bed.

'Darcy.' No response. 'Darcy.'

I lean in close to her mouth. No breath warms my cheek. *Oh dear God.* I'm reaching for her wrist to feel for a pulse when she wriggles her shoulders and lets out a long sigh before resettling into her original position.

My heart's banging against my chest. Castanese's prediction is getting to me. It's perfectly normal for someone in deep sleep to breathe shallowly. I need to get a grip.

It's seven thirty. Knowing Darcy, she won't be up for a couple of hours.

I check my Instagram. Jake has read my message but not replied. I shower, dress quickly, then leave the room, gently shutting the door behind me.

I'm about to go downstairs when I hear giggling from across the landing. A barefooted Chrissy, wearing just a

T-shirt, is coming out of Ed's room. He's leaning on the doorframe in his boxers. She runs a finger down his naked torso and leans in for a quick kiss. Before she reaches his lips, his jaw drops open at the sight of me. Chrissy turns. Her mouth forms an 'O' shape.

We stare at each other for a moment before I spin round and dive back into my room.

I expect Chrissy or Ed to knock and ask to speak to me and try to explain. No one comes. I sit on my bed.

Aren't Ed and Chrissy supposed to be the good guys? He, the family man, hands-on dad and attentive husband, and she, always Little Miss Follow-the-Rules.

'Bastards,' I say, not sure if I mean Jake or Ed or Chrissy.

Something about it, the easy affection, the lack of shame, tells me this isn't a one-off.

'Bastards.'

I can't face them or Noah right now. I pack my case and check the All Hallows Station timetable. I'll need to buy a new ticket but there's a train leaving in half an hour.

Darcy's still asleep when I creep out of the room, down the stairs and out of the house.

Leaves swirl in the wind, which whistles around my ears and stings my skin. The thin morning light outlines the grey hills to the back of the Dower House. I drag my case through the wet village streets, back to the station. I could do with a coffee but All Hallows' only café is closed.

A few people are already waiting on the platform, hidden under umbrellas, only the bright lights of their phone screens visible. More people arrive as I wait. It's busy for a cold Saturday morning. The train arrives and I take my seat.

HALLOWS HILL

The windows are all steamed up; there's no chance of seeing the Hags Ring on my return journey, for which I'm glad.

The direct trains to London start later in the day so I'll need to change in four stops.

My phone vibrates.

> Darcy
> > Where are you?
>
> Me
> > Feeling rough. Taking earlier train. Come to London next week xxx
>
> Darcy
> > I'll see how I feel x

I use the short journey from All Hallows to the main station to check on Castanese. Her website is surprisingly professional. Madame Castanese. The tenth-generation clairvoyant consulted by heads of state and royalty.

If our rulers are seeking out clairvoyants for advice it would explain why the world is in such a mess.

I scroll through pages and pages of endorsements.

Madame literally saved my life.

Since Madame told me business rival's methods, trade has flourished.

I always suspected my husband was cheating. Getting confirmation from Madame has helped me take the appropriate action.

Breaking up marriages – nice.

Now I know my little Emily's resting I've been able to move on.

Was little Emily the woman's daughter? Castanese has to be pretty twisted to make money out of grieving parents.

Weren't red flags flying when Noah researched her before booking?

I leave Castanese's website and do a general search. There are more recommendations on other sites, testimonies to her accuracy and insight.

Then I come upon another page. It's a reprint of a newspaper article from a Liverpool paper dated over fifteen years ago. A photograph shows a woman in dark glasses. She has long black straight hair with a severe fringe.

Four Years for Scheming Care Worker

Laura Eccles has been sentenced to four years in jail for altering the will of elderly dementia sufferer Edna Cunningham.

Care worker Eccles befriended the elderly widow, whose children lived several hours' drive away. Mrs Cunningham's previous will had disappeared and was replaced by a new one leaving everything to Eccles.

In February of this year, neighbours alerted the authorities when they noticed that Mrs Cunningham's upstairs windows were open and no one was answering the door. When police broke it down, they found the heating turned off and Mrs Cunningham in front of the window wearing only a thin nightdress. She died of pneumonia in the Royal Infirmary three days later.

The family were furious no charges were brought on this account. However, the CPS felt it could not be proved that Mrs Cunningham had not turned the heating off and opened the windows herself.

In his sentencing the judge characterised Eccles as 'A woman without conscience who prayed on the vulnerable.'

At first, I'm unable to see why the article appears in my search. Then I scroll down to the comments. Amongst the frequently expressed hope that Eccles rots in hell – and one assertion that this wouldn't happen if we euthanised the over-seventies – I come across a comment by a Matthew Cunningham.

> I am Edna Cunningham's son. Our family will never know if Laura Eccles shortened Mum's life. What we do know is the paltry jail term is now up and this woman is operating as a clairvoyant going by the name of Madame Castanese.

This is why it appeared in my search. I feel sick. Who the hell have we let into our lives?

Forgetting my anger towards them, I forward the link to our WhatsApp group.

Ed starts to write a reply, then stops. Darcy and Chrissy haven't read it yet. Noah has, but writes nothing in response. Why? Guilt? Embarrassment? If I found this so quickly, why didn't he? He has more reason for caution, in his position. Or did he leave all the arrangements to Penny? Maybe she's not as sharp as her resumé suggests. I'm ashamed of the flicker of joy this gives me and I damp it down.

＊＊

The main station where I have to change trains is rampacked with football fans as a local team is playing a match in London that afternoon. Boisterous fans chant, sing and swig from cans of lager, despite the early hour.

My hangover's starting to kick in with throbbing temples and the smell of beer turns my stomach. I need a can of cola and some Nurofen. The small kiosk on the platform will sell the former, if not the latter.

I buy a cola, a bottle of water and a bar of chocolate for any sugar crash later in the day. If I'd caught the later train, as planned, I'd have a seat booked. The chances of getting one without a reservation on this train are zero.

The tinny voice over the public address system announces: 'The ten twenty train to London Euston will be arriving on platform eight. First-class carriages are located towards the front of the train.'

There's no way I can stand all the way to London, being buffeted by a bunch of rowdy drunks. An upgrade to first class will be money well spent. Those carriages are at the front, and I have to move along the platform against the flow of the crowd, which would have been a challenge even if I wasn't lugging a suitcase behind me and didn't have a banging headache.

The packed platform makes it impossible to follow the public address instruction to 'remain behind the yellow line'. There's only a narrow strip at the edge of the platform that's clear for me to teeter down.

I manage to get about halfway along when I hear the

screeching of metal as the train pulls into the station. That's when I hear her. *Miaaa*.

No.

Not here.

Not now.

The crowd swells forwards. The gap in front of me disappears. I can't move.

The screeching metal is close behind me. *Miaaa*. I try to move away from the edge. The crowd pushes back. I stumble, fall onto my hands and knees, my head leaning over the edge. The train's coming. I leap up and step back, my heart thumping. A lucky escape.

It's then that two hands push hard into the centre of my back, propelling me over the edge. I throw my arms backwards to stop myself. It's not enough. Twisting, I fall sideways, my head turned towards the driver, his face stretched in horror.

You'll all be dead by Christmas.

I shouldn't have laughed at Castanese and I ought to have said goodbye to Darcy, Noah, Chrissy and Ed instead of rushing away.

Miaaa.

Why here? Why now?

Time slows. The Hags Ring stones spin around me. Bella closes her black eyes. Leanne laughs. The teeth of the skull scarf grin back at me.

It was supposed to be you.

And now, it is.

The shadow on the tracks below is not mine but that of a woman, bent and twisted, made of twigs and leaves. The shadow enlarges. The rails come closer.

Then someone grabs the back of my jacket and yanks me onto the platform.

The train whistles past, less than an inch from my face.

A broad and smiling middle-aged man hoicks me to my feet.

'Careful, love,' he says with beery breath.

I'm too stunned to thank him. He doesn't appear to think it's a big deal. Perhaps he doesn't realise he's just saved my life. He and his pals get on the train. I let everyone push past me and wait on the platform as the train draws away.

Then I let it sink in.

Someone tried to kill me.

NOVEMBER

Chapter 18

Home feels emptier than ever. After accepting that Jake wasn't coming back, I took his remaining possessions to the charity shop. To fill the empty space on his side of the wardrobe, I hung some of my T-shirts and jumpers there. It merely draws attention to his absence. The only person to fill the gap left by my husband is me.

No one's contacted me since I got home.

Chrissy and Ed will be whispering to one another about how to deal with me. Their lack of discretion suggests that Noah and Darcy already knew. Just like they all knew about Noah's engagement before me. They meet up without me, they keep secrets. I am no longer the group's glue. I'm the outsider. I'm Leanne.

I'm opening a bottle of wine in our kitchenette, when I get a message from Chrissy.

Let me explain.

I want to tell her what happened at the station and for her to listen and not give me a psychology lecture. I need someone to understand who and what Bella is. Conflictingly,

I also want reassuring she's not real, just a figment of my imagination, PTSD, something rest and relaxation will cure. Either way, Chrissy's justification for cheating on her husband isn't what I need right now, and I don't reply.

The kitchenette opens straight into the lounge. I take the bottle and sit on the worn chocolate-brown leather sofa. Jake and I bought this flat in an Edwardian mansion block over a decade ago. The previous owner, Mrs Rinaldi, wanted a quick sale so she could move to a bungalow near to her daughter in Kent. She sold it cheap and left all her furniture. Even ten years ago the décor was out of date and nothing has changed since. At first this was because Jake and I lacked funds and later it seemed pointless as we were going to move somewhere larger and leafier. But indecision left us stranded. Jake wanted to move out to Hertfordshire; I preferred to stay in London. Jake suggested we decorated anyway, it would make the flat easier to sell. I pushed back, never telling him how the thick carpets and statement walls remind me of being a young child, nestling on the sofa with my head on Mum's lap. A time when I felt happy and safe because my childhood had been both until that night on Hallows Hill.

Since then, all peace has been fleeting. Bella retreated when I was with Jake. Now she's back, always lurking, waiting to squeeze her way through the tiniest gap and re-enter my life. Even in her absence she is a presence, a constant anxiety that has me checking dark corners, steeling myself before opening doors or venturing out on autumn nights. And now she is the anticipation of two hands rammed into the small of my back, sending me tumbling towards the railway tracks and the flickering at the edge of the CCTV images shown to me by Constable Adams of the British Transport Police.

When I reported the incident, Adams had worn the face of a jaded teacher explaining long division to a particularly slow child. Grainy footage showed a crush of heads and bodies, in which the only distinguishable figure was me, teetering on the edge of the platform. Watching myself, I saw what a stupid risk I had taken, with nothing but a few inches separating me, the swaying football fans and the platform edge. It only took one fan to step back, and my attempt to avoid him, to cause my first stumble. I was up again quickly and that's when it happened. I flew forwards, out over the tracks, as the train screeched towards me.

Adams froze the picture, with me hovering in mid-air, like Wile E. Coyote in a *Looney Tunes* cartoon.

'I see this as an overcrowding incident. I'll speak to the station management, but I can't see that a crime has been committed here. In future, please adhere to the safety announcements.'

'I know it was deliberate.' My voice sounded weak and whiny.

The policeman linked his fingers and rested his chin on his hands.

'Is there something you're not telling me? Any reason someone would want to harm you? A disgruntled ex? A business dispute?'

What could I say? A sixty-year-old woman in an unconvincing wig has lain a curse upon me.

You'll all be dead by Christmas.

'Nothing like that,' I said.

He paused a moment and looked as if he wanted to ask

further questions. Then his phone rang. He answered it, grunted a couple of replies then ended the call before his attention returned to me.

'With the evidence available, I can't take this any further,' he said. 'All I can suggest is that if you do feel threatened again you should contact our colleagues in the Met.'

And that was that. For him at least. Not for Bella.

In last night's dreams, she cackled as I rewatched the footage, black and white save for the bright red McQueen skull scarf wrapped around the neck of a teenage girl who weaved in and out of the football fans. When she reached me, she flung out her arms, sending me flying over the edge of the platform. This time no one came to my rescue and I watched myself fall under the train. Bella smirked behind Constable Adams as he gave me that jaded expression once more and said, 'As I've explained to you several times, Ms Raine, playing the tape won't change the ending. You're already dead.'

Halfway down my glass of wine, I have a revelation. Bella feeds on fear and loneliness. She is a parasite, and a parasite requires a host. She must keep me alive until the next group of All Hallows teenagers choose the wrong night to chant the wrong words in the Hags Ring. That's why the man rescued me from the train tracks. She doesn't want me dead – yet.

Even as these thoughts form, a more obvious explanation screams at me.

You're losing your mind, Mia.

I nearly died because I took a stupid risk in walking along the edge of a crowded platform when someone slipped and put out their hands to stop themselves.

Chrissy not only explained about the psychomanteum and how external stimuli create powerful hallucinations, she also told me how our brains impose order onto chaos, creating patterns that do not exist. Castanese's prediction and the incident at the train station are two separate events. There's no link, no cause and effect. And as Ed said, if Castanese can predict the future what is she doing touring the country on dark autumn evenings? Why isn't she stationed in Downing Street or the White House?

I need to talk to someone. Darcy's number goes straight to voicemail. I'm too angry to call Chrissy or Ed and too embarrassed to call Noah after he overheard my conversation at the Dower House. I settle instead for a quick cyber-stalk of his fiancée, Penny French. According to Noah, she booked Castanese. Did she deliberately, or inadvertently, alert her as to who we are?

In her few online photos, Penny's more attractive than I remember. Not beautiful in the classic sense, but rake thin with regular features. She went to school in Bournemouth and studied data science at LSE. After which, she worked for a top bank, doing something with statistics. She joined Noah's company just under two years ago at the age of twenty-three.

I cringe at the thought of Noah recounting the overheard conversation I had with Chrissy. Penny's too young and clever to see me as a threat. More likely she pities me, the woman who's spent her life pining after a man who will only ever care for her as a sister.

I call Darcy again. She doesn't pick up and I don't leave a message. Bored, I order chicken dopiaza, pilau rice and an onion bhaji from my local Indian takeaway and start watching a French property show on Netflix. An elderly childless couple are seeking a vast Parisian apartment for several million euros. According to Ed, the interior of Noah's place is like these properties: tasteful and as minimalist as ostentation can handle. The next couple are searching for a beach house in the Caribbean. Azure waters lap across white sands. It serves to calm me a little, but I still jump when my landline rings.

'Are you all right, Mia?' Mum asks.

She usually rings on Sunday evening and is the only person not to use my mobile, so it shouldn't have been a surprise.

'I'm fine. Why do you ask?'

'Marielle Alderwell just called me. She wanted to know why Darcy's so upset. She said you met up on Friday. You didn't argue, did you?'

'For God's sake, Mum, we're in our thirties. Don't you think it's a bit ridiculous that you and Mrs Alderwell are getting involved in whatever's going on between me and Darcy?'

'You never stop worrying about your children. And Darcy's so fragile, I'd worry too, if I were Marielle.'

'Darcy wasn't feeling well. That's all.'

'John's a doctor,' Mum says. 'He'd know if she's unwell.'

'If it was something physical, yes. But as he's failed to spot the woman he's been married to for forty years is as mad as a box of frogs, I doubt he's going to recognise depression in his daughter. Darcy just needs to get out of that house and spend time with some normal people. She had more freedom when she was at school than she does now. She's coming to mine next weekend. That will do her good.'

'Marielle didn't mention it. Maybe Darcy hasn't told her yet. Anyway, I'm glad it's in London. What were you thinking of, going to the Dower House? Those people who pursued you before,' she says, 'the Crimson Circle, they're never going to go away. You shouldn't have met up on that date. If they find out—'

Although this is my exact fear, I'm defensive.

'How would they find out?' I ask. 'They've disappeared, haven't they? I check online all the time. Rex Pender's not been heard of for years and the Crimson Circle seem to have gone the same way.'

'People like that aren't going to disappear,' she says. 'They're obsessive. You don't want all that online stuff starting up again, do you? You must be more careful, Mia. No more anniversaries.'

That's an easy promise to make.

'By the way,' Mum always adds the questions she really wants the answer to at the end of phone calls, 'was Noah there?'

'Yes. He's just got engaged.'

'Natalie told me. Are you all right?'

'Why wouldn't I be?' I say tersely.

'As long as you are,' she says.

She doesn't believe me and we say our goodbyes.

My curry looks less appetising now it's cold and congealing, and watching the perfect lives of French millionaires is equally unpalatable. I pour another glass of wine and take out my laptop.

A quick search tells me there's no legal recourse to hold Castanese to account.

The 1951 Fraudulent Mediums Act has resulted in so few prosecutions it's fallen out of use. Now the only official redress is through general consumer legislation. Castanese and other 'seers' sidestep this with the disclaimer that their services are 'for entertainment purposes only'. The law can't touch them. Charlatans can operate without restraint, telling people what they want to hear to ensure they hand over cash again and again. But that's the weird thing: Castanese didn't tell us what we wanted to hear. She told us we were all going to die, and soon.

If someone thinks that after what happened to Leanne we're susceptible to this sort of suggestion, can they have used Castanese to frighten us? Given she has no qualms about cheating helpless old ladies, rinsing a millionaire like Noah and exploiting the death of a teenage girl isn't going to give her any sleepless nights. But what about the attempt on my life at the train station?

The newspaper article about Mrs Cunningham's death implied that in the middle of winter, Castanese deliberately dressed a vulnerable old lady in thin clothing, then turned the heating off and opened the windows. How different is leaving someone to die from actively killing them? And if Castanese doesn't like getting her manicured hands dirty, Leon is another matter. He treated her with an awe usually reserved for religious gurus, and our perceived disrespect enraged him. He could have followed me to the station or been there by chance and decided to act. I wish I could see the CCTV footage again.

It's getting late. The wind's up and the trees are swaying outside. I shut the curtains to block out the sight of them. I can't find anything else on Castanese, or Laura Eccles, as she was born. I return to the forums about the Hags Ring murder, which I regularly scan to check if there's any comments. No news of our meeting in All Hallows got out. Nothing on We Sleuth or True Crime Fanatics. All of This Is True, whose Hags Ring thread is usually dormant, has several new stories. Most are just rehashed conspiracies about sacrifice and pagan rituals from back when it happened. Then I scroll down and one post leaps out at me.

Do you know one of the Hags Ring five has died?

Nothing's written underneath. I reread it. It was posted five minutes ago. Is someone playing tricks? I pour more wine. When I look back, the post has disappeared. I scroll back and forth, trying to find it. I scroll faster and faster so the letters blur into streaks of black across the screen.

I rest my elbows on the table. The wine hangs heavy on my lids. I close my eyes for a second. When I open them again my heads on the keyboard. I've written a message.

ZZZZZZZZZZZZZZZZZZZZZZZZZZZZZZZZZZZZZZZZZZZZZ
ZZZZZZZZZZZZZZZZZZZZZZZZZZZZZZZZZZZZZZZZZZZZZ
ZZZZ

I pull myself upright and start to delete it. As I do, another message appears in reply.

TheForrester
Fall asleep? You need to wake up, Mia.

I rub my eyes. This can't be happening. No one knows the username TC123456 belongs to me.

My fingers hover over the keyboard. I shouldn't reply; it will confirm who I am. But this has to be more than a lucky guess. This person knows. Is Mum right – is Pender still out there, watching us? And if so, how?

I finish deleting the Zs, when another message pops up.

TheForrester
Five won't survive the frosts.

I shut the laptop.

Chapter 19

Halloween detritus litters my short walk to the studio on Monday morning. 'Scream' masks are getting shredded under bus wheels and a pigeon pecks at a discarded packet of jelly skeletons.

I have a few admin issues to sort out before I start work proper. But as soon as I'm on the computer, I'm drawn back to the true crime forum. Of course, the messages have gone. I half wonder if I imagined them. I flick back into work mode and answer a couple of emails before going to the easel and for three hours All Hallows and Castanese are forgotten. The vibrant pinks and oranges erase the grey skies and brown leaves of autumn.

At art college, my preference for slate grey and forest green, smears, swirls and forbidding shadows was criticised. One tutor asked, quite genuinely, if my colour vision was impaired. After that I painted in candy hues – children's characters, unicorns, fairies, will-o'-the-wisps – and overnight I became popular. I had a couple of exhibitions in small but influential galleries and an unnamed American pop superstar bought four of my pictures. Enough to place the deposit on our flat. Since then, the residual cool has kept me employed in dull but lucrative commercial work and I still have the odd exhibition.

I only stop painting when someone knocks at the door. It's Nadia, a sculptor, whose studio is next to mine. She doesn't sell much and so is grateful to make a bit of extra money fielding some of my clients' calls. She asks if I'm ready for lunch. I've not eaten today and my stomach's rumbling, so I follow her to the lobby area, where she's laid out leftovers from the Halloween party held at her flat over the weekend: pumpkin soup, cheesy feet and muffins with spiderweb icing. My appetite dwindles.

Nadia goes on to tell me how much fun the party was, even though they're too old to celebrate Halloween really. Her flatmate dressed as the Devil and she went as a witch. Seeing me tense she says, 'Oh, you're not religious, are you? I know some people disapprove.'

To hide my unease, I give her my stock answer. 'The commercialisation of ancient customs irritates me.'

'So you don't like Christmas either?'

'No.'

Though that festivity was ruined for a completely different reason. I take a muffin to show I'm not a complete killjoy. It's like sawdust in my mouth and I have to drink water to get it down.

'You know what? I could do with some fresh air,' I say. 'I'll eat this in the park, if that's OK?'

'Sure. No worries,' Nadia says.

The small park near the studio is usually kept clean. Today, a rat is gnawing at a pumpkin that's been split open, its orange flesh softened by the earlier rain. I find a bench as far away as possible, sit down and check my phone. The messages posted on the true crime forum have made me paranoid. I keep thinking one of my friends must have died. It's stupid, I know. If anything had happened, I would have heard straight away, but I do wish Darcy would get back to me. It's not just altruism that makes me want her to come at the weekend. The truth is, I don't want to be alone right now.

No one else has contacted me and I need to talk to someone about the messages.

I swallow my anger and try Ed.

> I don't want to fall out. Your marriage is none of my business.

Then I feel guilty because even though I don't like his wife, Molly, I do feel a little female solidarity. Especially when I think of Jake and Lisette in Harpenden. Ed texts me back straight away.

> Ed
> I feel bad, it was a one-off.

I don't believe him but I'm not up for an argument.

> Me
> I got a weird message on one of those true crime forums last night.
>
> Ed
> Ignore it.

I feel more nervous about texting Chrissy. We argued about Noah and now I know about her and Ed I'm unsure what to say. In the end I decide on:

We should talk.

Lastly, I text the person I really need to speak to, Noah. If I don't face him soon, I never will. And more importantly, he's the person with the skills to help me understand what happened with the messages. I don't mention them.

I have information. Get back to me.

He doesn't and the rest of the week ticks by slowly.
No further messages appear on the true crime forums.

On Friday, Nadia arranges for both of us to go out for drinks with a few others who share the space. I only go because another night in, staring at my laptop, waiting for the unknown person to pop up on the true crime forum, will send me insane.
The Bandit is a craft beer place, busy with local workers, most of them creatives ten years my junior. They're so carefree. I was never that light-hearted. Even before Leanne's death, there always seemed to be some lurking shadow that stole the sunlight. My friendships were never going to run the same course as these people in front of me, clinking glasses and laughing. Darcy, Noah, Chrissy, Ed and I were fools meeting up again like that. There were always going to be consequences. A dark mood overtakes me. I no longer feel like socialising. Home, my own flat, is where I want to

be right now, but Nadia spots me and is waving for me to come over.

She's talking to Austin, who's just finished a degree in business studies and is helping out with running the studio space. They've found a sofa and are huddled together, chatting. Their glasses are nearly empty and Nadia has a lock of hair twirling around her index finger. I suppose Austin's not so much younger than her – seven years perhaps. She's been out of a relationship for a while and has told me she's bored with dating apps. Right now, she's giggling about something, which produces a bemused smile from Austin. Her interest doesn't appear to be returned. When I sit down, Austin looks mildly embarrassed and Nadia a little flustered. She shifts a couple of inches away from him.

'We got you this beer,' she says.

'Thanks,' I say, looking at the cloudy liquid, which probably contains moss or fish bladders to make it more authentic. 'What have you two been talking about?'

'Austin was telling me he's a fan of yours.'

'Really? I don't think I've had a fan in over eight years.'

'I just love your aesthetic,' he says. 'Joyful without being mawkish, profound without being pretentious.'

I'm not sure if he's making fun of me, but Nadia seems so put out at the attention he's paying me, I think he must be serious. He becomes conscious of her staring at him and says, 'I'll get us another drink.'

When he's out of earshot I say, 'Isn't he too young for you?'

'Maybe he's too young for *you*,' Nadia says.

'Well, yeah, I'm nearly old enough to be his mother.'

I think of Leon's obvious attraction to Darcy. Maybe age

gaps aren't important but I want to make it clear I've no interest in Austin.

Nadia and I watch as the woman behind the bar ignores the other waiting customers and goes straight over to him. Her eyes uplift in a coquettish glance. Austin orders the drinks without any reciprocal flirting.

'You've either got it or you ain't,' I say.

'It's maddening when someone doesn't even realise,' she says.

'Oh, I think he realises,' I say. 'That nonchalance is a little too studied.'

Nadia merely raises her eyebrows.

My phone rings just as Austin is returning with the drinks. It's Noah.

'I have to take this,' I say and duck outside.

'I'm at your studio. Where are you?' Noah asks.

'I'm having a drink at The Bandit round the corner.'

'So you haven't checked WhatsApp?'

It can only have been twenty minutes since I did.

I open it to see a long note from Noah.

'Don't bother reading it,' he says. 'I'm on my way.'

Noah arrives, wearing dark blue jeans and a long wool coat. Like me, he's older than most of the crowd. Unlike me, he's more formally dressed but still manages to turn heads. Even though he spots us straight away, his eyes dart about the room as he comes over.

'I didn't realise you had company,' he says.

'Did you think I'd be drinking on my own?' I ask. 'You remember Nadia? And this is Austin.'

'Hi,' Noah says, barely acknowledging either. 'Look, can I talk to you, Mia? Alone.'

I smile apologetically at the other two, then follow him outside, where he pulls a packet of cigarettes from his pocket.

'I thought you'd given up,' I say.

'I have,' he says, lighting one. He takes a couple of drags before saying, 'I've been doing my own digging on Castanese.'

'And?'

'I'm not getting very far. Her mother worked as a medium, which is probably where she got the idea. I paid through the nose for the reading, but that sort of income doesn't account for her huge house in Cheshire. After she went to prison for fraud, she came out with nothing. She disappeared for a few years, then turned up fully formed as Castanese. Those comments about her being involved in that old woman's death have been wiped. I need to find out where she's getting all that money. Also, I can't work out the relationship between her and Leon. He's not her son and he's not her lover. What's he doing with her? He's only nineteen.'

'I wish you'd got back to me sooner,' I say. 'I need to tell you what happened on Sunday.'

I explain about the poster on All of This Is True knowing my name, claiming that one of us is dead and offering condolences. 'Those messages have disappeared. Is it possible to find out where they were posted from?'

'Not unless you're the forum's admin,' he says. 'Then you can trace the IP address. No one knew who you were until you accidentally posted, remember?'

'Can you find out who the admin is?'

'I can try.'

'And there's no chance someone in your office could be spying and tipped off Castanese?'

'We have a regular security sweep of all our equipment and our staff are vetted. No one knew about going to Castanese except Penny, and I trust her.'

I don't. Her online footprint is minimal. She could be anyone. And spilling our secrets doesn't have to be malicious. She could just be indiscreet, saying too much in chats with friends who are on someone else's payroll. I can't say this to Noah. Questioning Penny will appear as jealousy. I need someone else, Chrissy or Ed, to do it.

Noah drops his cigarette and stamps on it.

'If not a spy, who?' I ask.

Noah pauses, then looks at me sideways. 'You didn't do it, did you, Mia?' he asks.

'What?' I can't have heard him correctly.

He shrugs. 'I know the thing with Penny's upset you. But I told you a long time ago . . . I mean, you had a reason to be pissed off with me. Did you want to teach me a lesson? Don't marry that woman, Castanese said.'

I feel heat rise up my neck and my fingers start to tingle. 'You arranged for us to see her. You, Noah. No one else. And Darcy told *you* a long time ago. Did that change your feelings? Does Penny know you're still in love with her?'

I want this to hurt and anger him. He only looks sad and says, 'I've never been in love with Darcy, Mia. I'm just saying, you had time to go and speak to Castanese before dinner. I'm sorry, I shouldn't have asked. It's just something Penny said.'

'If Penny wants to help she can start by finding out who posted those messages.'

He looks as if he's about to argue, but instead says, 'Screenshot any more that come in and I'll get her to talk to the site admin. What were they called?'

'All of This Is True.'

'Right. And if Darcy comes down at the weekend, let me know. You can come over to the flat and meet Penny properly. I think we should all get to know one another.'

For the first time, I hope Darcy doesn't come, but I nod and say, 'That would be great.'

Noah has to go and jump on a Zoom meeting with someone in San Francisco so I go back to the others in the bar. Austin looks at me expectantly. I don't want to be alone tonight but I also don't want to get involved with someone I'm going to have to see every day at the studio. I mean, *am* I old enough to be his mother? If I was one of the teen mums you read about in the paper, then yes. Otherwise, we're in sister from another mister territory.

I down my beer and make my excuses. Feeling anxious after the push at the train station, I get an Uber for the short distance home, where I double-lock the front door.

Once inside I retrieve the remains of yesterday's pasta from the fridge and stick it in the microwave.

I can't believe Noah could think I have something to do with what happened at the Dower House. Is that how he sees me: self-centred, attention seeking and slightly cruel? Has he shared these thoughts with Darcy – is that the real reason she's not got back to me? And what about Chrissy and Ed?

Almost subconsciously my fingers reach for my phone and I start scrolling through the forums.

On All of This Is True I find the Hags Ring murder thread and click on it. Only old comments. Then, for no reason, my screen darkens and I see it: that dark sloe eye, staring back at me. The lid closes and opens again. Then just as suddenly it returns to normal brightness and a new post pops up.

TheForrester
Four buds remain.

It's disappeared before I can screenshot it. My heart's racing. I feel invaded, as if someone just smashed their way into my flat.

My landline rings. I race over and pick up.

'Hi, Mum.'

'Are you there alone, Mia?'

'Yeah, why?'

'Stay where you are. I'm coming down to get you.'

'What's going on, Mum?'

My mind wanders. Bernard? My stepbrothers?

'David, Darcy's brother, rang me just now.'

'Has something happened to John or Marielle?'

'No.' Her voice catches. 'It's not John or Marielle.'

The stench of forest floor, damp bark, rotten leaves and fungi spilling through split tree trunks overwhelms the flat. My head feels heavy and my lungs empty.

'I only just found out. They knew she was ill for some time but made a point of not telling anyone. Her heart gave way, darling. It's Darcy. She died this morning.'

I drop to the floor, letting the receiver fall from my hand. Mum's still talking – words I cannot understand.

Outside bus brakes squeal and horns wail. Through the

walls, I hear neighbours argue and televisions blare. Above it all, is Bella.

Mia, she calls, *Mia* . . .

Whilst the shadows leap from the corners and dance with glee.

Chapter 20

In the cemetery chapel, Darcy's family, the Alderwells, sit in the pew nearest the pulpit. Her father, John, and her brother, David, dwarfing her mother, Marielle. She has the same dainty build as Darcy, whereas John and David are tall and broad-shouldered. But David's shoulders hunch and from behind you'd assume he was the older man.

My pew consists of me, Mum, my stepfather, Bernard, and Ed and his wife. Chrissy sits on the other side of the aisle with her husband and Noah and his mother. Penny is absent. She hardly knew Darcy.

The funeral's been arranged in record-quick time. I've been back in All Hallows just over a week. Mum drove to London to fetch me.

I've spoken to Noah, Chrissy and Ed on the phone, but not left the house. Mum's been fussing over me, making my favourite childhood meals – spag bol, French onion soup, chilli con carne – all garnished with the tears she's unable to wipe away fast enough. Darcy was a second daughter to her; she was continually in and out of our house and ate meals with us most days because Mrs Alderwell always had her on a diet. Bernard was as demonstrative as he's capable of, squeezing my shoulder and telling me it's a terrible shame. He's kind in his own way. Right now he's holding Mum's hand and has tissues on standby in his pocket.

He drove us here today, and as we passed my old school, I saw some students running around on the playing fields, hockey sticks in hands. I was sure if I looked closely enough I'd see Darcy hanging back, chatting to the goalkeeper while our games teacher shouted at her to get involved under the threat of a detention we all knew would never come. Darcy was never punished. Perhaps it was her diminutive size or her beauty, but everyone wanted to protect her. Only sitting here on this pew, looking at her small coffin on the bier in front of me, I realise we can never really protect anyone.

The organ starts up, a droning rendition of 'Morning Has Broken'. As the vicar moves towards the pulpit, the door to the chapel bangs open. I turn around with some stupid notion it's Jake. But it's a young woman wearing a long black coat, underneath which I catch a glimpse of red. I know things aren't as formal as they used to be but who the hell wears red to a funeral? She takes a seat on an empty pew at the back. No one else seems to have noticed, and when the vicar mounts the pulpit I swivel to face him.

'We are here today to remember our sister Darcy . . .'

After all my tears of the past week, my eyes remain dry. The ceremony spools past my eyes like a film, a dramatic reproduction, not a real funeral. It doesn't seem possible that all of Darcy's life, her mischievous childhood, wild adolescence and twenties, quiet and disappointing thirties, could be held in such a small wooden box.

The vicar talks us through Darcy's fierce love of her family and her devotion to dance at which she excelled and would undoubtedly have succeeded, had her health allowed.

'Darcy was selfless. Knowing she'd never reach forty, she chose not to burden those beyond her immediate family with her diagnosis.'

Is that why she stopped working, stayed at home and eschewed men? She didn't want to drag anyone down into her misery? The same reason why she hadn't told me, her best friend, that she was ill?

'Darcy possessed the kind of loyalty that forged lifelong friendships and only a few weeks ago she spent a happy weekend with her oldest pals, Mia, Chrissy, Ed and Noah.'

No wonder Darcy shivered at Castanese's prediction. I'm amazed she agreed to meet her at all. What was she hoping for? A miracle – that she would live a full and long life? That's Castanese's bread and butter: desperate people looking for answers. But then why give us the answer no one wants to hear? *You'll all be dead by Christmas.*

The Alderwells aren't ones for speeches. They give no eulogies and no one else has been asked to speak.

As I see Darcy's coffin disappear behind the curtain, I think of that night on Hallows Hill, where she talked about another curtain, the one that exists between the worlds, and how, on certain nights, it could be lifted. The same words Castanese used. I have seen Bella, a woman long dead. Will I also see Darcy again?

When it's over and we stand to leave, I turn to the back of the chapel. The woman in the red dress is already at the door. The rest of my pew move slowly and by the time I manage to run outside, there's no sign of her.

Chapter 21

We drop the car off at Mum and Bernard's house and walk the short distance to the wake, which is being held at Darcy's family home. The Grange sits at the very edge of All Hallows village. John Alderwell's great-great-grandfather built it as a farmhouse, though the land has long since been sold off. Set back from the road behind wrought-iron gates, its grey limestone walls lend it a certain grandeur. That, and the length of time her husband's family has lived there, fuels Mrs Alderwell's fantasy that she's married into some sort of aristocracy. *Generations of Alderwells have lived and died at the Grange.* Her husband working as a doctor at the local hospital rather than taking his seat in the House of Lords, does nothing to dent this illusion.

I've never liked the place. Even as children, Darcy and I usually played at my house to escape Mrs Alderwell's endless snipes and barbs. How often do you want to be told *you're going to be thick waisted, just like your mother* or *you need that dress in a bigger size?*

Despite assuring Chrissy that these days Mrs Alderwell is just a sad old woman, automatically I suck in my stomach as we enter the house.

The screen between the sitting room and the dining room has been removed. Drinks are arranged on trays along a side table: red and white wine, sherry and whisky. No beer. A beige buffet of sandwiches, mini quiches and sausage rolls sits on the dining table.

Noah, Chrissy, Ed and I have agreed to meet later at the Wheatsheaf, a pub on the dual carriageway outside the village. Here, in the Alderwells' home, we skirt around each other, unsure how to interact in front of other people. We are the Hags Ring Five, reduced to four, united in grief, but not in how to deal with it. Darcy's death has left too many questions.

As I grab a glass of white wine, Chrissy's husband, Mark, sidles over to me. His self-importance has always irritated me, as does the way he takes Chrissy for granted, but I experience a sort of second-hand guilt for her infidelity. By staying silent, I am part of the deception.

'How are you coping?' he asks.

'I still haven't processed it,' I say. 'I can't believe she's gone.'

'I didn't know Darcy like you two did, but she always seemed so sad. I guess if she knew she was unwell, that would explain it.'

I look around and lower my voice. 'She was happy enough in London.'

Mark nods. I'm sure Chrissy's told him about the Grange and its occupants.

'How's Chrissy been holding up?' I ask.

'Not great,' he says. 'Don't say anything, but she messed up at work the other day. It's not like her; usually she's super thorough. I've told her to take some time off, but she's working harder than ever. The kids hardly see her.'

Even at Darcy's funeral, Mark's needs are paramount. This isn't about their kids. It's about his resentment of her career, even though it supports his idleness. I take a deep breath.

'Chrissy's coping mechanism has always been throwing herself into work,' I say. 'When she's calmer, she'll slow down.'

'She never slows down. Even before all this happened, she was on edge. And she came back agitated from that weekend away you had.'

I'm sure Chrissy won't have told him about Castanese. Does he have suspicions about Ed? We should have got our stories straight before the funeral, but it was the last thing on my mind.

'Do you know what it was that upset her?' he asks.

It could be any number of things.

'No,' I say.

Mark shakes his head. 'There's something wrong. Could you have a word?'

I feel like telling him to sort out his own marital problems, but not wanting to start an argument at the wake, I say, 'I'll talk to her tonight. We're meeting at the Wheatsheaf. Are you going to be there?'

'Gotta get back for the babysitter,' he says. 'But I appreciate it, Mia. Sorry to land this on you. I know you're grieving for Darcy, and Chrissy told me about Jake. Weren't he and Darcy—'

'That was years ago,' I snap.

'Sure. Sure,' he says. 'Do you think you two will get back together?'

'He's having a baby with another woman, so that's a no.'

Mark looks a little embarrassed and makes his way over

to Ed, who was drinking before the funeral and is now far too inebriated to have any inhibitions about making small talk to his lover's husband.

I'm considering getting another drink and joining Ed in oblivion when Darcy's brother, David, wanders over and pushes a plate of food in my face. His eyes are glassy and sleepless. I take a tuna mayo sandwich to be polite.

'I'm glad you came,' he says.

'Of course I came. Darcy was my best friend. I can't believe she didn't tell me she was ill.'

'She couldn't stand the thought of anyone feeling sorry for her. And once she'd made up her mind, well, you know how stubborn she is . . . was.' He looks away from me, trying not to cry. 'I thought she'd fainted when I found her. She'd done that before. Then when I touched her, she was cold. Quite cold. Mum was visiting a friend and Dad was on a late shift. I don't know how long she'd been there. I hate to think of her lying alone and knowing what was happening to her.' He rubs his eyes. 'Mum blames me. I went for a drink after work. If I hadn't . . .'

'Wasn't it always going to happen some time?' I ask.

'None of us thought it would be so soon.'

Using her daughter's death to guilt-trip her son is peak Marielle Alderwell. How a tiny, wizened woman gets two adult men rushing around doing her bidding, while their own grief goes unacknowledged, is a mystery.

I understand now why Darcy came home and stayed; she was too ill to work. But David could have escaped. He followed his father into the medical profession and one day he'll inherit the house, although with his salary he must be able to afford an equally large one if he chose. He's had girlfriends, but Mrs Alderwell always manages to break them up. Her anger at my turning David down was because she was outraged at the thought of anyone undervaluing her child. She would have hated me as a daughter-in-law. She would hate *anyone* as a daughter-in-law. David belongs to her.

I remember how every time I turned down an offer from David to take me out, he looked almost relieved. I think he just wanted some practice, and as Darcy's best friend I was around and easy to talk to. He's always been very shy and aware he doesn't share the family good looks. He has Mr Alderwell's height and bulk but he doesn't know what to do with it. He's lumbering, more like a man in his late fifties than his late thirties, with rounded shoulders, a soft belly and thinning hair. His face remains unlined, although its features, the same ones that made Darcy beautiful, are squashed together, giving him an odd cartoonish appearance. But plenty of average-looking men have wives and girlfriends. What's really putting women off is him living at home with his mother. Mrs Alderwell holds him captive. He's as much a prisoner as Darcy was.

'It's not your fault, David,' I say. 'It's your mother's grief talking. She doesn't really mean it.'

We both know this is a lie.

'I'm sure you're right,' David says. 'She's angry with everyone right now.'

I stare out of the patio doors at the end of the dining room, which look out onto a large, well-kept garden. Hallows Hill rises behind the fields beyond. The five stones of the Hags Ring are hidden from this angle. But I know they're there.

Darcy's bedroom faces the same direction. A silver birch

outside her window blocks the view of Hallows Hill. Still, she can't have avoided it completely. Not in this house. How could she stand it, day in, day out? One of the last autumn leaves floats from the tree and scrapes the windowpane. I shiver and turn away to see John Alderwell talking to Mum. They're friends from school. John is open-hearted and educated, the opposite of his wife. As well as being a medic, he's widely read and has an appreciation of art, even attending a few of my exhibitions and making intelligent comments. Bernard usually manages a 'very pretty' and 'that's supposed to be a person, is it?' Seeing me watch them, Mum smiles and John puts down his glass and comes over.

'You're looking at Darcy's silver birch. It's nothing but a skeleton at this time of year.' He gestures towards the bare white limbs. 'But it's beautiful in summer. Darcy made me plant it. She didn't like looking at Hallows Hill, for obvious reasons.' He glances to make sure Mrs Alderwell is out of earshot before continuing, 'We did think of moving away after it happened, but that seemed cowardly. And this is the house I grew up in and I want my grandchildren to grow up here too. It's not as if past generations of Alderwells, or of any family, haven't faced tragedy. With Darcy gone, I feel even closer to the Grange.'

'This is the first time I've been here without Darcy,' I say. 'It's just not the same.'

Next to me, David tenses. John doesn't appear to notice. He moves to the patio windows and puts a hand on the glass.

'You know Darcy was born premature?' he says. 'They had to put her straight into an incubator. We thought she wouldn't make it. She was always on borrowed time. I like to think we were lucky to have her as long as we did.'

Cant like this irritates me, and I'm surprised to hear it from a man as sensible as John Alderwell. If his wife didn't chain-smoke to keep her weight down, Darcy wouldn't have been premature. Did that early birth affect her heart? As a doctor, Mr Alderwell must know, but it's too cruel to ask him and he'll never say anything to his wife's detriment. All I can manage is a weak, 'I'll miss her.'

'Of course, you two were like sisters.' He pauses before saying, 'I hope you don't mind me asking, but Darcy told me something of what happened when you all got together the other week.'

David is fidgeting, moving crumbs of mini quiche around his plate.

'What exactly did she say?' I ask.

John lowers his voice again, 'Say nothing to Marielle, but Darcy told me you saw a medium and that you were very upset.'

I attempt to laugh it off. 'The medium, she was . . . very convincing. She talked about Leanne. It was horrible. But all a charade, of course.'

John fixes his face into a sympathetic expression, possibly honed on patients with embarrassing symptoms.

'The thing is,' he lowers his voice still further, 'the last time one of your friends died, you predicted it.'

'Not here, Dad. Not now,' David says.

I see the branch unfurl its twigs, beckoning towards me like fingers. Outside, the bare branches of the silver birch wave in the wind and behind them the mid-afternoon sun begins to drop behind Hallows Hill, reminding us of the approaching solstice.

You'll all be dead by Christmas.

'With Leanne, the boys spiked my drink with magic mushrooms,' I say. 'And Castanese's a fraud, a spiteful, manipulative charlatan.'

'If only Darcy had seen it that way,' John says. 'She was different when she got back home. Like she'd given up, somehow. Maybe she knew her time was running out. My poor girl.'

He drops his head. I place an awkward hand on his shoulder.

'I'm so sorry,' I say.

David moves to his father's side. 'Come on, Dad, let's get some more wine from the fridge.'

He leads John away, although they don't go in the direction of the kitchen.

As a doctor, an oncologist, Mr Alderwell must have seen hundreds of deaths. But no man expects to bury his daughter. I wonder if he's gone back to work. After his father died, he missed William Nicholson's cancer, which put in motion the events leading to Leanne's death. Perhaps I should say something to David, check that John's still up to doing his job.

I wander over to the drinks table. The white wine's gone so I switch to red. Ed is hovering nearby with Molly and Noah. Both men are drinking whisky whilst Molly sips on orange juice. She sees me and gives me a hug and, again, I experience that strange second-hand guilt.

'I'm so sorry,' Molly says. 'I know you were closest to her.'

She looks genuinely sad, though I'm pretty sure she didn't like Darcy. They were so different: Molly, even tempered, sensible and maternal; Darcy highly strung and prone to flights of fancy. Molly thought Ed had a crush on Darcy –

well, she was looking the wrong way. Chrissy, I notice, has attached herself to Noah's mother and comes nowhere near Ed, whose eyes are a deep pink. Whether it's through drink or tears, I can't tell. I give him a quick smile to let him know it's OK between us. He doesn't return it.

'How've you been?' I ask.

'Getting by,' Ed says.

'What about you, Noah?'

'I just keep busy. What else is there to do?' He glances at Ed. 'Look, we'll talk properly down the Wheatsheaf tonight.'

'Yeah,' I say. 'The Grange isn't the place for an open discussion and I'm not in the mood for small talk.'

'On that subject,' Noah nods towards the kitchen, 'have you spoken to Mrs Alderwell yet?'

It's odd, over the years we've ended up calling each other's parents by their first names, but Marielle will forever be Mrs Alderwell.

'I spoke to David and John just now,' I say.

'I know you don't like her but she's just lost her daughter,' Noah says.

I bite my tongue, thinking about all the ways Mrs Alderwell mistreated Darcy. She's the last person who deserves our sympathy. She constantly belittled her daughter and blamed her failure as a ballerina on indiscipline. *I'm the same weight I was when I stopped dancing There's no excuse for corpulence. Only fat women need a bra.*

Right now she's just inside the kitchen door, perched on a stool, her walking stick propped against the cabinet behind her. One hand holds a small glass of neat vodka – fewer calories – in the other she holds a cigarette, which she's sucking so hard, I'm surprised it doesn't vanish in one drag.

She senses my gaze and looks up. Normally, I take pains to avoid her; today, Noah's words carry some weight. I put my glass down and go over.

'I just want to say how sorry I am, Mrs Alderwell.'

'Shut that door, will you?' she says.

I'm not sure which side of the shut door she wants me and hesitate a moment, before stepping into the kitchen.

'I'm going to miss her,' I say. 'It's nothing to your loss, I know.'

She taps the cigarette into a nearby plate. Her eyes narrow.

'I don't know how you have the nerve,' she says.

I search her face for a clue to the source of this hostility.

'The hypocrisy,' she says. 'Don't think I can't see you're happy she's gone. You and Chrissy, both. No more competition for the Misses Mediocres.'

'Mrs Alderwell, I don't—'

'You were always jealous of my daughter – wanted what she had and when you couldn't get it you took it away from her.'

I understand David's warning. She must have been venting about me to him and he knew what to expect.

'I realise today is difficult for you—'

'You're the reason she never became a dancer – deliberately sabotaging her career.'

'Me?'

'Inviting Darcy back to yours, for those enormous meals. Stuffing her full of cake to make her as fat as you are.' She laughs. 'I still remember that ballet class you attended and watching you clumping about. You were like one of those dancing hippos in *Fantasia* next to my Darcy. She was so light and elegant. From day one, your friendship with her was nothing but a cover for your jealousy.'

'I admit I'm no dancer but I've never been fat. And if you'd fed her properly yourself, she wouldn't have come to ours to eat.'

Mrs Alderwell screws up her face. 'Your mother was just as jealous. She couldn't bear to see my child outshine hers.'

'Don't bring Mum into it,' I say.

She barely pauses for breath before continuing. 'And then you go and set yourself up so high you think you're too good for David. *You*, too good for *him*. He's a doctor, saving lives and you get paid money for those disgusting daubs.'

'I'm not arguing with you today, Mrs Alderwell. I wanted to offer my condolences. If they're not accepted, I'm sorry, and even if you won't acknowledge it, I was a good friend to Darcy.'

I put my hand on the door handle to leave.

'Don't you dare walk away from me.' Using her stick she pulls herself to her feet. '"I was a good friend." You believe it, don't you? You actually believe it. You took everything from her. Her dancing career. Her chance of happiness with a man.'

I let go of the door handle.

'What?'

'You're the one who poisoned Noah against her.'

'I never said anything.'

'And you stole Jake away.'

'*She* dumped *him*, then went off to Italy with that count.'

'She went to Italy to study. Jake was supposed to follow her and then you moved in, sniffing around him like a bitch on heat. Well, what's a boy that age going to do – travel across Europe for fine wine when there's cheap lager available in the corner shop?'

I ball my fists and keep my voice as calm as possible.

'I spoke to Darcy about Jake before we got together. She'd lost interest in him.'

Mrs Alderwell bangs her stick on the floor.

'My daughter had pride. Do you think she'd let you see how much you'd hurt her?'

'She was already seeing the count.'

'On the rebound. Any man would have done. She was heartbroken.'

I try to remember the order of events that summer. Had she started seeing the count *after* Jake, not before?

'And then, even though you have a husband you keep Noah away from her.'

'I have zero influence over Noah.'

'You're the reason he wouldn't have her. All that *we go way back, I can't hurt her, she's like a sister to me*. And then he got engaged to this Penny, and Darcy's heart was broken all over again. Really broken this time. I have the same heart condition as Darcy and I'm still alive and she's dead. Why? Because of you.' She pokes me in the shoulder with her cigarette hand and drops ash onto my dress. 'You, you, you.' Another jab with each word.

She raises her stick and I think she's about to strike me. I push it away. This unbalances her and she topples to the floor. I stand there, horrified at what I've done.

'Oh, Mrs Alderwell, I'm so sorry. Are you hurt?' I kneel down next to her.

Tears are streaming down her face. The only time I've seen her cry before was when Darcy announced she was giving up dancing.

'Don't touch me.' She slaps my hand away as I try to help her.

'I really didn't mean—'

'Get out. I can't stand the sight of you. No one here needs a reminder of your mediocrity, thriving while my daughter, my beautiful daughter . . .' She's overcome with sobs.

I'm reminded of the time I ran into Mrs Tattersall in the newsagents, and her telling me I should be dead instead of Leanne. I leave the kitchen and find David talking to Noah.

'Your mother's fallen over,' I tell him. 'She won't let me help.'

David races off to the kitchen.

I quickly locate Mum and Bernard.

'We need to go,' I say.

'So soon?' Bernard says. 'Isn't that a little disrespectful?'

Mum catches something of my urgency.

'Perhaps we ought to. It seems Marielle has taken a turn for the worse.' She nods towards the open kitchen door where David is helping his mother to her feet.

Mrs Alderwell catches sight of me.

'You killed my Darcy, just like you killed Leanne Tattersall,' she shouts.

Mum steps forwards. Bernard grabs her arm.

'You were right the first time, Sandy. We should leave. I'll get the coats. See you out the front.'

Outside the temperature has dropped. Mum and I huddle together to keep warm until Bernard arrives with the coats and we wrap up. Mum's lingering anger causes her to stride quickly up the drive. Bernard keeps pace with her. The day has exhausted me and I trail behind. Also, I don't want to discuss what's just happened.

How much Mrs Alderwell really meant and how much was down to grief is anyone's guess, but why did she make that accusation about Leanne? She never cared for her while she was alive, *that chubby cockney girl*. And after she was killed, Mrs Alderwell appeared to blame her as much as William Nicholson for the pain caused to Darcy. It was unbelievable how alert Mrs Alderwell was to slights on her daughter, and yet totally insensible of the fact that nearly all of Darcy's problems stemmed from having her as a mother.

As we leave, I spot a woman standing at the end of the drive, half hidden by a large laurel bush. She's staring straight at the house.

Mum and Bernard go through the gate and I follow. The woman moves forwards and I catch the flash of red beneath her long, black coat. The unknown mourner from the funeral. I hold the gate open for her. She doesn't move.

'Aren't you going in?' I ask.

The woman raises her head and gives me a look of pure hatred.

'No,' she says. 'I just wanted to make sure.'

'Make sure of what?'

'Make sure that Darcy Alderwell is dead.' Her voice is flat and hard.

'I'm sorry?'

She turns to me. A malicious grin spreads across her face.

'I'll come to all of your funerals. I need to make sure you're all really dead.'

I stand gaping at her. She gives me a sneering look, spins on her heels and walks off in the opposite direction to Mum and Bernard.

Chapter 22

On our way home we pass Arnold Court, the low-rise council block where Mum and I once lived. As we go by, a young girl's face pops up in the window. She's wearing a sparkly tiara and smiling. A small string tugs at my heart, because, despite living on Willow Avenue from the ages of six to eighteen, that house was never my home.

Mum had been lucky to get the Arnold Court flat after she moved us back from London. The other tenants were pensioners, all of whom made a fuss of me. My favourite was Mrs Bridges, or Dotty, as I was allowed to call her. She used to look after me while Mum went out to work as an auxiliary nurse. Dotty's daughter had emigrated to New Zealand and she never saw her own grandchildren. Her son lived in the UK, but his rare visits were short, and I'd hear them arguing in the kitchen. He was a chain-smoker and after he left, Dotty would open the windows and douse the place with lavender air freshener. With no real family of her own, I became a substitute. She made me fairy cakes and let me watch hours of children's TV. Unlike Mum, she never told me off or laughed at me for speaking to Lula, my imaginary friend. Mum felt guilty. She thought Lula was the result of my being lonely. But I don't remember feeling that way. I had Dotty and we frequently saw Noah and his mum, Natalie.

When Mum wasn't working, she'd take me to the park or we'd catch a train into the city and visit the Natural History Museum. On Fridays, I always got to choose my own dinner, spag bol followed by trifle. That flat, with its box bedrooms and two-bar fire in the lounge was my home. Not Bernard Collier's detached Victorian villa, however desirable the street or airy its rooms. Passing the small squat council block fills me with longing for those days, and it makes me sad that Dotty and all those pensioners must be long dead. Though, unlike Leanne and Darcy, they at least lived to see old age.

Back in the hall at Willow Avenue, Bernard takes our coats, which managed to get damp without it actually raining.

'I'll hang them in the utility room,' he says.

Mum stands in front of the mirror and brushes her hair with her hands.

'Who was that you were speaking to at the Grange?' she asks.

'Someone from school,' I say. Not a complete lie if the woman's who I think she is.

'Was she going to the wake in that red dress?' Mum says, turning from the mirror. 'She'd better hope Marielle doesn't see. That'll be another drama. Honestly, that woman. Even her daughter's funeral's just another stage set.'

I think about the harsh words Marielle directed at me and want to dismiss them as the irrational anger of a grieving mother. But do they contain a grain of truth? Was I not a good friend to Darcy?

Mum comes over and ruffles my hair. 'This day was hard enough for you without her ladyship putting on a performance.' She shakes her head. 'What was she saying to you?'

'She said I was a bad friend. I kept Noah from Darcy and stole Jake away from her.'

Mum frowns. 'Darcy and Jake – they were an item?'

'Only for a couple of weeks,' I say. 'Just before Darcy went off to Italy.'

'Why did you never tell me this before?'

'It wasn't important.'

'Marielle obviously thinks it was.'

'Are you siding with her now?'

'You know my opinion of Marielle Alderwell. I'm just surprised you never mentioned the thing about Darcy and Jake, that's all.' Mum straightens her dress. 'Right. Dinner. The food at the wake was inedible. Why don't you go and get warm in front of the fire?'

I go and sit down, wiggling my fingers to regain the sensation lost to the cold.

I didn't think I'd be justifying my marriage to Jake on the day of Darcy's funeral. She had loads of boyfriends – none of them lasted. After her ballet career faltered, Darcy started an art foundation course with the vague idea of becoming a photographer. That's when we started sharing a flat. But the course didn't suit her. She dropped out and got a job at a department store to pay the rent. There she was asked out by a series of rich men. That she took an interest in Jake, who was a student at the time, was out of character.

We met him at a party thrown by someone on my course. Straight away, he caught my attention. But when Darcy came over and said, 'He's hot. You'll have to introduce us,' I knew I didn't stand a chance. Darcy was film-star beautiful, and displaying both steel and vulnerability in equal measure made her irresistible. She always got the men she wanted, though that proved more of a curse than a blessing. I categorised her boyfriends into two types: the Bastards and the Spaniels. To the Bastards, she was nothing but a disposable trophy girlfriend. These were older, often married men, who called her up in the afternoon to spend a couple of hours in a hotel room with them. She'd come back complaining how they used her like a cheap tart, only to jump straight in a cab the next time they called. The Spaniels were closer to her own age. They worshipped her whilst she treated them like dirt. I remember one arriving at our flat with a suitcase because he and Darcy had planned a romantic weekend in Paris. She didn't turn up. Both myself and the guy were frantic with worry, convinced she'd been hit by a bus. As it turned out, she'd gone clubbing with another man and turned off her phone.

'I couldn't face spending three days alone with him, and Mo took me to the Ministry of Sound.'

Jake was neither a Bastard nor a Spaniel. He was kind but wouldn't take any of her nonsense. Then Darcy announced she'd met an Italian aristocrat and was off to Florence. The count was fifty-three years old. According to Darcy, it didn't matter that he was married because he was going to leave his wife and was just waiting for the right time to tell her.

Jake took it well, saying only, 'I thought Italy had got rid of its aristocracy.'

I needed someone to take Darcy's room and cover the

rent. Jake's tenancy had come to an end. It made sense for him to move in with me.

That summer was fiercely hot. Jake and I used to climb out of my bedroom window, lie on the flat roof, sunbathe and guzzle cheap wine.

One night, after drinking far too much, Jake admitted he'd always liked me. The week before I'd made a fool of myself with Noah after a similar excess of wine. He'd told me kindly but firmly that he would never see me as anything more than a sister. Jake didn't want a sister or a friend. He wanted me.

I said I'd have to clear it with Darcy first. She laughed when I told her. 'He's so dull, Mia. Why do you think I escaped to Italy?'

So I don't understand where Mrs Alderwell got it into her head that I stole Jake. Darcy didn't want him.

Unusually, Mum serves dinner on trays on our laps, rather than at the dining table. It's homemade steak and ale pie.

'Wine?' Mum asks. 'I didn't dare drink at the wake – scared of what I might say. Mia?'

I decline, having already had a couple at the Grange and knowing I'm meeting the others in the pub later.

Bernard fetches the bottle and, after pouring a glass for Mum and one for himself, he starts telling us about my stepbrothers' Canadian trip. They saw a bear on one of their excursions and they're glad to be back in a city now. Vancouver, I think.

Mum isn't listening. She's not touched her food, despite claiming to be ravenous, and when she's halfway through her wine she says, 'That woman. How John puts up with her, I'll never know. He's hen-pecked.'

'That's unkind,' Bernard says.

'Unkind but true. John won't have a word said against her – he worships the ground she walks on.'

'The same way Bernard won't hear a word said against you.' I've no idea why I'm defending Mrs Alderwell.

Bernard reaches over and squeezes Mum's hand. 'There's not a bad word I could say about Sandy. And it's natural for John to be protective of his wife.'

Marielle Alderwell exercises a strange charm over men. Her husband and son place her on a pedestal. Noah, however, is wary. They had a run-in after his brief fling with Darcy, although what Mrs Alderwell had to complain about, when it was Darcy who rejected him, I don't know.

Mrs Alderwell is one of the few subjects on which Mum and Bernard disagree.

'You know, it's a pity you can't call child protection in for adult children,' she says.

'Sandy,' Bernard says in a warning voice.

'It's no good pretending. That woman's a vampire. She sucked the life out of David and Darcy.'

'Not today, love,' he says.

'Yes, today,' Mum says. 'Darcy's dead and it's Marielle's fault.'

'That's going a bit far,' Bernard says.

'You know, when I first heard about that illness Munchausen syndrome by proxy, I thought that's what Marielle Alderwell has. Darcy was always sick with something or other.'

'I don't think even Mrs Alderwell—' I begin.

'We all want our children near us,' Mum interrupts. 'I'd love to have you still living here or just around the corner,

Mia. But you have to let them out into the world and become their own person. Marielle has done everything to clip her children's wings. Neither of them ever had a healthy relationship. David was engaged for a bit, until Marielle saw her off. She has some Oedipal pull over that lad. He's going on forty and he's never left home. Even when he went to university, he commuted. He didn't pick up any friends while he was there, as far as I can tell – is that normal?'

'David's a homebody. He's shy,' Bernard says. 'Not everyone's a social butterfly.'

Mum ignores him. 'It's all well and good following his father into medicine if it was his choice, but was it? Like Darcy with her dancing. Marielle bought her ballet shoes before she could even walk. She was so proud when she told me, like that's a good thing. Darcy was pushed and pushed. No wonder she broke.'

Bernard's given up trying to stop Mum and leans back in his chair, swirling his wine around the glass and letting her vent.

'When Darcy told her she wasn't going to dance any more, I thought good, she's escaped, but somehow Marielle reeled her back in.'

'I'm no fan of Mrs Alderwell,' I say, 'but you can't go around accusing people of having Munchausen syndrome by proxy. Tell me you've not been going around sharing your theories with anyone else.'

Mum looks down at her food.

'Mum,' I say.

'Only Natalie. And she agrees with me. She told me she was so glad Noah and Darcy didn't work out. Just because she didn't want the Alderwells as in-laws.'

Mum's generally kind-hearted, but once she takes a dislike to someone it's implacable. A slight to those she loves is felt far more deeply than any insult aimed at herself. I remember when our neighbour opposite falsely claimed my stepbrothers, Victor and Patrick, had snapped the heads off his roses. After that Mum refused to take parcels in for him, stopped inviting him to barbecues and, despite having zero interest in politics, she actively campaigned against him when he stood as a parish councillor.

I know better than to argue Mrs Alderwell's case and, given her attack on me at the wake, I'm surprised at finding myself tempted to do so.

Bernard tactfully guides the conversation back to his sons' trip and we spend the rest of the meal discussing their plans to carry on up to Alaska. After we've finished, Bernard takes the trays to the kitchen and I can hear him packing the dishwasher.

Mum pours herself another glass of wine, which is unusual. She rarely has more than one. The funeral must have been harder on her than she's letting on.

'I never thought I'd see this day,' she says. 'I always thought you and Darcy would grow old together. That was a comfort to me as you never had any siblings. I mean, you're not that close to Bernard's boys, are you? And you and Darcy were like sisters when you were younger. It's a shame that slipped away. Or maybe not.'

She looks sad. I feel like I should say something comforting but I don't know what.

'You weren't so close towards the end,' Mum says.

'She drew away from me.'

'So you didn't . . .?'

'Didn't what?'

'Have any inkling that this was going to happen.'

'I could see she wasn't well.'

'That's not what I mean.'

'What then?'

'It's just we walked past Arnold Grove earlier. It reminded me of Dotty.'

'I was thinking about her too.'

Mum furrows her brow. 'So you remember?'

'Of course. She was always so kind to me. She made me that ladybird cake for my birthday.'

'Anything else?'

'She let me watch old black-and-white films with her. I had no idea what was going on most of the time.'

'And that's all?'

'What else is there? What's Dotty got to do with Darcy?'

Bernard returns with coffees. I take mine. Mum refuses hers.

'You were saying about Dotty,' I remind Mum.

'It's nothing,' she say. 'With all that's gone on, I'm not quite myself today.'

I've arranged to meet the others at the Wheatsheaf at seven o'clock, and it's a surprise when the doorbell rings at six thirty. Bernard gets up to answer it. For a moment I have the irrational thought that it might be the woman in the red dress. But it's Ed who follows him back into the lounge.

'Hi, Sandy,' he says. 'I've come to fetch Mia.'

He's sobered up since the wake and goes over and kisses Mum on the cheek.

'Ah, Ed, a sad day. I always saw Mia, Darcy and the rest

of you terrorising the nurses at your old people's home one day. The rest of you better make it.'

'I'll do my best,' Ed says.

'Are you sure you don't mind me going out?' I say to Mum.

'Of course not. Go and see your friends, Mia. You must want to reminisce and you could hardly talk at the Grange. Besides, you're like a cat on a hot tin roof. Get out before you drive Bernard to distraction.'

Bernard shakes his head in amusement.

'Oh, Ed,' Mum says as we're about to leave the room. 'Did Marielle make a fuss about the woman in the red dress. She was just going in as we left.'

Mum can't have seen her walking away.

'I didn't see anyone in a red dress,' Ed says.

'She came and sat at the back of the chapel during the funeral,' I say.

'Her? She wasn't at the Grange.'

'Really? How odd,' Mum says.

Ed's too busy retrieving the vape from his pocket to see the pointed look I give him.

Chapter 23

The Wheatsheaf is a half-hour walk away. It's a typical November night with a thin mist hovering in the air and soggy leaves underfoot. At a quarter to seven the streets are quiet compared to London, where the pavements would still be crowded and the traffic bumper to bumper. I can see why Ed has stayed here to raise his children. They'll have the sheltered childhood we enjoyed. Or should have enjoyed. Leanne Tattersall's childhood wasn't sheltered. Nor was her sister, Cara's. Did her parents talk to her about Leanne, or was she a silent presence? Did they lay a place for her at the Christmas table or was any reminder of their daughter too painful? Cara was only five or six when her sister was killed. What memories would she have – a push on the swings, a birthday present? When she learned the truth, did she, like her mother, blame us? Is that why she wore red to Darcy's funeral? Because that woman had to be Cara Tattersall. No one else could hate us so much. I decide to wait until we're all in the pub to share my suspicions. Then I remember, we'll never *all* be there again.

Ed's as lost in thought as I am, puffing on his vanilla-scented vape. Eventually he says, 'I came early because I wanted to talk to you before meeting with the others. Clear the air.'

'You could have phoned. Coming round like that is a bit like being kids again. Can Mia come out to play?'

'Molly goes through my phone records.' He turns from me a little and sucks on his vape.

It takes me a moment to understand what Ed's trying to tell me.

'Chrissy's not the only one?'

'Don't judge me. Chrissy knows.'

'I'm guessing Molly doesn't.'

'She's so wrapped up with the boys and being this earth mother, I hardly get a look in. And now she's talking about having more kids, even though we only have sex about once every six months.'

'Would you accept that as an excuse from Molly, if she was the one having affairs?'

'Maybe. It's not like I haven't tried talking about it, but whenever I do, she just gets angry. I can't go without sex for ever. I'm not ninety. It's unnatural for a man my age.'

'And what about Chrissy?' I say.

'It's the same with her and Mark. Neither of us wants to break up our families, but I don't want to lead the life of a monk either. It's not like I feel good about it. But none of us are saints. Noah's got a fiancée and you wouldn't turn him down on moral grounds, would you?'

I feel my cheeks getting hot.

'For someone who wants to make up and clear the air, you're doing a lousy job.'

Ed stops walking. 'Yeah, I know. I'm sorry. My mind's fucked. It was even before I heard about Darcy. The thing is, Mia, someone's been sending me threatening messages. *I'm watching you. I know where you were last night. Watch your back.*'

'Molly teaching you a lesson?'

'Molly would just come out with it. I think it's Mark.'

'No way. You were chatting to him at the wake like you're old pals.'

'He doesn't know, only suspects. He's a coward, isn't he? Likes to sneak around. I've never known what Chrissy sees in him.'

'Not really the point,' I say.

'Do you think you could find out if it's him, Mia?'

'Me? How?'

'Ask him, subtly like. I wasn't the only one having a good chat with him at the wake.'

'Mark seemed more worried about Chrissy's work commitments than her fidelity,' I say. 'If Chrissy's not the only one, there will be other husbands.'

'Yeah, but it seems to coincide with me seeing Chrissy or contacting her.'

'I'm pretty sure it's not him, but he's going to ring me about something else soon. I'll sound him out then.'

'Thanks,' Ed says.

We've arrived in front of the pub and he puts his vape away.

The Wheatsheaf is where we first started drinking as teenagers. Long before publicans were tough on ID, we'd be downing halves of cider in a dingy corner furthest from the bar. It feels like I'm about to step back in time.

'Not a word about this to Chrissy,' Ed says. 'I'm not saying anything until I know for definite.'

'Sure. I don't think we're going to lack topics of conversation,' I say.

'You mean that train wreck of a wake. Mrs Alderwell's got a screw loose.'

'You don't know the half of it.'

'What do you mean?'

I see the woman in the red dress, a vicious smile spreading across her face. *I'll come to all your funerals.*

'Wait till we're together. You'll be needing a drink to hear this.'

Inside, the Wheatsheaf has been stripped of any individuality it once had. Its purchase by a chain means it now has the same décor and menu as a hundred other pubs across the country.

Noah and Chrissy are already huddled around a table. They sit up so suddenly when we arrive, I can't help suspecting they've been talking about us. Ed joins Noah in having a pint. Chrissy already has a bottle of red for me to share.

'It's weird but I was almost looking forward to the funeral,' she says, pouring me a glass. 'Like we could celebrate Darcy's life and move on. I can't believe it was such a nightmare.'

'I know, right?' Noah says. 'I mean, what the hell was going on with Mrs Alderwell? Why did you leave so quickly?'

I repeat what Mrs Alderwell said, that I was a terrible friend to Darcy and am to blame for her death. 'And she's still angry I turned David down. Then she raised her stick at me. I only meant to push it away but she fell over.'

'No way,' Noah says.

Ed starts giggling.

'It must have looked really bad,' I say. 'Did John or David say anything after I left?'

'None of us stayed for long after you went,' Chrissy says. 'But they know what she's like. No one's going to blame you.'

I don't repeat what Mrs Alderwell said about me keeping Darcy and Noah apart, but I do tell them about her accusation that I stole Jake away.

'I mean, Darcy dumped Jake,' I say.

Noah frowns. 'I thought he dumped her.'

'Weren't they on a break until she came back?' Chrissy says.

'That's not what happened,' I say. 'She left him, then went off with that fake Italian count.'

Noah doesn't look convinced.

'And what happened with Mrs Alderwell wasn't the craziest thing today,' I tell them.

'There's worse?' Ed says. 'I need another drink.'

I wait for him to get back from the bar before continuing.

'Did you see that woman in the chapel? She was at the back and wore a red dress under her coat.'

'The one your mum saw at the Grange?' Ed asks.

'Yeah, her. Well, she was spying on us from the end of the drive.'

'Who was she? A true crime nut or something?' Noah asks.

'I don't think so,' I say. 'She spoke to me as I was leaving and told me she'd come to the funeral to make sure Darcy Alderwell was dead.'

'What the hell?' Noah says.

'And that she'll come to all of our funerals one day.'

'Sick bitch,' Ed says. 'Who the fuck was she?'

I lower my voice. 'I'm not a hundred per cent sure, but I think it was Cara Tattersall, Leanne's sister.'

Chrissy gasps. 'It can't be. Why would she come here? She's too young to remember what happened.'

'You don't know what her parents told her,' I say. 'Or what she might have read online. She hates us.'

'But to come to Darcy's funeral?' Chrissy says. 'She knows what it's like to lose someone. After seeing what her parents went through, you think she'd have some compassion.'

'Not if she's been told we're responsible for her sister's death.'

'But . . . but . . . Nicholson.' Ed spreads his palms to express disbelief. 'It wasn't our fault.'

'Wasn't it?' I say. 'Sometimes I have to remind myself that we didn't actually kill her.'

'You can't think like that,' Chrissy says. 'Hey, you don't think she's been in contact with Castanese, do you? She knew about Darcy. Maybe she's keeping eyes on us somehow.'

'The Tattersalls probably still have friends in the village who would have told them about Darcy,' I say. 'But Castanese . . . nah, I don't see it. More likely Castanese looked her up after she found out our names.'

'It's possible,' Chrissy says.

'And if she knew about our meeting at the Dower House she could have come up and spied on us. What if she followed me to the train station and pushed me?' I think of those two hands in the centre of my back. Quite low. It could have been Cara, who I think's a little shorter than me. Or it could have been someone taller in a lunge position.

'You said you weren't sure if it was an accident,' Chrissy says.

Noah, who's been strangely quiet says, 'It can't all be coincidence. Castanese's prediction, that push at the station, Darcy's death . . . but I don't buy the whole thing about Leanne's sister. Unless . . .' he leans in, 'I mean we're working on the assumption that there's no sixth sense and supernatural.'

Chrissy rolls her eyes. 'Not this again. Study after study has shown—'

'None of those scientists were in that room with Castanese,' Noah says. 'And none of them were at the Hags Ring that night. I've tried to rationalise it. I just can't. You believe me, don't you, Mia?'

The thing is, Chrissy's explanation of sensory manipulation is convincing here in a busy pub surrounded by friends, but it cannot counteract the fear that squeezes my guts on windy nights when I hear the creak of tree branches outside the window and that feeling that there is another . . . what shall I call it? . . . realm, dimension. Castanese told me that the veil between the worlds is gossamer thin and, unlike her, I am not in control of raising it. Bella seeks me. I do not seek her.

No. I can't tread that path. These fears will consume me. The day has been emotional, I've had very little sleep and far too much alcohol.

'Chrissy's right,' I say. 'Whatever the answer is, it lies with the living, not the dead.'

Noah's look tells me I'm not fooling him any more than I'm fooling myself, though Ed seems satisfied.

'What Mia just said. A hundred per cent,' he says. 'These

things aren't a coincidence, but no to all this woo-woo shit. Someone has a grudge against us and the front runner is Cara Tattersall.'

'Does anyone know what happened to her after she moved away?' Chrissy asks. 'You live in the village, Ed. Who's still in touch with the Tattersalls?'

Ed splutters on his pint. 'God knows. Since my parents moved to Haverton, I don't know anyone in the right age group.'

He gets up and goes to the toilets.

'Mia, Noah, ask your mums,' Chrissy says.

'No way,' Noah says. 'It was really tough for our parents back then. Mum hates being reminded. We never talk about Leanne.'

'Well, you're going to have to,' Chrissy says. 'If Cara's a threat, your mum would want to help you, right?'

'I think we need to find out if Cara *is* a threat before I dump a load of unnecessary stress on Mum.'

'Same,' I say.

'Well, can you at least check her out? You've got the most resources, Noah.'

He bristles at this.

'I'll have a look,' he says and swigs his pint to mask his irritation.

Is it the assumption that he's got money to do everything that riles him or because no one else is buying into the 'woo-woo shit', as Ed puts it?

Ed returns from the toilets sniffing and with white powder around his nostrils.

'For God's sake,' Noah says. 'Can't you at least be discreet?'

Ed wipes his nose with the back of his sleeve.

'No one's gonna notice in here. Want some?' He taps his top pocket.

'No,' Noah says angrily.

'All right, just asking,' Ed says.

'Ed, please. Not tonight,' Chrissy says.

'You know what?' Noah says. 'I'm sick of talking about Mrs Alderwell and Cara Tattersall. Today's supposed to be about Darcy.'

Ed raises a glass. 'To Darce.'

'We all follow.'

'To Darcy.'

Noah manages to keep Ed off the cocaine and we drink and reminisce about Darcy. We laugh at how cheeky and funny she could be. A talented mimic, she used to tease the teachers but in such a sweet and charming way, no one took offence. What a daredevil she could be, climbing to the top of the local water tower just because someone bet that she'd be too scared. And how she changed from a carefree, rebellious girl into a cautious, serious woman, almost scared of life. Of course, her illness must have been weighing on her, something we didn't appreciate at the time. At various points in the evening, we're all in tears and we carry on until the pub rings last orders.

I'm pretty drunk by the time Chrissy and I totter back together. Her Airbnb is just round the corner. A flat this time, not the Dower House. I did offer her a room at Mum's, but she used the same excuse as she had before. She wants a place to herself so she can have a proper lie-in. I suspect the real reason is that she expects Ed to join her later.

'So how long has it been going on with you two?' I ask.

Chrissy shrugs. 'For years, on and off. I mean, it's just sex.'

'What if Molly or Mark finds out?'

'They won't,' she says. 'You mustn't think we're meeting up all the time. At most it's once every couple of months.'

We've reached the driveway to Mum's house and I give Chrissy a hug.

'Just take care,' I say. 'I don't want to see anyone hurt.'

'It's you we worry about, Mia. You never talk about Jake.'

I puff out my cheeks. 'There's not much to say about that.'

'And how are you feeling about Noah getting married?'

The truth is, all the pain associated with Darcy's death has blotted much of that out.

'It's for the best,' I say, and in this moment I mean it.

We promise to meet up again soon and as I go in for a hug, another smell obscures the floral scent of Chrissy's perfume: a rank heavy smell of decay and putrefaction, mouldering undergrowth and fly-blown flesh.

Miaaa.

I pull back. The streetlamp haloes Chrissy's head, and behind her the bushes shiver in the still air and whisper my name.

Miaaa

Darcy is gone. Bella can't want more.

'Are you OK, Mia?' Chrissy asks.

'Yeah, just too much wine,' I say. The smell intensifies and the buzzing of a thousand insect wings fills my ears.

'You take care, Chrissy,' I say, then hurry to the front door, dive into the house and lock out the night behind me.

Chapter 24

Mum wakes me by swishing open the curtains. The cold morning light floods in and I'm left with only faint impressions of my dreams – spinning stones, snapping twigs, the swirl of dry brown leaves. I haul myself up onto my elbows.

'Hangover?' Mum asks.

I groan in response.

She nods to the bedside table where she's placed a mug of tea, a glass of water and two paracetamol. Drinking the tea succeeds in lifting some of the fur from my tongue.

'It's like you're a teenager again,' she says and smiles. 'I kind of miss those days. I wish it wasn't only funerals that brought you back.'

Mum rarely mentions my neglect. If only she'd move away from All Hallows, I'd visit more often. But on this point she and Bernard cannot be swayed.

'You can always come to London,' I say.

'You know Bernard hates cities.'

'This isn't the nineteenth century. A woman can travel alone, without her husband.'

'I don't like leaving him,' she says.

'Is he unwell?'

'Bernard? He's fit as a fiddle but he gets so much stress at work and then there's everything he does for the Conservation Club. He takes far too much on. It grinds him down sometimes.'

'Surely he can manage one weekend without you.'

'We'll see,' she says.

Mum thinks I hate All Hallows because it reminds me of Leanne's death. I can't tell her it's because here, Bella is closest, in every tree and hedgerow. And after what happened last night with Chrissy . . . I shudder, not wanting to think about it.

'I'd better get up. My train's at twelve,' I say and swing my legs out of bed.

'Cooked breakfast?' Mum asks.

'Thanks.'

'I'll have it ready in half an hour.'

After a shower, I'm starting to revive and I sit down to breakfast with a full appetite. As we eat, Bernard happily chats away about the golf tournament he's organising for All Hallows Conservation Club. The group helps keep the village in good order, promoting eco-friendly practices, maintaining country footpaths and such like. It's obvious to me that whilst it may be hard work, Bernard enjoys it and doesn't find it stressful. But then Mum's always been a worrier.

I'm mopping up the egg yolk with a hunk of crusty bread when the doorbell goes. Mum's finished her food, so gets up to answer it.

'I wasn't expecting to see you,' I hear her say.

Bernard and I exchange quizzical looks before John Alderwell steps into the kitchen. He's flushed and slightly out of breath.

'I'm sorry to disturb you while you're eating,' he says.

'That's quite all right,' Bernard says, standing up. 'Take a seat, have a cup of tea.'

As fellow golfers and members of the Conservation Club, Bernard and John are on friendly terms.

'Thank you, I won't. I can't leave Marielle for too long. You understand?'

'Of course,' Bernard says. 'How can we help you, John?'

'I came to speak to Mia, actually.'

'Me?' I say, my mouth still full.

'In private, if that's all right?'

I wipe my mouth and glance at Mum. Is this about my altercation with Mrs Alderwell? I really don't want another confrontation, but I can hardly turn him down.

'Use the lounge,' Mum says.

The last round of toast remains uneaten and I lead John across the hall to the front room. My hand shakes on the handle as I open the door. I tell myself not to be so stupid. He can't hurt me.

Although Mum's house-proud and the lounge is well dusted, it has the stale air of disuse. Mum and Bernard prefer to sit and watch TV in the small room off the kitchen, they call the snug.

I offer John a seat. He declines so I also remain standing. He seems as nervous as I am and brings his hands together in front of him, locking and unlocking his fingers.

'I've come to apologise, Mia,' he says. 'Marielle's behaviour yesterday was unforgivable.'

'She's just lost her daughter. She's not herself.' I say these words to make him feel better because we both know Mrs Alderwell is always sour and vicious.

'Even so, the last thing Darcy would have wanted is for her best friend and her mother to be on such bad terms. I did ask Marielle to come and apologise to you personally.'

'There's no need.'

'There's every need,' he says. 'Unfortunately, yesterday was too much for her and she's in bed. She has to take strong painkillers for her arthritis. They leave her pretty groggy. I just feel so bad. You were Darcy's best friend. After the family, you'll be feeling this the most.'

'You don't have to apologise, John, really.'

'Anyway, I wanted to give you this.' He hands me a parcel wrapped in brown paper. 'It's something Darcy wanted you to have.'

The sticker attached to it is cheap, the type you use for labelling freezer boxes. 'Mia' is written on it in Darcy's small neat handwriting. Tears fill my eyes and I can't stop them tumbling down my cheeks. All the grief, the years and years of memories, crash in on me and I have to sit down. John hands me a tissue.

'Marielle was so wrong. You were a good friend to Darcy. The best. And I want you to know, that if there's anything I can do for you, if you ever need help, all you have to do is ask. I see you as a second daughter – family – and I know David shares my sentiments.'

Through my tears, I snuffle out my thanks.

'I'd better get going,' he says. 'As I said, I can't leave Marielle for long. Have a safe journey home.'

I don't see him out, just clutch Darcy's parcel and lie

back on the sofa. The crying has made my headache return. Bernard hears the front door shut and comes into the lounge. I wipe away my tears.

'What did John want?' Bernard asks.

'He came to apologise for Mrs Alderwell's behaviour.'

'That's the least he could do,' he says.

'It's not his fault.'

'I suppose not.' Bernard shifts his weight to one leg. 'Are the Alderwells the real reason you hardly ever come home?'

'It's nothing to do with them.'

'Your mother wants you to live your own life. Sandy's not another Marielle Alderwell who needs to control her children. But none of us are getting any younger and Darcy's death proves that we don't know how much time any of us have left.' He comes and sits on the arm of the sofa. 'She doesn't say it, but Sandy misses you and it does hurt that you make so little effort to see her. You're her only blood family. Her father died young too, and her mother . . . well you know about her.'

Actually, I know very little about my grandmother. I only met her once. Mum borrowed a car and drove me a considerable distance to a large Victorian hospital. There we visited an elderly lady in a cotton nightdress. She mumbled incoherently and had spittle running down her chin. Sudden movements and bangs caused her to flinch and her frightened eyes would dart about the room. Her oddness scared me at first, but when Mum left the room to talk to a nurse my grandmother fed me sugared almonds and muttered soft words into my ear. I can't remember what she said, nonsense most likely, but I found it calming. Looking back, I think she had dementia. She must have died soon after that as there were no further visits. The only time I recounted this memory to Mum, she became visibly upset so I never mentioned it again.

'Was there bad blood between them?' I ask Bernard.

'It wasn't that. Your grandmother's illness was difficult for Sandy to accept, especially as a nurse. This was something that happened to her patients, not her family.'

'Is Mum worried she'll go the same way?'

Bernard looks confused. 'Of course not.'

'But there's no guarantee.'

The look of confusion remains. 'Of course. No guarantee. But it's you she worries about.'

'Me? I've got years left. And if it does happen, I doubt Mum will be around to see it.'

'Hmm . . . indeed.'

We've strayed from our original topic.

'But I understand what you're saying and I'll make an effort to come back more often.'

This satisfies him. He slaps his thighs and stands up.

'I'll drop you at the station,' he says. 'You don't want to walk in this cold.'

Mum is nearly in tears when I leave and I feel guilty all over again. At All Hallows Station the train is delayed by twenty minutes. The station is too small to merit a waiting room and I slowly freeze on the open platform, while I jam my back to the railings to make sure no one can push me. The only other people there are a couple of teenagers, far too engrossed in their phones to pay any attention to me. The train arrives. This one's direct to London. I board and as we chug out of the village Hallows Hill rises into view.

Yesterday's rain and mist have cleared and the five stones stand proud atop its summit, black against the white sky.

I have a double seat to myself so spread out and open the parcel Darcy left me, untying it and pulling back the brown paper to reveal some silk fabric. It's her red McQueen skull scarf, the one I longed for so much, the twin of the one Leanne was wearing the night she was killed.

Darcy knew she was dying. Did she leave this because she knew that I once coveted it? Or is it a sign she knew what I had done? Did she make up the parcel before or after we saw Castanese? John Alderwell might know the answer but I can't intrude further on his grief and he'd want to know the reason I was asking.

I hold the scarf to my face. It releases a faint waft of Darcy's Coco Mademoiselle fragrance. The silk is soft against my skin; then I realise the skull is next to mine and it seems like a sick joke. Why did you do this, Darcy?

Someone comes and sits next to me and I have to wrap the scarf back into the brown paper. As I do, I notice something else. An envelope. Will this explain why she left me the scarf? I tear it open. Inside are several sheets of A4 lined paper, the sort from a cheap refill pad. I unfold them. It's not a letter.

Like her, Darcy's handwriting was, small, neat and delicate. I have no problem deciphering the words. 'The History of the Hags Ring'.

Chapter 25

The History of the Hags Ring

As the second son of the fourth Viscount, Arthur Verne-Fontaine's prospects were modest, the family fortune being insufficient for him to live idly. He would have to make his own way in the world. With no appetite for exertion beyond bloodsports and womanising, his pecuniary outlook appeared unpropitious. That was until his elder brother, Richard, died in a hunting accident at the age of twenty-three. Arthur had been riding behind him when he was thrown and broke his neck. Another version of this event exists only in whispers and I will not repeat it here.

Arthur's father died young and so the fifth Viscount Verne-Fontaine succeeded to the title at just twenty years of age. He gave his steward full rein in running the estate, leaving Arthur free to pursue his many pleasures; delighted to throw off the appellation of vices previously attached to them by his father.

The new Viscount spent little time on the All Hallows Estate, preferring London, Lucerne and the company of the Hellfire Club, whose ill reputation far exceeded anything they actually performed. Black masses and devil worship were for show, to amuse themselves and shock the establishment. When several members decided to reject these antics in order to belong to the very establishment they once despised, the group disbanded.

Arthur Verne-Fontaine was not dismayed. For him, the Hellfire Club lacked ambition, and he created another group, more secretive and serious. The Crimson Circle.

They quit London for Arthur's estate, All Hallows Court. In such relative seclusion, their activities bore no scrutiny and Arthur's ambitions grew.

This writing isn't Darcy's style. She must have copied it. And yet, if a book detailing the activities of Arthur Verne-Fontaine exists, I'm amazed I haven't found it. I have trawled libraries and archives searching for anything that might confirm local lore. I found nothing resembling this document and Darcy wasn't one to spend hours scouring dusty archives.

I read on.

The Hags Ring was constructed on land strewn with Iron Age burial mounds. A fellow member of the Crimson Circle, Redford, claimed this was an auspicious spot for what they intended. Follies were too common on eighteenth-century estates for anyone to think raising the Hags Ring stone circle was anything other than playful. Few in that remote area had heard of the Crimson Circle and those that had were too in fear of their new overlord to speak out.

Rumours of strange behaviour began to spread across the district. The Viscount would starve himself, deny himself sleep. Injuries appeared on his flesh with no explanation. The mutilated carcass of a goat was found near the Hags Ring. All the cooks and kitchen maids were dismissed from All Hallows Court and soon strange green smoke emanated from the kitchens, accompanied by the sharp smell of sulphur.

When an old woman who'd worked for the Verne-Fontaine family was found with a pitchfork driven through her, amusement turned to outrage. The body was discovered near her cottage, but there was no blood on the ground beneath her, whereas inside the Hags Ring stones, darkest crimson stained the earth. Her family made no complaint and were later gifted the deeds to their small farm, which in the past they had only rented.

The parson was scandalised. The Viscount's behaviour offended both man and God. He threatened to report Verne-Fontaine to the courts and the Church. Arthur stated that any such action would oblige him to reveal to the bishop the nature of the parson's relationship with his handsome young curate. The parson retired to live with his brother in Shropshire and the post was left vacant.

The rumours spread further afield. The Viscount's uncle travelled post, all the way from London, to castigate his nephew. Arthur was besmirching the family name. It was said he was consorting with demons and trying to raise the Devil. Arthur only laughed.

'This is God's work, Uncle. The Devil would flee in fear.'

His uncle left.

It was nine months after Arthur dismissed the cooks, by which time his ribs poked through his skin like some street urchin and most of the servants had left, that he first heard of Isabella St John, the daughter of a local farmer. It was not, however, her reputation for beauty that cast Arthur as her suitor. He had espoused the pleasures of the flesh along with liquor and rich food. No, it was because Isabella was said to be a seer. A true seer. She had told Jenny Martin when her husband was going to die, and Mrs Rogers that her next pregnancy would be twins.

Isabella had been told she must never read her own future. Only evil could come of it. But then evil can always thread its way into our lives and she had no reason to suspect the true purpose of the Hags Ring stone circle.

The text finishes here. It's not torn off, there's nothing scribbled out. Darcy just stops. Why? What was the true purpose of the Hags Ring? I need to know why she copied this out. Where did she find it? And, just as importantly, when did she write it – before or after we met with Castanese?

By the time we pull into Euston Station, I've read it three times. On the Tube back to my flat I see an advert for *The Sleeping Beauty* ballet. A slender dancer lies inert upon a sumptuous bed. Her petite frame and long dark lashes remind me of Darcy, who won't wake when kissed by the handsome prince. I should have jumped in a cab.

I read the manuscript one more time when I arrive back at the flat. I think of ringing Noah or Chrissy. They're both smarter than me. Did Darcy leave them this, too – or anything? But then I don't know what Darcy told them about me. The McQueen scarf changes everything. I need to find out as much as I can before I ask Noah and Chrissy.

Chapter 26

Back in London, the days inch by and all I do is slouch from the bed to the sofa and back again. I find a channel showing old black-and-white movies like the ones I used to watch with Dotty when Mum and I still lived in Arnold Court: *Sunset Boulevard*, *The Servant*, *A Streetcar Named Desire*, which I now realise was hardly suitable for a four-year-old. As I can't be bothered to shop or cook, Deliveroo becomes my best friend: Persian stews, Vietnamese pho, anything warm and hearty.

Mum rings a few times and I have to fake a certain level of cheer. Noah, Chrissy and Ed don't get in touch. They have their own support networks. I have no one. Apart from Nadia, who met Darcy once, no one else knew her. If I talk about her, acquaintances will nod and make sympathetic noises, then get back to more important topics: squabbles with their other half, stress with the boss, another Tube delay. They don't want to hear about Darcy, how funny she could be at times and how callous at others. No one's interested in my reminiscences about the times she and I laughed and cried together, shared our dreams, and how, for reasons I'll never understand, we drifted apart.

HALLOWS HILL

***

Nadia sends repeated texts telling me I really need to sort some issues out with an overdue project. On Friday, I somehow manage to shower, dress and drag myself to the studio.

'You look dreadful,' she says when I arrive. 'Have you been ill? There's a bug doing the rounds. Austin's been off most of the week too.'

'I'm fine,' I say.

'Good. Well, read your emails.'

Once in the studio, I turn on my Mac and make a few adjustments to an image a client has issues with. It doesn't take long and soon I'm back checking the true crime forums. Tumbleweed. For about the hundredth time I reread 'The History of the Hags Ring'.

I've typed the whole thing into my laptop and searched for matches through plagiarism software. Nothing comes up. Where did Darcy get it? Is it a work of fiction?

I've double-checked Darcy's account with the factual data available. Arthur Verne-Fontaine did make a mésalliance in marrying Isabella St John, the daughter of a local tenant farmer. The fifth Viscount would have been expected to marry someone of his own rank or, failing that, a wealthy heiress. Choosing Isabella suggests something odd did occur. If he'd merely found her attractive, he could have kept her as a mistress.

The notion that Isabella, the Bella in the All Hallows legend, was sacrificed, doesn't tally with the documentation, which shows she died in childbirth.

The identity of the woman found in the Hags Ring in the 1940s was never discovered but locals named her Bella because her fate mirrored the putative one of Isabella Verne-Fontaine. Then there's Leanne. She was killed in the Hags Ring. The Crimson Circle claimed Nicholson carried out a sacrifice. Again, there's no evidence for that. He suffered from psychotic hallucinations. He wasn't capable of planning anything so intricate. Leanne was simply in the wrong place at the wrong time. But Darcy must have thought the original Bella was significant in Leanne's death. Why else would she write this down and leave it for me? I go round and round but can't find an answer. In the end I turn off the computer and decide to go home.

Outside, Christmas lights sparkle in the darkness, and already mince pies and yule logs take up far too much shelf space in the express supermarket I stop off at to buy a few essentials. I can't live on takeaways for ever. 'Jingle Bells' is being piped through the shop's sound system. I leave, swearing to get my groceries delivered next time.

The alley that snakes between the blocks of flats shortens my journey home by about five minutes. I always tell myself I shouldn't walk through it after dark but I always do and it's not even six o'clock yet.

The soles of my shoes slapping against the wet pavement ring an echo against the alley walls. Soon, though, it's not an echo but a second set of footsteps. I pause. The footsteps stop. As I start walking again. So do they. Is it her – Bella? I turn around. A streetlight casts my shadow back along the concrete paving slabs. There's no second shadow, no flickers in the corner. Whoever is behind me is real. I think of those two hands planted firmly in my back, propelling me towards the on-coming train. *You'll all be dead by Christmas.* I spin round and run, skidding round the corners and sprinting far beyond the mouth of the alley until I'm in front of my block of flats. Looking back, I see a figure at the alley's entrance. It's difficult to make out but I'm sure it's a woman.

I step forwards. The figure retreats into the shadows.

I take another step.

'Cara,' I shout. 'Is that you?'

The figure pauses a second, then shoots off into the darkness.

Chapter 27

'Pack a bag and get a cab over here,' Noah says when I tell him. 'You don't know it's Cara. But this woman turning up at Darcy's funeral is one thing, turning up at your flat is another. Whoever she is, you can't take risks.'

I'm unsure about staying at Noah's. I don't want to hand Ed a reason to call me out for hypocrisy. He claimed I wouldn't turn Noah down even though he has a fiancée now, and the truth is my feelings for him are muddled.

Noah senses my hesitancy and adds, 'Penny's here.'

I grab a few items from the bedroom and book an Uber. Although it will stop Ed from making insinuations, Penny's presence will be awkward.

The ugly grandeur of the River Heights Apartments is just as I remember. The building towers over the Thames, its glass front reflecting the dark flow of water below. A uniformed concierge gives my shabby canvas holdall a dubious look when I lug it to the reception desk. He calls up to Noah and looks incredulous when I'm admitted into the company of such an esteemed captain of industry.

This level of security only comes with being rich. In my

block, Cara Tattersall could easily make it to my front door by pressing every buzzer and pretending to be a pizza delivery.

Penny opens the door, barefoot and tousle haired. A stark contrast to the buttoned-up, schoolmarmish assistant I remember. Her clear, soft, make-up-free skin reminds me how puffy and blotchy my own face must be. She invites me in and, as I brush past, the oversized man's shirt she's wearing releases the faint spice and citrus scent of Noah's aftershave.

'Noah waited until you got here safely before jumping on his call to the States. It's important, apparently,' Penny says and rolls her eyes. 'Aren't they all? Anyway, he'll be out in fifteen minutes or so.'

'Nice of him to let me disturb you instead,' I say.

She grins. 'No worries. I've been working since six this morning. The break will do me good.'

The hall opens into a lounge where a cream rug covers the floor, beige linen sofas are strewn with ornate silk cushions, and canvases – Basquiat, Warhol, Rothko, all originals – hang from the walls. Floor-to-ceiling glass doors running the width of the room lead to a terrace overlooking the river. To the left the bright lights outline the skyscrapers of the City's banks and stock market traders.

'Wow,' is all I can say.

'Amazing, isn't it?' Penny says. 'I don't think I'll ever get bored of that view.'

I wouldn't either and revise my opinion about the place being ugly.

'I'm just about to make a cup of tea and have a snack,' she says. 'Have you eaten?'

'Not since breakfast.'

'Leave your bag here. Let's see what we've got in.'

I dump the holdall by the door and follow Penny into the kitchen, which is immaculate and gleaming white apart from a dark splash next to the coffee machine. I sit on one of the barstools placed under the high, central table. Meanwhile Penny rummages through the fridge. It's full of green leaves and bottles of kombucha. Has she weaned Noah off his passion for junk food? She's easy and relaxed as she brings pots of hummus, olives and baba ghanoush to the table. I notice she uses one of those teapots with an infuser when Noah makes his in a mug with a teabag. And neither the décor in here nor in the lounge is to Noah's taste. No girlfriend has got this far before. But then Penny's not his girlfriend, she's his fiancée. A platinum and sapphire ring sits on her finger. The stone catches the light and throws tiny blue beams across the white surfaces. Penny spots me looking at it.

'We chose it together,' she says.

'It's beautiful,' I say. 'Sorry I've not got round to sending you an engagement card.'

'With everything you've been through? Don't apologise. Losing Darcy like that, I can't imagine how difficult it must be. I know you five were practically siblings.'

She means to be kind but it riles me that Noah found it necessary to emphasise his brotherly affection.

'It was a shock,' is all I say.

Penny starts carving a pavé loaf and placing the slices in a toaster. She's facing away from me when she says, 'Noah was so worried when you rang up about this girl. Cara, is it? Do you really think she's following you?'

'She must be. It can't be a coincidence, her lurking in the alley near my flat.'

Penny shudders. 'That would creep me out. Maybe talk to a lawyer – get a restraining order. Noah should be able to help you.'

'I can't prove it was her.'

'No?' she says, and something I don't quite like crosses her face.

Does she think I'm making this up? Perhaps as an excuse to come and stay with Noah now my husband's left.

To try to prove I'm not lying I ask, 'Did Noah tell you Cara came to Darcy's wake?'

Penny nods. 'He said someone outside sort of threatened you. The whole thing's upset him more than he's letting on.' She checks it's still just the two of us before continuing. 'Honestly, I hope that whoever this woman is, she *is* in on it with Castanese, because Noah's starting to worry me. He really thinks he's under some sort of curse. Darcy's death has done something to him and it's more than grief. I don't understand why he's started believing in all the mystical stuff. You don't think it's real, do you?'

'Of course not,' I lie.

'Noah's the most rational guy I've ever met. For him to buy into Castenese's smoke and mirrors, it must have been . . . I dunno, it must have seemed authentic.'

'But I thought you suggested it.'

'Me? I told him about Castanese. There were some top executives at the bank I used to work for who swore by her. It was all on the sly, of course – you can't have clients knowing you're investing their money on the whim of a mystic. Noah was fascinated. He decided he had to see her.'

Did Noah put this all on Penny in order not to admit it was really him who believes in the afterlife and the occult? My hand drifts towards my hair to remove an imaginary twig. I stop just in time and clutch the teacup, so I'm not tempted again.

'Castanese's very convincing,' I say. 'You'd believe anything when you're in there. It's only afterwards you can analyse it. I mean, you don't have to know *how* a magician pulls a rabbit out of a hat to know it's a trick.'

My phone rings and I'm glad to have an excuse to look away because I'm unsure how convincing my sceptical face is. The call's from an unknown number. I cut it off.

'Do you mind me asking how you booked Castanese?' I ask.

'Not at all. Well-known people like actors and musicians often want to make reservations for restaurants or holiday homes and things like that, without the press and public learning about it in advance. So they use a third party to book it. Obviously, Noah's not a celebrity but it's often better that rival companies don't know his plans. I used the same people for Castanese. There's no question of a security breach. It would ruin their business.'

She pushes the dips towards me and appears to be on the verge of saying something else when Noah appears. His shirt carries the same scent as the one Penny's wearing and I have to remember not to hold our hug for too long. He looks me in the face, which must look drawn because he says, 'Not sleeping?'

I shake my head.

'Me neither,' he says. 'Penny's got me meditating. It's not helping.'

'It takes practice,' she says. 'Noah wanted to take pills. I'm mean, no way.'

I think of Darcy's blue pills and her deathlike sleep at the Dower House. Did they contribute to her death? Between insomnia and sleeping pills, I choose insomnia.

Noah sits next to me and reaches across to pinch some of Penny's toast.

'Hey, get your own,' Penny says, only in jest, and she starts slicing some more bread.

'Are you OK, Mia?' he asks. 'Being followed must be scary.'

'I was more angry than scared. I nearly chased her back into the alley. But she could have had a knife or anything.'

'Yeah. Don't engage,' he says. 'Have you thought about calling the police?'

'It was dark. She was a long way off. I couldn't swear it was her. And even if I could, she's not committed an offence.'

Noah looks relieved. He doesn't need any more drama.

'Ed's going to ask around All Hallows,' I say. 'To see if anyone's still in touch with the Tattersalls. In fact, I should call him and warn him about Cara.'

'We don't know it's her,' Noah says.

'We know it's someone.'

Ed picks up on the second ring and I put him on speaker. He sounds harassed; I can hear shouting in the background.

'Are you sure it was her?' he asks when I tell him.

'As sure as I can be,' I say.

'Yeah, I'll keep an eye out.'

I can tell this is a bad time. Ed's not taking it seriously and he wants me off the phone.

'Listen, did you ask around about the Tattersalls? Is anyone in the village still in touch?'

'Molly's been asking at the garden centre. Nothing so far.' Something crashes in the background followed by the sound of children's shrieks. 'Look, I've got to go. I'll call you as soon as I've any news.'

Next I try Chrissy. She doesn't pick up. I think it's her when a phone rings. But it's Penny's.

'Smithson,' she says to Noah. 'Sorry, Mia, I've got to take this.' She leaves the kitchen and goes into a room off the lounge.

Noah helps himself to more toast and pours a cup of tea. 'Has anything else happened since you left All Hallows, anything to make you nervous?'

'Something strange did happen,' I say and tell him about John Alderwell's visit and the package from Darcy with the McQueen scarf and the handwritten account, 'The History of the Hags Ring'. 'Did she leave anything for you?'

'Nothing. Why would she leave you that old scarf?'

'Not sure.' It's reassuring that Noah has no idea of the scarf's significance.

'And that story – what's it got to do with anything?' he asks.

'If she wrapped it up for me after we saw Castanese it was probably because she was upset and obsessing about Leanne. But if it was before . . . I don't know.'

A door clicks to the right of us.

'Look, do me a favour and don't mention this in front of Penny.'

I agree, although I don't see why she would care either way.

After Penny gets out some cheeses, she opens a bottle of wine. I decline and stick to tea. I need to keep a clear head.

When the unknown caller rings again, I hold the phone up for Noah to see.

'Do you recognise this number? This is the third time they've called. Maybe it's Cara. If she's got my address, my number's got to be easy, right?'

He exchanges a look with Penny. Do they think I'm making this up?

'Shall I answer it?' Noah says.

'If she's stalking us and recognises your voice, she'll know where I am. You must be easy to find.'

'I'll answer,' Penny says.

'I don't want you involved,' Noah says.

'She'll not recognise my voice. I've never done a TED talk.' Penny takes the phone.

'Hello.'

There's a short exchange. 'I'm Noah's fiancée . . . yes, she's staying with us. She'll explain.' She hands the phone back to me.

'It's Chrissy's husband.'

You'll all be dead by Christmas.

I grab the phone.

'Mark, is Chrissy OK?'

'As far as I know. You never got back to me after the funeral. Why are you at Noah's? What's going on?' Mark says.

I tell him about Cara Tattersall showing up near my flat. 'You ought to warn Chrissy. I can't get through to her.'

'You and me both,' he says. 'Listen, Mia, do you think Chrissy's having an affair?'

I nearly choke.

'Just a minute,' I say.

This conversation needs to be private. I slide off the chair, exit the kitchen, cross the lounge and open the large glass doors to step out onto the terrace. The wind's cold and strong up here and I huddle against the wall and attempt to make myself smaller.

'Why do you think she's having an affair?' I ask. 'You and Chrissy have been together for ever.'

'Maybe that's the problem. We got together too young. We should have played the field before settling down. She's pretty unhappy with me right now.'

I scrunch myself up against the glass, bracing against the cold. The sight of the dark waters below makes me feel still colder.

'Do you suspect anyone?' I ask.

'A colleague, I think.' I breathe a little easier. 'She tells me she's working late at their London office, which is near King's Cross. So why does her Find My Friends app say she's near Liverpool Street?'

'No one's going to meet in the heart of the financial district for a romantic liaison,' I say.

'You know as well as I do that some people get together in broom cupboards. And she's got a burner phone.'

'Are you sure it's not just a work phone?'

'It's one of those old Nokias. What firm hands those out?'

'I didn't see it in All Hallows.'

'Chrissy had her own room, didn't she?'

I remember her late night phone call, heard through the walls. At the time, I assumed she was talking to Mark. Maybe it was someone else.

Noah comes out onto the terrace with a parka jacket and places it over my shoulders. He raises his eyebrows as a question. I give the tipping hand signal to let him know it's so-so. He hovers by my side for a moment before returning to the lounge.

'I mean, is there something else going on I should know about? Did she seem strange or off to you?' Mark asks.

'If you want to know what Chrissy's up to why don't you just ask her?'

'These days I can't ask her if she wants a coffee without her biting my head off. But I need to know where I stand. She didn't say anything when you went out for that drink after the funeral, did she?'

'To be honest we just talked about Darcy, not so much about our own lives. It wasn't the right time. And really, Mark, I don't feel comfortable talking to you about Chrissy behind her back.'

'Please, Mia. I'm going nuts here. And it's not good for the kids.'

My goddaughters, Layla and Macey. I don't want them to suffer.

Ed's at home with his kids, so it's not him she's meeting. I try and think of another reason for burner phones and fake overtime. Another lover? I look across the river. The City towers loom black against the inky sky. Shrines erected in devotion to the great God Mammon.

'Chrissy said you have money problems.'

'Oh, she found time to complain about me being unemployed, did she?'

'I'm trying to help, Mark.'

'Well, yeah. Things are difficult. We had to borrow money

off Chrissy's parents to pay last month's mortgage, and the girls' school fees are in arrears.'

The lights of the Gherkin, the Walkie Talkie and the Shard glisten in the distance. *Love of money is the root of all evil.* An idea, one I don't want to contemplate, rises in my mind. Have you done what I think you have, Chrissy?

'I'll try and meet with her, Mark. But I can't promise anything.'

'Cheers, Mia. I appreciate it.'

Noah is watching me from the lounge and signalling for me to come inside.

'I'll get back to you when I know anything, Mark.'

I end the call and hurry back indoors.

Noah's waiting for me.

'What did Mark want?' he asks.

Penny hands me a fresh mug of tea, my fingers curl around it, appreciating the warmth.

'Chrissy's behaving strangely,' I say.

Noah can guess what this is about, but I can tell he's not told Penny about Chrissy and Ed, and I'm pleased he doesn't ask any more questions. Because I don't think an affair is the reason for her burner phone. And I'm not ready to share my theory with Noah yet.

Chapter 28

I tell Noah and Penny I'm in need of an early night. The bedroom they show me to has the feel of an upmarket hotel; with a white shagpile carpet, mirror wardrobes and an ensuite bathroom, it's luxurious, but not homely.

'I left towels out for you,' Penny says. 'Let me know if you need anything else.'

I thank her and we say good night.

I do my usual scan of the true crime forums – there's nothing new – before getting down to the research I really want to do. I start with the two words Chrissy used at the Dower House, necromanteion and psychomanteum: the rational explanations of why I saw Bella.

According to some strands of Greek mythology it was the river Acheron, and not the Styx, across which Charon ferried the dead. On its banks stood a temple dedicated to Hades and Persephone, king and queen of the Underworld. It was called the Necromanteion and there, following elaborate ceremonies and preparations, including the ingestion of narcotic substances, devotees could speak with their dead ancestors.

The next word is psychomanteum, a modern ritual

inspired by the ancient Greek one. An American psychiatrist and physician placed the subjects of his experiments in a small dark room with a mirror and a candle. The subject would be asked to think about a deceased relative. Under these conditions many reported seeing and speaking to the dead. The doctor thought this method helped people deal with grief. Later he started to believe that his patients were genuinely talking to their dead loved ones.

I think of the darkened room and flickering candles at the Dower House. Had the suggestive environment created my vision? I also note that the obsidian ball Castanese claimed was cut from the same Aztec mine as the mirror used by the Elizabethan alchemist John Dee was identical to ones that can be purchased from Amazon for under twenty pounds.

As I scroll through endless posts about contacting the dead, I come across another experiment. Again in the United States, it involved participants who had already claimed to have seen psychic phenomena, creating a ghost. They were asked to invent what characteristics this ghost should have. He would be male, between thirty and forty and speak with a Southern accent. When they performed a seance, this man, who had never existed, came and spoke to them.

If you were to combine the two experiments, the psychomanteum and the creation of a ghost, what would you have? Something close to what we experienced around Castanese's table. And what then: a book, a podcast, a TV series? Because the person quoted at the end of the article I read is Christine Banks. Why had she never told us she had a professional interest in this area? I'm beginning to think she used us in an experiment. As a psychologist, she'd know how to leave the breadcrumbs so that Noah ended up thinking it was his idea. Then she could prime Castanese.

If my theory is true, then telling me about the necromanteion and the psychomanteum was a mistake made by someone unused to deceit who'd drunk too much wine.

I text Chrissy.

> Me
> Can we meet tomorrow?
>
> Chrissy
> Too busy
>
> Me
> It's important. We can go to that Italian near Paddington.

The restaurant is one of her favourites and with it being close to the station, she can just jump on her train straight home afterwards.

> Chrissy
> How about The Golden Buddha Covent Garden? Won't be able to stay long.

I've no idea why this venue suits her more than the Paddington one, but I agree.

A sliver of guilt nags at me. Springing these accusations on one of my friends feels like some cheap reality TV stunt. But if Chrissy's been exploiting our trauma to make money and further her own career, maybe she deserves it.

Chapter 29

Nearing the end of November and London has fully surrendered to Christmas. I have to elbow my way through armies of shoppers, weighed down with endless bags from which sprout bright ribbons and shiny paper. In Covent Garden Piazza, jugglers, dancers and mime artists vie for the attention of tourists. Vaping revellers spill out of the pubs, office workers scurry towards the Tube and the homeless huddle in doorways. Why did Chrissy choose this place? She hates crowds. The Italian near Paddington Station would have been quieter and more convenient for her.

Across the windows of The Golden Buddha Thai restaurant Santa and his reindeers fly between giant snowflake stickers. Inside, holly wreaths and pine fronds cover the walls. I find Chrissy in a corner, half hidden by the Christmas tree, a bottle of wine and an empty glass on the table next to her. She doesn't notice me at first and is frantically tapping on a phone, which she whips into her bag the moment she sees me.

As we hug, I notice shadows smudging her eye sockets.

'You're late,' she says.

'The crowds were bad.'

'I ordered for you 'cos I can't stay long. Fried sea bass and beansprouts, right?'

'Thanks.' I could really do with something more substantial like a red chicken curry and sticky rice, but I'm not here for the cuisine.

Chrissy waves the waiter over. He brings another glass to the table and pours for me.

'How long for the food?' Chrissy asks.

'On its way, madam,' he says and ducks away.

'Noah told me you're at his. Do you really think it was Cara Tattersall?'

'I'm not sure any more.'

'How's it been, living with Noah and Penny?'

'I've only been there a few nights. I'll go home soon.'

Chrissy gives me a knowing look, which is beyond irritating.

'We should have met at Paddington,' I say. 'Covent Garden's hell at this time of year.'

'I like it.' She checks her watch. 'What's going on, Mia? You said it's something important.'

I've gone over my approach. I need to be direct and leave Chrissy with no wriggle room. If my suspicions are correct and she's betrayed us, I have a right to be annoyed. But seeing her drinking so quickly and looking ten years older than she did less than a month ago, I'm finding it difficult to be angry. All I can think of is how kind she's been to me over the years. It was Chrissy who convinced me to stay on at art college when I was ready to leave because I'd made no friends in the first term. She said I should forget about Noah, I could do better, and she assured me that I was still Darcy's best friend, even though she was spending more time with Leanne. If Chrissy did set us up with Castanese, it could only be financial desperation that drove her to it.

'It's kind of awkward. I don't know where to begin,' I say. 'I'm not angry with you, whatever you've done.'

A crease forms between her eyebrows.

'What are you talking about, Mia?'

'Mark called me last week.'

The crease deepens.

'Why would Mark phone you?' She refills her glass and drinks.

'Because he's worried. He thinks you're having an affair.'

Chrissy nearly spits out her wine.

'What did you tell him?'

'Nothing, of course. But he knows you've got a burner phone.' I look at her bag where she stashed it earlier. 'But that's not for Ed, is it?'

'It's a work phone.'

'An old Nokia?'

She doesn't meet my eye. 'My client has security concerns.'

'What client?'

She shifts in her seat. 'Suddenly you're interested in my professional life? You didn't even know I'd had papers published before.'

'Just tell me what's going on, Chrissy.'

The waiter arrives with our food. We sit in silence as he arranges the dishes. Then Chrissy pushes some rice around her plate and I wait for her to speak.

'We're in a mess, financially,' she says. 'Mark buries his head in the sand but the mortgage is four months in arrears, I can't cover this term's school fees for the girls and Mark spends money like we're both hedge fund managers rather than a university lecturer and an unemployed artist. We'll have the bailiffs in if we carry on like this. I've had no choice but to take on extra work.'

'Are you allowed to do that?'

'Not according to my contract. I was approached by a company to do something off the books. Hence the burner phone, as you call it. I didn't want Mark to know because he's already touchy about not working and he can never keep his mouth shut. Calling you is a perfect example.'

'Isn't it better he knows about the extra work rather than thinking you're having an affair?'

'It's better we have a roof over our heads,' she says. 'If he'd just stop being so precious and get a job. Everything's beneath him or not quite what he wants. He's the one who insisted the girls go to private school. I'd have been quite happy sending them to a state one. But now they're there, I don't want to pull them out. Anyway, if this comes off we may not have to.'

'If what comes off?' I ask.

Chrissy looks at me suspiciously. 'Why are you suddenly so interested?'

I try to make my next question sound less accusatory. 'Does this work have anything to do with Castanese?'

'Huh?'

'You told me about the psychomanteum,' I say. 'The place where people go to talk to the dead.'

'Where are you going with this, Mia?'

'I've been trying to work out how Castanese could have known we were coming? Only one of us could have told her. Don't you agree?'

'I'm not sure.'

'I checked with Penny how she made the booking. It was through a third party. Castanese couldn't have known who we were and some of the things she told us wasn't information available on the internet. Did Darcy let slip what she was planning?'

'Wait, you think I contacted Castanese?'

'Someone must have done. It can't have been Darcy and I know it wasn't me. That leaves Noah, Ed and you.'

'Have you gone around accusing them of creating this . . . this . . . I don't know what you'd call it.'

'You know exactly what to call it. You explained it to me. It was a psychomanteum.'

'You're not serious, Mia. I was trying to talk you down. You totally freaked after Castanese spoke to you. The psychomanteum was just a way to make you understand how the senses can be tricked. I didn't create it and I found out what Noah had planned at the same time you did.'

'Darcy didn't tell you?'

Chrissy puts down her fork. 'No one told me, and even if they did, what have I got to gain?'

I take a long, slow sip of wine.

'I'm asking you again, Chrissy. What's this job that's paying so well?'

'You think I was paid to help Castanese? No one pays good money for cheap parlour tricks.'

'People pay money for books and podcasts. There's never been more interest in the occult and true crime. Put them together and bang – you've got a hit. Did you record what went on in there?'

'Mia, you're going too far.'

'Or isn't it that sort of entertainment? Are you telling

your clients it's real and you can get the same results for them? What better demonstration than revealing unknown details of a famous murder case?'

'I had no contact with Castanese until that day at the Dower House. None whatsoever. And anyone watching a recording of that would assume it's rigged.'

'The only one of us with the expertise to pull that off is you. And how many people with your knowledge of psychology have four deeply traumatised friends to use as guinea pigs?'

'I don't know what's got into you, Mia,' Chrissy says and rubs her forehead. 'What happened at the Dower House was fucked up but it had nothing to do with me.'

'Then why all the lying and sneaking around? It isn't like you, Chrissy. If you'd just come clean . . .'

'You think you're Sherlock Holmes when Inspector Clouseau is nearer the mark. This isn't about you.'

'Who is it about? Noah?'

Chrissy stops for a moment. 'Why do you think it's about him?'

'I'm right, aren't I? What is it, business rivals trying to freak him out, get him off his game?'

'Stay out of what you don't understand. You have plenty of money coming in. You don't have kids. No one's relying on you. Get off your high horse.'

She stands up and snatches her coat from the back of the chair.

I reach over and grab her arm. 'Chrissy, please. Whatever's going on, whatever you've done, we're all here for you.'

She gives me a scornful look, shakes her arm loose and marches out of the restaurant.

I sit there stunned for a few seconds. The cold draught of air from the door as Chrissy leaves brushes the Christmas greenery. A red holly berry turns into a black eye glinting at me. The spiked leaves wither and curl. I jump up and race out after her.

'Chrissy. Chrissy.'

I spin this way and that, trying to spot her, but she's lost in the swirl of the crowds. Nearby, the bells of St Paul's Church begin to chime. A drunken rendition of 'Fairytale of New York' starts up in one of the pubs.

'Chrissy,' I yell at the top of my voice.

Footsteps run towards me. I spin round.

'Chrissy?'

It's the waiter.

'The bill, madam, the bill.'

I follow him back into the restaurant and settle the bill, leaving a big tip and wondering how I've handled everything so badly.

Back outside the church bells continue ringing through the night air.

Chrissy is nowhere to be seen. I walk towards St Paul's. And just for a moment I see a flicker of white fabric before it disappears behind some shrubs in the graveyard garden.

Chapter 30

Back at River Heights, I find Noah and Penny in front of a screen, poring over some performance report with an investor in Dubai. They work long hours and rarely leave the apartment. People say opposites attract, but Noah and Penny are so similar: driven, focused. They seem not to require the rest most of us need just to function. After around eight in the evening, all I'm good for is the latest Netflix drama. Noah and Penny only pause for dinner before continuing to work until the early hours of the morning. It's impossible not to feel like an interloper. And I'm annoyed how difficult I find it, being a constant witness to their intimacy. The casual kiss on the cheek, the way they interlace feet whilst answering separate emails, pulls at a thread deep within me. One that should have frayed down to nothing long ago. Cara Tattersall can't camp out in a North London alleyway for ever. It's time for me to go home.

I've convinced myself that the sheet I saw in St Paul's graveyard belonged to one of the street performer's costumes. Chrissy will be fine. Still, the incident's left me agitated and I need to keep myself busy so go into the studio.

After ignoring Nadia's increasingly sarcastic voicemails for the past few days, her greeting of, 'Good of you to make it,' is no surprise. I don't rise to the bait and just ask, 'What's been going on?'

'You nearly lost the Jenson account. They're not paying until you make the agreed changes. It's only because Austin sweet-talked them that they didn't walk away.'

'That was good of him. I'll get on with it.'

At my desk, I fire up my computer and start manipulating the image as Jenson have requested. The changes weaken the impact, in my opinion but the customer is always right, however questionable their taste.

Halfway through the afternoon, Nadia comes in with the peace offering of a flat white and a biscotti from the overpriced coffee shop next door.

'I'm sorry I was snippy with you earlier. It's just I've been dealing with your clients all week. Did you take all this time off because of your friend?'

'How do you know about that?'

She looks confused. 'You went to her funeral, remember?'

'Yeah, of course.' I was thinking of Chrissy.

Mark's been calling me all day. I've not answered because I'm not sure what to tell him.

'Is there something else?' Nadia asks.

Where do I start? My husband's left me, the sister of a murdered schoolgirl is stalking me, and instead of helping Chrissy, I've made things a hundred times worse.

'Life's just a bit complicated right now,' is all I say.

'If you want to talk about it . . .'

'Honestly, Nadia, the very last thing I want to do is talk about it.'

Austin pops his head round the corner.

'Hi. Glad you're back. Jenson are chasing again. Can I tell them you'll have it done by the end of the week?'

'Sure,' I say.

He's about to disappear when I call out to him.

'And, Austin, thanks for taking care of all of that while I was away. I appreciate it.'

He nods and looks pleased with himself.

Once I've finished the coffee, I switch off the computer and go back to my easel, losing myself for a few hours layering a canvas in pink and mauve. As soon as I move into a darker pallet, I sense Bella's presence, just over the brow of a hill or in the barn I've started to sketch out. When she begins whispering in the hum of the central heating, I turn the canvas and decide it's time to go.

At gone seven, Nadia's already left and I'm surprised to find Austin still here.

'No home to go to?' I ask.

'I prefer to stay at work and keep busy,' he says. 'London's lonely when you don't know anyone.'

'Maybe we can attend one of my clients' Christmas dos,' I say. 'You'll meet people there.'

'Thanks,' he says, without enthusiasm. 'To be honest, I don't think I'm cut out for the art world. I'm starting to think I should get a corporate job, earn loads of money and just buy the art I like.'

'You should go and work for my friend, Noah. He's loaded and so are half his employees. His walls are covered in paintings that could pay off my mortgage.'

'Noah Campbell, who we met the other night? He's in tech, isn't he?'

'Yeah, but you don't have to be technical. They need people with business ideas too. I can have a word if you want.'

'Really?' He seems genuinely excited. 'That would be great.'

'In the meantime, you really should go home and get some rest. Nadia said you've been ill. You look like you've lost weight.'

'I had a stomach bug, I'm fine now,' he says. 'By the way, I heard about your friend's funeral. I'm really sorry. Nadia said she was a real character.'

I laugh. 'That's one way of putting it.'

'What was she like?'

'Darcy? Impossible. Wonderful. Just a mix of everything. It's sad she ended up like that.'

'Like what?'

'Living with her parents, never doing any of the things she planned to do when she was younger. Not the ballet, not the photography. I know she wanted to marry and have children but that never happened either.'

'But Nadia said she was really pretty.'

'She never had any problem attracting men. She had lots of boyfriends, but none of them hung around. Strange, out of all of us, I thought she'd be the one to succeed.'

'Not Noah?'

'We took it for granted he'd do well. But Darcy, you had to meet her. She had charisma. Wherever she was, people noticed her, wanted to be with her. But it never translated into anything. I saw an advert on the Tube for the ballet of *Sleeping Beauty*. The dancer looked so much like her, it seemed cruel.'

Austin's eyes slip towards the clock on the wall. So he's not that keen on staying and I'm boring him.

'Anyway, never mind me jabbering on. I'll lock up. You go and get some rest,' I say.

He fetches his coat, then pauses at the door.

'Your friends, Noah and Darcy, did they never date each other? It seems natural as they're both so charismatic.'

'We're more like family,' I say.

'Yeah, I get it,' he says. 'Night, then.'

I lock the door and set the alarms. I don't really want to go back to River Heights just yet. As I should start thinking about Christmas presents; I browse a few shops instead. I've always hated Christmas, ever since the age of six when Mum told me I was getting the best present ever. I assumed it was the bunny I'd been told was impractical because we lived in a small flat with no garden. It turned out to be a new family. I'd noticed that Dotty had started looking after me more often. And once or twice I spotted Mum being dropped off back at the flat by a man in a large blue car. But the revelation that Mum was going to marry Bernard and I would be getting two stepbrothers came as a shock.

For as long as I could remember, it had just been Mum and me. I lost my father at eighteen months old and have no memories of him. My grandparents all died young except for my maternal grandmother, who I only met once. The point is, Mum and I were happy. I didn't need or want a new family.

Disappointingly, I wasn't locked in the cellar and starved. Bernard turned out to be mild-mannered and generous. The boys lived with their mother and only visited every other weekend. But before they came into my life, I had Mum all to myself. She cooked the food I liked. Her free time was spent entertaining me. I could never work out why she married. There seems to be some fondness between her and Bernard, but nothing approaching love. Financially she was better off. Bernard had a good salary and a large house and she was able to give up the low pay and long hours she worked as an auxiliary nurse. Apart from having to share Mum with him, I blamed Bernard for Mum banishing Lula from my life. Did I want my new father to think I was still a baby, Mum asked. And so I stopped speaking to Lula. Soon she faded and went the way of all imaginary friends. In return I got an enormous room with a queen-sized bed, a desk and my own books. It's selfish of me to resent Bernard.

I see a bottle of single malt in an expensive presentation box and I buy it for him.

I stick my earbuds in and put on a playlist of summer music to drown out all the festive dross pouring from the shop speakers. No sooner have the first bass beats of 'Hey Ya!' started playing than a call cuts them off. Mark again. I nearly send him to voicemail, then decide I may as well get it over with.

'Look, Mark, I didn't have time to have a proper chat. But I think the burner phone . . .'

'I don't give a fuck about the burner phone,' he says. 'Chrissy's just texted me. She's being followed. It must be that woman you told me about. The Find My Friends app says she's on the south side of the river going east towards London Bridge. I can't get there in time, Mia. You have to help her.'

Chapter 31

I press my earbuds in securely and keep Mark on the phone as I elbow my way through the streets and try to hail a cab.

'She's just texted me. "I'm sorry",' Mark says.

'What the hell does that mean?' I ask.

Chrissy is never cryptic. Why did I let her leave the Thai restaurant before getting the truth out of her?

'Something's very wrong,' Mark says. 'How far away are you?'

I've gone about thirty yards and I need to cross to the next street before the traffic's even travelling in the right direction for me to hail a cab. The Tube might be faster.

'I'm at least twenty minutes away,' I tell Mark.

'Can't you get there any quicker?'

'I'm going as fast as I can, Mark. Call her on the other line.'

'That's what I'm doing. Hang on, she's moving. She's passed London Bridge. She's still south of the river, heading towards Tower Bridge.'

I think of that dark water swirling below Noah's flat and the glimpse of a white sheet I caught in St Paul's graveyard garden. A dread comes over me.

I dash between moving traffic to get to a cab that's pulling up outside a pub, pushing two tourists out of the way to leap in.

'Welcome to London,' one of them says sarcastically.

'Tower Bridge,' I yell at the driver.

We get to the end of the road before grinding to a halt. The traffic lights change twice without us moving an inch.

'Can you take another route? This is an emergency.'

'If you know another route, let me know,' the driver says.

'What's happening? Where are you?' Mark says in my ear. 'Chrissy's still on the move. Why won't she pick up?'

We finally lurch through the traffic lights and stop again.

'We're kind of gridlocked,' I tell Mark.

'Then get out and run.'

The cabbie's unimpressed when I ask to be let out.

'I just let that other fare go for you.'

I offer to pay him a big tip and he won't unlock the doors until it's gone through. Then I jump out and run across the stationary traffic. I dive down a side street in the vague direction of the river, find myself at a dead end, then set off again in the other direction. I get back and run along the main road. Between the buildings I can see Tower Bridge, lit up like an alternative Christmas tree.

I'm out of breath before I've gone even half the distance and curse giving up my gym membership. The pavements are thick with people, many of whom exclaim and swear at me as I dodge and weave among them. A bike courier punches my arm when he has to swerve around me as I lurch out into the road to get round pedestrians.

My lungs are bursting, my legs heavy.

'Chrissy's on the bridge. Where are you?' Mark asks.

HALLOWS HILL

'I'm close.'

I've slowed to a fast walk, faint and dizzy with exertion. I step into the road only to be yanked back. A double decker bus comes straight past my nose.

'You need to be careful,' says the woman who saved me. She has an American accent. 'They drive on the other side here, you know?'

I haven't enough breath to thank her. I check the road this time before ploughing forward.

I finally reach the bridge, where I scan for Chrissy. She's nowhere to be seen.

'I'm here; I can't see her,' I say.

'She's stopped,' Mark says.

I run onto the bridge. There's crowds of tourists stopping and taking photographs. An icy rain has started falling and umbrellas are beginning to go up. It's impossible to see anyone's face.

'She must be there,' Mark says. 'I can see her phone on the app.'

I wiggle through the crowds. It's nearly impossible to spot an individual. I draw back from the edge of the road, remembering what happened to me at the train station.

Then there's a great screech of brakes followed by screams and shouts.

'What was that?' Mark asks.

I use the last of my energy to sprint the short distance to where a bus has come to a halt and a crowd is forming.

'No. No. No.'

'What's happening, Mia?'

'Chrissy.'

'Mia, what's going on?'

I force my way through to the front of the crowd.

I stop. My knees give way.

Chrissy is lying next to the bus, her limbs splayed at odd angles. The blood pooling beneath her head mixes with the rain, forming dark rivulets that run down the cambered tarmac towards the drain.

'Let me through. I'm a doctor.' One woman comes to the front. Someone grabs me by my armpits and drags me backwards so I'm propped up against the railings.

'What's happening? What's happening?' Mark shouts in my ear.

I can't talk. I can't move.

Chrissy is no longer visible. The crowd has closed in around her. One figure peels away. And turns towards me. The light is behind her.

'Cara,' I say.

She pulls the hood low over her head and sprints off. I try to follow but my legs are made of lead and I collapse after just a few feet.

Sirens wailing in the distance become Darcy's screams.

I'm on top of Hallows Hill again with Leanne Tattersall bleeding out at my feet.

Chapter 32

What did we raise that night on Hallows Hill? Some malevolent force we call Bella. No harm was intended, but a silly childish dare has tainted my entire life. She is a constant torment – lurking in the bushes outside Mum's house, slithering behind the Christmas decorations of a Thai restaurant, and now in the hospital, hissing my name through the squeak of stretcher wheels and dancing in the lone, wind-tossed tree in the courtyard beyond the reception area.

A policeman, talking furiously into his radio, walks past. I think he's here for Chrissy, but he's ushered into one of the cubicles further down where some drunk is kicking off.

I press myself into the hard plastic chair back and grip the cup of tea someone placed in my hand. The hospital has phoned Mark and he's on his way. I couldn't face it. The only person I've spoken to is Mum, who says she's coming down. She'll not get here before ten.

In the courtyard, the scrubby tree branches wave gleefully in my direction.

'Why have you done this?' I ask.

'Who are you speaking to?'

I look up to see Noah.

'Sandy phoned me. Is Chrissy going to be OK?'

Shock has made the past few hours feel like a bad dream. Seeing Noah here, grey and shaken, makes them real. I leap into his arms and we cling together. My tears mingling with his.

'They can't tell me anything at the moment.'

'How can this be happening, Mia?' he says. 'I don't understand. Why was she on Tower Bridge?'

I let him go and blow my nose, then tell him about Mark's phone call, my race across London, the bus, finding Chrissy in a pool of blood and seeing someone fleeing the scene.

'Was it her?' he asks.

'Bella?'

Confusion runs across his face.

'No, Mia, not Bella. The woman from Darcy's wake.'

'Yes, of course. Cara Tattersall. I meant to say Cara. All this is messing with my head.' In the courtyard, the scrubby tree shakes its branches. 'I saw someone running away.'

'But was it the same woman?'

I open my palms in despair. 'Whoever it was wore all black – the joggers, the hoodie, the gloves. And I only saw them in silhouette, not their face. It could have been anyone really, but I'm sure it was a woman.'

'You told this to the police?'

'They've not spoken to me yet.'

'Where are they? They came to the accident, right?'

'Yes,' I say, more because I know they must have been there rather than because I remember their presence. I did hear sirens. Or were those the sirens of another night long ago?

'Did they question anyone, or try and find out who the person was who ran away?'

'I don't know.'

My answer irritates him.

'Mia, if you don't push this, it could get dismissed as absent-minded woman wanders in front of bus. And we know Chrissy wasn't like that. There'll be CCTV on the bus and the bridge. We need to get the police to check it.'

'They'll not find anything,' I say. 'The same thing nearly happened to me with that train, remember? The officer dismissed it as an overcrowding incident.'

'I'd forgotten about that,' he says.

And if it hadn't been for that American tourist, Noah could have been sitting here for both of us.

'Do you think what Castanese said was true?' he asks.

'No,' I say, far too quickly.

Noah holds my gaze. 'You said Bella just now. Why?'

'You know why. All this reminds me of what happened to Leanne.'

'We disturbed something that night,' he says. 'Something that should have been left alone.'

'Stop talking like this, Noah.'

'Stop pretending like you don't know. You, of all of us. We did something that Halloween and, for some reason, it's come back to us. Darcy's dead, Chrissy's injured. Who's next?'

I feel the pressure of hands on my back and see the intercity express hurtling towards me, then the red metal of a double-decker bus whizzing past, an inch from my nose.

'I'm next,' I say.

'No, Mia. We're not going to let that happen. We're going to talk to the police and tell them everything.'

A nurse hurries past. I try to catch her and ask about Chrissy. But she's too fast and goes into another corridor. Noah gets up and talks to the woman at the reception desk. I don't hear the conversation but can tell she's doing her best 'as soon as we know anything' pacifying face. Finally, a nurse does come over.

'It's Mia Raine, isn't it?' she says. 'Mrs Banks's husband and parents have arrived.' She looks awkward. 'They've asked if . . . they say they would prefer to be left alone.'

Noah and I look at each other.

'They don't want us here?' Noah asks.

'Grief is an unpredictable emotion. At this early stage, when they're still in shock, as you must be, it's best to let them have their way.'

'Grief, shock . . . early stages . . . has Chrissy . . .?'

The nurse looks even more awkward now.

'I can't say any more. Perhaps you should go and get some rest. It's going to be a long night.'

'They really don't want to see us?' Noah asks.

'I'm afraid not,' she says and leaves.

'Why wouldn't they want us here?' Noah asks when she's gone.

'It's probably a mix-up,' I say.

Since Darcy's death, I've got to know Mark a little better, and although I don't exactly like him, I know he loves Chrissy and that's enough for me. And Chrissy's parents are like her, kind and sensible.

'I'll text Mark. Let him know we're waiting here,' I tell Noah.

'Good idea. He'll want to speak to you at least. You were there. The police should have interviewed you already. I'll call my solicitor in the morning. There must be standard ways of dealing with this or offering evidence to a case.'

Noah's always looking for solutions. As if a thorough police investigation will fix Chrissy. He doesn't realise Bella is always two steps ahead.

While Noah goes to fetch coffee for us, I try to digest the nurse's words.

Grief. If Chrissy has died, surely the nurse can tell us. Or is it only family?

Noah returns and sits next to me. The hospital strip lights cast a deathly hue on everyone and he looks worse than before. He took his time coming back and I wonder if he phoned Penny. I'm jealous that he has someone to call and comfort him, and jealous that that person is not me.

A door further down swings open and I see Mark. He's with his father, who I recognise from his and Chrissy's wedding. I nudge Noah and we run over. Mark turns round when I shout his name.

'What's happening? Is she going to be OK?'

Mark stares at us for a moment before saying quietly, 'Her parents are on their way. We're waiting for them before we switch the machine off.'

'No,' I say.

Mark steps towards us.

'What's wrong with you – your little group? I used to tell Chrissy to break free. You take and take and give nothing back. You dragged her down with all your shit. You know what? I was glad when Darcy died. She was a leach. And you're no better. Tomorrow I'm going to have to tell the girls their mother's dead and it's your fault. Just like with Leanne.'

'That's not true,' I say.

'Chrissy told me what happened that night.'

'William Nicholson killed Leanne.'

'Did he? Did he really? Because Chrissy used to think there was far more to it than that.'

I'm too stunned to speak.

Noah stands between us. 'You're in shock, Mark. Go and wait for Chrissy's parents.'

Mark's father starts to lead him away.

I take one step past Noah. Mark spins back to face me.

'I see you, Mia,' he says. 'I see you.'

His father glowers at me. I stop in my tracks. Then Noah pulls me back down the corridor towards our seats.

'He didn't mean it, Mia.'

'Yes, he did,' I say. 'Chrissy blamed me.'

'If that was true she wouldn't have been your friend.'

I wonder if she had tried to detach herself. If it was really her hectic work schedule and kids' birthdays that kept her from meeting up so often. And now I'll never know. A machine is forcing air through her lungs while her brain, that brilliant innovative brain, is no more.

I look out towards the courtyard and the tree and expect to see Bella there, flitting between the branches and peeping round the trunk. But through the glass all I can see next to the tree is my own hollow-eyed reflection staring back.

DECEMBER

DECEMBER

Chapter 33

There's a moment after I wake to my central heating humming and soft cotton sheets brushing against my skin that I am content, warm and cosy in my bed and last night's icy rain is forgotten. Then a punch to the guts. Chrissy is dead.

Mum came to the hospital and took me back to my own flat. She put me in pyjamas and tucked me up in bed as if I were a little girl. I can hear her now, pottering about the kitchen. The aroma of coffee drifts under the bedroom door.

My limbs are tired and heavy. Still, I get up and haul my way to the kitchen. Mum says nothing, pours me a cup of coffee and motions for us to move to the sofa in the lounge. Her eyes are red. She's known Chrissy as long as I have but will save her tears for when I'm not around. It makes me feel weak as mine spill down my cheeks.

Mum heaps sugar into her coffee mug and, without looking up, says, 'Is there anything you want to tell me, Mia?'

I'm still half asleep and can only reply with, 'What do you mean?'

She taps the spoon and places it to the side.

'Ed's wife has been going around asking if anyone is still

in touch with the Tattersalls. Darcy and Chrissy die within a few weeks of each other. So I'm asking you, is there anything you want to tell me?'

I cover my face with my hands. 'I don't know where to start.'

'The beginning.'

'I don't know where the beginning is.'

'How about what really happened on Hallows Hill that night?' Mum asks.

'I can't . . . I don't know. What happened after that . . . I'm not sure what is real and what isn't.'

'Just tell me what you saw.'

'We never told anyone because we thought we were in enough trouble as it was, but Ed and Noah tricked me into drinking a hot toddy laced with magic mushrooms. You know what the Hallows Hill dare is. You go up to the Hags Ring and call for Bella three times and then she comes and tells your fortune. Well, this time, she came.'

Mum raises her hand to cover her mouth. She looks more frightened than I am.

'And then I saw her again at the Dower House.' The fungal smell of her presence fills my nostrils as I speak. 'She let me know we were all going to die.'

'And did you see anything else?'

'Like what?'

'I don't know, that's why I'm asking.' There's an edge to her voice I don't understand, as if she's sure I'm holding back information, but this time I'm not.

Mum sits quietly taking it all in before asking, 'You saw Chrissy the night before she died?'

'Yes.'

'And did you have any inkling of what was going to happen?'

'You asked me that after Darcy died. Why do you think I'd know?'

'No reason,' she says.

The thing is, I did receive a sign that Chrissy would die and I chose to ignore it. That white sheet, the shroud. But I didn't see it with Darcy. And Chrissy's could have been a real sheet. In Covent Garden, with all the street performers, it may have been someone dressing up, part of their act.

'I was worried about Chrissy,' I say. 'She seemed harassed and she was drinking a lot, which is unlike her. I didn't know she was going to die.'

Mum purses her lips.

'Mia . . .' She stops and looks to the window. A grey dawn is breaking over the rooftops. 'Who else knows about you seeing Bella?'

'Darcy, Noah, Chrissy and Ed knew about the first time on Hallows Hill. I told Chrissy about the time at the Dower House because she's a psychologist and I wanted a rational explanation. She gave it to me.'

'Anyone else?'

'I accidently said her name to Noah at the hospital. I meant to say "Cara", but it just came out.'

Mum leans closer to me and puts a hand on my arm. 'Listen to me, Mia. You mention this to no one else. No one. Ever.'

'You believe it's real then?'

'I don't,' she says. 'But there are other people, dangerous people, who do. Since Darcy's death people have started talking about Leanne again. Some woman I've never met approached me and asked me straight up if Leanne had been a sacrifice. I gave up a lot to try and protect you, Mia, because even before Leanne's death there was all sorts of talk about your involvement with I don't know what you'd call it . . . witchcraft . . . the occult.'

'Before Leanne's death? But I'd never done anything like that before. It was a stupid dare. Every kid in All Hallows tried it at some time or other. We were just unlucky.'

'There's more to it than that, Mia. Do you remember Dotty, the old lady who babysat you?'

'Of course.'

'She used to put all sorts of strange ideas into your head.'

'Like?'

'That imaginary friend you had, Lula. She kept saying she was a spirit, that you had the gift, and you know how people gossip in a village.'

The gift. The same words Castanese used about me at the Dower House. Mum's still staring into her coffee cup and doesn't see my look of horror.

Lula. I remember Dotty being accepting of my imaginary friend and a memory comes back to me.

Dotty came in and muted the television. A cartoon was on and I was watching the images of Road Runner, feet awhirl, as he sped away from Wile E. Coyote. Dotty was talking and I wished she'd shut up, but she was being insistent, something about Lula. My friend came and went as she chose, and right at that moment she wasn't there and Dotty was spoiling my enjoyment of the cartoon. I squealed with laughter as Wile E. Coyote rushed off a cliff, still running until he looked down and saw there was no ground below him. On this realisation, gravity took hold and he crashed to the canyon floor.

'Are you listening to me, Mia?' Dotty was saying.

'Huh?'

She turned the television off.

'But . . .'

'This is important, Mia,' Dotty said. 'You know what Lula said about Mrs Lyons – has she ever told you anything about Paul, my son?'

I looked at her blankly. 'Why would Lula say anything about him? She doesn't know him.'

Dotty leant back and looked relieved. 'You're sure? I need to ask her something.'

'She doesn't know him,' I repeated.

Dotty looked relieved.

'Good girl.' She switched the television back on just as Road Runner zipped past a rock that Wile E. Coyote had flung across his path.

A memory tucked away as irrelevant but now it seems so strange. I'd forgotten the names Mrs Lyons and Paul. Why have they just come back to me? And why was Dotty asking me about Lula, not as the harmless invention of a kid with an overactive imagination but as a real person? Like Castanese, she must have thought I had the gift. But why?

'You said Lula existed because I didn't have enough playmates. And anyway, I stopped talking to her after we moved in with Bernard and you took me to that psychologist.'

Mum can't meet my eye as she says. 'I'm just worried what would happen if it got out you'd seen a medium who predicted Darcy's and Chrissy's deaths . . .' She shudders. 'I mean if Rex Pender heard about it . . .'

'Rex Pender? Is he still alive?'

'I've heard nothing to the contrary. He was obsessed with

you. Wrote you letters, came to the house, loitered around your school. We had to involve the police. You weren't leaving your room at the time so it was easy to keep from you. But if Pender hears about this it could set him off again. That's why I'm telling you now; so you understand that what you see, or what you think you see, has to be kept quiet. Tell no one. Not even Noah.'

'You're not serious.'

'Darcy and Chrissy are dead. Of course I'm serious, Mia.'

'Do you think Pender had something to do with their deaths?' I ask.

'I think he'll use their deaths as a reason to contact you.' She sighs. 'I do wish you'd worked things out with Jake. I'd feel you were safer living with someone.'

'It's not like I didn't try,' I say. 'Not all relationships can be like yours and Bernard's, all polite and considerate.'

'For someone intelligent, you can be incredibly stupid sometimes,' Mum says.

Her anger takes me by surprise and I'm unsure of its cause.

I look hard at Mum. She's aged since the summer. The skin around her neck and jaw has loosened and her eyes are losing their brilliancy. While many women her age are still groomed and glamorous, Mum seems happy to drift into her senior years without a fight. A sudden fear of losing her grips me. Without Jake, she's my last anchor. Darcy and Chrissy are gone, Ed has his own family and soon Noah will join him. I will be Auntie Mia, an occasional visitor and old family friend. Who will I have to turn to on days like these when I'm so lost and in need of comfort?

'What you said about giving up a lot to protect me, what did you mean, Mum?'

'Never mind. Forget what I said.'

'You meant that you married Bernard so I would have a secure upbringing in a nice house and not have to be farmed out to neighbours while you went to work.'

'That's not why I married him.'

'Did you ever love him?'

She takes a sip of coffee and looks back to the window. The streetlamps are beginning to extinguish. A flock of pigeons takes flight from the roof of the opposite building.

'There are different types of love,' she says. 'Bernard's been a good father to you.'

I snort.

'He's done his best to look after you, Mia. Never once questioned the money I spent on extra art lessons. Financing your degree at a London college would have been impossible without his support. He's never mentioned it. Not once. When people turned against you after Leanne's murder, he stood up for you. However bad it was, it would have been ten times worse without him. Has he ever said anything to you? Asked you to be grateful?'

'No.'

'Well, then, you should show him a little more appreciation.'

'But, Mum, you were young when Dad died. You could have married anyone.'

'That's not quite true.'

'Wouldn't you have liked someone who shared your interests: art, books, music? Bernard likes golf, single malt, the *Sunday Times* crossword and that's it. You and John Alderwell should have married. You've far more in common. I never understood why he chose Marielle.'

For some reason this dispels her bad mood and she giggles like a schoolgirl.

'Don't underestimate Marielle's charm. She was very beautiful when she was young. Even more beautiful than Darcy. Starvation diets and cigarettes have ruined her looks. And she wasn't always so sour faced. As people get older they're distilled down to their essence.'

'Whisky in Bernard's case. Vinegar in Marielle's.'

'That's unfair,' Mum laughs. 'Bernard has one small glass after dinner. You make him sound like a drunkard. And Marielle, I put it down to disappointment. Her whole life she wanted to be a ballerina and when her chance came, injury ruined it.'

'Maybe she just didn't have the talent,' I say, thinking of what Darcy told me about her own career.

'Whatever the truth, when I moved back to All Hallows after London, she wasn't the woman she is now. She'd lost both her parents in under a year. Her career was over. The man she had wanted to marry, a choreographer, left her for someone else. She was vulnerable. That's what John saw in her as much as her beauty. Some men need to be needed. It inspires devotion in them in the same way an infant's dependency inspires a mother's love. That's something I could never have given John, and if he has regrets . . .'

'Regrets? Did you two used to be a couple?'

'God no. I knew him from around the village. We talked a few times. It was a silly crush on my part. Then I met your father in London and that was that. By the time I came back to All Hallows, John was married and David was already walking. But John was always kind – helped me out once or twice when I fell behind on the rent. And he'd drive me over to see my mother in the old people's home because I didn't have a car and there was no bus service over that way. Sometimes he'd bring round a bottle of wine and have a chat.'

'I bet Marielle loved that.'

'I don't suppose John told her, even though it was nothing more than friendship. You see, I was pretty lonely back then. Not many people wanted to socialise with a widow with a young child in tow. We couldn't always go and see Natalie and Noah. Frequently they were away visiting Eric, wherever he was in the world. Things changed when I married Bernard. I hate to think where I'd be without him. You see, when you talk about love, Mia, you're really talking about passion, which stays alight about as long as a matchstick in a blizzard.'

What Jake and I had was more than passion, but our light still flickered and died.

I lay my head on Mum's shoulder.

'I still can't believe this is happening. Darcy and Chrissy.'

Mum strokes my hair.

'I know it's selfish, but after all you've told me, I can't help just being grateful it wasn't you. Please, darling, get away for a while. Abroad, even.'

'I'd feel like I was abandoning Chrissy. I know she was pushed. And I know it was Cara Tattersall who did it. She's not going to give up. Unless I stay away forever she's going to come after me.'

'I just can't lose you, Mia, you know that. It would kill me. Didn't you say you'd been staying with Noah?'

'It's been a bit awkward with Penny being there.'

'Awkward is better than dead. Call him.'

'I'll think about it.'

When Mum goes for a shower, I do ring Noah, not to ask if I can stay with him but just to hear his voice, to make sure he's safe and well.

'The police are coming here to speak to me,' he says. 'You should be here too.'

I agree to go over. Mum's pleased when I tell her.

'Well, that's one weight off my mind.'

I leave out that I'm not going to be staying there.

'Natalie doesn't seem too keen on this Penny, Noah's engaged to,' Mum says. 'What do you think of her?'

I give a noncommittal shrug, ignoring Mum's knowing look. 'She's nice enough.'

The buzzer goes to let us know the cab's downstairs. Before she leaves, Mum makes me promise to call or text her twice a day. I tell her I will.

Then I'm left alone, wondering how I'm going to explain to the police that the sister of a murdered girl killed my friend last night.

Chapter 34

In the Uber over to Noah's I google Leanne Tattersall and our names. Nothing new. Have none of these people who used to comment on our lives, careers and marriages not noticed that two of us are dead? Somehow their current silence is more unnerving than their previous clamour.

A search for Rex Pender and the Crimson Circle returns only old results. And as for Cara Tattersall, it's as if she never existed. No pictures. No profile. No work records. How is that possible? To avoid having any digital footprint takes meticulous planning over many years, which makes the Cara-shaped hole on the internet even more sinister. I put my phone away and listen to the local news bulletin on my driver's radio.

'Fatal accident on Tower Bridge' barely gets a mention. It's a small item after the announcement of some city councillor embroiled in a corruption scandal and a football manager getting fired.

It's ironic that after so many years of fearing publicity, the lack of it puts me on edge.

**

The River Heights concierge doesn't recognise me at first. I must look even more bedraggled than before. He does, however, appear slightly less surprised than last time, when Noah agrees to let me up to his apartment.

He opens the door in sweatpants and a T-shirt. Stubble shades his chin and, for the first time, I notice the lines around his eyes. In the lounge is an empty pizza box and some half-eaten garlic bread.

'Penny's stuck in Zurich,' he says. 'I've not been able to sleep.'

'You should have stayed at mine. Mum was there.' I add the latter sentence so he doesn't think this was another type of invitation.

'Sandy's good like that. I wish my mum had come down. I can't be buzzing about in my own head right now. I need someone to talk to. All of it's going round and round. Darcy, Chrissy, Castanese. It all goes back to Leanne – and Bella.'

I remember Mum's caution to tell no one about seeing Bella.

'It's too soon to make sense of it,' I say to deflect from the topic. 'Have you spoken to Ed?'

'No. Molly says he's distraught, which is a euphemism for blind drunk.'

'He needs to stay at home until he's sober. He can't go around blurting stuff out in All Hallows. Mum says since Darcy's death all those rumours about Leanne being a sacrifice have resurfaced and are doing the rounds. And just wait till they find out about Chrissy.'

'He should move away. Even Haverton would be better. But you know Ed, he hates change.'

'Look, Noah, before the police get here I have to tell you something about Chrissy. I think she set up the whole thing with Castanese. Or maybe Castanese realised who Chrissy was and contacted her before she came to the Dower House.'

'What makes you think that?'

'Money,' I say and explain about the psychomanteum and the possibility of lucrative podcasts and publishing deals. I leave out the bit about my seeing Bella.

'If she needed money she could have asked me,' Noah says.

His reaction lacks the outrage I expected.

The intercom buzzes.

'That'll be the police,' he says. 'I told them you'd be here.'

'What am I supposed to say?'

Noah looks confused. 'The truth.'

'About Castanese? About the psychomanteum.'

'That's not part of the truth.' He moves towards the door.

'If someone online or in the press makes the link to Leanne, there's going to be trouble. We should come clean.'

'My people can handle the press. And online's been quiet,' he says.

'Too quiet,' I say.

Noah pauses on his way to the front door.

'If they don't mention Castanese, there's no need for us to. Will Mark have said anything?'

'Chrissy made a point of not telling him,' I say.

'Good.'

Someone raps on the door. Noah takes a deep breath before opening it. I go to sit in the lounge, at first on the sofa facing the window. Then I change my mind and choose one placed at right angles to it.

A man in a grey suit appears. He's younger than expected. Thirty at tops.

'Detective Sergeant Lacon,' he says. 'Ms Raine? May I take a seat?'

'Please,' I say, though it's not my place.

He sits facing the window and takes in the view across the Thames, trying not to look too impressed.

'This isn't your usual address,' he says.

'Noah's letting me stay here. I was pretty shaken up.'

'Of course,' he says. 'I'm very sorry. It must have been terribly traumatic to find your friend like that.' He looks at Noah. 'She was your friend too, I understand.'

'We were all at school together.'

'All Hallows Secondary School.' Something in his voice puts me on alert. 'And your friend, Leanne Tattersall, was killed by a patient who had escaped from the local mental health facility.'

Lacon waits for us to respond. Neither of us does.

'Understandably, Mr Banks is distressed. In the account he gave to us, he seems to think Leanne's death has relevance to his wife's accident. Leanne's sister, Cara, contacted you recently, is that correct?'

'We don't know it was Cara Tattersall,' Noah says quickly.

'But she fits the bill,' I say. 'The woman who turned up at the funeral of our other friend, Darcy, was wearing a red dress and said she'd enjoy coming to all our funerals. Then, about a week ago, I thought I saw her lurking around in the alleyway near my flat.'

'But you didn't report it to the police.'

'It's not illegal, and anyway I didn't get a good look at her. It was dark.'

'So it might not have been the same woman?'

'You think I'm being followed by two different people?

The woman at the funeral and the woman in the alley. She ran away when I spotted her, just like on the bridge.'

'We'll come to that,' he says. 'I want to ask you about the report you made to our colleagues in British Transport Police. There was an incident on 1 November this year. You believed someone tried to push you in front of a train.'

'The station was full of football fans. Nothing was clear on the CCTV and after I spoke to your colleague, I tried to convince myself it must have been an accident. But now . . .' I look to him to interrupt. He sits with his hands resting on his knees, leaning slightly forwards and giving no indication he's about to speak.

Noah's phone rings. He's about to switch it off, then checks the screen again. 'I have to take this.'

Lacon looks annoyed.

'Ed?' Noah says.

We can all hear Ed shouting incoherently down the phone.

'Bastard won't let me in.'

'Ed, calm down. Where are you?'

'In your lobby or whatever you call it. Snooty twat's all like, I think you'll find that's a different Noah Campbell. Are there two of you now?'

'Let me speak to the concierge.' Noah moves towards the kitchen and all I can hear is 'Apologies . . . terrible shock . . . send him up.' When he returns he looks nervously at me, then at Lacon. 'Ed's another friend of Chrissy's. He's rather drunk. He wasn't a witness or anything. I'll just make him a coffee and get him to lie down.'

Noah looks over to me. Even for Ed this is too early in the day.

'You all must have been very close,' Lacon says.

'We were,' Noah says.

Lacon returns his attention to me.

'You share everything with your friends. What did they think about the incident at the train station?'

'They were concerned but thought it was probably an accident. Was there any CCTV of what happened to Chrissy?'

'We're still examining it,' he says. 'Can you tell me what you saw last night on the bridge?'

'By the time I got there, it had already happened. Chrissy was lying in the road. I nearly fainted. Someone propped me up against the railings. That's when I saw her. The woman running away.'

'Could you identify this woman if you saw her again?'

'I didn't see her face. She wore her hood up and the light was behind her. Even her hands were covered.'

'What about her build? Tall, short, thin, fat?'

'I was sitting down so it was hard to judge, but medium height maybe. She was wearing a padded jacket and baggy sweatpants so I couldn't see her build.'

Lacon blinks away his irritation at my vagueness.

'Mr Banks rang you to say he'd received a text stating that his wife was in danger and that she was being followed. Is that correct?'

I nod. 'That's why I was at Tower Bridge. Mark was tracking her phone.'

'Why do you think Cara Tattersall would target you when William Nicholson killed her sister?'

'There were a lot of things said at the time. It's like that in places the size of All Hallows. People gossip and they blamed us for what happened.'

'I don't understand.'

'We were all meant to go to the standing stones on top of Hallows Hill that night. As a Halloween dare. Stupid, I know, but we were teenagers.'

'When teenagers behave sensibly, it's time to worry,' Lacon says.

'The thing is, Leanne didn't turn up when we were supposed to meet and we left without her. The dare involved being inside the Hags Ring – that's the stone circle – as the sun sets and we didn't wait. There was a misunderstanding. Leanne took a different route and she ran into Nicholson.'

'It seems a stretch to blame you,' Lacon says.

There's a knock at the door. Noah stands up. 'That will be Ed.'

I try to concentrate on Lacon.

'People always want someone to blame,' I say. 'And there were all these rumours that we were involved in Satanism and Leanne was a sacrifice. But it was a dare. Pretty much every kid at our school did it at one time or another. We weren't into the occult or anything. It was just something kids in All Hallows did. A rite of passage.'

'It was bad luck Leanne's murder happened at the same time you were playing this game,' Lacon says.

'A one in a million chance. And it was Halloween. This guy called Rex Pender created a band of nutjobs called the Crimson Circle. They became obsessed by us and thought we were followers of the Old Ways, whatever that means. It all got out of hand. My mum kept me off school and away from the internet. It's only later I learnt all of it.'

'I see.'

At this point Ed stumbles into the room. He drops his

keys, including one for his car. Noah swipes it away before Lacon turns round.

'Look – police,' Ed says. 'Here to do fuck all, as usual.'

'Ed, DS Lacon's here to help.'

'Sure he is,' Ed says. 'Fill in all the right forms and then say it was an accident. Like with Darcy.'

'Darcy was ill,' Noah says.

'That's what they want you to think.' Ed taps his nose in an exaggerated fashion.

'Let me get you a coffee, mate.' Noah hauls him towards the kitchen.

'Sorry about that,' I say. 'He and Chrissy had a thing when we were young.'

Lacon gives a wearied smile. 'I understand.' He watches Ed's back slump down on one of the kitchen stools before Noah closes the door. 'You were telling me about the village rumours.'

'None of it was true,' I say. 'But Leanne's family wanted someone to blame. They thought Nicholson had "got away with it" as he was found guilty of manslaughter, not murder. And he died not long afterwards. They needed someone to be angry at.'

'They came after you?'

'Only once,' I say. I can still see the hatred on Mrs Tattersall's face as she dashed the magazines from my hands in the shop that day. 'They moved away from All Hallows the following year. But whatever they told Cara, she hates us.'

Noah returns to the room, careful to close the kitchen door behind him.

'Have you found Cara?' he asks.

'Not yet,' Lacon says. 'Given what you've told us, you should be careful. Although in a place like this . . .' He indicates the flat. 'It's going to be difficult to get in unnoticed, as your friend Ed has just demonstrated. We'll find Cara Tattersall, though it's possible she has nothing to do with it. You've no positive proof the woman you saw at the funeral is Leanne's sister, or even if this is the same person who's been following you. And it could well turn out that Mrs Banks's death was an accident. Unfortunately at this time of year, with the festive season upon us and people out drinking, it happens a lot.'

'But I saw that woman, the one in the puffer jacket.'

'As I said, we're going over the CCTV, and if there's anything suspicious we'll follow up.' He stands. 'I really am sorry about your friend. After all you went through as teenagers too, it must seem like you're cursed.'

Noah flinches at the word but Lacon's eyes are on me.

'It's been difficult,' I say. 'But you will find out who did this?'

Lacon pulls a pained expression.

'It's not the best time to mention this, but it'll come out eventually. It appears Mrs Banks had been selling on data from the psychological experiments she did at the university and passing the results to foreign companies along with the details of those involved. She was about to lose her job and would almost certainly have been facing a criminal prosecution. On top of that her blood alcohol levels indicate a high level of intoxication. Unless there's strong evidence to the contrary, this will be labelled as an accident at best.'

'At best? You mean you think it was deliberate – a suicide?

Chrissy would never do that. She's not like that and she loves her girls too much.'

Lacon stands up.

'Of course, you're better placed to know her state of mind,' he says, though his words carry no conviction. 'I'm sorry for your loss. I really am. We'll keep you informed.'

Noah shows the detective to the door, then comes back and sits next to me. 'Chrissy was so law abiding. If she sold data from her work, what else would she sell?'

I had accused Chrissy of exactly this, but now it seems impossible she would do such a thing.

A thud comes from the kitchen. Noah races to the door to find a chair turned over and Ed sprawled across the table trying to stuff coffee grounds into his mouth.

'What the hell, Ed?' Noah takes the jar away and pulls him upright. 'I can't believe you drove in this state.'

'I didn't hit anything,' Ed says.

'Not the point. You could have killed yourself, or someone else. Where's the car?'

'I left it on the pavement.'

'I'll go and get it before it's towed away. And you're not going anywhere until you've sobered up.' Noah goes out to the balcony to make sure Lacon's left. When he's sure he's gone, he rushes off with Ed's keys.

Ed doesn't seem to know or care about the panic he's induced.

'I bloody loved that woman,' he slurs. 'I would have married Chrissy.'

'Why didn't you?'

'Too clever for me,' he says. 'That's something that old bitch Mrs Alderwell got right for once. Far too clever.

Chrissy went off to uni and I stayed in All Hallows. Before I knew it she was with that wanker Mark. I love Molly but she ain't Chrissy.' He starts to cry.

I help him to his feet and try to walk him to one of the bedrooms as he mumbles to himself.

'Dunno why Noah's trying to save me. He can't even save himself. Castanese knew. She knew. We're all gonna die.'

'She's a fraud, Ed,' I say.

His head flops onto my shoulder and he becomes a dead weight. I'm not going to get him as far as a bedroom, so tip him onto the nearest sofa.

He's snoring before I take off his shoes.

Ed, who along with Chrissy seemed the most cynical, now believes. Was that always the case and he hid it, or is this the effect of Chrissy's death combined with alcohol?

Noah returns, shaking his head.

'I've just spent ten minutes calming the concierge down and persuading him to let me use the parking space allocated to one of the vacant apartments. What was Ed thinking? We could have had two deaths in two days. He needs to see someone about his drinking. It's way out of control.'

I lean down and pick up a packet of white powder that's fallen from Ed's pocket.

'And the rest,' I say.

Noah takes the packet to the bathroom and I hear the toilet flush.

Ed moves in his slumber. 'We're all going to die,' he mutters.

The thing is, Ed's right. Two of us dying within a month of Castanese's prediction cannot be coincidence.

***

Between us, Noah and I haul Ed to one of the bedrooms and leave him to sleep it off.

'I have to call Penny,' Noah says. 'Let her know what's going on.'

He goes to his office. I amble into the kitchen, make a coffee and click through to All of This Is True. I expect the Forrester to have learnt of Chrissy's death and to have posted brags about their foresight. When I get to the forum, I can see the Forrester *has* posted, but it's not related to Chrissy's death.

The hairs on the back of my neck rise as I read the first line.

It's the same document that Darcy hand-copied and left to me, along with Leanne's scarf.

> As the second son of the fourth Viscount, Arthur Verne-Fontaine's prospects were modest...

I scan down to the place where she broke off.

> Isabella had been told she must never read her own future. Only evil could come of it.
> But then evil can always thread its way into our lives and she had no reason to suspect the true purpose of the Hags Ring.

Unlike Darcy's account, the Forrester's narrative doesn't stop here.

> Within its stones the vengeful spirits of the dead could not be countered by man or God. For Redford had chosen his site

well. The stones were cut from the ruins of an ancient Greek temple dedicated to Hades, the god of the underworld, and angels would not tread on such unholy ground.

Of course Isabella had misgivings about her marriage, yet a young woman of such low birth could not refuse a man of Verne-Fontaine's rank. She had little affection towards him and it soon became apparent that their indifference was shared, which made Verne-Fontaine's wish to marry her seem even more perverse. Soon, however, she began to perceive the reason for his choice.

He regularly had her tell fortunes. She could not help him with gambling, had better accuracy at predicting the weather, but where she excelled was in foretelling death. She always knew when someone was going to die. In the preceding days, they would appear to Isabella to be wearing a shroud. On one occasion, Verne-Fontaine was sure she had made a mistake. Redford was now a permanent fixture at All Hallows Court, a strong and healthy man of thirty. On seeing him striding across the yard one day, Isabella gasped. Verne-Fontaine knew at once what this meant and berated her for stupidity. Redford was in the prime of life. Three days later he was crushed to death beneath the wheels of a dray cart when crossing the street in Haverton. Verne-Fontaine never doubted her again.

Moreover, Isabella appeared to be immune from harm. When the carriage she was travelling in overturned, the coachman and her two fellow passengers were gravely injured. She walked away without so much as a scratch. Verne-Fontaine learnt that while the half of her family that survived smallpox had deeply pitted skin, hers was smooth and unmarked.

It was as if she had a guardian angel watching over her.

Shouldn't such providence be granted to those of high birth, who could better exploit it?

At first when Isabella made her predictions, Verne-Fontaine would praise her and shower her with gifts. But soon this behaviour changed and he began to enforce upon her the exacting regime he himself followed. She was starved, made to sit naked in an unheated room in winter and deprived of sleep. When she complained he beat her.

Once she ran back to her parents' farm. Her mother fed her and tried to hide her away. But it took little time for Verne-Fontaine to discover her whereabouts and he threatened the family with eviction, should they aid her again.

After that, Isabella was rarely seen and those that did glimpse her said the happy, plump, pretty girl was gone, replaced by a thin miserable woman, who cursed her own existence.

Then news got out that Isabella was with child. Although the house had no servants by this time, it was noted that extra eggs and milk were being ordered and Isabella had been spotted with a swollen belly and she was allowed to roam in the gardens near the house.

Just before Christmas old Mother Pratt was called upon to aid with the birth. Normally she dealt only with the peasantry and it was a great shock for her to be called to the All Hallows Court. The birth was straightforward and Mother Pratt reported that Isabella had given birth to a bonny baby girl and both mother and child were doing well. What a Christmas present for the Viscount. The village hoped that, with the blessing of a child, the Viscount would cast off the bad company he kept and return to the church; that he would restore All Hallows Court to what it had been, and re-employ the staff, so that his family and the land could prosper.

It was on 22 December, the shortest day of the year, that a shepherd discovered Isabella's body in the Hags Ring. Her heart had been pierced with a thin blade. His horror at the sight sent him running back to the village, but when he returned with several other strong men, the body had gone.

The Viscount let it be known that Isabella had died from a fever following the birth of her child. The shepherd must have been drunk, or perhaps he had eaten the liberty cap mushroom, known to induce terrifying visions. No one had the courage to contradict Verne-Fontaine's account.

Isabella was buried after Christmas. The coffin laid in the Verne-Fontaine vault was said to be extraordinarily heavy for such a slight woman. Cynics said it was because the Viscount had overcompensated for the empty coffin with a surfeit of lead.

Whatever the truth, from that day forward, both the Viscount and the village prospered. Arthur Verne-Fontaine became a very rich man. All his speculations reaped bountiful profits. A new steward was employed to properly manage the estate. Servants returned to the hall and contentment to the village.

When all was well with the world, who would want to dwell on the death of a farmer's daughter?

After the fifth Viscount was widowed he sought another wife to give him an heir. A girl could not inherit and Arthur would not countenance his cousin, the son of the pompous uncle who came from London to lecture him, becoming the next Viscount. So he married the daughter of an earl, a plain, broad-hipped girl that Verne-Fontaine considered suitable for bearing children. Like everything since Isabella's death, his guess was correct. She bore him seven children, five boys and two girls. Isabella's child was fed, educated and ignored. When she asked to marry a local farmer, Arthur did not oppose the match. He viewed it only as the daughter returning to the sphere to which her mother belonged. The Viscount gifted her husband a farm on the far edge of the estate and then he forgot about his first-born child. She no longer bore the Verne-Fontaine name, nor did she mix in the same circles as her half-siblings, who would give him the grandchildren of high birth he desired.

I reread the description of Isabella seeing a shroud several times. That I am not the first person in All Hallows to see this portent of death, terrifies me. Can the similarity between my visions and Isabella's be mere chance? I long for Chrissy to explain it away and miss her more than ever.

Then I go back and try to understand the rest. This version corresponds to the one I'd heard through the village. That Verne-Fontaine killed his wife in a ritual. But the Forrester's account is more specific, detailing the reason for their marriage, his mistreatment of Isabella and why he wanted her dead – to take her angel from her and replace Isabella as its master. The Hags Ring was constructed in order to remove its protection. An angel could not enter the land within the stones, which belonged to the underworld. It was a mish-mash of religions and beliefs. I was reminded of what the woman interviewed in the newspaper articles at the time of Leanne's death – Oleana, I think her name was – had said about Rex Pender: that he's not a true pagan. He bends other belief systems to fit his own. Well, in that respect, he was treading in the footsteps of Verne-Fontaine.

The document makes concrete the idea that's been fermenting at the back of my mind.

'Where are Ed's keys?' I ask Noah when he returns from his phone call.

He holds them up. I take them from him.

'What do you need those for? I've already moved the car.'

'We're like sitting ducks, just waiting here for Cara to pick us off one by one,' I say. 'The police aren't going to find anything in the CCTV footage. We need answers. Can I borrow a hoodie?'

'Are you cold?' He throws me one that's been slung over the back of a chair.

'No. I'm taking Ed's car.'

'Where are you going? I don't think you should go poking around, Mia. The police have got this.'

'No, they haven't,' I say. 'I'll send you a link to a post on All of This Is True. Read it and see what you make of it. I'll phone you later.'

Chapter 35

Ed's car is in the corner space of the underground car park. A silver Ford Mondeo, it's sufficiently anonymous for my purposes and I set the Sat Nav for the place listed as the main business address on Madame Castanese's website: Benton-on-Sea.

Grief is a luxury I cannot afford. Two of us are dead. Noah just says we're cursed and Ed's solution to everything lies at the bottom of a glass. I'm the only one trying to stop this. Whatever this is.

I crawl across town before pressing my foot to the floor and flying up the M40 and the M42, zooming past the exit that would take me to All Hallows, before hitting the M6, then turning off towards the seaside town of Benton.

I park on a residential street away from the seafront. Before I get out of the car, I send the All of This Is True link to both Noah and Ed. Then I write down all my suspicions about Chrissy's new income stream as a reminder to Noah and to see if it will ring any bells with Ed once he's sobered up. After that I pull Noah's hoodie on. I'm immediately enveloped in the subtle citrus of his aftershave. I take a moment to savour his scent, then flip the hood over my head and get out of the car. Cara has taught me one trick: red dress for display, dark hoodie for concealment. I'm not as anonymous as she was. My jeans do not hide me as loose joggers would have done and my white trainers have a distinctive mauve 'V', but my face is sufficiently concealed that I can't be identified from a distance or a CCTV camera.

Few places are more depressing than a seaside town in winter. The light drizzle and slate-grey sea mirror the depression hanging over the streets. The ice-cream kiosks and knick-knack shops are boarded up. The whirr, lights and screams of the funfair are a distant memory. The only bar open is the Waikiki, which sees nothing ironic in being named after a Hawaiian beach whilst blaring out country-and-western music and offering 'a pie and a pint' for five pounds.

I bear away from the front and wind through the backstreets until I come to an alley; halfway up which hangs a small, hand-painted sign.

Madame Castanese – Practitioner of the Arcane Crafts

I did consider making an appointment but she doesn't allow online bookings and I'm worried she would recognise my voice on a call. I could just go and knock, but no doubt Leon guards the door. He wouldn't let me sneak in, hood pulled low across my face.

I hover at the entrance to the alley, looking like some loitering drug dealer, but luckily Benton's residents pay me no attention and hurry past, anxious to get out of the now insistent rain. I'm hesitating about what to do when the door opens and Leon steps outside. He doesn't look my way and walks off in the opposite direction. I have a split second to decide, then dart towards the open door before it swings shut. The raindrops pitter-patter, masking the sound of my trainers on the wet paving stones.

A low-lit, windowless corridor awaits me. I'm not sure what course of action to take. It's possible Castanese is not here at this time of day. And it's only when the door bangs shut behind me that I realise it's the type that locks on both sides. Until Leon gets back, I'm stuck here, and then what?

Coming alone wasn't ideal, but Ed's too drunk and Noah's too cautious. I have my phone and can call the police if the worst comes to the worst, though what they would think of me I don't know.

I listen for Bella's hiss as I move along the corridor and my soles scuff the cement floor, but she's quiet today. I can hear something else, however. A jingly-jangly song playing on a radio. It's coming from the end room. I tiptoe closer and lean in. The La's 'There She Goes'. Not what I expected in a space dedicated to the arcane crafts. Someone clears their throat.

'You can come in when you've finished spying.'

Castanese doesn't bother hiding her Scouse accent this time. I check to see if there's a camera. It's hidden if there is. I consider running away, then remember the door is locked. I steel myself. Isn't this why I'm here: to confront her and find answers?

'I haven't got all day,' she says.

I peel back my hood and push open the door.

She's standing behind a table, in the process of lighting a cigarette. The wig is gone, which shortens her by a few inches but she still towers over me. Her cropped grey hair exposes her face with its cavernous cheeks; she's far older than I thought her at the Dower House. Beneath lashes swathed in thick mascara her eyes are sharp and appraising. Despite me taking her by surprise, between the two of us, she's by far the more composed. All the questions I've prepared flee my mind and I can only gawp.

She takes a long drag on the cigarette and exhales slowly.

'It always amazes me that when you tell someone lies, they'll accept it. Tell them the truth and oooo,' she sucks air through her teeth. 'That's when the problems start. Your friends have died. That's why you're here, right?'

'How could you know that?'

'I'm a medium.'

'Bullshit.'

She gives me a cold smile. 'You know it's not.'

'Someone tipped you off about who the reading was for at the Dower House. You'd prepared all that stuff about Leanne.'

'Do you know how many people I get coming through hear? Politicians, billionaires—'

'Yeah, Leon gave us the spiel.'

'People like that don't pay if they're not getting what they want. But you came to me thinking you were so superior.'

'You're telling me these politicians and billionaires don't think they're superior?'

'Not in the way you did.'

'We're no different from other people.'

'You misunderstand me, dear. By "you", I didn't mean your group, I meant you specifically.'

It takes a moment to comprehend her meaning. That it was my attitude or something I did to make her turn against us. 'Why me? What did I do?'

'Tell me what frightens you most – that I'm a charlatan and these deaths are orchestrated, or that I have the gift and I'm merely reporting what will be?'

I'm stumped.

'I'll let you into a little secret, Mia. I'm a mixture of both.' Castanese appears to be enjoying herself. 'I do have the gift but it comes and goes. When it fails to materialise I have to rely on other talents. People will pay all day to listen to what they want to hear.'

'Like those old people you defrauded? They thought you were their friend because you told them all the right things. You were employed as a carer and you did everything but.'

This needles her.

'Oh, so you're capable of some research. Well, you're wrong. I did care for them. More than that, I was their friend. I'd take their calls long after my shift finished and listen to how they were frightened, or anxious, but mostly they were lonely. Their children and grandchildren hardly visited. Some of the daughters would pop by once a week and make out they're some sort of martyr for looking after their own mother. They were all just hanging around, waiting for their mum to die so they could sell the house and use the money to build some hideous extension or go on a luxury cruise.'

'You exploited them.'

She shakes her head. 'I made sure their last few years were filled with fun and laughter and they rewarded me. No one was conned or coerced. Of course, when someone like me is speaking in front of a jury and it's my word against Mrs La-di-da-middle-class, they choose her version of events. I went to jail and they got their money, which was all they were interested in, not their parents' welfare. So you tell me, who's the grifter?' She shrugs. 'I learnt my lesson after that. My business is legitimate. The law can't touch me.'

'When you're telling your clients what they want to hear, do you tell most of them they're going to be dead by Christmas?'

She smiles again, back in control of her emotions. 'I told you, dear, you were different.'

'In what way?'

She taps the ash from her cigarette. 'You're right. I did know you were coming. Chrissy told me.' She holds my gaze without flinching. It's impossible to tell if she's lying or not. 'She wanted to perform an experiment. But I had my own one in mind. I told you that the gift comes and goes, but that night I saw clearly. That night I knew all of you were going to die and the reason I knew is because you brought someone with you into that room at the Dower House, didn't you?'

'I don't know what you mean.'

'I think you do. She spoke to you before I did.'

Before me the branch unfurls and the bright green buds wither to brown.

'Do you know what people would do to have the gift you scorn? You waste your life in pastels when your colours are red and black. Yes, I've seen your paintings. They'd be vomit inducing from anyone, but from you? Who do you think you're kidding? Maybe yourself, no one else. When you've discovered your true calling come and see me. I'll get you some real work.' She leers at me through nicotine-stained teeth.

'Two of my friends are dead,' I say. 'You'll forgive me if I don't join in the joke.'

'We all die. Life is only the waking hours between two long sleeps. With so little time left, are you sure you want to spend it with an old lady in a dying seaside town?'

She's guiding this whole conversation. This isn't what I came here for.

'Who killed Chrissy?' I ask.

'How should I know?'

'Was it Cara?'

'Who?'

'If you have any information then you need to go to the police.'

'I know no more than you. You'll all be dead by Christmas. I don't tell you this to upset or hurt you but because it's the truth. I'm neither sad nor sorry. None of you seem like pleasant people to me. You let your friend Leanne die, and you can cut it anyway you want, make excuses, but that's what happened.'

'You must know something,' I say.

'Far less than you do and if you can't work it out, how do you expect me to?' She stubs out her cigarette. 'That night on Hallows Hill when Leanne died wasn't the first time Bella had spoken to you, was it?'

'Bella is a myth.'

Castanese raises an eyebrow. 'Bella, as you understand her, is a myth, Mia. Have you ever heard of a guardian angel?'

It's my turn to sneer. 'Like a fairy godmother.'

She tilts her head to one side. 'That's how they show up in children's tales.'

'And you're telling me this is what Bella is? If that's the case I've nothing to worry about. I won't die by Christmas.'

'They're not invincible. Look at what happened to Isabella Verne-Fontaine.'

I don't want to give her the satisfaction of raising my curiosity.

'You're such a fraud.'

She gives me a long, hard, appraising look. 'In that case,' she says, 'we've nothing more to discuss. Leon will show you out.'

I spin round. I hadn't noticed him enter the room. For all his bulk, his movement is stealthy.

'I need to know exactly what Chrissy told you,' I say.

She turns her back to me.

'You need to leave,' Leon says.

'But—'

He moves to stand in front of me. 'Out.'

'Just a moment.' Castanese takes a step towards me. 'If Bella's a myth and your visions are just the product of an overheated mind, who's Lula?'

'How do you—' I stop.

She turns away again. 'That's all for now. Leon will escort you to the front door.'

I'm still in shock as Leon shunts me out of the room and, clutching my arm, marches me down the corridor.

Before ejecting me he pulls his face close to mine. 'I'm following Madame's instructions not to harm you. But if I see you back here, or anywhere in this town again, it'll be a different story.'

I yank my arm from his grasp.

'Who are you?'

'You need to leave.'

'Who is *Madame* to you? Your mother, your lover?'

He balls his fists. I think he's going to launch himself at me. Instead he steps back and lets the door slam in my face.

I walk back down the alley. The rain drenches the hoodie, soaking my hair. On the promenade the sea and sky are indistinguishable, the Waikiki bar lights struggle against the gloom and Dolly Parton is begging Jolene not to take her man.

The streets leading back to the car are empty. I check to make sure Leon isn't following. He isn't. Still, I'm glad I'm not taking the train. Was it him that day at the station? There's a bristling violence to the man, as if he's just waiting for an excuse. But why? The only person who could hate us that much is Cara Tattersall, but Castanese looked blank when I mentioned her.

Back inside the car, I pull the sodden hoodie off and set the heaters to full blast. The rain bouncing off the windscreen forces me to drive slowly.

Castanese's words go round and round in my head.

You brought someone with you into that room . . . that wasn't the first time Bella had spoken to you, was it? If Bella is a myth . . . who's Lula?

Only after Chrissy's death did I learn that a second person once claimed I have the gift. Dotty, the old lady who looked after me when we lived in Arnold Court. She's long dead and there's only one person who knows my imaginary friend was called Lula.

I head back down the motorway, but this time I turn off towards All Hallows. It's dusk by the time I near the village and the Hags Ring stones stand like ghosts, barely visible through the rain and fading light.

Chapter 36

I called from just outside Manchester to tell Mum I was coming. She told me to be discreet.

'Now isn't the best time for you to be in All Hallows.' She wouldn't tell me why.

I leave Ed's car down the road from the house rather than on the drive. It's ludicrous taking these precautions, as if I'm some sort of fugitive. Mum, however, deems it necessary and has gone to the trouble of switching off the automatic outside lights. When I arrive she ushers me through the front door before hugging me.

'What's happened, Mia? Are you hurt?'

'I'm fine,' I say, a little taken aback. 'Is all this necessary, the secrecy, the lights?'

'It's easier if people don't ask questions and that includes Bernard. I don't want to burden him.'

'I'm a burden now?' I ask.

'Come into the kitchen,' she says.

There's a pot of tea waiting for me on the table and some homemade biscuits.

'Why did you take Ed's car?' Mum asks.

I explain about him turning up drunk in London.

'I do worry about him,' Mum says. 'I bumped into him the other Saturday at around ten in the morning. He reeked of whisky. I suppose it could have been from the night before, but I don't think so. Poor Molly and the boys.'

'He always had a thing for Chrissy,' I say. 'It's not that they were ever going to get together, but maybe he was hoping one day . . . I don't know. Drinking's his way of coping. Or not coping.'

'And how are you doing, Mia? Why are you here?'

'I'm on my way back from Benton-on-Sea. I went to see the medium, Madame Castanese.'

Mum looks anxious. 'I told you to stay away from anything like that.'

'I need to know the truth. What you told me after Chrissy died didn't sink in. I was too upset. But since, I've been thinking about Dotty. You said she started rumours about me even before Leanne died because I used to speak to my imaginary friend.'

Mum doesn't answer.

'Two of my friends are dead. I'm being followed. Keeping information from me is no form of protection. Castanese knew about Lula. How? Only you and Dotty knew her name.'

She puts down her tea. 'Sometimes I think we should have left All Hallows, but I'm not sure that would have kept you safe.'

'Safe from what?'

'I was so naïve. I thought it was good of Dotty to look after you. She didn't ask for money – said it was her pleasure – and I couldn't have worked if she hadn't, and we'd have been even poorer than we were.'

'We weren't so poor, were we?' I say.

'I always tried to make it seem that way. You didn't know all our clothes were second-hand and I had to dash around the supermarket just before they closed, buying up all the damaged and outdated produce. But we got by. The thing is, Dotty wasn't looking after you out of the goodness of her heart. It was Lula she wanted.'

'You never answered my question before, Mum. You never told me why Dotty was so sure Lula wasn't simply an imaginary friend.'

Mum lowers her eyes and takes both my hands. 'Do you remember there were only eight flats in that block and all the others were occupied by pensioners? There was one lady, Marjorie Lyons, she was a little younger than the others. In her early sixties, I think. Anyway, she kept that long-haired rabbit you liked to play with.'

Mrs Lyons, the name Dotty had said to me in connection with her son, Paul. Her rabbit was the reason I was so set on having one of my own for Christmas the year Mum surprised me with my new family. And another memory stirs, then evaporates when I try to bring it into focus.

Mum takes a deep breath. 'The thing is, the day before Mrs Lyons died you told Dotty she was wearing a . . .' The moment before she says it, I know the word she's about to use. '. . . shroud. I mean what five-year-old even knows the word "shroud"? The next morning, Dotty noticed that Mrs Lyons's mail was still stuck through her letterbox at noon. After that, she came to me and told me what you had said. She claimed you had the gift.'

'Gift' – another word to unnerve me.

'Dotty wasn't one to keep things to herself. People started

avoiding us. The hospital said they no longer required my services.'

'That's totally ridiculous.'

'It's not ridiculous if people believe it. Those women in the seventeenth century didn't really sour milk and blight crops. They were still hanged for witchcraft.'

'That was four centuries ago.'

She ignores me. 'Before the railway was built, this village was a fraction of the size it is now. There were just a few old families who intermarried for generations. Bernard's was one of them. Dotty's was another, and the Alderwells, of course. After the village expanded the old families married out but they still kept their secrets and banded together. The Conservation Club is the remnants of those people.'

'What has this got to do with Lula?'

'The girl found murdered up at the Hags Ring in the 1940s, the one they called Bella.'

'What about her?'

'She was a girl who'd fallen pregnant to one of the Verne-Fontaine sons. Marriage was out of the question. The old Viscount pulled strings to get his son sent overseas immediately – not difficult in the middle of a war. After the child was born, the girl went to All Hallows Court and screamed curses at them. That night a stray Luftwaffe bomb destroyed the hall and most of its inhabitants. Two days later the girl was found in the Hags Ring, murdered.'

'The Verne-Fontaines at the hall had been killed and the son was abroad. So who did it?'

'No one knows who, but the Conservation Club know why and what her real name was.'

'So who was she?' I ask.

Mum takes both my hands and looks at me with scared eyes. 'Her name was Lula.'

Outside the trees rustle in the wind. I want to cover my ears. *She* is laughing. *She* is coming for me.

'Dotty must have told me that name,' I say.

'You called her Lula long before you met Dotty. As soon as I understood why she was taking such an interest, I got you away from there.'

'By marrying Bernard?'

'Bernard's head of the Conservation Club. No one would harm his stepdaughter. Although after Leanne died, it did become difficult. If only you hadn't gone to Hallows Hill that night.'

'If you'd told me half of this, I never would have.'

'It's too late. I did what I did. And you're still here. But with all that's going on, you need to stay away from All Hallows. Even Bernard is starting to have doubts.'

'What doubts? What are people saying?'

'People are saying you're dabbling in the occult, which is true.'

'Twice. I've done it twice.'

'And both times people have died.'

'This isn't about the occult. It's a campaign against us by Cara Tattersall.'

'You know it's more than that,' Mum says. 'There is something . . .'

'What else aren't you telling me?'

'People know about Darcy and Chrissy. Someone brought up Leanne's death at the Conservation Club and mentioned your name. Which is why you coming here tonight wasn't a good idea.'

'What aren't you telling me?' I repeat.

The front door clicks open.

'You see, Rex Pender—'

'Hey, Sandy, what's happened to the lights?'

Bernard's home. We were too busy talking to hear his car.

'I must have knocked the switch when I was hoovering,' Mum calls back to him.

She hurries me to the back door and opens it for me to slip out.

She calls me back for a moment.

'Rex Pender had met you long before that night on Hallows Hill. He's Paul Bridges, Dotty's son.'

She shuts the door and I hear Bernard come into the kitchen.

Chapter 37

Rex Pender knew about me and knew about Lula even before Leanne's death. I remember him sitting down and asking me questions and Dotty shooing him off. The leather-jacketed man with cropped hair looked nothing like the one with long hair and a beard I remember from the newspapers. But it was him. It's not something Mum could have made a mistake about.

The car's parked around the bend so they can't see me from the house, nevertheless I drive off to a small lane without streetlights, pull over, get my phone out and do my research.

The last mention of Rex Pender is over ten years ago. He had been due to speak in a series of lectures at a college near Worcester: 'Vernal Equinox: Spiritual or Commercial'. His previous provocative statements caused speakers and attendees to question his inclusion. They claimed he brought the whole pagan movement into disrepute with notions of necessary sacrifice. Pender withdrew from the conference claiming 'bed-wetting virgins' weren't worth his time and effort. More exciting plans were afoot – a commune for like-minded people. After this, he disappeared.

I'd read this before, but I'd been too passive, expecting his name just to pop up. A different approach is needed. I scan the names of the people who had raised objections to Pender's appearance at the conference. The most unusual one, the easiest to search for, is Oleana Jenkins. I remember her mentioned when I looked up the news report from the time of Leanne's death. I have no problem tracking her down to a group in Cumbria who volunteer to maintain footpaths. The group is always looking for new members. There's a phone number in the contact details at the bottom. I take my chance.

After a couple of rings, a rather tired voice answers.

'Hello.'

'Hi. I'm calling about the Wistfell Volunteers.'

'It's a bit late. Maybe you could ring back in the morning.'

'Tomorrow?'

I must sound disappointed because she says, 'Actually, it's fine. We always need more people. Let me just take your details.'

She shuffles around in the background and I feel bad because I'm approaching her under false pretences. When she comes back on the phone, I come clean.

'The thing is, I'm not ringing about the volunteering,' I say. 'It's about another matter.'

Silence.

'You used to belong to a pagan group in Worcestershire.'

'That was a long time ago,' she says. 'I attend church these days. And I can only advise you to stay away from people like that, whatever your interest.'

'It's not them I'm interested in. I'm looking for someone. His name is Rex Pender. He's—'

'I know who he is.'

'Do you know where to find him?'

'That man is dangerous.'

'I'm Leanne Tattersall's friend. The name the press gave me was Maria Collier. I remember you speaking to the *Haverton Herald*, telling them that Pender was not a real pagan.'

'The only thing that man truly believes in is his own self-interest. A couple of years before Leanne's death I'd been skirting around the fringes of his group. I thought it was alternative and exciting. I soon saw through him. What he did, taunting that poor girl's parents, showed him in his true colours. That's why I had to do something when he was going to give a speech at the conference all those years later.'

'But do you know where Rex Pender is now?'

'Rex Pender!' She snorts down the line. 'I hate that name. You know that's a joke, right?'

'A joke?'

'It's not his real name. He's called Paul something or other – Bates or Briggs.'

'Bridges.'

'Yes, Bridges. That was it. Well, Rex obviously means King and Pender is a nod to Penda, England's last pagan king. Talk about delusions of grandeur. Everything about him is a fraud. He said such outrageous things, no one looked at the man. Saying someone's into the occult is a bit like saying they're into religion. I mean, which form? Christianity, Hinduism, Islam? Because Pender's into everything. It started off with that faux paganism, only one up from *Lord of the Rings* cosplay. Then he combined it with Enochian magic – that's angels and stuff.'

'Angels?' This is starting to ring alarm bells.

'It goes back to the Book of Enoch, one of the Apocrypha, the books that didn't make it into the standard Bible. John Dee and Aleister Crowley were into it. Crowley claimed to have followed a ritual to raise his guardian angel. I heard that's what Pender's up to these days.'

'So you do know where he is?'

'You need to keep away from that man.'

'Please, Oleana. I need to find him. Leanne was my friend. This isn't idle curiosity.'

'OK, but you need to take care. I'm still in touch with a few people in the movement. Pender has started a community in Pelham Chase. There are permanent residents and he makes money running retreats, promising them God knows what. My friend went but left pretty quickly. Pender claims he can help raise people's guardian angels to bring them good fortune all their lives. For an exorbitant fee, of course. All types of people go there: royalty, politicians . . .'

The same claim made by Leon about Madame Castanese. Do they know each other, share a client base?

'Can I talk to your friend, the one who left?'

'She's too afraid. They really messed with her head.'

'Then can you help me find him? Pelham Chase is pretty big.'

It's one of the largest forests in the area. I have vague memories of a school trip there, where an earnest young man in corduroy trousers eulogised about toadstools and beetles.

'Why's everyone interested in Pender again, after all this time?' Oleana asks.

'Someone else has been asking after him?'

'A woman phoned me back in the summer.'

I take a deep breath and try to keep my voice steady as I ask, 'Did you meet her?'

'No. It was just a phone call.'

'Did she give you her name? Was it Chrissy?'

'No, not Chrissy.'

'Cara?'

'Not that either.'

I think of Castanese and her matching boast about attracting politicians and royalty. But how would she have introduced herself.

'This woman, did she have a Scouse accent?'

'More Scottish, but I couldn't place it exactly. I do remember her name because it was slightly old-fashioned. What was it?' Oleana clicks her tongue. 'I've got it. Lula. Her name was Lula.'

Chapter 38

In the car I ring Noah. I want him to know about Pender. He's living in the middle of Pelham Chase – surely that means he's the Forrester. Noah doesn't pick up. I try Ed, who does answer. He sounds sober but tired.

'Are you back in London?'

'No. All Hallows.'

'Me, too. I got the train home. Molly was about to lose it. Are you just dropping the car off?'

'It's a bit more than that. I'll tell you when I see you. You don't mind about the car, do you?'

'No. I shouldn't have driven. It was so stupid.'

'The thing is, Ed, can I borrow it tomorrow?' I ask.

'I need it for work. Soz, Mia.'

I check my watch.

'I'll drop it back now. I can still catch the last train home.'

Ed lives in a detached four-bedroomed house. Most people would think it a great place to raise their kids: big garden, good state schools, access to the countryside. But most people aren't best friends with a tech millionaire. I know Ed feels he's fallen behind and not made much of his life.

Though a steady job, a doting wife and two cute kids should be enough.

He opens the front door as I pull onto the drive.

I jog up to him, keys in hand. Ed looks terrible. His eyes are bloodshot, his face puffy.

'You don't need to tell me I look like shit. Molly's already been there.' He cracks a smile. 'Come and have some tea.'

I check my phone. I've forty minutes until the last train and Ed's house is ten minutes from the station.

Molly's already in the kitchen, with a cup of fruit-scented tea at the breakfast bar. We kiss and she says, 'You've not come to take him to the pub, have you?'

'Just returning the car.'

'Where did you go?' Ed asks.

I look at Molly, unsure what to say.

'We tell each other everything,' Ed says. Then busies himself making my cup of tea. I think of the night at the Dower House with Chrissy and the anonymous threats he's been receiving. He doesn't tell Molly everything.

'I know about that medium,' Molly says. 'Madame Castanese.'

'That's who I went to see.'

Ed stops mid-stir.

'Mia, is that safe?'

'I'm here, aren't I?'

'You need to be careful.'

'What would you say if I told you the craziest encounter I've had today wasn't with Castanese but with my mum?'

'Sandy? What did she have to say?' Ed asks.

'Too much. Not enough. I need to speak to you both. You live here. Have you heard all these rumours?'

I repeat what Mum told me about Bella being a real person and all the old villagers knowing her true name was Lula. I leave out the part about my imaginary friend.

'It sounds like a lot of old women with too much time on their hands,' Ed says.

'That's sexist,' Molly says.

'But true,' Ed says.

Molly rolls her eyes.

'You've not heard anything, Molly, at the garden centre?'

'People know I'm married to Ed. They wouldn't say anything in front of me, and when I asked around about the Tattersalls, no one admitted to being in touch. It could simply be the truth.'

'Why do you care so much about these rumours? You don't believe them, do you?' Ed asks.

I repeat what Mum said. 'It's not that I believe them, but other people do so I have to take them seriously. I haven't told you the last part. The reason I asked to borrow the car tomorrow.'

'Where do you want to get to?'

'I tracked down Rex Pender. I'm going to talk to him.'

'You should stay away from that guy,' Ed says. 'He's into some dark shit and it's like you said, it's what he believes that counts.'

'We need to speak to him. I wasn't the first person to try and track him down.' I tell them about Oleana Jenkins. 'This person who phoned called herself Lula – the name of the woman who was murdered in the 1940s.'

'That's fucked up,' Ed says. 'Who do you think it was?'

'I thought it might be Chrissy or maybe Cara Tattersall, but Oleana said she had a strange Scottish accent.'

'Probably strange because it wasn't really Scottish,' Molly says. 'When I was a teenager me and my mates went through a phase of making prank calls. We'd always put on accents to hide our real voices.'

'That's what I thought,' I say.

'Do you really think it could have been Chrissy?' Ed asks.

'She was desperate for money. Noah told you about the experiment, the psychomanteum?'

'Yeah, but I don't buy it. Chrissy wasn't like that. Why would she contact Pender? And as for Cara, she must hate him as much as we do.'

'There's only one way to find out.'

'No, Mia,' Ed says. 'I've already lost two friends. You can't go wandering off into the middle of a forest on your own.'

'So are we just going to sit around waiting to find out who is doing all of this? It will be too late by then.'

'Why don't we speak to Noah?' Ed says. 'He can pay people to do it.'

'Noah's being weird. It's like he doesn't want to admit what's happening. He's not going to help. I'm going to find Pender and speak to him.'

'I'm not lending you my car for that.'

'Fine. I'll hire one.'

Ed looks at Molly. She shrugs.

'OK, if you're going, I'm coming with you.'

'You said it's dangerous.'

'It's less dangerous with two of us. And we'll have Molly at the end of the phone in case we need to call the police. Right, Molls?'

She nods.

'I think you need to do this,' she says. 'And I've got a Mace spray.'

'Why the hell do you have that?' Ed asks.

'You were working away and there was a series of break-ins.'

'It's illegal – where did you get it?'

'The dark web. You can get anything there.'

My preconceptions of dull Molly are evaporating.

'I'm married to the mob,' Ed says.

We agree it's easier for me to stay the night than go back to London. I borrow a T-shirt to sleep in and Ed takes my clothes to the utility room to be washed overnight.

Molly and I make up the bed in their spare room.

'Thanks for being cool about Ed coming with me. I'll feel safer with him there.'

'He needs to stop brooding and do something, take his mind off alcohol. Honestly, Mia, I love him, but how much am I supposed to put up with? He's always drunk too much, but since Darcy's death it's gone through the roof and yesterday he was drinking before I got up and then disappeared with the car. We have two kids. I have to think of them.'

'Ed knows he has a problem.'

'He needs to fix it,' she says. 'He's becoming paranoid.'

'In what way?'

She shakes the duvet, then smooths it down.

'He doesn't trust anyone. He asked me if I thought Noah and Chrissy had arranged that whole business with Castanese. And then he said he'd started thinking again about what happened when Leanne died.'

'In what way?'

'I'm not sure. But I know he and Noah had an argument before he left London. He wouldn't tell me what it was about. These days he's permanently stressed. And that just makes him drink more.'

'I'm sorry, Molly. I didn't know you were dealing with all of this.'

'Chrissy's death hit him harder than Darcy's, and not just because it was the second one. He loved her, didn't he?'

'We were all a bit in love with one another at some stage,' I say. 'It's inevitable when you're all teenagers together and your hormones are racing. It's not real, though. He loves you, Molly. Chrissy was just nostalgia, like listening to an old radio station.'

'He does that too,' Molly says.

I'm getting into bed when Molly returns with the Mace spray.

'I'm giving it to you. Ed's all fingers and thumbs; he'd probably end up spraying himself. And if anyone finds it, you didn't get it off me.'

'Cheers, Molly.'

I feel bad about not liking her before.

Chapter 39

Pelham Chase, once the hunting ground of medieval kings, is still one of the largest forests in the country despite the encroaching farmland. Even though it's only an hour's drive from Ed's house, we stop off for a coffee, both wanting to delay the encounter. More than William Nicholson, who came into our lives then was gone, Rex Pender has lingered in my consciousness. His disappearance created a vacuum that sucked in all manner of evil imaginings.

I'm at the wheel. Ed said he was too tired to drive. I suspect the truth is that he had a surreptitious drink before we left. His breath was suspiciously minty when we got in the car.

After our coffee, we drive for another half-hour before Pelham Chase comes into view. Our route skirts the edge of the forest, trees to one side and farmland to the other. After another fifteen minutes we reach the small layby described by Oleana. If it had been summer, vegetation would have hidden the post with three black stripes.

We undo our seatbelts and sit in silence. My hands shakes as I turn the key to switch off the engine. Ed appears far calmer. Dutch courage perhaps. Cold air rushes in when I open the car door and our breath billows out in white clouds. Along with the Mace spray, Molly lent me her walking jacket, for which I'm grateful. Although it's too small for me to zip up, it's warmer than just a hoodie.

Ed wears only a light jacket and doesn't appear to be affected by the cold.

'Is that it?' He points to the narrow path opposite.

After learning that the camp was in Pelham Chase, we took some time to find it on Google Earth. From the satellite picture I could see we needed to walk straight from the post to the centre of the woods. But it's much harder to find on the ground than from above. The path we start along disappears under brambles almost immediately. We take another that splits and it's unclear which is the main way through. Several times we end up faced with thickets of holly and we have to backtrack and take another route.

Sodden leaves cover the forest floor. My trainers' tread is insufficient and I slip and slide while Ed strides forward in his thick walking boots. Though it's daylight and the ground flat, it reminds me of that trudge up Hallows Hill all those years ago, where I fell and hurt my wrist and nearly turned back.

Our progress is slow; Ed has to keep stopping and waiting for me. The distance, which looked only a few minutes' walk on the map, is taking us far longer as we wind through the forest over uncertain ground.

Once I fall over because something swoops through the trees. I duck and lose my footing before realising it's some sort of hawk. Ed helps me to my feet.

'Do they normally attack humans?' I ask, brushing dirt and leaves from me.

'It must have seen some prey in your path. We probably disturbed a mouse or something.'

I wipe my hands on my jeans and look up. The hawk has gone.

We carry on in silence for another ten minutes before something else begins to bother me: the definite sensation of being watched. I stop and stare around. The branches are bare but there are enough tree trunks and clumps of bushes to hide behind.

'Can you see anyone, Ed?' I whisper.

'No. Keep walking.'

His strained voice tells me he too is starting to feel on edge. I rummage for the Mace spray in the bag slung across my body.

We're moving faster now, getting used to the terrain, though with speed we're noisier; twigs snapping beneath us. I realise that all the forest looks the same and if we were to get lost, it would be difficult to find our way out. I check my phone, which is down to one bar of reception and shows us as a dot of red in a sea of green, giving us no clue as to which way we should be going.

The trees become denser as we move forwards. Some are choked by ivy and we have to weave around holly bushes, their branches bright with red berries.

The sensation of being watched becomes more intense. I can feel eyes boring into the back of my head. I tap Ed to stop and a moment after we do, a twig cracks behind us.

Ed and I look at each other.

We can't see anyone.

'Who's there?' I say. Ed looks at me as if I'm insane. 'We know you're following us. Just come out.'

From behind separate tree trunks, two figures appear dressed almost like medieval peasants in grey trousers and wool tunics with separate hoods. An instinctive dread grips me. It's as if we've stepped into another age. My hand tightens around the Mace spray, I'm now holding behind my back.

'What do you want?' I ask in my bravest voice.

The two figures walk forwards. I can see now they are both men in their twenties.

'You're trespassing,' one says.

'This is public land,' Ed says. 'You don't own it.'

The two exchange a look.

'You need to come with us.'

'We're not going anywhere,' Ed says. 'What authority do you have?'

'We have natural authority over this wood.'

I start to bring the Mace from behind my back. Then the other one speaks in a more conciliatory tone.

'Excuse Drew,' he says. 'Some people hear of us and come to gawp. They want to make Instagram posts or create a podcast. We don't take kindly to publicity.'

'We're just going for a walk on a public right of way,' Ed says. 'We've no interest in podcasts.'

'Then you're not here to see Rex Pender?'

I can't help glancing at Ed.

'That's a shame,' the man continues. 'Because he was very much looking forward to meeting you, Mia.'

I'm too shocked to be cautious.

'How does he know I'm here?'

'He sees many things. You should come with us.'

I look at Ed.

'If you don't wish to see him, we will lead you back to your car.'

Another glance at Ed and he gives a faint nod. I stash the Mace back in my bag.

'Good,' the man says 'I'm Adam. Follow me. You're going the wrong way.'

The path is narrow and we have to walk in single file. Adam leads us and Drew walks at the back. I need to talk to Ed but I can't. How the hell did Pender learn that we were coming? The only people who knew about our journey were myself, Ed and Molly. Oleana hated him, and wouldn't have warned him, even if she had known we were making this trip today. The thought of *you know how* nags at the back of my mind. I damp it down. No one can see into the future.

Miaaa.

I stop so suddenly Drew crashes into the back of me.

'Why did you stop?' he asks.

I look around. There's no movement in the trees, and the branches are fixed still against the sky, which is turning from blue to grey. Is s*he* here? I think again about turning back. Ed and Adam look at me expectantly.

'I just needed to catch my breath,' I say.

Drew's face is a picture of disdain. I'm a soft city dweller who can't even walk half a mile without getting out of breath.

I scan the woods again and say, 'I'm ready to move on again now.'

Adam sets off at a slower pace this time.

As we move on, the woodland changes from the bare branches of deciduous trees, mostly oaks, to a darker canopy of pines.

After a while their sharp, sweet scent mingles with that of woodsmoke, which intensifies the longer we walk. Finally we arrive at a circular clearing with a log fire smouldering at the centre. A wooden lodge stands to one side and a couple of marquees and multiple tents are dotted around elsewhere. About twenty to thirty people are standing around, dressed in a similar fashion to Adam and Drew: dark wool tunics with separate hoods. They all turn and look as we pass. Their stares frighten me because they are not ones of hostility, but of wonder.

I reach for Ed's hand again as we cross the clearing and stand at the steps leading up to the lodge.

'Wait here,' Adam says.

Drew stands in front of us, his arms crossed. This is obviously some sort of cosplay for him. He's not a guard and we are not his prisoners. But then if we wanted to leave now, would we be allowed? It's irrelevant. I'm not going to leave. Having come this far, we need answers. If Pender is behind what's happened he needs to know we're on to him.

Adam steps outside the lodge. 'He'll see you now.'

Drew stands to one side and we walk up the steps. Like me, Ed has his chin held high as we try to exude a confidence we do not feel.

The lodge has only the door and one small window for light. The fire at the far end of the room produces far more smoke than heat and the fumes scratch at my throat. Pender stands with his back to us. He wears a black cape whose hem brushes the floor. His attitude reminds me of Castanese. It appears no theatrics will be spared in the creation of his persona as a mystic or guru. He swishes round to face us.

Despite being thinner and more lined than the photos I remember, this is unmistakably Rex Pender. The intense stare that seemed to reach out of the pages of newspapers is even more disconcerting in real life. I have the physical sensation of his eyes drilling into me. His cape actually makes him look like an old-fashioned schoolmaster. All he needs is a mortarboard. This comic image rescues me from my basic dread of the man. He's a fraud, an attention seeker. Like any of these mystical cult types, he preys upon the vulnerable and makes them feel part of something important.

He examines us both, scrutinising me more intently than Ed. I make sure to look directly at him as he does so.

'You've grown since I last saw you,' he says.

Ed takes this to mean since we had our photographs taken as teenagers. He does not know Pender has been watching me from the age of four.

'You interest me intently, Mia. You always have. But you already know that, don't you?'

I'm not going to be drawn in. We're here to question him, not the other way around.

'We want answers,' I say.

'You should have come two decades ago. I can't help you now.'

'I'm not asking for help.'

'Then why are you here?'

'Because two of our friends are dead,' Ed says. 'And we think you know why.'

Pender gives us a pitying look and brings his hands together beneath the folds of his cape.

'Everyone dies. Do you think you and your friends are any different?'

'One was murdered.'

Pender shrugs his shoulders. 'I still fail to see why you're here. I could have foreseen your friends' deaths but I could not have prevented them. The hour of our last breath is determined long before our first.'

'Cut the bullshit. We're not some of these paying saps.' Ed motions towards Pender's acolytes. He speaks slowly and clearly when he asks, 'Have you had any contact with Cara Tattersall?'

Pender's eyebrows rise. 'I can think of no reason to communicate with that unfortunate girl.'

'What about Madame Castanese, also known as Laura Eccles?' I ask.

'Ah, *Madame*,' Pender says in a sarcastic voice. 'I have always enjoyed her company. What strange divertissements she offers. Did you enjoy them?'

'How did you know we saw her?' Ed asks.

'Mia would not have mentioned her had you not,' he says. 'And was the redoubtable Leon with her? A lost youth who's found his calling. Poor boy, he's looking for a mother figure, wouldn't you say?'

I don't like the smile about his lips. 'What do you know about Leon?'

'Madame provided him with a home when others would not and, after being abandoned by his own parents, he couldn't be more grateful. He considers her to have great gifts, and he's not wrong. It's just a pity fortune-telling isn't one of them. But just as the untrained eye will care nothing if the *Mona Lisa* is the original or a print, Madame's talents satisfy most. One of life's little mysteries is why someone with so little talent should have so much ambition.' Here he looks at me. 'And those with the greatest deny its existence, trample it under foot and search for reasons, any reasons, that explain away their foresight. Even coming deep into the forest and seeking out a man considered to be an enemy.'

He's staring at me, but Ed's too angry to catch the meaning of his words. 'If we find out you have anything to do with it—'

'I've not left the Chase in five years.'

'You could have sent someone.'

'Like some sort of Mafia godfather? And why would I do that? Unlike many, I hold nothing against you, quite the reverse. You, Mia, should have come to me long ago and it would never have come to this.'

'Come to what?' I say.

He smiles again. And there's a rustling outside the lodge.

Miaaa.

She is here. The rustling becomes louder and louder until I want to put my hands over my ears.

'Is she calling you, Mia?' Pender asks. 'Just let her in.'

'No,' I shout. The leaves fall silent. 'Castanese's not the only skilled trickster,' I say. 'You're fleecing vulnerable people.' I look at the rag-tag group assembled in the room. 'And you promise them what? You should be prosecuted for fraud.'

His entourage starts to bristle but Pender only looks amused.

'Not everyone is as fortunate as you, Mia, to have someone watching over you. You call her Bella, do you not – your guardian angel?'

'She's not an angel she's a . . . a . . .'

Ed is looking at me open mouthed.

'Witch?' Pender says.

'An unidentified murder victim,' I say.

Pender laughs. 'You don't believe in that any more than I do. She speaks to you, doesn't she?'

'No.'

'She drives you mad.'

'You don't know what you're talking about.'

'Let her in, Mia. The cat doesn't scratch at the door once you've opened it. Your resistance causes your anguish.'

'I didn't come here for this bullshit,' I say. 'I came to find out who you've been talking to?'

'Many people.'

I'm close to losing my temper and have to turn away from him.

Ed steps in.

'We know you spoke to someone about us. A woman.'

This only amuses Pender more.

'A woman? As an unmarried man, my liaisons require no lies or subterfuge. Can you say the same, Edward Fields?'

Ed's face drops

'And you, with the alluring Molly at home. Men, I despair of them, don't you, Mia?' he says in a mocking tone. 'Don't worry, you're too good for Jake anyway. He's no better than your friend here.'

Ed looks furious.

'Was it Chrissy who came to see you?' I say.

'The deceased Mrs Banks? No, she did not.'

'Then it was Cara Tattersall.'

For a moment he doesn't look so smug.

'No,' he says.

'You're lying.'

'For someone with such talents you're remarkably slow-witted, Mia. All your troubles stem from the same source. You're blaming the wrong people. You should learn who your friends are. You're angry with me. When that anger subsides you should come and find me. We could achieve so much together.'

It's my turn to laugh. 'You think I'd ever come here and join your flock of sheep? I don't think so. I'm here to find information, that's it.'

'But you're asking the wrong questions,' he says. 'Your mind is so closed to ideas beyond those taught in your school science lab that when the truth is lain before you, you dismiss it. Your friends died because they were destined to do so. As you were told . . .'

I take a step back. Pender isn't going to give us any useful information and he's enjoying toying with us in front of his followers. Well, I'm not going to give him the satisfaction.

'I've learnt what I came to find out,' I say. 'We're going.'

'Are you sure of that?' Pender says.

'Come on, Ed.' I walk out of the lodge.

Ed looks confused but follows me. I get to the edge of the clearing and am unsure which way to go.

Pender calls from the lodge.

'Wait, I will accompany you. We don't want you getting lost in the woods. Adam, you will come with me.'

Reluctantly I accept the offer as I really have no idea how to get out of the forest.

Pender takes the lead. He must be in his sixties but walks at speed and is far more sure-footed than I am. Drew also joins us, though no one asked him. None of us speak. I try to concentrate on both my footing and what Drew and Adam are up to. I have my hand on the Mace spray the whole time. However, after a much faster journey than on the way here, I can see the road and Ed's car up ahead.

Pender stops about two hundred yards from the edge of the forest.

'Adam will take you the rest of the way. First I must speak to you, Mia.' He draws me away from the others. 'The problem is, Mia, you think an angel is like the ones you see on Christmas cards: beautiful, dressed in white with a halo. In truth they are vengeful and jealous. Think about why those around you die.'

'I'm not interested in your pseudo-religion.'

'You need to face the truth, Mia,' he says. 'In the meantime, take this.'

He hands me a cardboard cylinder about twelve inches long and an inch in diameter.

'I'll leave you now, Mia,' he says. 'Think about what I've said. Come back any time.'

Without waiting for a response, he turns and walks back the way he came.

I long to examine what's in the cylinder, but this isn't the place, and I stick it in my bag instead.

Adam and Drew take us back to the road. I expect them to leave the moment they've accomplished their task, but they stay with us to make sure we go.

'You should show more respect,' Drew says.

'To Pender?' Ed says. 'He should be in jail.'

'You have no idea who he is. You're just closed minded, ignorant, like the rest of the world.' Drew steps towards Ed.

Adam intercedes. 'You can't expect him to understand.' He turns to me. 'Though you should, Mia.'

Ed's looking at me suspiciously.

'I've no idea what you're talking about,' I say.

'I've wanted to meet you for so long. We go through so much here,' he says. 'All of us – we starve, we stay awake for days, just to get a glimpse. But yours comes to you, unbidden.'

I start to feel sick.

'It's true, isn't it? You raised your guardian angel that night on Hallows Hill.'

'You've been lied to,' I say.

'If you came and lived with us, we could learn,' Drew said.

'That's not going to happen.'

'There are people . . .' Drew says. Adam gives a slight shake of the head. Drew either doesn't see or chooses to ignore him. 'There are people whom no one would miss.'

It takes me a moment to catch his meaning. They think Leanne's death raised Bella. They actually believe in human sacrifice. Seeing my thoughts, Adam speaks.

'We harm no one. And we never will.'

Drew's eyes exude a zealotry no reason can counter. Adam appears more grounded.

'How much have you given up for this?' I ask. 'Can't you see he's exploiting you?'

'What I gave up was of no value. I have gained everything,' Adam says.

'I've seen things I could never have believed,' Drew adds.

'Anyone can do that with the right edibles,' Ed says.

'You have seen nothing and you never will,' Drew says. 'But you, Mia . . . do you know what people here would do to have what you have?'

A dead woman rustling in every branch and bush. Nausea swells in my guts.

'Pender is a sick fantasist,' I say 'He's stealing your money and brainwashing you. Get away from here before your whole lives are ruined.'

'A ruined life.' Drew gives me a slow steady stare. 'How is yours going, Mia?'

I think of my empty flat. The pink and mauve fairyland canvases I despise. The constant anxiety and endless lies.

'As I thought then,' Drew says. 'I'm not the fool here.'

We walk the couple of hundred yards to the car. Adam looks to the sky. The grey is giving way to white. 'We'll have snow tonight,' he says. 'So beautiful, but less fun when sleeping under canvas. Enjoy your warm beds. Snuggle up with your certainties. You have until Christmas.'

He turns and walks back into the trees.

As we drive away, the first flakes of snow start to fall.

Chapter 40

Ed insists on driving back. He's revving the engine before I've even buckled up my seatbelt and we screech off the moment it clicks. The roads are narrow and wet and Ed's driving is erratic. I grip my seat and pray he's sober.

'Why did you leave when you did?' Ed asks.

'Pender wasn't going to tell us anything. I just wanted to get out of there,' I say.

'Really? 'Cos you were having a nice cosy chat with him on the walk back. What was it he couldn't say in front of me?' Ed asks.

Until I know what it is myself, I'm reluctant to tell him about the cylinder lying at the bottom of my bag next to the Mace spray.

'He just repeated that I should come and join them,' I say.

'Wankers,' Ed says as he crunches the gears. 'New Age wankers. Posh kids cosplaying King Arthur.'

I close my eyes as we pitch into the first bend. Telling Ed to slow down will only irritate him. I try to keep my voice calm as I ask, 'Do you think Adam is Pender's son? They don't look alike, but the way he speaks makes me think they're related.'

'He definitely thinks he's second in command. Vice-dickhead or whatever. I bet he's planning to take over whenever Pender kicks the bucket. But he's gonna have to wait. Wiry fuckers like that always live for ever.'

We take a small hump at speed and momentarily lose contact with the road.

'We should find out who he is,' I say. 'I never considered that Pender could have children.'

'He's probably got hundreds of bastards sprayed around the country. Strange, isn't it? All these cults have different and conflicting beliefs, but the one thing they can all agree on is the spiritual necessity of boning girls half their age.'

I would laugh out loud if we weren't approaching a tractor, crawling up the steep hill ahead, knowing Ed's going to try and pass it over the brow. Is Castanese's prediction going to be fulfilled now on a country road in the middle of Worcestershire? Ed drops a gear and slams his foot to the floor. I close my eyes as I'm flung back in my seat and I don't open them until Ed changes up again and we dive down the opposite side of the slope.

It's snowing harder now with great fat flakes flying towards the windscreen in mesmeric spirals. I glance at Ed. He's leaning forwards, his eyes fixed on the road.

'What bothers me is not what's going on in the camp but how he knew we were coming,' he says.

'That bothered me, too.'

'The only people who knew were you, me and Molly,' he says. 'So how did he?'

'Oleana Jenkins probably guessed we were going there, but she hates him.'

'What about Noah and your mum – did you tell them?'

'No way. They would have tried to talk me out of it.'

Ed says nothing for several minutes. I look out of the window and watch the landscape whizzing by and realise Pender can't be the Forrester. There's no equipment out there and barely any phone reception. Someone else is on the All of This Is True site and has identified me through the TC123456 username.

I should be pleased Ed's concentrating on the road, only his jaw is clenched and he's breathing hard. We lurch into another corner. This time Ed loses the back end and we skid for a few yards before he manages to pull it straight.

I can't keep quiet any longer. 'Slow down. You'll kill both of us at this rate.'

'Help complete Castanese's prophecy?' he says.

'We don't believe in that,' I say, even though these were my exact thoughts a few moments ago.

'Darcy and Chrissy are dead,' he says.

Where was Ed's mind wandering during those minutes of silence?

'And then you turn up at my house late at night with some woo-woo shit about knowing Bella's identity.'

'Mum told me that.'

'I've lived in All Hallows my whole life and no one told me Bella's true identity. Why does Sandy get to know? Why do you?'

He spits out the words 'true identity' in a sarcastic tone and his repeated glances over to me drag his concentration from the road. I don't want to argue with him right now, so say nothing.

'In the Dower House, you shared a room with Darcy,' he says. 'You must have noticed she was ill.'

'Not how ill.'
'She didn't confide in you?'
'No.'
''Cos she confided in me when I dropped her home later that day. She was upset you'd gone without saying goodbye.'
'I know I should have stayed, but I was confused.'
'Darce was never as close to me as she was to you and Noah. But she needed to talk. I thought she was being paranoid but it all makes sense now. Do you know what the last thing she ever said to me was?' He looks straight at me. 'She said; don't trust Mia.'
'What?' I swivel in my seat. 'She would never say that. We were close. Like sisters. She came to me with everything.'
'Then why was she scared of you?'
'She wasn't.'
'She thought you set the whole Castanese thing up.'
'Why would I do that?'
'She couldn't figure that out either. But she was dead less than a week later. It's not paranoia if they really are out to get you.'
'Darcy died of natural causes.'
The white outlined hedges whizz past the car window. At least Ed's eyes are on the road now, his hands wrapped in a fist over the steering wheel.
'How did Pender know about my other women and about Molly?'
'Ed, if you've been playing the field, I can't be the only one to have found out.'
'And all this stuff about Cara Tattersall. Strange you're the only one to have seen her.'
'We all saw her, at Darcy's funeral.'

'I saw a woman I didn't recognise. Who said she was Cara Tattersall? She could have been anyone.'

I had assumed Cara was the woman in the red dress who sat at the back of the chapel and was loitering outside the Grange during the wake. I have no proof of this woman's identity. Nor do I know if she's the same person who stalked me in London and pushed Chrissy in the path of a bus.

'I might be wrong about Cara. But even if I am, what exactly are you trying to say, Ed?'

'I'm saying there's a gaping hole at the centre of this puzzle and only one person fits the missing piece.'

'You can't be serious? What have I got to gain? It was Chrissy's experiment.'

'So you keep telling us. But she never mentioned the psycho room—'

'Psychomanteum.'

'—to anyone else. And now she's dead. Other than Chrissy, the only person we know was definitely on Tower Bridge that night was you.'

'Ed, you know I'd never hurt Chrissy.'

He swings the car across the road and we skid to a halt in the gateway to a farm track.

'Just like you wouldn't hurt Leanne?'

'I didn't hurt Leanne.' I can hear the hesitancy in my own voice.

'I didn't think anything of it at the time. But they never found Leanne's phone.'

I want to say something, but my throat's suddenly too dry.

'My phone bill showed I'd sent Leanne a text on the afternoon before her death. It wasn't on my actual phone so must have been deleted. I was pretty wasted that day. I thought I must have sent it and forgot. The thing is, I wasn't close to Leanne. There was no reason for me to contact her. I told Chrissy. She said to forget it. We didn't want any more gossip. I didn't suspect anyone in particular, until now.'

I swallow and try to get some moisture into my mouth.

'It's not what you think.'

'You dropped in to see me and Noah that day. What did the text say, Mia? Did you tell her to take a different route, lure her towards Nicholson?'

'It's not what you think.'

'What then?'

I don't answer.

'Your mum used to work as an auxiliary nurse at Heartlands Hospital,' Ed says.

'That was years before Nicholson was admitted.'

'She must still have had friends there.'

'Do you really think that me and my mum planned to have Leanne murdered?'

'You never liked her – were always jealous. Everyone could see that,' he says.

The wipers whisper through the snow falling on the windscreen. *She* is trying to talk. I block her out.

'Chrissy worked it out. Noah told me what Mark said at the hospital and Pender always knew. That's what he was talking about all those years ago and what you two were bonding over back in the forest. A sacrifice.'

We stare at each other in silence. The only sound is the swish of the windscreen wipers still trying to whisper my name.

Darcy was scared of me. Ed thinks I'm a murderer.

'I saw you that night in the Hags Ring and at Castanese's, Mia. You saw something the rest of us didn't.'

'I was drugged.'

'Not in the Dower House. I only pieced it together after seeing you in that camp, with Pender treating you like some visiting dignitary and hearing you talking about Bella like she's real.'

He's so angry right now. How can I make him see reason?

'It's been hard for all of us since Darcy and Chrissy died,' I say. 'You've been hitting the bottle, not to mention the coke. It's made you paranoid.'

Ed smashes his hand against the steering wheel, making me jump.

'Seven of us were up on Hallows Hill that Halloween. Four are dead. Leanne, Nicholson, Darcy, Chrissy. That's not paranoia. That's fact.'

'We need to stick together, Ed. Not turn on one another,' I say.

His mouth splits into a sardonic grin. 'What's planned for me, eh? Was something supposed to happen to me last night, in my sleep. Or was I supposed to die in that forest?'

'You're one of my oldest friends.'

'Just admit it's you doing it,' he shouts.

I shake my head.

'Get out of the car,' he says.

'We're in the middle of nowhere.'

'Get out.'

The headlights shine upon the bushes lining the road and I see something that frightens me far more than Ed's temper.

'Please, Ed, you are in danger, but not from me.'

He reaches across and pulls the door handle. 'Out. Darce was right not to trust you.'

I pick up my bag from the footwell, moving slowly, hoping he's going to change his mind. He doesn't. The second I'm out of the car he slams the door. The wheels spin, showering me with mud and slush. The car skids across the road, picks up speed and soon its taillights are streaking away. I stand still, watching until they disappear over the brow of the next hill.

The snow is falling heavily now. Without Molly's coat, which is on the car's backseat, the hoodie won't keep me warm. But it is not the cold causing me to shiver. Before I exited the car I caught sight of Bella in the hedge bordering the road, her sloe eyes turning upon me as, in the headlights' beam, a white cloth drifted across the road.

Chapter 41

The cold kills what's left of my phone battery. In my dark clothing, I'm invisible to the cars whipping past at seventy miles an hour, oblivious to the wintry conditions. I have to press myself into the hedgerow each time one rushes by, bringing me into closer contact with *her*.

Miaaa, she calls. The falling snow carries her voice. *Miaaa*. Her talk is insistent but indecipherable.

This area of the country is sparsely populated. I do bang on the door of one farm and ask to use their phone but they shoo me away. In my soaking wet, mud-spattered clothes, I must look like some sort of vagrant. The farmer tells me they patrol the barns.

'So don't try hiding out there.'

I trudge on.

Ed will be home by now, maybe taking a hot shower, while Molly fixes him a hearty meal, though it's more likely he's in front of the fire, still in his dirty clothes, drinking whisky, or worse. As so often happens, Ed stumbled upon a truth, that other, supposedly cleverer people, overlook. I did not like Leanne and I did send her a text that day.

She came from London, which in our provincial

village seemed achingly cool. She wore her hair short and asymmetrical when we all aimed for Hollywood flowing locks. We thought our Top Shop clothes were the height of fashion. She trawled market stalls and charity stores to create her own unique look. She spoke fluent French, had lost her virginity to the bassist in an almost famous band and never got ID'd in pubs. She made us feel how small and narrow our lives were. This dislike would have remained abstract, had she been adopted by one of the more popular groups at school. But for some reason she chose to hang out with us. And more specifically Darcy, who gobbled up all her tales of London life and imagined this as her future, hopping in and out of black cabs around Soho and falling out of nightclubs with minor celebs. I later found out that Leanne came from Beckenham, a sleepy suburb that doesn't even have a London postcode. It didn't matter. To Darcy, Leanne was a bona fide It Girl.

  Suddenly I started finding out that Darcy and Leanne had gone all the way to Birmingham to go shopping together and later had a double date with two sixth-form boys. At Christmas, Leanne was going to take Darcy to London, where they could stay with her aunt. This was a period when Ed and Chrissy were dating, and after Darcy rejected him Noah had no interests beyond smoking weed and playing Xbox.

  I was lonely and I blamed Leanne. If she was so cool why was she stuck in this dull backwater with the rest of us? And why did Darcy now prefer her company to mine?

  When I tackled Darcy she laughed, told me that she was allowed more than one friend and my jealousy was plain stupid. I should have other friends too. We couldn't always be together. She was off to ballet school next year and what was I going to do then?

It was Leanne who came up with the Halloween dare. Having sensed hostility from me and a few others, maybe she thought this would be a bonding experience that would help her fit in with the rest of us, not just Darcy. Noah agreed at once, pleased for us to hang out all together like we used to. Because the group, our immovable solid group, had begun to drift apart. And whatever Darcy said, I wasn't the only one who found this frightening. For this reason, everyone agreed that, like countless other All Hallows teenagers, we would go up to the Hags Ring and call for Bella. And but for two things, like countless other All Hallows teenagers, it would have remained a joke, a silly escapade we laughed about later. But on that night, William Nicholson escaped from the Heartlands Hospital and I decided to play a trick on Leanne.

For her birthday, back in September, Leanne had bought Darcy a fake red and white Alexander McQueen skull scarf. Leanne had a matching one in black. Darcy cooed over her scarf far more than the DVD of Matthew Bourne's *Swan Lake*, I had bought her. And she did look fabulous in it: cool, chic and elegant; she wore it constantly. Other girls remarked on it and Leanne always chimed in that she was the one who had bought it. It wasn't that I never saw Darcy at all or that she wouldn't hang out with me. What bothered me was she and Leanne doing things on their own. I felt that Darcy was slipping away. Other people started noticing and began asking Leanne, not me, if Darcy was coming to a party or if she had seen her at the weekend.

In fact, on that Halloween, Darcy hadn't been round to my house in several weeks. The expedition to the Hags Ring was already planned, so I wasn't expecting her when she turned up mid-morning.

'I've got something to show you,' she said. 'Look what Mum got me.'

I was anticipating something ballet related. Instead she got out her birthday present from Leanne.

'A fake scarf. So what?'

'No,' Darcy said. 'Not a fake.'

I leant over and touched it. It was smooth and light beneath my fingers and released a faint powdery scent.

'Real silk,' I said.

'Real McQueen,' Darcy said.

She slung it round her shoulders and posed in front of the mirror. I knew nothing about designer clothes but I could tell the difference between this and the one Leanne had gifted her. It moved differently as Darcy sashayed about, caressing her shoulders and dispersing light over her face.

'Mum reckons knock-offs are tacky,' Darcy said. 'She hated me going around in that thing Leanne got.'

The fake scarf had fallen out of the same bag and lay crumpled on the floor. Darcy's scorn made me conscious of my poor taste for ever having been impressed by the thing. And yet . . .

Darcy saw me looking at it. 'You can have it if you like.'

I swept it up, pulled it around my shoulders and joined Darcy in front of the mirror. We were as different from one another as the scarves. One precious and exquisite in its beauty, the other everyday and unremarkable. I should have been jealous, but I was elated. Discarding Leanne's present seemed an indication that Darcy was tiring of their friendship, which, like the scarf, had been a cheap imitation of the real thing.

Darcy left my house soon after that as I had promised Bernard I would drop my stepbrothers at their friends' birthday party while he played golf. I was walking home through the village, proudly wearing Darcy's scarf, when I bumped into Leanne, taking her younger sister, Cara, to the park.

'Why are you wearing that?' she asked, sounding slightly hurt.

Having been shunted aside to make way for her, I enjoyed saying, 'Darcy didn't want it any more. She gave it to me. I mean it's not my thing really. Knock-offs are so tacky.'

'What's tacky?' Cara asked. She was about five or six and looked up at me from under a fur-lined hood whilst hugging a Hello Kitty bag to her chest.

'Tacky means cheap and nasty,' I told her.

Leanne's lower lip jutted out as she said, 'If Darcy didn't want it, she should have given it back to me, not to you. And as you think it's *cheap and nasty* . . .'

The thing is, I loved the scarf and wanted to keep it. But I couldn't lose face so I pulled it from my shoulders and tossed it to her, cursing my temper for getting the better of me. If Darcy asked, I'd tell her Leanne demanded to take it back, which was true, sort of.

Leanne fingered the scarf, as if searching for some flaw in the once-beloved present. 'You hate that I'm friends with Darcy, don't you?' she said.

I shrugged. 'Makes no difference to me. We've been friends since we were four. A fake scarf's not going to change that.'

Leanne searched for Cara's hand.

'But it was a present,' she said. I thought she was going to cry.

'Not all presents are for life,' I said and walked away.

If only my triumph over the scarf had satisfied my need for revenge. I didn't like Leanne hanging around with Darcy and I didn't like her assuming she was part of our group. After taking my stepbrothers to their party I dropped in on Noah. Ed was there. The cider was already flowing, the room stank of spliff and they were brewing something disgusting in one of Natalie's pans, a concoction they planned on taking to Alicia's party later. With The Strokes on full volume, they barely paid me any attention. Ed's phone sat on the side. The temptation was too great. No one bothered with passcodes back then.

> Change to plans. Meeting at the Royal Oak car park not Roundels. See you there. X

I sent it to Leanne, then deleted it. I knew there was no phone reception in the Roundels car park. When we didn't turn up, Leanne wouldn't be able to contact us, and she'd go home. And if she said anything later, well, it was Ed's phone.

I've tried to excuse my part in this but I should have realised that a girl coming from the other end of the country into a small community, who had known each other most of their lives, would try hard to fit in. And if that meant making her suburban upbringing into some cool and edgy boho existence, who could blame her? I didn't know she would run into a killer. What were the chances? But I should have considered that a teenage girl out after dark, alone on an empty hillside, would be vulnerable.

Now I realise why Darcy bequeathed me that scarf. She knew. She must have done. Did Chrissy? Does Noah? Did they, like Ed, come to the conclusion that this was more than a prank?

Has some fit of teenage pique led me to this point: friendless on a dark winter road at night?

Chapter 42

My fingers and toes lose all feeling as I trudge up and down never-ending hills, their white tops glowing in the moonlight now the snow has stopped falling. Cold bores into me. The exhaustion is overwhelming. Hypothermia kills trekkers in the Arctic and the Himalayas. I can't die of it here, on the low rolling hills of an English shire, can I?

To quell my rising panic, I concentrate on Ed's missing piece of the puzzle. If I don't fit, who does? The most obvious answer is Cara Tattersall. And though Ed doubts her role in any of this, I do not. Her complete absence from social media is suspicious in itself. Is she living off grid at Pender's camp, perhaps? Everyone looked the same under those hessian tunics and hoods. Surely Cara would never go there. She must hate him, the way he mocked her parents and claimed there was a justification for her sister's killing. But who knows how Leanne's death affected her? Maybe she resented the sister she barely remembered but upon whom her parents spent all their anguish.

Who else? Oleana Jenkins? I only have her word she hates Pender. If she's still one of his followers, it would explain why he knew of our arrival.

He's also a friend – or at least an acquaintance – of Castanese, who could have approached Chrissy. It still pains me to think Chrissy would sell us out like that, however much debt she was in and however great her professional ambitions. I'm not convinced she could do it.

And something else is nagging at me. Like most teenagers, I was fairly self-obsessed and Mum frequently reminded me that *it's not all about you*. Even on my wedding day and when I've opened exhibitions, I've repeated this mantra to myself. But now, I'm starting to think it *is* all about me. Dotty, Castanese and Pender have all singled me out as different – special. And Adam from Pelham Chase knew I had seen Bella and he thought she was an angel. Why would he think that? It makes no sense and I'm back to where I started.

My eyeballs are stinging in the frosty air as I climb yet another hill. At least from the top of this one I can spot pub lights glinting in the distance.

Inside the Crooked Staff, the landlord looks at me dubiously and it's only my American Express card that convinces him I'm not a vagrant.

I ask for the number of a nearby taxi firm.

The barman laughs. 'Out here? At this time of night?'

'I've no other way of getting home.'

He calls a cab from the nearest town and tells me it'll be here in two hours. No hot drinks are available and I have to make do with a cola and a packet of peanuts as I sit in the corner shivering in my wet clothes.

My fingers are so stiff with cold I can barely prise the top from the cylinder Pender gave me. Inside is a scroll. It's written in an ornate hand, like some ancient parchment, but the stiff white paper is obviously modern.

For many generations the Verne-Fontaines prospered. Until the 1940s, when a misstep by the twelfth Viscount's son threw the family into turmoil. Hugh Verne-Fontaine's roving eye was the stuff of raillery amongst his peers. This levity wasn't shared by the girls whose reputations lay in tatters after their seduction on the basis of false promises. Hugh, however, did at least acknowledge his children and provide for their basic upkeep. But eventually, the old Viscount had had enough. Hugh was his heir, and if the All Hallows estate was to remain intact he'd need to learn to use both his capital and his loins in a responsible manner. When yet another farmer's daughter, heavy with child, turned up at All Hallows Court, claiming Hugh had promised her marriage, his father lost patience. He pulled strings to have his son sent overseas immediately, not difficult in the middle of a war. Soon after the girl gave birth she went back to All Hallows Court and was turned away. The curses she screamed down upon them could be heard on the other side of the village. That night a stray Luftwaffe bomb destroyed the hall and most of its inhabitants. Two days later the girl was found in the Hags Ring, murdered.

But this time it was not at the hands of the Verne-Fontaines. Whilst the villagers had sympathy for the girl's plight when she was the victim of Hugh's seduction, they now feared her.

All Hallows lay far from the city and was not on any German bombers' flightpaths. It had to be more than bad luck that the Court was destroyed on the same night this girl cursed it. Its destruction was a disaster. The village's prospects depended on the Verne-Fontaines.

One villager now saw the fifth Viscount's treatment of

> Isabella in a very different light. The guardian angel granted her was dangerous under the command of a commoner. The fifth Viscount had acted to save All Hallows, both the Court and the village.
>
> The next day the girl was found inside the Hags Ring. She had been slain, her heart pierced by a thin blade. When the police from Haverton investigated the crime, they were met with silence. No one would say the girl's name. So they called her Bella, in a nod to the murdered eighteenth-century viscountess.

There's nothing to back up these claims. Any woman's identity could be grafted onto the unknown victim. The document only refers to her as 'the girl' so it's impossible to check if such a person existed.

What I do notice is that this piece employs the same style as the document given to me by Darcy and the one sent by the Forrester. Is Pender its author? It echoes his pompous tone.

I read it again. Whoever wrote it, Darcy, the Forrester and Pender all thought that the fates of Isabella Verne-Fontaine and the unknown victim in the 1940s somehow relate to me. Both women were said to have a guardian angel. Pender and Castanese believe I do too. Both women were murdered in the Hags Ring. The documents have been given to me as a warning I'm in danger. But how could Darcy know?

By the time I get a taxi to the nearest train station, travel on the slow train to London, hop on the Tube and get back to my flat, I'm dead on my feet.

A hot shower does something to lift the chill. I let the water run over me and imagine it washing me clean, not just of the dirt of Pelham Chase, but of all my sins: Leanne,

Darcy, Jake. I wish I were religious, so I could confess and throw myself on the mercy of some deity, but the only person who can forgive me is Cara Tattersall and she wants me dead.

After my fingers start to wrinkle, I get out of the shower and crawl into bed. The flat's warming up and I can smell hot dust rising from the radiators, but I'm still freezing.

By turns the room is too hot and too cold. I twist beneath the covers, throwing them off and on again as, in fractured dreams, my dead father comes to me. His face is that of the photograph Mum keeps but never puts on display. He is far younger than I am now, his hair still dark, his skin smooth and unlined.

'What's this mess you've got yourself into, my girl?' He looks both sad and amused. 'You made the wrong friends and ended up with the wrong dad. Bernard's nice enough, but he's a boring bastard.'

I laugh along with him until he turns into Rex Pender.

'The wrong friends and the wrong father, indeed,' he says. 'You should have come to me. To Pelham Chase. If you joined me you could escape your fate. You have until Christmas.'

Finally, and inevitably, Isabella Verne-Fontaine stands before me, her beautiful face hollowed out by malnutrition, her white dress drenched in the blood bubbling from her torso. She reaches for me. I pull back. A tear runs down her cheek before she transforms into the Bella I know. The woman of twigs, leaves and spiders' webs.

'Leave me alone,' I say.

'Never,' she says. The black, sloe eye still carries Isabella Verne-Fontaine's tear. 'I'll never leave you, Mia.'

Chapter 43

I wake to the smell of citrus and spice. Christmas? The mattress dips as someone sits at the end of the bed. I don't know why it comes into my head but I say, 'Dad.'

The figure moves closer.

'Mia, it's me.'

I open my eyes to see Noah's face, crinkled in concern.

'You weren't answering your phone. I couldn't get any sense out of Ed. So I used my key and came here.'

It takes me a moment to realise where 'here' is. Mrs Rinaldi's floral wallpaper tells me I'm in the bedroom in my flat.

My head throbs and my mouth is dry. I lie back down.

'What day is it?'

'Saturday.'

Three days. I've been lying here for three days.

'I was just about to call a doctor,' Noah says.

'No,' I say and drag myself to my elbows. 'I just need to rest.'

'You're dehydrated,' he says. 'Your lips are cracked.'

He passes me a pint glass of Robinson's Barley Water. Noah's mum, like mine, uses this as her cure-all, along with camomile tea. It's cool and refreshing and I finish it in a few gulps. Noah refills the glass from a jug on the side table.

'Sandy said you were up in All Hallows a couple of nights ago. Did you take Ed's car back? What happened?'

I let my head loll back onto the pillow and rest my eyes. 'Ed thinks I killed Chrissy.'

Noah doesn't sound shocked. 'He accused me too and said I'd set up the whole thing with Castanese – never came up with a motive why I'd do it. Molly said Ed's getting paranoid. With the amount he drinks and snorts it's not surprising.'

That at least is different because Ed had no problem ascribing a motive to me. It's not all down to alcohol and drugs.

'Not only did I kill Chrissy, I flirt with Molly when we meet. Then he went on a tirade about what a pretentious twat I am and how I lord it over all of you with my money before he opened a bottle of Saint-Émilion without asking and deliberately spilt it all over my cream rug. After that I caught him trying to steal my car keys. I don't care about the rug or the car, I care about Ed. He's still my mate. What's happening to him?'

'Even before all this happened, he was struggling. Chrissy's death was the last straw. And I know it's not your fault, Noah, but it's tough for him seeing you do so well while he's leading the quiet commuter existence of Mr Average.'

'Ed would hate my life. The long hours, the stress. He loves his job and he loves Molly and the boys.'

'People always look at what they don't have. I mean, I always wanted to be Darcy. Even after she ended up unemployed and living back with her parents. The mad thing was, she wanted to be me and, like Ed, she would have hated my life. She never liked London. She didn't like work much. What's to be jealous of?'

Noah looks serious and doesn't say anything.

'What?'

'Nothing,' he says.

'Not that thing about Jake, Mrs Alderwell was banging on about at the funeral. He and Darcy only went out for about five minutes before she dumped him for that old, fake aristocrat.'

Noah still says nothing. I wonder if I've hit a nerve. His teenage relationship with Darcy was short-lived. When she went to ballet school in France he waited for her return. Did it hurt that the moment she came back, she started dating a junior doctor who had his own car? Have the decades and Darcy's death not erased his pain? Am I not the only one who can't move on?

Noah changes the subject.

'So were you with Ed in Pelham Chase?'

'He told you?'

Noah looks sheepish. 'It's only 'cos I was worried about him. But I took a leaf out of Mark's book and put Find My Friends on Ed's phone. He was too drunk to notice me use his face to open it.'

'You can't do that, Noah.'

'You didn't see the state of him. By the time he finally stormed out of my flat he was incoherent. I was convinced DS Lacon would end up fishing him out of the Thames.'

'Well, you ought to turn it off. We can't spy on each other. Talking of which, did you find out who the admin is for the All of This Is True site?'

'With everything that's been going on, I forgot. I'll ask Penny to get someone on to it.'

'When I found out Pender was in Pelham Chase I thought he must be the Forrester, but there's no electricity out there and barely any phone reception.'

'That's why you went to Pelham Chase? To see Pender?' Noah stares at me, open mouthed in disbelief. 'Why would you do that?'

'The police are going to put Chrissy's death down to an accident. We're all in danger. But I'm not just sitting around waiting for something to happen. I went to see Castanese. She hinted that Pender knew something.'

Actually it was Mum who hinted at this, but I don't want to drag her into it and have to reveal my connection to Pender through Dotty. Nor do I want Noah to know about Lula.

He shifts his position on the bed. He's still horror-stricken at my decisions.

'We agreed Castanese's a fraud and now you're dragging Pender back into our lives. Why would he want to start all of this up again now? He's been quiet for years.'

'People pay to go and stay at the camp in Pelham Chase. You should see them. They think they're Robin Hood and his Merry Men, all dressed like medieval peasants, and Pender's there done up in a cloak like Gandalf or something. He promises to raise their guardian angels. They believe that's what happened in the Hags Ring that night.'

'Because Leanne died?' Noah says.

'Because you became very wealthy. As did the fifth Viscount after he sacrificed his wife. At least that's what happened in the unofficial version.'

'Why can't people see through it? Pender has to be breaking some law or other.'

'If his followers are over eighteen, and they're there of their own free will, I don't see who can touch him. The thing is, Pender got right under Ed's skin. It was on the way back that he really turned on me.'

'This is insane. We have to stick together,' Noah says.

'Maybe Ed's safer up there with Molly. The state of him driving around the countryside like that – I thought we were going to end up smashed into a tree or upside down in a ditch and our frozen bodies not found for three days. He probably did me a favour, throwing me out of the car.'

'I'd offer to pay for him to go to rehab but he'd just throw it in my face.'

'Let him calm down first. He must know neither of us would ever hurt Darcy or Chrissy. I'll check with Molly he's OK.'

I call her. She doesn't pick up, but she does send me a text.

> What happened in Pelham Chase? Ed's spiralling. The Alderwells are threatening us with the police. Can you speak to them?

I show Noah.

'Why would the Alderwells want the police to speak to Ed?'

'I bet he's been making the same wild accusations to them as he has to us. I'll have to call John.'

'Don't,' Noah says. 'Mum told me John's been looking really gaunt and sick. He's not coping with Darcy's death and all of Mrs Alderwell's demands. Call David instead.'

I'm reluctant to call David. That whole thing about us getting together still hovers over me and I don't want to encourage him. Then I remember that was years ago. His sister, my best friend, has died. Surely I can ring a man I've known most of my life without him thinking I've changed my mind and now want to marry him?

David, can we talk about Ed.

He gets back to me after a few minutes.

I'm in London tomorrow for a conference. Meet me at the Garden Café for lunch.

It's an address in Soho. I'm still weak but don't feel I have a choice.

See you there.

Noah takes the phone and reads the text.
'Good,' he says. 'Because there's another reason I wanted you to speak to David, and you're not going to like it.'
'Spill,' I say.
'This *you'll all be dead by Christmas*. We've assumed Castanese knew Darcy was ill. But Darcy had the same condition as Mrs Alderwell and she's still with us despite her chain-smoking.' He pauses. 'I talked it over with Penny. This only makes sense if Darcy didn't die of natural causes.'
The same thought has been nagging at the back of my mind. Was Darcy really that ill? In a sequence of predicted

deaths, Darcy's occurring so soon after we saw Castanese cannot have been a coincidence.

'Darcy was living with two doctors,' I say. 'Surely they'd know if something was wrong or the symptoms didn't match her illness.'

'But what if they did match? Someone with medical knowledge could arrange it.'

'Or someone married to a medic,' I say almost to myself.

'Mrs Alderwell? Munchausen syndrome by proxy? Yeah, Mum came up with that, too. I never bought it myself. And she wouldn't kill Darcy.'

'Not deliberately, but maybe she went too far with whatever she'd been giving her to make her ill.'

'But we're talking about a deliberate poisoning,' Noah says. 'Someone who wanted Darcy dead.'

'Which could be engineered if someone knew what Mrs Alderwell was up to.'

'I guess . . .' He doesn't sound convinced. 'You can ask David.'

'Oh, sure. "David, was your mum poisoning your sister?"'

'OK, not like that. And we don't know it was Mrs Alderwell, or anyone. We just need to see if it's a possibility.'

'Even if you're right, there's no proof,' I say. 'The police aren't going to open an investigation based on a prediction made in a crystal ball by a convicted fraudster.'

'They might if two doctors started to question the cause of death. Try and raise it with David tomorrow. He likes you. He'll want to help.'

'The Alderwells have enough to deal with,' I say. 'I can't lay this on them. I just want to know what Ed's done.'

'Well, just hint at it. Say how sudden it was and weren't they surprised.'

'You should speak to him.'

'I don't think batting my eyelids is going to have the same effect.' Noah flutters his lashes.

I can't help smiling. 'I'll see how it goes.'

Noah pushes a strand of hair behind my ear and smiles back at me.

'You're made of tough stuff, Ms Raine.'

I lean my head against his shoulder and wait for him to say he'll stay with me. But he kisses my forehead, reminds me to drink plenty of fluids, before telling me he needs to get home.

'Let me know how it goes with David,' he says.

Chapter 44

I'm still feeling weak and lightheaded when I arrive in Soho. It's bright with Christmas decorations and crowded with shoppers, their bags overflowing with clothes, toys and trinkets.

The chalkboard in the café David's selected advertises its seasonal sandwich: turkey with pork stuffing and cranberry sauce. The walls are tastefully draped in tinsel and, pleasingly, no greenery, but a nutcracker styled as a soldier sits on a shelf next to a sugarplum fairy in arabesque. It reminds me of Darcy, her hopes and dreams. As Castanese said, we're all going to die. But did it have to be so soon? And why did life crush her so that her existence shrank down to the four walls of the Grange?

I spot David sitting in the window, his shoulders stooped, his shirt crumpled. He, too, is staring at the sugarplum fairy, no doubt thinking the same thoughts as me.

Bells jangle as I open the door. David looks up. I force a smile and wave. He waves back but does not stand, so I don't go in for a hug and, instead, take a seat on the opposite side of the table.

Considering I've known David since I was two years old, and he asked me out on a regular basis from the ages of fifteen to twenty-two, it's odd how little I know him. Unlike Darcy, he never appeared to fight Mrs Alderwell's attempts to control his life, a house cat to her caged jaguar. In a rare moment of intimacy, David once told me he never married because no woman could live up to his mother. So it's a surprise he didn't take Mrs Alderwell's side over my supposed attack on her at the funeral. And even more of a surprise that he's willing to talk to me now.

He appears agitated and has trouble looking me in the eye as I ask him how his medical conference is going and he makes a bumbling reply about AI diagnoses, which I don't understand.

The waitress comes over. We both order the seasonal sandwich and a flat white.

'How are Marielle and John?' I ask.

'Mum's zonked on anti-depressants. She won't see a therapist.'

'And John?'

'He's busy looking after Mum. I don't think he's had time to grieve himself.'

'I'm so sorry about what happened at the funeral,' I say.

David shakes his head. 'Mum has strange ideas. It really wasn't your fault Darcy never married.'

I'm shocked. It never occurred to me that Mrs Alderwell blames me for all of Darcy's romantic failures, not just Jake.

'Darcy could have been with anyone she wanted,' I say.

'Not quite anyone,' David says pointedly.

'So you think it's my fault too?'

'We don't choose who we fall in love with,' David says. 'Look at Ed. Happily married, but in love with Chrissy all this time.'

Again, I'm shocked. I had no idea David knew about Chrissy and Ed. I only found out a few weeks ago myself.

'It's Molly I feel sorry for,' David continues. 'When was the last time you spoke to Ed?'

'A few days ago.'

'How did he seem?'

'Agitated. He's drinking too much. Chrissy's death hit him hard, especially as the family are freezing us out. They've made it clear we won't be welcome at the funeral.'

'I've spoken to Mark,' David says. 'He's flailing around, angry at everyone. A bit like Ed really, only he's not drinking. And as for Ed, I can get him a referral. He's obviously in need of help but he has to stop coming to our house. He's been to the Grange twice now and accused us of being in league with Pender and harming Darcy. Mum and Dad are struggling as it is, without all this drama.'

'He's made similar accusations to me and Noah. I know it's the last thing your parents need.' Seeing how drawn and tired David looks, I add, 'And you. How are you?'

He gives a sad smile. 'Sometimes I'm just about to go into Darcy's room to tell her something. And then I remember she's not there. That's when it hits me that she's never going to be there.'

David removes his glasses and rubs his eyes.

'When I saw her at the Dower House, she was so thin,' I say.

'Darcy's always been too thin.' He pauses before continuing. 'But her health did deteriorate after you met up on Halloween. She was tired and stayed in bed most of the time.'

'She didn't go out at all?'

'No.'

'Or take phone calls?'

'I don't know about that. Why are you asking all of this, Mia?'

'It's just . . . I don't want to distress you but I think Leanne Tattersall's sister, Cara, came to Darcy's funeral. The woman who had a red dress under her coat.'

'I didn't see her. That whole day's a bit fuzzy.'

'She spoke to me and made it clear she blames us for Leanne's death. I was wondering if she had contacted Darcy or could have harmed her in any way?'

David looks agitated. 'Harmed? What do you mean, harmed?'

'Is there any chance Cara could have been in contact with Darcy and made her condition worse?'

'By causing her stress?'

'I was thinking of something a bit more direct. Perhaps she contacted your mum. Was Mrs Alderwell the one responsible for making sure Darcy took her medicine?'

David stops, his cup halfway to his mouth. For a moment he looks angry, then pity takes over his face.

'I can see where you're going with this, Mia. The thing is, I see a lot of grief in my job. It affects everyone differently. Many people struggle to accept death. They look for someone to blame – like Mark.'

'Chrissy was killed only a few weeks after Darcy's death. And I've received threats on this forum dedicated to the Hags Ring murder. This isn't me struggling to accept Darcy's death. I need to know if there's a chance Cara or an unknown person could have hurt Darcy.'

'Following your logic, Cara or the "unknown person" must be a serial killer.'

'I know it sounds far-fetched.'

'For good reason,' he says.

'What if she poisoned her or something, and they weren't looking for a specific substance at the postmortem.'

David leans back in his seat and brings his hands across his belly, twisting his thumbs.

'Darcy was ill. She had the same condition as Mum but in a far more serious form. I'm a doctor – I would recognise signs of poisoning, as would Dad.'

'And Chrissy?'

'I've spoken to Mark. The postmortem showed Chrissy died of injuries consistent with a road traffic accident. She also had high blood alcohol levels. The university was about to dismiss her and she would have been facing criminal charges. Nothing suspicious was found on the CCTV images. In truth, if Mark wants someone to blame he could look at himself. It's his laziness that made them desperate for money. Deep down he knows that, which is why he's so quick to blame everyone else. I'd hate to have to put you in the same bracket, Mia.'

'But I saw someone running away.'

'An opportunist thief. Chrissy's phone and purse were missing. This is a difficult time for all of us. Don't make it worse.'

'But—'

'Drop it, Mia. And please don't go to my parents with this. They're both fragile right now. They'll think these are accusations, like Ed's. Darcy was your friend, but she was their daughter and they're never going to get over this.'

'I understand, David. And I really didn't come to stir up trouble only . . .' I can't go into everything with Castanese and Pender. He'll think even worse of me than he does now. 'I know you think I'm making it up, but can you promise me one thing?'

'What?' He looks irritated.

'If Cara does ever try to contact you, you'll let me know?'

'Sure,' he says in a way that tells me he thinks this is highly unlikely. He glances at his watch. 'I have to go back to the conference.' He pushes his uneaten sandwich away and stands up. 'And now you need to promise me something in return, Mia.'

'Anything.'

'Keep off those damn forums. They're populated by the spiteful and the insane. And if you don't want to become one of them, you need to stay away.'

We say goodbye. David must be more agitated than he appears because he leaves without paying. I signal to the waitress to make up the bill while I finish my coffee and text Noah to tell him what David said.

As I look up from my phone, I see a face pressed against the window. We stare at each other for a moment. She looks as shocked as I am. I grab my phone and take a picture. Then Cara Tattersall starts running.

I throw thirty pounds onto the table and sprint after her.

She's on the other side of the road by the time I've exited the café. I dive through the crowds, knocking into an older woman, who shouts at me to look where I'm going. I dash towards the alley Cara just darted down. It runs between a pop-up vintage store and a bubble-tea café before taking a right-angled turn. Overflowing bin bags line the walls. Two rats disappear under one of them. I slow to a walk as I enter the alley and approach the corner as quietly as possible.

I stop and listen. Nothing. Then I hear the distinct crunch of glass under foot. She is there, just around the corner. I want to say, *I know it's you, Cara, why are you following me?* but my mouth is too dry and the words stick in my throat.

A shadow falls across the alley, the outline of a woman made of twigs and leaves.

Miaaa.

I'm back on the train station platform, the tracks rising up to meet my fall as they whisper.

Miaaa.

That shroud I saw on the lonely road in Worcestershire was for me. Tightness grips my chest and I can scarcely breathe because I know, I just know, that if I turn that corner, I'm dead.

I take one step back. Then another. Before turning on my heels and fleeing. I don't stop until I'm near the Tube station. As my breathing slows, I try to reason with myself. It was not a premonition, only my mind gathering facts. A woman predicted my four friends and I would be dead by Christmas. Two of those friends are already in their graves and someone has tried to push me under a train. Cara Tattersall has made her hatred of us clear and has been stalking me. Following her around the blind corner of an alley would have been idiotic. My reaction had nothing to do with Bella's warning.

At least now I have her picture – proof she exists.

I send it to Noah. Then after a couple of seconds I send it to Ed with the message:

I know you don't believe me but this is Cara Tattersall.

My phone beeps. It's Ed.

Liar.

Then another text.

> Ed
> I know you met David and I know why. You're working for Pender. So is he.

For a moment, what he says makes sense. If someone did harm Darcy, where easier than from within the family, but then I think of the quiet, stolid David.

> Me
> David would never hurt Darcy.
> Ed
> What about you?
> Me
> Me neither.
> Ed
> Sure about that?

Then a text from another number.

> Noah
> Tracked Ed's phone. He's in the Green Man pub. That's on the parallel street to where you met David.

> **Me**
> He can't be.
>
> **Noah**
> He is.

Two streets away with Cara Tattersall here. Not a coincidence. Who knows my movements? Why have they lured Ed here? I turn away from the Tube and start jogging towards the Green Man.

I call Ed. He has to stay where he is. Cara is coming for us. It rings three times before going dead.

I turn right, down a short side street and then onto another main street. The Green Man is on the corner.

The crowds seem to multiply and the shopping bags increase exponentially the more frantic I become. I reach the pub just as Ed picks up.

'Ed,' I say.

He doesn't speak and I can't hear the background buzz of a bar or any street traffic, only a slight scrape and shuffle. Inside the pub, Ed's nowhere to be seen.

'Ed.'

There's still noise coming through his phone but he's not replying.

Then a loud bang.

'Ed.'

No reply.

I daren't get off the line and text Noah instead.

> **Me**
> How could he know? Are you sure he's here?

Noah
Yes.

It's then a man runs to the bar and says, 'Better call an ambulance, mate. There's a couple collapsed in there.' He jabs a thumb toward the toilets. 'I don't think they're breathing.'

I run to the toilets. Sprawled across the floor is Ed, and next to him lies Cara Tattersall. Their eyes are open and unblinking. Their pupils constricted to pinpricks.

Chapter 45

Two off-duty doctors burst into the toilets and start CPR on Ed and Cara. The glance they exchange a minute in tells me it's hopeless. I feel numb. The scene in front of me appears at a distance as if viewed through a telescope. The lifeless bodies on the floor, the frantic chest compressions of two work colleagues meeting up for Christmas drinks, leaves me unmoved. I exit the toilets and take a seat in one of the nooks opposite the bar. Half the clientele have left and the staff are standing around looking at each other blankly.

The paramedics arrive and run into the toilets, followed a couple of minutes later by two police officers. One of the bar staff brings me a cup of tea. She places it on the table nervously.

'Did you know them?' she asks.

I incline my head.

'I'm so sorry.' She pushes a packet of biscuits onto the saucer and returns to the bar.

Shortly afterwards the police officers come back down and clear the pub's remaining customers.

'You'd better leave, miss,' one says. 'They're going to move the bodies. You'll find this upsetting.'

I hear the words but can't seem to move my limbs.

The bartender who brought the tea says something to him.

'Edward Fields was your friend?' the policeman says.

I nod. He mistakes my lack of responsiveness for something else.

'If you've taken any of that stuff, you'll need medical attention.'

'I haven't. We were on the phone. Then I heard him fall and I came in here and ran to the toilets. Ed was . . .' I can't say the words.

The officer sits down next to me.

'Can I take your name?'

I tell him. He notes my address and date of birth as well.

'I'm sorry about your friend. It looks like he got a bad batch of cocaine most likely cut with fentanyl. The paramedics say the deaths are consistent with an opioid overdose. We need to find where it came from so that other people don't die. Have you any idea where they got it from?'

'I think she brought it – Cara Tattersall.'

The police officer frowns. 'Cara?'

'The woman who's in there with him.'

He calls over to the other officer, who's taking down the names and addresses of the bar staff. She breaks off and comes over.

'Ms Raine says the woman we found is called Cara Tattersall. That isn't the name on the ID she was carrying, is it?'

The other officer shakes her head. 'Her credit cards say Annaliese Reynolds. Did you know her under another name?'

'It's complicated,' I say.

She looks as if she's going to ask another question, but her radio buzzes and distracts her.

The male officer quizzes me again about where Ed got the drugs. The bar staff confirm I only arrived just before calling for help. My attempts to persuade him that Ed was deliberately targeted meet with scepticism. And when I raise Chrissy's death a few weeks ago, he looks sorry for me, but unconvinced of a wider plot.

I hear the other officer put out an alert for a batch of fentanyl-contaminated cocaine. But I know there will be no more victims. Making a drug user's death seem like an accident is an easy murder, like yanking the cable of a tightrope walker. No one's looking for a killer beyond blatant stupidity. But I don't understand Cara's death. Did she deliberately kill herself, or did she try to do some complicated sort of switch and fail?

How will Molly feel, not only losing her husband but knowing he spent his last moments in a toilet cubicle snorting cocaine with a young woman he was obviously hoping for a bit more of later?

Once the police say I can go, I turn off my phone and try to feel something. I think about Ed. Funny, happy-go-lucky Ed, who would always tell you not to worry, not to get stressed. Life always seemed so easy to him. Of all of us, Leanne's death affected him the least. Sure it was sad, but why were we tormenting ourselves, we couldn't change the past, we couldn't know the future; enjoy the now. How did that Ed turn into the angry, suspicious man who threw me out of his car on a dark lonely road in the middle of nowhere? The drink and drugs were the symptom, not the cause. And I realise that, like everyone else, Ed was playing a part. Fake it till you make it. Only, like the rest of us, he never could.

Chapter 46

Christmas is less than a week away and Noah and I are the only ones left. For the second time in under a month, I went chasing across London, glued to a phone, only to find my friend dead at the end of it. I'm beginning to understand Ed's last words to me.

Darce was right not to trust you.

Distrust me, not because I am dangerous, but because knowing me is dangerous.

Pender said my angel was jealous. Does Bella want me to herself as I once wanted Darcy to myself?

Back at my flat I check the All of This Is True forum.

It's as if the messenger can read my thoughts.

TheForrester
Do you foresee them or do you cause them Mia?

How do they know?

I grab a screenprint seconds before it disappears and send it to Noah.

I pace up and down the room. None of this makes sense. I wish I could talk to Chrissy. She would give me a rational explanation for Bella's appearance before someone dies. Or is psychosis the only rational explanation? Should I be seeing a psychiatrist?

I ring Mum. She's in disbelief about Ed and wants me to come home.

'I'll only put you in danger,' I say. 'But you need to answer a question, and you have to be one hundred per cent honest. Did you ever believe I have the gift?'

She takes a moment to answer.

'Dotty was a lonely old woman who talked nonsense. I didn't believe her. But you used to scare me. I thought the thing with Mrs Lyons was a coincidence, but one weekend Bernard's uncle came. He seemed perfectly healthy, but you said he was in a white sheet, when he was wearing blue jeans and a maroon jumper. He died unexpectedly of a heart attack the next day. The white sheet reminded me of the shroud Dotty told me you said Mrs Lyons was wearing the day before she died. I took you to a child psychologist. She said you had an overactive imagination. I didn't dare hint at anything more. Not after what happened to your grandmother.'

I take a moment to try to understand the significance of this. The old woman who fed me sugared almonds.

'I remember we visited her once in hospital.'

'It was no place for a child,' Mum says. 'But she knew she was dying and asked to see you. I didn't feel I could refuse. It's the worst decision I ever made. After that visit you started seeing Lula. The same name she gave the woman haunting her – the reason they locked her away.'

I remember her dry lips brushing my ear, whispering words I no longer remember. Only now I hear them.

'Lula will come to you. She will protect you.'

No. I still have an overactive imagination. This is not a memory, it's a reaction to what Mum's just told me. I never recalled these words before. It's not real.

'That place . . .' I say.

'It was a psychiatric hospital. Your grandmother was sectioned when I was just eighteen. I was terrified the psychologist would diagnose you with whatever she had and that, like her, they'd place you in an institution.'

Bernard told me as much when he spoke to me the day after Darcy's funeral, but I hadn't been listening.

'It seemed to calm down after we moved in with Bernard,' Mum says. 'You were forbidden from talking about Lula. But then Leanne happened and it all started up again. Did you see anything before Darcy, Ed and Chrissy died?'

What can I say – that I'm as crazy as my granny? It's not too late for some doctor to section me, lock me away and drug me up to the eyeballs. And I'm not insane because whatever visions I had told me the truth. Three of my friends are dead.

'I didn't see anything,' I tell Mum. 'It's just after all that's happened, I'm trying to make sense of it.'

'Are you sure, Mia?'

'Yes,' I say, and get off the phone as quickly as possible.

I don't leave the flat for two days. I daren't even trust Deliveroo drivers and have to survive on pasta and tinned tomatoes. There's wine in the fridge but I stick to coffee. I need to keep a clear head and make sense of what's happened. Lunch with David, seeing Cara, then the phone call. I look at the picture of Cara. A pretty young woman, slender with glowing skin and delicate features. She's been living as Annaliese Reynolds, which is why we never found her. She doesn't much resemble Leanne. But then many siblings look different. On the third day I get a text from Noah.

Check this out. I'm coming round to pick you up.

Underneath is a web link to the Gerrard Tait Talent Agency and one of their actors. The photograph matches the one I took at the Garden Café four days ago. She graduated from an elite drama school. More importantly, she was born in Cardiff. This definitely isn't Cara Tattersall under a different name.

I'm trying to understand the implications of this when Noah calls me and tells me he's outside in his car.

At rush hour the main road is a river of red and white lights. Noah and I don't talk about Ed. Swollen eyes, hollow cheeks and three days' worth of stubble tell their own story. Noah was closer to Ed than the rest of us. The boys formed a group within a group. There were things they couldn't or wouldn't share with us and, as neither of them had brothers, I guess they became each other's.

Noah bangs the steering wheel and honks in frustration at the slow-moving traffic.

'Come on. Come on,' he says.

'Why would this Annaliese Reynolds target us?' I ask. 'Why come to Darcy's funeral and follow me to my meeting with David Alderwell or take cocaine with Ed in a pub toilet?'

'That's what we're going to find out.'

I read her agent's profile again. Annaliese can do accents – Welsh, London, RP and Standard American. She can dance cabaret and ride a horse. None of which appears to have found her much work. All the jobs on her CV are for walk-on parts and commercials.

'Do you think she has some connection to Castanese or Pender?' I ask.

'How the hell should I know?'

Noah jams the heel of his hand on the car horn again, causing several pedestrians to stare at us.

'The thing that keeps coming up with Castanese and Pender is royalty, politicians, celebrities. That doesn't apply to Annaliese. Did you find anything else about her beyond her agency's profile?'

'Only that she's not Cara Tattersall. I was never sure why you were fixated on Leanne's sister.'

Noah weaves the car through the side streets until we get to a row of Georgian houses. We pull up outside one with multiple doorbells, indicating it's been broken up into flats.

'The top one,' Noah says. 'Annaliese shared with a girl called Sara she went to drama school with. Neither of them gets any acting work, yet they can rent a two-bed flat in an expensive part of London.'

'Family money?'

'Let's find out.'

Noah presses the 'C' bell. We wait a moment before hearing footsteps on the stairs.

A young woman in a grey T-shirt and navy joggers answers the door. Her hair is pulled back tightly and, like Noah, she has swollen, red-ringed eyes. She looks us up and down. 'I'm not changing my gas supplier,' she says.

'It's Sara, isn't it? We're here about Annaliese,' Noah says.

'No comment.' She goes to close the door. Noah jams his foot in it.

'We're not press either,' Noah says. 'Ed, the guy Annaliese was with, he was my best friend. I'm just trying to understand what happened.'

Sara hesitates, looking at me.

'I'm not Ed's wife,' I say.

She looks relieved and opens the door a fraction, scanning the street before inviting us in.

Whether it's because she's young or because she's too distraught to keep the place in order, pizza boxes and empty beer cans are strewn across the lounge and clothes lie in heaps on the floor. What the mess can't hide is that this is a high-end flat, in an expensive neighbourhood. The rent must be a stretch for two rarely employed actors.

Noah and I sit on the butter-coloured leather couch and are careful not to disturb the Siamese cat stretched out on it, extending and retracting its claws. Sara sits on a matching armchair opposite.

'I'm sorry about Annaliese,' I say. 'Were you close?'

She shrugs. 'We knew each other at drama school and ended up in the same boat as so many of our classmates – going to auditions, getting nowhere, working odd jobs. Neither of us could face going back to live with our parents so we got this place together.'

I look around at the artwork. None of it's mine but I recognise some of my contemporaries and even their limited prints are expensive.

'How do you get by without any work?'

'Like I said, odd jobs.' She calls to the cat. It ignores her.

She's being evasive and my mind can't help speculating on the most obvious profession for two young, attractive women to make serious amounts of money.

'Do you know how Ed and Annaliese met?'

'You're good friends of his, right? So you know his wife?' Sara asks.

'Of course,' Noah says.

'Then you should ask her.'

Noah and I look at each other.

'Molly introduced them?' I ask.

'In a manner of speaking,' she says.

Noah shifts in his seat. He's becoming agitated. Obfuscation and double talk drive him crazy and, as the last thing we need is for him to get snippy. I step in quickly.

'We can't talk to his wife right now, you understand? They have kids and she'll have to talk to the police, I guess. Can you just tell us what you know? We've been friends with Ed since primary school. This has been really difficult for both of us.'

Sara sighs. 'OK then, but you have to understand, it's not escort work or anything like that.'

I hold up my hands. 'We didn't say anything.'

'I've been called a whore before. Annaliese and I both have. Even by the people who employ us.'

Next to me, Noah's mouth is open.

'We're not here to judge you,' I say. 'We just want to know what went on. It's not escort work and you say Molly knew about Annaliese.'

'She paid for her.'

'To date Ed?'

'Not exactly. We're actors and I know some people have

a problem with what we do, but if you're not a cheater, you've nothing to worry about.' She looks straight at us, as if this makes everything clear. When it's obvious we have no idea what she's on about she says, 'It's decoy work.'

'Decoy?' I say.

'Our agency sends girls somewhere, usually to a bar, to chat up a guy, to see if he'll take the bait.'

'And Molly did that?'

'Must have. It's nearly always the wife or girlfriend.'

'But you don't sleep with these guys.'

'Christ, no. We're told where to meet them, we flirt with them and see how far they'll go. Exchange numbers. Agree to another meet up. Book a bedroom there and then. It's all recorded and sent back to whoever's paying.'

'And do you know who's paying?'

'The agency deals with that. Annaliese told me about Ed because the request was weird. Not the first one. Meet some middle-aged guy in a bar and see if you can get him to exchange phone numbers. That's normal. I mean, we sometimes discuss our mark – that's what we call the guys we're sent to meet. But it's just so predictable and run of the mill.'

I imagine them sitting here laughing over a bottle of Prosecco at the poor saps who actually think they have a chance with a hot girl half their age.

'Was it normal to do cocaine?' Noah asks.

Sara looks wary.

'That's the weird bit. We're not supposed to take drugs or get drunk. Only . . .'

'Only what?'

'The client wanted to know if Ed was doing drugs. She

paid three times the going rate. A bag of coke was couriered round here. There were strict instructions that Ed had to take it on his own; she mustn't be seen to partake.' A sob rises in Sara's throat. 'The thing is, Annaliese has a bit of a habit. I don't think she could resist.'

'Have you told the police this?' Noah asks.

'They've not been in touch,' Sara says.

'You need to contact them. This was murder.'

'It was an accident. His wife couldn't know the coke she got was no good. Especially if she wasn't used to buying it.'

Molly had suspected Ed's infidelities, but would she set him up with another woman and send him cocaine? Or was the instigator in this case not a wife or girlfriend but someone else with a grudge?

'Did Annaliese do anything other than decoy work?' I ask.

'I told you, we're not escorts.'

'That's not what I meant. Was she ever given jobs that required her acting skills that didn't involve being a decoy? Anything outside London?'

'Last month she had to go to the Midlands and act as a mourner at someone's funeral.'

The woman in the red dress.

'She felt bad about that. She said she wouldn't do it again. But they paid her well for travelling.'

'And what about other work? Following someone, for example.'

'I've never been asked to follow someone and neither has Annaliese. She'd have told me.'

'Are you sure?'

'Look, we get paid to go around in designer clothes and

drink champagne at other people's expense. There's no way Annaliese would go hanging around underground car parks or whatever. It's just not her.'

From what Sara's saying, it wasn't Annaliese lurking around in the alleyway near my flat and she was certainly not the person who chased Chrissy to her death.

'And this decoy agency, what's their name? How do I contact them?' Noah asks.

'I can't give you their name. That's one of the rules. They're very discreet, for obvious reasons.'

'Sara, if Annaliese hadn't died she'd currently be in a prison cell on a charge of manslaughter,' Noah says. 'Your employers don't give a damn about you.'

She looks around the flat. 'It's the only money I have coming in. I'm going to struggle as it is without Annaliese's share of the rent.'

'Do you really want to carry on doing this, after what's happened?' Noah asks.

'What choice do I have?'

He hands her his card. 'Contact me. I might be able to find you something,' he says.

Sara turns the card over. 'I've heard of you,' she says, obviously impressed. 'You'll really help me?'

'We're growing and always looking for ambitious young people. And really, this career you've got going isn't ever going to be long term, is it?'

She shakes her head and I realise she's far younger than I first thought, closer to twenty than thirty. The decoy work probably seemed exciting, like being in a spy movie rather than grubby barrel scraping.

'So can you tell us who they are?' Noah asks.

Sara's shoulders slump. 'They're called Hansfords. They don't have a website. Only a number. Word is passed through discreet recommendations.'

She shows Noah her phone and he copies the number.

'Thanks,' he says. 'My recruitment people will be in touch about available positions.'

'Why did you do that?' I ask when we're outside and back in the car. 'You could have just threatened her with the police. Withholding evidence or something.'

'I felt sorry for her.'

'What she does isn't illegal but it's kind of immoral.'

'We've all been young and stupid,' he says. 'And it was the easiest way to get the information. Why do I feel someone's one step ahead of us? They probably knew we'd come here. Just like they knew Ed would meet that woman in London and snort coke.'

'It still doesn't make sense, though. Why did she come to the café I was sitting in? And why come to the funeral?'

'We need to speak to Hansfords.'

He rings the number. No one answers and there's no voicemail option.

We sit in the car, silent for a moment.

'Do you still think it could be Cara Tattersall?' I ask eventually. 'I mean, she wasn't Annaliese, but she could be living under another name.'

'I think you've become obsessed with Cara. You're only looking at this one way.'

'We should at least find out where she lives,' I say. 'We don't know who she is, or what she's been doing for the last twenty years. She could have paid Annaliese.'

'I was thinking about Mark,' Noah says. 'If he found

out about their affair, he could have wanted both Chrissy and Ed dead. Do we actually know he was at home when Chrissy died?'

'The police must have checked,' I say.

'Not if they think it was an accident.'

'Ed did tell me someone was threatening him. He thought it was Mark, but I just don't see it. I don't like Mark, but I wouldn't have him down as violent. And what about Darcy? It can't be him. Whoever it is knows us really well and they're not going to stop.'

'I've been thinking the same,' Noah says. 'Maybe if we can make it to the end of the year, we'll be OK. I'm thinking of going to San Francisco. We have work over there. Can you get away?'

I've nowhere obvious to go. No family or work abroad.

'Dunno,' I say. 'France, maybe. I need to think about it.'

'You could come with us,' he says. 'All that Californian light could take your work in a new direction.'

I imagine Noah and me on the beach, the sun setting, his hand dusting sand from my skin. Then I imagine Penny with us.

'We'll see,' I say, and take out my phone.

I don't bother checking the other forums; I go straight to All of This Is True. Forrester has written again.

Two buds left

'Our answer's here,' I say. 'Did you ever find the admin for this site?'

'I'll get on it,' he says.

HALLOWS HILL

***

Noah drops me at my flat and tells me to call him once I'm inside. I check every room, then double-lock the door and call Noah to let him know I'm OK.

'You take care too,' I tell him.

Bella is not here and if the trees are talking their noise is drowned out by the unrelenting rain spattering the windows.

Where is Ed now? On a metal table, having his organs extracted and weighed. I think of Molly trying to explain to the boys why Daddy isn't coming home. Will she blame me, as Mark did with Chrissy?

After running on adrenaline all day, my limbs are now heavy and the rain acts as a lullaby. I'm falling asleep when suddenly I sit bolt upright.

The rain has stopped. A branch is tapping at the window.

I strain my ears. I can't hear her, but somehow I know Bella has come to me.

My phone light is on although I didn't hear it buzz. I've five missed calls and a voicemail from Noah: 'I found out where the forum posts come from. I can't tell you over the phone. I don't want you to do anything stupid.

And then he texts again.

I've found her. Come.

SOLSTICE

Chapter 47

I panic when Noah doesn't answer his phone. It's 21 December. We have three days left. I'm unsure what to do. I still have the keys to his apartment and so decide to head there. At eight in the morning with the traffic bumper to bumper in the driving rain, it's easiest to catch the Tube. My carriage is crammed with commuters and the atmosphere soon becomes hot and humid as moisture rises from their sodden coats. I loosen my collar and raise my chin to try to find some cooler air as sweat drips down my back.

I found out where the forum posts come from . . . I don't want you to do anything stupid.

What stupid thing does Noah fear I'll do?

Once we've crossed central London, the carriage empties. The sweat on my back has started to dry and I'm shivering even before I exit the station into the rain that has now turned to sleet. I hurry along the Thames path. At high tide the river laps against the top of the wall and the wind whistles along the water, digging deep into my bones as if it's in league with Bella in attempting to sap the last of my resolve.

I pull my coat tight around me and lean in to the wind.

At River Heights the concierge nods. By now he's used to my bedraggled form blighting the lobby's chic lines.

As I take the lift to the penthouse, it floats before me. The white sheet. The shroud.

Noah.

I rush to his apartment.

The entrance hall air carries an odd, metallic smell. My instinct is to flee. Instead, I force myself forwards, treading as silently as I can.

There's no sound but I sense a presence. I inch along the corridor, then onto the lounge's parquet floor. A dark stain has spread from behind the sofa and across the cream rug. It has to be the red wine Ed spilt. Noah told me about it. Only this wine is still pouring, its crimson stain creeping towards me.

I step forwards. Noah lies face down on the floor, blood oozing from beneath him. Beside him, her clothes as bloodied as his, kneels Penny.

I take one more step. My coat catches a glass on the low side table and sends it crashing down. Penny spins around. I'm the one that should be frightened, but the terror's in her eyes. She jumps to her feet. I raise my hands to defend myself only to see Penny running away from me towards the balcony. She darts outside and shuts and locks the door behind her.

I crouch down next to Noah. It's impossible to tell if he's breathing or not. I phone 999 and give them details of our location and the situation. The operator stays on the line.

Looking up, I see Penny out on the balcony. Can she be Cara? I suspected her all along, but Noah was so certain. How could he have missed it?

I'm not sure if I'm angrier with him or her as I charge to the balcony and bang on the doors.

'I've already called the police,' I yell. I don't know if she can hear me through the glass and above the high wind that's buffeting her hair.

She starts phoning someone. I search for the key. Behind the fronds of a house plant, in an enamelled dish, lies a second one. I hold it in my hand and raise it up to show Penny.

I'm not sure what I'm going to do. She's younger than me and works out at the gym.

She's still on the phone talking frantically to someone. Who?

Rage overrides my caution and I unlock the door and step out into the icy air.

'Cara,' I say.

She takes a step back.

'It was always you, wasn't it, Cara?'

'She's here, come quickly,' she says into her phone.

Her eyes don't leave me as she speaks and starts backing away and climbing the balcony wall. What's she doing? We're in the penthouse; the drop will kill her. Then I see she's aiming to leap to the adjacent balcony about five feet away.

High in the sky, behind Cara, strong winds push the grey clouds together until Bella's form appears: her matted hair and jutting chin.

'No, Cara, don't.'

Whatever she's done, I don't want her to die. I run to stop her. She only sees a threat.

'I knew it was you,' she says before launching herself into the air.

Her jump is powerful, her arms and legs flailing, propelling her towards the other balcony. For a moment it looks like she's going to reach it. Then I hear Bella's high-pitched scream as a gust of wind catches Cara and blows her off course. She misses the balcony rail by an inch and is carried towards the river, where she crashes into one of the cast-iron lampposts lining its banks. Her body wraps around once before being flipped downwards, smacking on the wall and tumbling into the water below. Her body is visible for only a second before it disappears beneath the softly lapping waves.

All that's left is a spray of blood on the river wall.

Chapter 48

I stare at the spot where Penny disappeared into the river, expecting her to bob to the surface and cry for help at any moment. But the grey waters of the Thames roll on by to the sea with no trace of her. After I'm sure she's not coming back, I return to the lounge.

Noah's still bleeding, which means he must have a heartbeat. Remembering some Girl Guide first aid, I roll him over onto his back and apply pressure to the wound using my hands and a light jacket left thrown across the sofa. I keep my palms pressed down hard close to his heart, begging him to live. After what seems an eternity, the paramedics arrive and take over. A moment before they place an oxygen mask over his face, Noah opens his eyes.

'She came back,' is all he says before his eyes close again.

The paramedics rush him downstairs to the waiting ambulance.

When the police arrive, I tell them how I came across Penny covered in blood. How she ran from me and tried to jump to the next balcony.

'Why did she do that?' I ask DS Lacon, the same policeman who came to speak to us about Chrissy's death.

'Panic,' he says. 'She called the emergency services before you. Did you know that?'

That's who she was on the phone to. But Penny always seemed so self-contained. I can't imagine her panicking.

'Why did she call the police?'

'She found Noah bleeding and unconscious and was aware of someone else running from the apartment. She thought it was you and you'd come back for her.'

'I thought she killed Noah.'

'That's what I mean about panic. Whoever killed Noah would be drenched in blood and we know from the concierge that you arrived a few moments after Ms French called nine nine nine. If she'd stopped to think, she would have realised it couldn't have been you.'

He's very matter of fact. That's what dealing with murder and violence as part of your day job does to you. You forget that to most people this is an aberration, their worst nightmares realised, not just another day at work.

'This is the second time you've come to this apartment,' I say. 'Since then Ed's died and Noah's been stabbed. Do you believe me now about Chrissy – that what happened on Tower Bridge was more than an accident?'

Lacon takes a deep breath and looks out of the patio windows and along the river to the high towers of the City's financial institutions. 'It's too soon to make assumptions,' he says.

'I told you back then that Cara Tattersall was behind this. Now I know that's Penny French's real name.'

'Ah, he told you?' Lacon nods in approval. 'I did tell Mr Campbell the best thing he could do was come clean.'

My brow furrows. 'Noah knew?'

'He called me after I left that day and said he wanted to tell me there was no mystery to Cara's whereabouts. She'd changed her name to avoid the true crime fanatics and some guy called Pender, who was obsessed with the case. Noah was worried how you'd react.'

I sit there, stupid and blank. I've been blind. After Castanese and the Dower House, I immediately suspected Penny, and every time I hinted at it, Noah nudged me away. Then I fixated on the woman in the red dress at Darcy's funeral.

But how did Cara come into his life? Did he seek her out or did she seek him? And then they fell in love. It seems insane and I have a thousand questions.

Noah would never have agreed to hurt any of us. It must have been Cara acting alone and Noah not wanting to believe her capable of violence. Then he found out the forum posts originated in his own apartment and he could no longer ignore the obvious. When he confronted her, she stabbed him. That's why he didn't want me to do anything stupid. He was going to deal with her himself.

I tell Lacon all of this. He remains sceptical.

'That hardly tallies with Ms French calling the police. And why would she shy away from a physical confrontation with you if she's no fear of a tall, athletic man like Mr Campbell?'

He has a constable lead me away before I can ask any more questions. As I'm leaving the apartment, the forensic team come in. Their white plastic overalls appear wildly incongruous set against the fake cheer of the tinsel and the

Christmas tree with the illuminated angel atop, or is it a fairy? I think of Darcy – 'just like a fairy' is how people used to describe her dancing. She was the brightest, best and first of us to fade. Then Chrissy, clever and determined. After her, Ed, the fool who dared speak the truth. Meaning that Noah and I are now the last surviving members of the Hags Ring Five, and his life hangs by a thread.

But the shroud I saw as I exited the lift was not for him. It was for Cara.

Downstairs in the lobby another detective is questioning the concierge.

'We've never had a crime in this building,' he's saying. 'And the delivery seemed genuine. I checked with Mr Campbell, before allowing the rider to go up. It all seemed legit. He uses that pizza company all the time when Ms French is out. He told me not to tell her about it, because she's so keen on health food.'

My escorting officer whisks me past, out into a waiting car and I'm unable to hear any more.

At the hospital a forensics officer comes and finds me to scrape under my fingernails and bag up my clothes. In their place, she gives me a pair of loose jeans and a mildewy jumper. I'm kept in overnight and treated for shock. In the morning a young female officer tells me they'll be doing a more in-depth interview at the station at a time and date to be decided. But for now I can go.

The problem is, where to? Not Mum's. I can't bring this chaos to her door. What I really want to do is stay close to Noah at the hospital. Then I think of his mum arriving. Natalie will blame me, just as Mark and Leanne's parents did. I thought their criticism unfair. Now I know they were right. I am to blame for their loved ones' deaths. Like Typhoid Mary, lack of intent doesn't diminish culpability. Mary Mallon died in enforced quarantine after having infected hundreds and killing an estimated fifty people. Should I be similarly incarcerated, for the good of the general populus?

In the end I decide to go home, shower and change out of the musty clothes. Then, unable to settle, I go out and wander the streets, trying to get my head around what's happened and why. I'm starting to come around to DS Lacon's way of thinking. It couldn't have been Cara. There was no weapon at the apartment, as far as I could see, and a pizza delivery guy went up not long before Noah was stabbed. This is the more likely assailant. But who could it be? There's no one left, no one who fits the hole at the centre of the puzzle Ed talked about.

It's 22 December, the shortest day. Three days until Christmas. Three days to figure it out or, if Bella's prediction is accurate, both Noah and I will be dead.

Passing a café, and tempted by its warm, orange glow and the promise of strong hot coffee, I press my nose to the window. But no, I can't be around people right now. And I remain outside, shivering in the icy rain and trying to order my thoughts.

I've found her.

Who did Noah mean? He already knew who Cara was. Did he mean he's seen through her, found the real Cara. Or was it Bella he saw?

Then I remember the other message.

I found out where the forum posts come from. I can't tell you over the phone. I don't want you to do anything stupid.

The anticipation of finding out where the posts came from and the shock at the attack on Noah have made me forget to do my regular checks. As soon as I do, I see the message waiting for me on the All of This Is True forum.

I told you to wake up Mia. It's almost too late.

The fairy lights twinkling in the café window give rise to a sudden realisation. Only one person could have done this.

I scroll through my phone. No messages, but an email from Noah. He must have sent it after I didn't respond to his texts.

Your laptop has spyware. Probably your phone too.

Underneath he's written several paragraphs on how he went about finding the IP address of the account sending those messages to me on the All of This Is True forum. It means nothing to me and I skip to the bottom, which tells me where the messages came from. Not from his apartment, not even from London.

Unconsciously, I think I always knew. But as Chrissy once told me, external stimuli can cloud your reason. The spyware knows I've read this information. Another message pops up.

The Forrester
So *you* figured it out. Meet me at the Hags Ring before dusk.

Here it is then. The piece that fits the hole at the centre of our puzzle.

Chapter 49

As I drive north, the sleet turns to snow, the mist to fog. By the time I reach the Hags Ring, it's mid-afternoon. On the shortest day of the year, that means it will be dark soon. I leave my hire car at Roundels car park, from where we started our trek all those years ago. Plunging temperatures freeze the fog to a thick soup and the glare of the torch beam bouncing back at me means I can see better with it switched off. Just as I do, I catch sight of a white sheet floating through the trees. A shroud. My shroud.

I navigate the route to the summit of Hallows Hill by memory.

The snow and heavy air seem to both deaden and amplify sound. My breath echoes and swirls around me as I make my way through the tunnel of trees. This time I do not turn at the soft thud of footsteps behind me and the scent of rotting vegetation infusing with the fog.

Castanese was right. I had been Nicholson's intended victim, lured into the stone circle to rid me of Lula's protection. Verne-Fontaine's structure was anything but a folly.

At the summit, I can just about make out the nearest

stone to the tree line. The tallest of the Hags Ring, Noah. My heart bangs against my ribs as I approach. No one will come while I stand outside the stones. I must leave my shield.

I step into the circle, turning slowly to each of our stones, me, Noah, Ed, Chrissy and finally the smallest slenderest stone.

Then I wait.

It's recognition, not surprise, that makes me cry out when Darcy slides from behind the stone pillar, her light ballerina poise allowing her to skip over the icy ground. I'm unsure which emotion is stronger: elation that my oldest friend is still alive, or hurt at the knowledge of how much she must hate me, how much she must have hated all of us, in order to do what she has done.

'Stay in the circle', Darcy once told me. I'm only just starting to scratch at the significance of those words.

I start moving towards her, then halt. Her appearance has altered since we last met. Her lips are bloodless, her cheeks, sunken. Only the brilliance of her eyes reveal that it's not illness that has enacted this change.

'You took your time,' she says, mocking laughter in her voice. 'Why did you decide to come? Loyalty? Nostalgia? Guilt? Can't turn down a dare?'

I want to run at her and scream, why, why, why? But the icy fog has cooled both my blood and my mind.

'It's *my* motivation you think we need to discuss here?' I say.

She smiles. 'You know what the worst thing is, Mia? You never appreciated what you had: talent, success, a doting husband, a loving mother. Even your stepfather cared for you. All I had was a middling talent for ballet, spun out far beyond its limits and still I failed in my mother's eyes. And all the while I had to watch you wriggle and squirm, trying to escape her, a gift you considered a curse. She should have bound herself to me.'

It takes me a moment to work out what she means.

'You think Bella is a gift? I could have ended up in some sort of asylum, like my grandmother.'

'Only because you're too stupid to understand who and what she is. The Hags Ring. People call it a Verne-Fontaine folly, when there's no room for ornament in my family.'

'*Your* family?'

'Yes. Verne – the old French for the alder tree, Fontaine – meaning well. Alderwell. I'm surprised no one ever put two and two together. Dad's family is of an illegitimate line, of course, but after my grandfather got rid of Lula for him, the fourteenth Viscount acknowledged their kinship and named him as his heir after his son, Hugh, died. But then he had to flee to Buenos Aires and our lands were covered by an ugly 1950s housing estate. So we had to resort to the ancient methods to regain our fortune.'

Verne-Fontaine. Alder-Well. Both obvious and obscure. Like having two doctors in the family to declare you dead, when you're very much alive. Perhaps there was someone in Darcy's coffin. A Jane Doe or maybe, like Isabella's, it held only lead.

'If you'd accepted David's marriage proposal, none of this would have needed to happen.'

'Then Bella would have been an Alderwell too, or should I say a Verne-Fontaine?' I ask.

'Bella, if that's what you choose to call her, is an ancient force. She binds herself to individuals. And don't sneer at the

Verne-Fontaines. You're one too, Mia. Haven't you worked out who Lula's bastard child was?'

'My grandmother.'

'Grandfather tried to track her down years ago. But there were thousands of illegitimate children born in the war. They were sent all over the country, even abroad. It was impossible. It's only because Dotty babysat for you and recognised who your imaginary friend was that we were able to work backwards and find her. I doubt your grandmother even knew she was adopted. Lula must have known what was coming. She sent her guardian angel to her daughter. And the Alderwells remained poor and obscure.'

'And you thought if you killed me, Bella would come to you?'

'Worth a try.'

'You pushed me at the train station.'

'It seemed too good an opportunity to miss. I didn't plan it. I just wanted to see where you went. I had an idea you were already in touch with Pender. It's very much his style to play a double jeu.'

'And not yours, Darcy? Or should I say the Forrester. The details of the Dower House file had spyware. You were watching everything I did.'

She shrugs. 'I do what I have to. And anyway, the attempt at the station was pointless. She protected you. After that I knew the path I had to take. Which is why you're here.'

'I understand why you want me dead. But why the others, Chrissy, Ed, Noah?'

'Because we named the stones after them. A silly mistake years before I understood who I am and what the stones were. Pender worked out that the stones' namesakes had to be eliminated for them to act as a shield. He also advised that we followed a strict regimen of self-denial: abstinence from food, alcohol and sex as well as self-flagellation. He's an excellent scholar – has access to all sorts of documents and archives. He helped Dad with primary sources for "The History of the Hags Ring". You read his manuscripts?'

'John wrote those?'

'Yes.'

'And the reason he's gaunt is because like you, he's starving himself. You're all Pender's acolytes now. Starving, isolated and sleep deprived. You know these are classic conditions for brainwashing.'

Darcy closes her eyes. 'Pender has been useful. He was the one who told Dad about you in the first place, years ago when Dotty Bridges had to look after you. You don't think I wanted to make friends with the clumsy kid from ballet, do you?'

I shake my head. 'We were friends, Darcy, whatever you say. You can't fake what we had, not over all those years.'

She gives a dismissive flick of the hand.

'Remember it as you choose,' she says.

'One thing I don't get is Leon. Who is he?'

'You saw the look he gave me at the Dower House. What child doesn't idolise his long-lost mother?'

'Mother?'

'I only slept with Noah to keep him from you. Nothing to do with Bella. I was just sick of you always getting everything you wanted. A teenage boy with a little cider inside him isn't hard to seduce although I made sure he thought it was the other way around. The pregnancy wasn't planned, but it turned out for the best. Guilt is a hard taskmaster. Noah would never go near you after that.'

'So you never went to ballet school in France?'

'Noah begged me to keep the child, but Pender told me to give it to Castanese. She could raise him and he might be useful to us later. But I made sure that when we reconnected he grew to hate his father. I told him how Noah took advantage of a naïve teenage girl and demanded she have an abortion. He would have happily killed Noah, but I wanted that very special pleasure.'

I can see now all sanity has deserted Darcy and, as I suspected, she's come here to kill me. She pushed Chrissy under a bus, tricked Ed into snorting fentanyl and dressed as a pizza delivery boy to stab Noah. She may be small and undernourished, but she can move quickly, and I'm ready for her when she produces a blade from behind her back. I reach for my Mace spray and hold it up in front of me. Darcy doesn't stop her approach. I'm about to press the release when two pairs of hands grab me and it's flung from my grasp.

John and David Alderwell have crept up on me through the fog. John looks triumphant, David apologetic. 'If only you'd said yes to me.'

He and John hold me fast. Darcy points the tip of the stiletto knife at me.

The odour of dead and rotting vegetation fills the circle. Even the Alderwells can smell it.

'Is she here?' Darcy asks, her eyes saucer wide.

Outside of the circle, Bella is screaming, but Darcy can't hear. She approaches in slow measured steps.

A calmness settles over me. This is how I'm going to die.

John and David grip me tighter. When Darcy's close enough she holds the thin blade vertically before lowering the tip until it is parallel with my heart. Then she slides it through the thick padding of my coat. I cry out as the cold tip pierces my skin and it comes to rest a quarter of an inch into my flesh. Darcy's so close now, I can feel her warm breath against my cheek. 'It really should never have come to this.' Her lips brush my skin as she speaks.

I squeeze my eyelids shut and wait for the fatal thrust.

Suddenly the blade is withdrawn. I open my eyes to see Darcy airborne. Leon's arms are around her waist, flinging her away from me across the Hags Ring. She smacks into one of the stones and slides down it. John Alderwell lets go of me and launches himself at Leon, rugby-tackling him to the ground. I wriggle free from a stunned David and dive for the Mace spray. He's an instant too slow. I twist around and release it into his eyes. He staggers back screaming in pain, and crashes into a stone.

After the surprise attack, Leon easily out-muscles John Alderwell, his grandfather. He pins him to the floor while twisting towards his mother. 'I hate you,' he says. 'I was never your son, only a pawn.'

Darcy pulls herself to her feet, the knife still in her hand.

'We're all someone's pawn, Leon,' she says.

It's just me against Darcy now. I haul myself upright and point the Mace spray in her direction.

'Why now, Darcy, after all these years? After you failed with Leanne, why not just let it go and get on with your life?'

A maniacal grin invades her face.

'My family wasn't lying. I am ill. I wouldn't have made

forty. But I wanted a chance to live properly. The life I could have lived. The life I should have lived with Bella at my side. I'm not going to fade away like Mum, or end my days on a hospital bed stuffed with tubes.'

'It's too late, Darce.'

'I've made my choice,' she says.

Her head tilts skyward. She raises the knife, and I realise it was not my shroud floating through the trees on my route up to the Hags Ring. Before I can stop her, she pulls the knife down hard and thrusts it into her ribcage, just below her breast.

The blood isn't obvious at first. The blade is so thin and her coat so thick, the metal's nearly clean when it's withdrawn. The first sign of the lethal wound is a crimson circle forming in the snow beneath her feet.

She slumps down at the base of her stone.

Leon cries out but remains astride John, pinning him to the ground. David knocked himself out when he crashed into Ed's stone.

I'm the only one free to go to Darcy. Her eyes are shut but her mouth expresses an emotion I've never seen on it before. Contentment.

A NEW YEAR

Chapter 50

Haverton Herald

Police Review Leanne Tattersall Case

As a result of recent events at the Hags Ring, police are reviewing the Leanne Tattersall case as evidence comes to light that John Alderwell brainwashed his patient into committing the murder. William Nicholson, who was not of sound mind, killed Leanne by mistake because she was wearing Mia Raine's distinctive McQueen skull scarf.

Meanwhile both John and his son, David, are on remand for their involvement in the second attempt on Ms Raine's life, as well as perverting the course of justice and falsifying a death certificate. They were, however, allowed to attend the funeral of Darcy Alderwell, their daughter and sister respectively, at All Hallows Cemetery chapel. Additional mourners included Darcy's son, Leon Eccles, her mother, Marielle Alderwell and her oldest friend, Mia Raine.

Chapter 51

Noah is on the mend. As am I. We have spoken several times over the phone, although he is too tired for long conversations. Penny never hid her origins. As the easiest to find of the Hags Ring Five, Noah was the one she approached to learn about her sister. Her impressive qualifications – and I'm guessing a measure of guilt – led him to offer her a job. He never told us because he thought we would find the reminder of Leanne's death upsetting, Darcy in particular. Then when romance blossomed and they became engaged, he planned to tell us. But the events at the Dower House and my fixation on the unknown assailant being Cara Tattersall, held him back.

Mum and Bernard come and sit with me every day. They don't talk about the Alderwells. The subject is too painful to me. And whilst I would expect nothing less than daily visits from them, I've had several other, unexpected visitors.

Jake came carrying a bouquet of chrysanthemums. Until the decree absolute, I am still his wife and he feels some obligation towards me. The flowers came with a request that we sell the flat. With a baby due in the next couple of months, he and Lisette need the money to purchase a house. Nadia tells me my fame, or possibly notoriety, have increased the value of my paintings. So I won't be left homeless.

The second surprise visitor was Mrs Alderwell. She has to use a wheelchair now as her arthritis and osteoporosis have worsened in the short time since I last saw her. She brought nothing and said little. I see now how her small cruelties blinded me to what was going on in that house. She was ruled and dominated by her husband and children. Her snide comments and digs were an attempt to wrest a tiny amount of control back into her life. Her desire was never for Darcy to be a dancer or a wife, it was for her to escape. She apologised for her former harsh words and wept an hour over her daughter.

Leon brought roses and chocolates. He's let his hair grow and the resemblance to Noah is more obvious. He's not been to see his father. He feels it would be too overwhelming at the moment, as he's just coming to terms with his mother's deceit. Illegally adopted by Laura Eccles – or Madame Castanese, as she prefers – he lived with her until the age of four before being sent to a care home for several years while she served her jail sentence. When he contacted Darcy, she was delighted to tell him how Noah was a brute who took advantage of a naïve and vulnerable young girl. Consequently, he despised his father and worshipped Darcy. The reason he followed her up to the Hags Ring was to keep her safe. Only to learn that, like the rest of us, he'd been her fool. It must have hurt, knowing your conception and birth took place merely to be used as a puppet on someone else's stage. For this reason he is cautious about meeting Noah.

And my assurances of how kind he is count for nothing. Darcy was, after all, my best friend.

The real shock is Pender. He strides into the room flanked by Austin, the intern from my studio. I give him a double take.

'We had to keep an eye on you,' Pender says with a smile of amusement.

I won't give him the satisfaction of showing alarm or distress. He cannot hurt me here.

'Given how blind I've been to betrayal by my friends, I'm not going to be surprised by that of a nodding acquaintance.'

'Indeed,' Pender says.

'So he's got you starving,' I say to Austin, seeing how emaciated he's become. 'No sleep? Self-harm? Contemplating murder? It won't work. There's no such thing as a guardian angel.'

'And yet you're still here,' Pender says. 'Despite multiple attempts on your life. Others around you drop like flies. But you survive. Are you telling me that's luck?'

'I'm telling Austin that luck cannot be found in following an aged charlatan. Any visions you've had are probably due to LSD and sleep deprivation. You should read Christine Banks's papers on the subject.'

'*Touché*,' Pender says, giving a little bow. 'What I understand now is that an angel is assigned and cannot be stolen. I came to shake your hand and tell you I'm going to leave you in peace.'

I refuse to take it. I'll not shake the hand of a murderer, which he is, morally if not in law.

'Get out, Austin, while you can,' I say.

He follows Pender from the room though I sense a hesitancy in his manner.

HALLOWS HILL

***

I've begun to realise we did raise evil that night on Hallows Hill, but it was not Bella. She's been with me since the day my grandmother died. The evil was in Darcy, and it was not of a supernatural nature but firmly of the corporeal world. Evils too commonplace to remark upon: jealousy, ambition and a need to dominate.

As for Bella, I no longer fear her. I know she will always be with me, and she will always protect me.

Chapter 52

It's a cool spring day when I climb Hallows Hill. I am not alone this time. Mum, Bernard, Noah and Leon are with me.

At the top I have a clear view over All Hallows, the rooftops glistening from the recent rain: the Dower House resplendent behind its iron gates; the Alderwells' former home, the Grange, with its 'For Sale' sign.

I stand back from the Hags Ring and watch workmen adjust and readjust the chains attached to the stones. Then the heavy machinery growls into action; lifting each stone, which is half the height again below the ground.

Given its grisly history and renewed interest from a younger generation of occultists, the Conservation Club of All Hallows in agreement with the local council has decided to remove the Hags Ring Folly. Trees will be planted and the only stone will be a small memorial one dedicated to Isabella, Lula and Leanne.

Once the stones have been taken away they will be broken up. But as they hoist the 'Mia' stone, one of the chains comes loose and it crashes to the ground, sending tremors through the earth. The crew work to reattach the chains more carefully and it is lifted away. But a small piece has broken off, perhaps weakened all those years ago when I chiselled my name into it. When everyone's eyes are diverted, watching the large stone lifted onto the truck, I pick it up and pocket it before strolling back down Hallows Hill.

Acknowledgements

Firstly, I'd like to thank my editor, Kate Bradley, as well as all the team at Harper Fiction for their hard work on *Hallows Hill*. And I have to mention my agent, Sandra Sawicka, who made all of this possible. Thanks also to Syd Moore for her wise words on an early draft.

Much love to Keith, who is one of my first readers. You always give great feedback and are super supportive.

And finally, to Mum, to whom this book is dedicated. Your unwavering support and your encouragement always spur me on.

If you enjoyed *Hallows Hill*, don't miss Olivia's Isaac-Henry's chilling novel, *Sorrow Spring* . . .

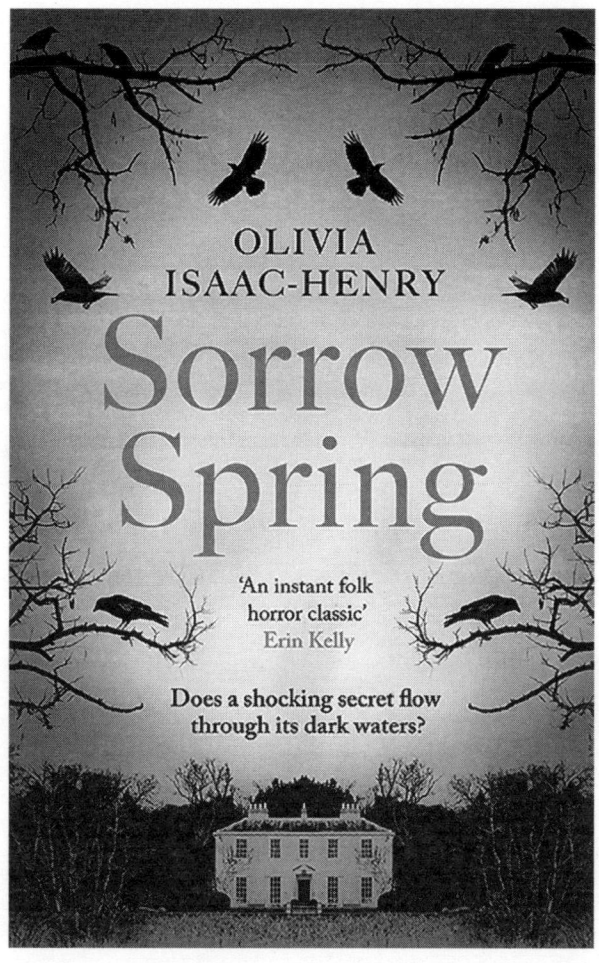

Available now